"Let me come with you," Sebastian said.

"No!" Julie cried, trying to withdraw from his grasp.

"You can leave Paris, Julie, but you cannot run away from the fact that you are a flesh and blood woman. Oh, Julie, you know how much I want you! You have a heart as well as a mind. Don't ignore it. You say you are protecting yourself from grief. But if you protect yourself too much you will never live at all."

"I will do as I see fit," she began, but he stopped her words with a kiss. She tried to push him away, but he held her firmly until her resistance melted. The sweetness of their first kiss came rushing back, and then it was too late. All her cautious practicality, her precious talent for survival, fell away, and a strange new recklessness took its place.

No matter what befell, she thought, she would not waste this happiness. She would gather it greedily and live for the moment. The future would have to take care of itself.

"Let me come with you," he whispered again, and this time she knew she would not deny him.

Dear Reader,

This month we bring you the promised second half of the very special miniseries that began last month. In Kristin James's *The Gentleman*, you met Sam Ferguson, older brother of hero Stephen Ferguson. This month, Sam has his own story, *The Hell Raiser*, written by bestselling author Dorothy Garlock, writing here as Dorothy Glenn. Sam is rough and tough where Stephen was smooth and polished. In fact, Sam epitomizes the West itself—so it's a real surprise when the one woman who can tame his heart turns out to be a polished Eastern belle. *The Gentleman* and *The Hell Raiser*, two very different heroes—and two equally perfect books!

This month also introduces a new author for the line, Mollie Ashton. And in coming months, look for favorites Bronwyn Williams, Caryn Cameron, Kathleen Eagle and more. The past has never been more alive—or more romantic—than it is every month, right here, in Harlequin Historicals.

Enjoy!

Leslie J. Wainger
Senior Editor and Editorial Coordinator

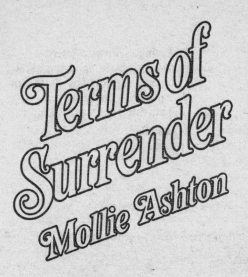

Terms of Surrender

Mollie Ashton

Harlequin Books

TORONTO • NEW YORK • LONDON
AMSTERDAM • PARIS • SYDNEY • HAMBURG
STOCKHOLM • ATHENS • TOKYO • MILAN

In loving memory of Berdj...
who never stopped believing in me,
whose love, support and optimism
will stay with me always.
This one's for you, babe.

Harlequin Historical first edition May 1990

ISBN 0-373-28646-5

MOLLIE ASHTON

was born in England and came to the United States in 1960, but still has family in both England and France, a circumstance which makes it very convenient for her to make historical research trips to both countries. She realized that she was destined to write about the French Revolution when she discovered that her oldest daughter had been born on the 150th anniversary of the Battle of Waterloo. Mollie has published several Regencies, including one for Harlequin, and has published four contemporary romances under the name Moeth Allison.

Prologue

Paris—Year II of the Republic, Pluviose (February, 1794)

I am Julie, Marie-Louise Juliette de Sainte Aube, and in a moment this nightmare will end and I shall wake safe in my bed at Sainte-Martine.

She lifted her face to the dry, biting day. The cold at least was welcome. Perhaps it would steal under her wrap, pierce her merino bodice and numb the terror brimming in her heart, just as it was numbing her lips.

Her eyes were shut tight, but she had no way to defend her other senses. The crack of the whip and the clatter of hooves and wheels on cracked paving stones, the brutal jolt and sway of the tumbril that forced her to grip the rail and brace herself, the taunts and obscenities from the crowds lining their route. Worst of all, if she lowered her face she caught the smell of doom. Forty aristocrats riding in a cart used for carrying pigs to the slaughterhouse. They stood tall and stiff-shouldered, their fear masked with rage and arrogance, but no perfumes could disguise that visceral odor of mortal terror.

She could only lift her face blindly to the cleansing cold, repeat her desperate canticle and force herself to believe it.

"I am Julie. I am Marie-Louise Juliette de Sainte Aube, and I am safe in my bed at Sainte-Martine. This is only a nightmare and in a moment I will wake. I am Julie..."

But when the tumbril halted, her eyes opened inadvertently, and despite every effort of will, the dream was still upon her. They had stopped in a city square lined with ruffians, soldiers with muskets holding back the mob. A scaffold mounted on a platform cast its long shadow over the square.

Her bones softened as she surrendered to the truth. The summons to Paris, the papers she had signed; she had dreamed none of it. The marriage contract that was to protect her, the prenuptial agreement safeguarding the Sainte Aube properties; it was all real enough, but it no longer mattered. Papa's plan had failed. All that counted now was that she had heard mass before the journey and been confessed.

"The guillotine," murmured a young man in claret-colored brocade. "Thank God for the wooden lady with the sharp embrace. They say she's quick and painless at least. One moment you are hearing the howls of the *sans-culottes*, and the next, choirs of angels—assuming, of course, that heaven is your destination."

"Claude Henri de Vinces Chaumier, aristocrat, parasite, enemy of the people of France."

At the summons of the tumbril guard, the young man turned to whisper directly to Julie. "They call my name, *mademoiselle*. Courage, it will be over soon." He touched his fingers to his lips and then to hers. Then he turned and threaded his way through the other occupants of the cart in an eerie minuet. Two soldiers, their uniforms threadbare and dirty, led him to the steps of the scaffold.

Julie turned from the sight of the guillotine and found herself staring at another fellow prisoner, a small woman with the imperious bearing of a duchess. Her stone-colored eyes had passed beyond hope, beyond fear, to some unimaginable territory of acceptance. There were creases and ink stains on her emerald silk skirt, but her wig was immaculately powdered. "Behold the new government," she said, her eyes sweeping over the scene. "God help France if—"

The rest of her words were drowned in a long roll of drums, followed by an unearthly silence, and then a sound as loud and sudden as a cannon shot as the blade came to rest. Julie sucked in air and expelled it in a scream, but it came out soundless. The spectators cheered, at first perfunctorily, then their cry swelled to a tumultuous crescendo. Steadfastly she kept her back to the scaffold, but she could not stop the picture that sprang unbidden to her inner eye. A sack suspended from the base of the scaffold served as the receptacle. The executioner had plunged his hand into it, drawn out the severed head and held it aloft for the spectators. It never failed to bring a great roar of approval.

Dear God, was there no more pity in France? Was human decency to be— Her thought froze at the sound of the guard's voice.

"Marie-Louise Juliette de Sainte Aube!"

She turned slowly towards the sound of her name, and in a lucid moment of utter detachment, she was amazed that her body moved without a tremor toward her death. So this is how it is done, she thought. Like a puppet controlled by invisible strings, she made her way to the back of the tumbril. She stood at the very edge, where the gate had been lowered to form a ramp, and found she could go no farther. A heavy lethargy descended on her, weighting her legs and dulling her senses. Was she swooning? she wondered. Was her body anticipating oblivion? Whatever the sensation might be she accepted it unresisting, for it erased all fear. Swaying slightly, she waited, knowing they would pull her down the ramp soon enough, but no longer caring.

Slowly sounds began to penetrate her isolation. Sounds without meaning at first. Reluctantly she became aware of raised voices, then words.

"She was not taken from the Conciergerie but from a house on the Ile Saint-Louis." The voice came from below her, where a captain stood in altercation with the tumbril guard. "It's an obvious mistake, Corporal. She's had no imprisonment and no trial."

"She needs none. Are you turning royalist on me? A Sainte Aube is an aristocrat. She's on my list and she's not for release."

"Fool, this is the seal of the Tribunal. If you can't read you can at least recognize that! Do as I order or you'll answer to Citizen Robespierre for it."

"I can read well enough, Citizen Captain . . . well enough to know my chain of command—and I don't report to you!"

"Your zeal is to be commended, Corporal, but in this instance the captain is right." An elderly man came forward. He was neither aristocrat nor ruffian but an important-looking bourgeois, dressed in plain, well-tailored black. His voice held such authority that he did not need to raise it to be heeded.

"You will release her immediately to me. She is no longer a Sainte Aube. She is Citizeness Farroux, my wife."

Chapter One

Paris—Year VI, Frimaire (December, 1797)

The tall town house on the Ile Saint-Louis had its best vistas from the third-floor bedrooms. On the south side, the windows faced the left bank. Over the carefully trimmed treetops one could see the Faubourg Saint-Victor, a prettier sight from the distance than it was on closer inspection. In consideration for her husband's sensitivity to the cold, Julie had chosen the north-facing rooms for her own. On a clear day she could see the city sprawling out from the right bank, broad avenues and mean winding streets, church spires and taverns, massive buildings of pale gray stone, even the ruined towers of the Bastille. Seen through the angular window frame and the swirling humidity of the river, it looked less like a city than a large painting, a study in muted grays with washes of deep green. The sharp edges of reality were softened as if with an artist's brush, or so she fancied. She preferred it that way.

But that morning it was not the view that occupied her. It was her dressmaker. Julie's gaze turned from the flimsy white gown Claudine was patiently holding up to the sketch that lay on her bed. Taking up the sketch, which was a page torn from a fashion magazine, she scrutinized it once more. It depicted a woman wearing a waistline fashioned so high and a bodice cut so low that her breasts billowed above the neckline like plump twin cushions.

What woman would want to be seen in public like that? But this was the same illustrious publication, *Madame*, to which Queen Marie Antoinette had subscribed—the very arbiter of Paris fashion. Only the name had changed; as *Citoyenne*, the magazine still reigned supreme among the chic.

Claudine was holding up a faithful copy of the sketched gown, fashioned in white muslin lined with silk, and her arms were getting tired. She rustled the dress a trifle impatiently.

"Come, Citizeness, if I am to finish it before tonight, there is no time to lose."

"It seems so thin for this time of the year, Claudine."

"But for a formal soiree, muslin is a must. You will arrive in a fur mantle, of course. But the house will be crowded and overheated. There will be dancing. I promise you, after a few moments you will wish to discard even your silk shawl. Now, please!"

Julie cast one more dubious look at the page, then set it down and untied the neck strings of her morning robe. "But, Claudine, I cannot hope to fill the gown so. My bosom is not that shape."

"No bosom is that shape, my little one. It is all in the art of the *couturière*. You shall see. Take off your robe. And now your chemise."

Naked save for her pantalets, Julie stepped into the skirt. Claudine drew it up to waist level and fastened the hooks at the back. Before she fitted the bodice, she studied her client with a professional eye. The young unblemished breasts rode firm and naturally high on her rib cage. Cunningly concealed in the bodice lining were flaps and tie strings to coax those breasts higher still, until Julie's form was exactly as the fashion demanded. And fashion was one of the few civilized amenities that had survived the revolution. As Claudine's fingers worked deftly, deepening a dart here, a seam there, bracing the cross flaps, she silently thanked God for the survival of her trade. They could strike down royalty and outlaw the use of titles. They could banish the Christian calendar and replace it with absurd ten-day weeks

and a year that started in September. They could turn
France upside down, but they could not destroy fashion. In
fact business was booming since General Bonaparte's victories. At last Paris had found a real reason to celebrate . . . it had been a long time coming. "Done," she said
at last.

Trailing clouds of white skirt across the Chinese carpet,
Julie hurried to the mirror.

"Who would have dreamed it!" she exclaimed, beaming
at her own reflection. "It's magic, Claudine. You have made
me voluptuous."

"But wait!" Claudine gathered up the train, gave it a
twist and showed Julie how to hold it casually over her arm.
Julie saw the skirt tighten, smoothing her hips and clinging
to her legs in a wickedly sinuous line. Her laughter pealed
out into the room.

Claudine stepped back to relish the moment. Incredible!
She had taken care of the girl's wardrobe for more than
three years, and it was the first time she had heard her laugh.
Indeed, it was the first time the citizeness had agreed to show
more than a mere sliver of her shoulders. But what could
one expect of a young girl married to an old stick like Farroux? And no lovers yet, judging by her manner. At all
events, she would cut a delicious figure tonight. Lustrous
dark hair and rosy skin, and at last a style that made the
most of her.

Carefully Claudine removed the dress and hurried away
to finish it with loving care. If the girl didn't find a lover
tonight, no one was going to blame the dress for it.

Bonaparte had conquered half of Italy and returned to
Paris with a treaty giving the French Republic dominion
over the Adriatic and much of the Mediterranean. His pre-
sentation of the treaty for ratification by the Directory was
staged as a great public ceremony. Not since the heyday of
the monarchy some ten years since had Paris enjoyed such
festive splendor. The general was to be received with full
honors by the entire legislative assembly, with the Directors
robed in the togas of ancient Rome. In the audience, there

would be as many spectators as could be packed into one hall. Only the court of the Palais du Luxembourg was big enough.

Her husband, Guillaume, had left earlier that morning, but the guests would not be admitted until noon. Julie had ordered a carriage for eleven o'clock and had invited her friend Anne-Marie Cassat to ride with her.

"Did Guillaume set off in a toga this morning?" Anne-Marie asked.

Julie shook her head, her lips curving a little at the thought. "Only the five Directors will be in Roman costume. Guillaume wore a black cutaway coat and white breeches, just as your papa did."

"I suppose the general will wear his full-dress uniform. Don't you just adore the cut of an officer's coat, Julie?"

Riding across the bridge to the left bank with a girl of her own age chattering beside her, Julie felt almost content. The nightmares—once so relentless that she had dreaded closing her eyes—were infrequent now. Often she would enjoy a whole month of untroubled nights, and as a result both her health and her spirits had improved.

Sometimes she still felt pangs of regret that she had not known her father better, but she could hardly pretend that his death was a keen loss; she had seen him so rarely when he was alive. As a child she had always assumed he didn't care for her, but his final acts had proved he cared very much. That in itself was a great comfort. She was protected and well provided for—and in such a precarious world, that was more than enough.

Guillaume was, of course, hardly better as a husband than Charles Sainte Aube had been as a father, but she knew better than to complain of trifles. Guillaume was not young, not handsome, not even amusing, but he demanded little of her and he was not unkind. She could not reasonably ask for more than that.

She was under no illusions. To Guillaume she was a clause in a contract, a clause that brought him all the ancestral property of the Saint Aubes, and as such he respected her. That the property had escaped sequestration was attributable to his genius as a lawyer and a legislator, and as such, she respected him. Her duties, to oversee the servants and be a good hostess, were little enough. The remainder of her time she could spend as she chose.

Sometimes she felt inner stirrings in response to the hot looks in a young man's eyes and she would fantasize a romance, but never for long. Inevitably she would remember the long, long shadow of the guillotine, and her dalliance would die a quick death. Yes, she was unendingly grateful for what she had.

In gratitude, she spent much of her time reading newspapers and pamphlets, trying to become knowledgeable about the times so that she would not shame Guillaume before his well-informed guests. But she was not naturally inclined to politics, and the mechanics of the present government seemed particularly complex. She was intuitive and artistic by nature, not a pragmatist, but she did at least try.

She turned to look through the carriage window as they swung into the Rue de la Harpe. There was heavy foot traffic on the road now, as well as carriages, hackneys and even country carts. Banners fluttered gaily along the way with legends welcoming the young victor. *Vive Napoléon! Bienvenu, Général!*

Overnight, it seemed, the man had become famous. "In a country with neither god nor king," Guillaume had said the other night, "this hotheaded general has arrived at the perfect moment." Everyone was ready to adore him.

Even Anne-Marie was still bubbling over about the hero of the hour. "Mama says he is only twenty-eight and quite romantic, with soul-piercing black eyes. Has Guillaume ever seen him?"

"General Bonaparte? Yes, once."

"And?"

Julie shrugged, unable to contribute anything remotely glamorous. "He speaks with a foreign accent and he is quite short, I understand. Every one of his officers towers above him."

"Bernard is short, too. I do hope flat pumps will stay in fashion, at least until the wedding. I caught sight of us standing together in a mirror. He tops me barely by two fingers." Anne-Marie patted her lavender bonnet and made a moue. "It's a flat coiffure and pumps for me. Oh, Julie, I wish you would tell me what the wedding night is like. I mean really tell me."

"Certainly not. It is your mother's privilege to tell you that."

"All Mama will say is that the first time hurts a little but it gets better and I may learn to like it. Well of course one learns to like it. Why else would every other wife in Paris have a lover? I mean to say, that is a purely voluntary act and sometimes quite risky."

A disconcerting warmth rose from Julie's throat, flushing her creamy skin up past her cheeks to her temples. She began to babble at random to cover her embarrassment. "Really, Anne-Marie! Just because we've had a victory, you can't—I mean to say—really, the times are very grave. France is awash in problems. The most terrible arguments in the assembly every day. No one knows from one day to the next if this— Well, you are a deputy's daughter after all!" Julie twisted her fingers together in ever-changing combinations. "Do you have nothing more important to discuss than wedding nights?"

Anne-Marie widened her round blue eyes in amazement. "You can't be serious! What else should concern me thirty days before my marriage? Now, be a good girl and stop lecturing. Just tell me, for pity's sake. How was your first night?"

Julie turned to the window once more to hide her face. "Believe me," she said carefully, "after one look at the wooden lady, it was more than welcome!"

Anne-Marie bounced on the seat, then flung herself back against the upholstery with a sigh of exasperation. Julie didn't expect her to be satisfied with that answer, but for the moment at least, the chatterbox was prepared to drop the subject.

With a sigh of relief, Julie sat back. Smoothing her wrinkled gloves over her fingers, she felt the hard band of gold beneath the silk. Perhaps one day, if they remained friends, very close friends, she would consider telling Anne-Marie the truth.

Chapter Two

London—December, 1797

Sebastian Ramlin rapped on the hackney roof and leaned out of the window. "It's a rare day for the time of year, driver," he called out. "You can pull over now. I have a mind to walk the rest."

Jumping down from the carriage, he handed the driver a shilling, turned his back on the wide thoroughfare of Park Lane and took a narrow alley leading to Shepherd Market. It had been some years since shepherds had gathered there. The relentless building in the town had reduced the once green patch of common land into a stubby little cul-de-sac lined with shops, notably a hatter, a chandler, a spicer and a barber shop. In the cobblestone center were the stalls.

Hands thrust deep into the pockets of his greatcoat, Sebastian walked with the slight sailor's roll that always marked his first few days ashore. It was the end of the day and those of the chicken and geese vendors who still had livestock were beginning to cut their prices, but the produce stalls were still doing a brisk trade. He idled through the fruits and vegetables. After solid months of pickled cabbage between distant ports of call, it was pleasant to wander through the pyramids of pale celery, artichokes, freshly pulled potatoes smelling richly of the soil, and rosy winter pears.

Then the apple barrow caught his eye, and the apple vendor, a slender young girl with a lusty voice. "Fresh Kentish apples. Best in the world," she cried. "Russet for eating and green for cooking. Better than physic for what ails you! Buy my juicy Kentish apples!"

He bought a russet from her then leaned against the chandler's doorpost to eat it, watching the girl ply her wares. She had a round country face and a dazzling smile, and she smelled pleasantly of crisp, tangy apples.

The barber emerged from his shop, razor in hand, and strode up to the girl's wheelbarrow. Sebastian could not hear their words above the vendors' cries, but it was plain the man had not come as a customer. A short, stocky fellow, he was menacing the girl in some way. Then, as she burst into tears, he gripped her arm and dragged her toward his shop.

Sebastian tossed away his apple and in a few swift strides intercepted the barber in his doorway. "Stop bothering the girl, bully," he ordered, gripping the shorter man by the shoulder.

Furious, the barber turned, quickly adjusting his expression at the sight of a London gentleman. "Sir, I'm not bothering 'er. Polly 'as *agreed* to let me pull 'er eyeteeth. *Agreed* fair an' square."

Sebastian blinked. "Pull her teeth! But they're splendid. I'll wager every one of them's sound as a bell."

The barber rubbed the mole on his nose and stretched a smile not likely to inspire confidence in his dental services. "Indeed they are sound, sir. I'm paying 'er 'alf a guinea for 'em. She won't get no better offer than that. Mistress Broxley is in my shop with two eyeteeth needs pullin'. If I can put 'ealthy ones in the wounds, they'll likely take root and she'll 'ave no gaps."

"And even more likely, they'll not take root," Sebastian replied hotly. "Good God, man, teeth are not carrots! I know your kind of quackery. The only certain thing is that this girl—this mere child with as sweet a smile as you'll see in a month of Sundays—will suffer God knows what torture, and she'll have ugly great gaps in her mouth for the rest of her days."

The barber's mouth tightened, the corners disappearing into his jowls. His voice rose with wounded dignity. "I'm no butcher, sir. There's a full glass of gin for 'er as promised—before I lay a 'and on 'er. She'll not feel much of anything after she gets that down 'er gullet, and besides . . ."

Ignoring the rest, Sebastian drew the girl gently away from the shop front and bent to her ear. "Do you really want to do this, Polly?"

She snuffled into her sleeve then raised a tearstained face. "Oh, yes. I need the money, sir. Me mother is poorly and me father is passed on. There's four of us still at home and there's not much profit in apples."

Sebastian put an arm around her shoulder and felt the slight tremors that shook her body. "But you struggled and wept when he tried to take you into the shop."

"Didn't want to go before dusk. After sunset was what he said. After me apples were sold. But the lady came early. I didn't want to leave me barrow unattended."

"No, no, of course not. I understand." She was fourteen at the most. Hardly finished growing. . . . His arm was still around her shaking shoulders. She felt like a fledgling fallen from its nest. It was unthinkable. "If God had meant us to sell our teeth, he'd have made them replaceable like hair," he told her, and glanced behind him.

The barber stood beside his pole, making stropping motions with the razor blade against his brown smock as he rocked back and forth on his feet. Clearly he could hardly wait to get his hands on the girl.

"I've got a better bargain for you," Sebastian said quickly. "If I give you half a guinea, will you promise to keep your teeth where they are?"

Her trembling increased. "What else must I do for the half guinea?"

He felt the soft places in his heart painfully stirred. "Nothing, by God," he said, more sharply than he intended. "Nothing, I swear it. Just keep that promise."

She nodded her head, bereft of words, as he walked her back to her apples. But when he handed her two crowns and a shilling, she rewarded him with her luminous smile and slipped the coins into her apron pocket. "Bless you, sir. I didn't really want to do it."

"I guessed as much," he said solemnly, and bid her farewell.

Striding toward Berkeley Square, he felt exhilarated. A tiny victory had been won. He hated poverty with a passion. "The poor will always be with us," Domenico always said. "By all means be charitable, but don't expect to change the world, boy. And don't impoverish yourself in the process." Sebastian knew there was wisdom in those words, but the kind of poverty that drove the Pollys of this world to sell the teeth right out of their mouths he could not abide.

His expression sobered as his thoughts turned to the state of his own pocket. For ten years he had driven himself to put a great distance between himself and poverty, but the last voyage had been a disaster. With all Europe at war, alliances could shift in the blink of an eye, and sea trading had become a risky business. Profits could be eaten up in a dozen unpredictable ways—heavier customs bribes, diverting expensive cargoes to minor ports that could not pay the freight, extra weeks under canvas as a result of evading hostile fleets. This trip could have made him sole owner as well as master of the *Celandine*. Instead, he would have to sell his one-third share in the clipper to pay off the crew and insure the next venture.

"Compulsive gifts to apple girls will have to be curbed," he muttered, and walked into Benson's Gentlemen's Club to distract himself for the evening. Tomorrow would bring a hard day of bargaining at Lloyd's and facing unpalatable facts with Cecil.

"Allow me to buy you a brandy," he said an hour later. He had won five guineas at backgammon from a Frenchman. Little Polly Apples had brought him luck. He was not so naive as to consider the gaming tables a solution to his problem, but it was after all a game of vingt-et-un that had given him his start in trading.

Now, as was only proper, he would converse with his gaming companion over a glass or two, then Sebastian would agree to some further play to allow the loser to recoup his losses.

The man was a marquis, but without the haunted expression one had come to expect these days of the displaced, disinherited French aristocrat. In fact this one seemed reasonably content with his exile—almost as if it were a matter of pure choice. He was extravagantly dressed in green velvet and wore a prodigious amount of jewelry, even for the French. A trifle too well fed, he hid his excess blubber behind expensive tailoring.

He was not a companion Sebastian could warm to particularly, but winning money off a man demanded a sporting response, and so he entered into a friendly conversation.

"The last time I was in London, the city had many of your countrymen, sir," Sebastian said. "Now they seem to have dispersed. Some have returned to France, I hear. At any event, you are quite a rarity these days."

"A few returned," the Frenchman said, "but they were fools to do so. Myself, I shall not return until the Bourbons regain the throne," he added, flicking a speck of lint from the dark green velvet of his sleeve.

"You are confident that will happen?"

The marquis shrugged. "I believe so, but at all events, my properties and my future are secured."

How in God's name could that be? Sebastian wondered. It was a tantalizing statement, and he dearly wanted to pursue it, but he had been raised as a gentleman, and breeding demanded that he make some personal disclosures in his turn. "For my part," he offered, "I would be glad for any solution that would leave Europe at peace. War is ruining my business."

"And your business is . . . ?"

"Shipping. Until this last voyage, I thought of myself as a mariner and a trader. Now I believe blockade runner would be a more accurate description. The wars are costing me dear."

The marquis finished his brandy in one long gulp. "Property, my boy. When you have liquidity, I would advise you to put it in land."

Sebastian's dark brows knitted in puzzlement. "That is astounding advice from a Frenchman in these times. Has your property not fallen prey to the Republic, *monsieur*?"

"I have no qualms." The nobleman's smooth perfumed cheeks became plumper than ever with his smile. "No qualms at all. I have married my daughter to a man who will keep my estate intact, a man who has sufficient clout in the new Republic to do so."

"At this moment, perhaps," Sebastian muttered, "but I fail to see how that could reassure you. The Republic has seen three governments rise and fall in as many years—as I know to my cost. As soon as I reach an agreement with some official he is out of office, and the agreement is useless."

The Frenchman leaned forward until they were nose to nose across the gaming table, filling the air with his cloying scent. "Yes, *governments* rise and fall, my friend, but not my son-in-law. That is the beauty of him. He is as secure now as he was in King Louis's court. He swears unswerving loyalty to the prevailing power of the day. He has a . . . how shall I say . . . ?"

The marquis paused, waving his arm in the air as he groped for the right word. ". . . a kind of enduring inconspicuousness—a great political gift. I am quite confident he will keep his seat in the government until his death."

Once launched on the subject, the man became unstoppable, drawing Sebastian into a curious tale of deception and double-dealing.

The marquis had but one child, a daughter whom he had apparently rarely seen. Her mother had died in childbirth. She had been consigned to the care of a nurse and governess, sent to a convent school at the age of nine and had spent all the summers of her girlhood in England with her late mother's family.

At the height of the Reign of Terror, the marquis had escaped to England but had left his daughter, then approaching her sixteenth year, in the convent. He had sent a messenger there, summoning her urgently to Paris for the purpose of fulfilling a marriage contract that supposedly would preserve the family estate and save the marquis from the guillotine. The bridegroom was a lawyer with a powerful position in the new Commune.

Remaining safely in England himself, the marquis had deliberately misled the girl to believe first, that he would meet her in Paris, next, that he had been executed shortly before she arrived, and last, that his dying wish was to see her married according to his arrangement.

As far as Sebastian could tell, the monstrous deception had no other purpose than to assure the plan's success by shocking the poor girl into unquestioning obedience. The plan had succeeded. The girl was duly married—and was still under the false impression that her father, the man smiling so complacently across the gaming table, was dead.

"Should the Republic prevail," he concluded airily, "I shall continue to live in England and receive partial revenues from my land. But should the Bourbons return, it will be an easy matter to reclaim every acre. Thanks to my son-in-law, none of the land will be sold off to the peasant farmers." His expression seemed to demand admiration for a brilliantly conceived and executed plan.

Sebastian had difficulty believing what he heard, but staring at the greedy, self-congratulatory face, he knew he had heard aright. He was filled with such an urge to strike this vile and shameless creature that he remained silent for some time, struggling to calm his violent reaction. When he spoke, it was only to murmur icily, "Your daughter has courage, sir."

"My daughter does as she is told." The marquis stroked his chin. "Of course, if she were to give birth to an heir, my claim would be somewhat distanced, but there is little chance of that." He paused, obviously wanting to be questioned further, but Sebastian's curiosity was at an end.

The Frenchman's urge to boast, however, was not. "You see, sir, my son-in-law has been twice married and as yet is still childless. He is well into his sixties now, and I have every reason to believe he is incapable of siring an heir. So! As I have proved in the very worst of times, land is always salvageable, my friend, providing you have wit enough to protect it. Always, there is a way. Invest in it when you can."

Always a way, Sebastian thought, provided you have more greed than scruples. A wave of disgust shook him, but, remembering his own circumstances, he held his tongue. "Sound advice," was all he said, "but I shall never have the wherewithal for land as long as the wars continue."

"Perhaps I can help. In fact, it is very like, *monsieur*, we can help each other."

Sebastian had little inclination to enter any bond with this creature, but in his current plight, noble high-handedness was a luxury he could not afford. The Frenchman might have no redeeming features as a human being, but he obviously had a canny nose for profit. Sebastian was in a bad fix, and it wouldn't hurt to disguise his distaste and listen closely. For the hour that followed he was careful to see that Charles Sainte Aube won back every last farthing of his five guineas.

Through the window in the deputy's antechamber, Sebastian looked down at the Tuileries gardens. Four years ago when famine threatened the city, the gardens had been stripped and turned into a potato field. They seemed decorative enough now, their complacent lawns and shrubs well tended. Watching the glossy carriages sweeping down the side boulevard that skirted the gardens and the elegant women walking their dogs on the white gravel paths, it was hard to believe that Paris had ever known strife or hunger or bloodshed. But there at the far end of the long green rectangle was the Place de la Révolution. Instead of a guillotine, a chestnut vendor stood near the center of the square, surrounded by strutting pigeons. Yes, it was hard to believe....

He returned to his straight-backed chair and rubbed his temples. What was even harder to believe was that he was here. He, Sebastian Ramlin, was about to trade favors with a man he had met only once, scarcely ten days ago, and had heartily disliked. He was about to approach Deputy Farroux with a letter of introduction written by the marquis. And in return for the letter, Sebastian would send the marquis fresh news of his daughter. Not that Sainte Aube gave a fig for his daughter's health or well-being, that was clear. His sole concern was that she should remain childless. And he could not have news of her in any natural manner because, for reasons of his own, he wished to remain dead to her. With the utmost distaste, Sebastian had given his word he would not violate the confidence—in the unlikely event that he should meet the unfortunate woman.

Sainte Aube had burdened him with a long account of exactly why it was crucial that she not bear her husband an heir. But the minute complexities of French estate law combined with his own distaste for the whole business had resulted in Sebastian forgetting the line of reason. It seemed as rapacious and unnatural as the rest of the deception. Why had he allowed himself to be dragged into such a shabby affair? he asked himself, knowing the answer full well.

If the underwriters at Lloyd's had been less stringent, if there had been even the slightest glimmer of a solution that would allow him to honor his maritime partners and save some part of his fortunes, he would have spurned the Frenchman's proposition. He had left his agent in London with his partner Edward Cecil, both casting about for a better solution, but there wasn't much hope. He owed it to his creditors and himself to leave no stone unturned, he assured himself, yet he felt tainted by the circumstances.

The door opened, and Sebastian looked up to see the secretary who had ushered him into this room. "The deputy will see you now," he said, and led the way to Farroux's chamber. The room was smaller, less imposing than he had expected, and dark with filled bookcases, some of them blocking the windows, but the large lacquered desk with its stacks of documents was magnificently carved of fine mahogany and bore every sign of weighty matters of state.

The elderly man who rose briefly from behind the desk was as dry and serious as the chamber itself. A thin, grizzled bachelor, Sebastian would have guessed, rather than a thrice-married man. Guillaume Farroux seemed born to be a state functionary, without passion, humor or warmth of any kind, a man circumscribed by the letter of the law.

Sainte Aube's letter of introduction lay before him. He glanced at it through half-moon spectacles and wasted no time in greeting beyond a perfunctory handshake. "What is it you want from me, Citizen Ramlin?"

"License to ply my trade in the Mediterranean, sir, without let or hindrance."

Farroux asked for more details and listened attentively while Sebastian summarized his enterprises as both a mariner and a trader. "And now that a French general has brought the key Italian ports into French domain," he finished, "it is to the Republic I must apply."

"General Bonaparte is a Corsican," Farroux pointed out with unnecessary pedantry.

"But an officer in the French army nevertheless." Sebastian knew he was in for a session of tedium and reminded himself that Farroux was a lawyer, obsessed by detail like most of his tribe. Whatever effort of patience was required, he would remain polite and imperturbable.

Farroux gave a dry cough. "Customs matters are not in my department, Citizen."

Sebastian groaned inwardly at the all-too-familiar phrase.

"However...there are—just faintly possible, you understand—some...yes, some avenues I might explore, providing..." Farroux let the ensuing silence hang heavy in the air, as graphic a hint of bribery as an open palm.

Sebastian hastened to come in on cue. "Whatever it costs, if my ship has free trading restored in Mediterranean waters, I assure you the money can be raised."

Farroux shook his head. "This is not a question of money or licenses, Citizen. It is rather a question of—" He broke off abruptly and stared at Sebastian as if he were seeing him for the first time as a human being rather than one of a thousand applicants. "When you are not at sea, where do you make your home?"

"I have rooms in London. I regard my guardian's house in Cornwall as my home."

"How long will you stay in Paris?"

Till hell freezes over, if there's a chance of success. "Until my mission is completed or proved to be in vain," he answered evenly. Whatever the old fox had in mind, he would play along until he came out with it.

"How well do you know Charles Sainte Aube?"

Sebastian hesitated, wondering what answer Farroux most wanted to hear, but since he had no way to judge, he gave the truth. "Very little. We met just once over a game of backgammon at my London club."

Farroux's pale blue eyes narrowed. "He is not a man to grant favors freely. What did you have to offer in recompense?"

"Simply news of his daughter. Nothing more."

Farroux paused as if digesting some complicated and weighty information. After a few moments, he rose. "I suggest you see me again in three days. My secretary will arrange a time. I need to give the matter some consideration." With a curt nod, he brought the meeting to a close.

Grimacing in the mirror a week later, Sebastian struggled with his recalcitrant cravat. He was on his way to the Tuileries yet again. After three cat-and-mouse sessions with the wily old man, he was still none the wiser. This time, he resolved, would be the last. Farroux wanted something from him. If it wasn't money, it was probably intelligence. Sebastian had already decided he would not be pressed into espionage—it required more deception than he was capable of. He had always considered his forthrightness more of a handicap than a virtue, but in any event, if that was the way the wind blew, they were both wasting their time.

Throwing his mantle about his shoulders, he left his rooms on the Rue Manche and headed ill-humoredly for his rendezvous. This time, he would direct the discussion.

"With all due respect to your office, Deputy, I must protest at the treatment I have received at your hands," he began, refusing to sit. "I come not as a supplicant but a man of trade—as vital to the ports of the Republic as those ports are to me. I have offered to buy licenses and you have denied me, yet you still insist you can smooth my path. You have compelled me to dance attendance on you three times without ever explaining yourself. Now state your case as plainly as I stated mine these seven days since and be done with it.''

"My dear Citizen Ramlin, I am not unaware of your impatience." Farroux offered a wintry smile. "Perhaps you will better understand my reticence when you know what it concerns."

He had been waiting a week to know, but he bit back on the angry retort that sprang to his lips. "You have my ear, sir," he said through clenched teeth.

"As I told you, I am in no direct position to grant official licenses. Neither trade nor foreign affairs is within my brief—and even if they were, there are no licenses to be had at this time." Under his black coat, Farroux's shoulders made a small circular movement. "However, I do have some influence with the foreign minister, and there are certain amenities I can offer—amenities, I might add, which will not only open certain sea roads but quite possibly, given the appropriate set of circumstances, contribute substantially to your prosperity in a number of—"

"If those appropriate circumstances require my services as a spy for the Republic," Sebastian broke in, "do not waste your breath."

"They do not," Farroux said softly.

"Then what in God's name do you want of me?"

"It is a delicate matter and you—"

"And you have more than paid delicacy its due, sir. Speak out."

Farroux's thin dry form seemed to shrink in the chair and his head drooped. When he raised his head to speak, his lips sagged, his closed eyes were no more than little mounds of slack gray wrinkles, and his voice quivered. The important state elder had become a pathetic and tired old man.

"I want you," he began, faltered painfully, then started again. "I want you to seduce my wife."

Chapter Three

Julie sat in the crowded carriage lost in her thoughts. She was squeezed between Anne-Marie on her left and Bernard Seurat on her right. Facing her sat Anne-Marie's parents, Justine and Laurant Cassat. It was an uncomfortable ride in a carriage meant only for four, but she was accustomed to it and generally enjoyed the voluble company. Guillaume could never get away from affairs of state to come home in time to leave with her for the theater, and since the Cassats often attended on the same evening, to ride with them had become commonplace. It spared her the indignity of arriving at the theater unescorted.

Tonight she would not have minded a solitary ride instead. Indeed, the last place she wished to be was between Anne-Marie and her betrothed. She saw the surreptitious glances passing between them and knew they longed to touch and whisper together. But they were not yet wed, and propriety—at least for an unmarried girl—must at all costs be served.

"You are very silent tonight, Julie," Bernard said.

"I was merely thinking about *Così fan tutte*," she replied. It was the opera they were about to see, but it was far from the object of her thoughts. She had been thinking how fortunate Anne-Marie was. She teased Bernard mercilessly about his short stature, but it was quite obvious the two were in love. It seemed to Julie lately that she was surrounded by lovers. Every afternoon when she walked Ton-Ton along the embankment she would pass couples idling beneath the trees, engaged in amorous conversation. At Talleyrand's soiree there had been... She shifted restlessly, impatient with herself. She had spent far too much time dwelling on that night.

Ever since the reception she had known a deep discontent. In ten days it had not dissipated. Every wife in Paris had a lover, Anne-Marie had said. It was a gross exaggeration of course, but still...she was twenty and...missing so much. Was her life to continue forever in the same unremarkable way? And what if it did? she wondered. What did it lack now that ten short days ago had seemed negligible, not worth consideration? It was a comfortable enough round of duty and pleasure—safe, unexciting. Why should it suddenly vex her? Precisely why was safety no longer enough?

Justine Cassat wore a fur-tipped cape over her gown and a jeweled bandeau from which rose an ostrich plume, flopping absurdly to the sway of the carriage. No doubt *she* had a lover, though she sat primly enough beside her husband discussing the Austrian whose operas were lately in fashion.

"I just adored his *Don Giovanni*. I hope this new one is as amusing. It's the first performance in Paris, so he'll probably be conducting it himself."

"The composer is dead," Julie said.

Justine Cassat looked crestfallen. "Why how sad! I thought he was quite young. When did it happen?"

"Six years ago, *madame*."

"Ah, Julie the industrious! How would we lazy ones fare without you? You can be relied upon to read the newspapers, to be informed and, above all, to take your pleasures seriously. I'm sure you are studiously prepared for this evening at the opera. Now tell us the plot."

Madame Cassat's remarks were accurate. But something contrary in Julie resented them. They made her feel deadly dull, as seriously virtuous as an English maiden aunt. At that moment, nothing could have persuaded her to admit that she was indeed well prepared for the evening's entertainment.

"I'm afraid tonight I am no more prepared than you," she said with a flighty sigh. "We shall all have to rely on the program when we get there, *madame*." She was surprised to hear herself twice using the old honorific. She was usually so careful. But no one seemed to notice. Many people were slipping *monsieur*s and *madame*s into their conversation these days, just as they were reverting to conspicuous displays of wealth in their dress and their entertaining.

Again her mind flitted back to Talleyrand's house, as it had repeatedly these past few days. The salon, so brilliant with candlelight, lavish food and bejeweled guests...

She had felt gay and reckless that night in her revealing muslin gown, and as light-headed at the prospect of meeting General Bonaparte as if she had switched heads with the giddy Anne-Marie. Perhaps it was the gown affecting her mood, or the gala atmosphere of the reception—or possibly the result of that morning's ceremony, where she had caught tantalizing glimpses of the general and had been awed by the august body assembled to honor him. Whatever it was—and she had tried many times to explain it away—she had not felt such tingling anticipation since she was a child.

The evening had not disappointed her. She had loved the music, the dancing, the gay conversations and the flattery of several young men. The height of the evening had been a brief interlude with the general.

She knew from Guillaume that Bonaparte was short but had a commanding presence, that he was brave and well loved by his men and officers. That he was also gallant and handsome, no one had ever mentioned. Nothing she had read or heard had prepared her for those splendid chiseled features, the grave and gentle charm of the man and the riveting eyes. Anne-Marie had said something about soul-piercing black eyes, only they were not black at all but a subtle grayish blue, and to be the object of their gaze, to feel oneself lost in their depths... For a few minutes she had quite lost her wits, had found herself acting the coquette—all smiles and blushes and provocative remarks.

The general had done nothing to provoke such foolish behavior. Upon learning her name, he had smiled and commented, "My brother Joseph has a wife named Julie, a sweet lady who has given me a lasting fondness for that name." It was the most banal, the most innocent of salon chatter, yet she was charmed to share such a personal trifle about his family. His gaze then left hers and settled dreamily somewhere beyond her left shoulder as he murmured, "Indeed, Julie's sister Désirée would be my wife if Josephine had not stolen my heart before the betrothal."

Julie saw the intimate gleam in his eyes when he spoke of his wife. "I should be enchanted to meet her," she murmured politely.

"She is traveling back from Italy—I insisted she take a safer route than I, but alas, she will not arrive for several more days." His voice was hoarse with such open longing that Julie envied the woman. Momentarily she was overwhelmed by bittersweet intimations of what it must be like to fall headlong in love.

She had not been quite herself since that night. She had sensed herself vulnerable to a sudden attraction as never before. It was alarming to find herself so suddenly susceptible. Alarming to think she might one day be attracted beyond her power to resist. She had always depended on her head ruling her heart, and with God's help, it always would. And yet now she felt so deprived that she was hard put to dissemble the busy, fulfilled young wife. It was as though for the space of five minutes she had actually felt what love was like. And in those five minutes, security, comfort, predictability—all the blessings she had clung to so gratefully these past four years—had become utterly meaningless.

Now, in the quilted little cocoon of the carriage, it was an effort to be sociable and unmannerly not to participate in the conversation. Bernard had already remarked on her silence. She did her best to overcome her malaise and contribute some token words for the remainder of the ride but gave a sigh of relief when the carriage came to a halt.

The large quadrangle where the theater stood was a favorite pleasure spot. Once the enclosed gardens of the Palais Royal, it was now a pleasing area of cafés, gaming houses, winehouses and expensive boutiques, linked together by colonnaded walkways and miniature gardens. Brilliantly lit by flaring torch lamps, it was as lively in the evening as by day. Leaving the carriage, the party continued on foot through the gardens and cafés to the theater, which lay at the north end. They mounted the steps and crossed the portico graced with fluted marble columns. Once inside the foyer, they parted ways to go to their respective boxes.

Guillaume was already seated when Julie entered their box, and she collected herself enough to greet him appropriately. "How splendid," she said. "You are already here. For once we shall be able to enjoy the entire performance together."

Guillaume rose and helped her remove her mantle. "I'm afraid not, my dear. I shall have to leave at the intermission. I left my secretary preparing some documents that must be signed and on their way to the Vendèe tonight. Forgive me, but you will be returning as you came, with the family Cassat." He gave a thin smile of apology and drew the velvet curtains, closing them off from the passageway. "I will hear the overture, however, and attend the first act."

Seductive music filled the theater, but Julie found she could not lose herself in it. The flute was decidedly thin in tone and the violins harsh. The theater was not built for musical productions, but Mozart was not considered serious enough to warrant the Opéra, she imagined. Peering into the orchestra pit, she noted that the wig of the *chef d'orchestre* was awry.

Peering into her heart, she was painfully aware that she cared little that Guillaume had arrived on time, and even less that he would soon be gone.

Sebastian sat in his heavy greatcoat outside the Café Mireille. The *garçon* had eyed him oddly when he insisted on an outdoor table on a winter night. But while the air was chill, the little plaza was sheltered from the wind and tolerable enough with his seal collar raised. It was calming to watch the evening pleasure seekers stroll through the gardens, and to listen to the street fiddler beguiling the passersby. To sit inside would mean sharing a table and he was not in a sociable mood. His grasp of the French language, serviceable enough in a customs house, had been sorely exercised this past week—along with his patience. Indeed, everything upon which he based his life seemed lately to have been put in question.

He watched the steam rise from the hot coffee laced with brandy and, after the *garçon* left, settled back to his thoughts.

I want you to seduce my wife. That was the precise point when he should have left. He had gone over their conversation a dozen times since, remembering Farroux pouring forth in broken sentences his inability to sire a child, his desperation, his begging. A combination of incredulity and language difficulty had made it hard to follow the rapid flow of impassioned words. Now Sebastian understood only too well, and he had dwelt much on the irony of the situation.

He could serve Sainte Aube with simple assurances that Farroux and his wife had no heir. He could serve Farroux by providing him with an heir.

What in God's name had he stumbled into? An alien world where fathers regarded their children as pawns and husbands pandered for their wives. He wanted no part of it, and yet . . . And yet if he could bring himself to take this seriously, if it worked, the prospect was tempting. He wrapped his hands around the tall cup of coffee, brought it to his lips, then set it down again, a wave of repugnance enveloping him as his last encounter with Farroux returned to his mind.

Marriages of convenience, yes, that was the norm in the landed classes everywhere. But this? It was too bizarre. Even before he had fully understood, his instinct had been to turn on his heel and leave the chamber without uttering a word.

He had actually turned to leave when Farroux called him back in such pleading tones that he had frozen in his tracks. He had vastly underestimated the man's powers of persuasion.

"My wife is a lovely young girl who has nothing to look forward to in her barren marriage except widowhood, sir. Yes, widowhood, and perhaps at an age past hope of children by a new husband. She has no romance in her life, no gaiety. None of the elements that young women live for. It would surely be a kindness on your part to provide some."

Sebastian knew a specious argument when he heard one. It was hardly concern for his wife that prompted Farroux's proposal, it was pure self-interest. Sebastian despised it in Farroux but knew nothing save his own self-interest kept him listening.

"If you would once see the lady, you would realize this is a far from unpleasant undertaking. And when she is with child, all my influence will be at your disposal, I swear it.

"I offer you a trade, sir. My political power for your virility. I do not expect your answer this moment, merely that you will consent to lay eyes on her and then decide. Why do you look so askance? Is it too much to ask that you look upon her?"

"But ... but what of your wife?" Sebastian had spluttered. "A girl of tender years? A girl who has led a sheltered life? Is she to be a brood mare put out to stud? Can you seriously believe she would accept such a crude arrangement?"

"Not knowingly, Citizen. In no wise would she accept it. She is obedient and willing, but not without spirit. I believe her delicacy would be grossly offended."

"To put it plainly, sir, she would be disgusted—with you and with me."

"Of course. She must never know this was planned. It will be a chance romantic encounter, a seduction. God knows it is common enough in Paris. And God knows, she is ripe for the occasion. It astonishes me that she has been faithful this long. I can only put it down to her youth and innocence, and perhaps to her keen awareness of my position and her fear to jeopardize it."

"In that case, sir, you have a wife of incorruptible virtue and all my efforts would be futile. I will hear no more of this." Sebastian turned once more to leave, but the older man clutched his sleeve with surprising strength.

"For pity's sake, she is flesh and blood, man! Twenty years old! Look at me, then look at yourself. No one is incorruptible."

Those last words hit home. Sebastian had not come this far in his dreams of a trading empire by making a virtue of incorruptibility. What was so remarkable about a liaison with a married woman? It would hardly be his first. But the resistance in him, the distaste, was inescapable. He had surely reached a line he could not cross.

His romantic relationships had always been warm-blooded and genuinely affectionate while they lasted. To dissemble to a woman he had never laid eyes on, a woman for whom he could conjure not the slightest sentiment— His thoughts broke off abruptly, for the latter was not altogether true. He discovered he had already developed a deep compassion for the lady. Any woman burdened with such a father and such a husband could not help but stir his pity. Compassion had softened his heart toward this woman, even without meeting her, and he could feel himself slipping into a dangerous pit.

"No," he told Farroux after a long silence. "I am no moralist, but I do have some scruples. Your proposal is offensive in the extreme and I must decline."

At that, Farroux rose, walked around his desk and, hands clasped behind him, stared at Sebastian with the air of a cross-examiner. "So you have never committed adultery, sir? Never caused a wife to deceive her husband?"

"I cannot claim that. I have on occasion relieved a lady of the infinite tedium of her marriage, but—"

"But always decently behind the husband's back. Is that it?"

Sebastian's silence was answer enough. Farroux pounced on it like a hungry fox.

"So it is simply the fact that you are not deceiving me but have my sanction that so offends your sensibilities, is it?"

Sebastian paused, knowing he was no match for a professional equivocator. He stared at his boots, less concerned about his showing in a verbal fencing match than about identifying his own true feelings. He spoke guardedly. "It is rather the fact that I would be deceiving the lady that offends me. A romance should be entered into only for reasons of the heart."

"Don't preach me the ethics of adultery, sir! Reasons of the heart, indeed! Is your heart spoken for? No? Then I suggest you think again. Only see her. Then give me your answer. And if that answer is yes, a banker's draft will seal our bargain. Four thousand louis d'or should buy you at least some time. If and when you get her with child, then you can expect your real reward. I can guarantee the sea roads will be yours."

Sebastian found that his cup had grown cool in his hands as he thought. A stream of theatergoers had already passed his table. A ticket admitting him to an orchestra seat lay in his waistcoat pocket. The theater stood a few steps away at the far end of the colonnade. He was usually a decisive fellow with a taste for adventure, but he had never felt more timorous. Had he grown fainthearted at twenty-seven? he wondered. Why did he have the fancy that impending doom sat with him at the table? Were the dire consequences he sensed connected with accepting Farroux's proposal or with rejecting it?

If he chose, he could see Madame Farroux in the lower box to the right of the stage, seated with the deputy. If he chose, he could make up some pretext to approach her during the first intermission when the deputy would absent himself from the theater. And yet he sat there postponing the decision as if it might be the last he would ever make.

The stream of theatergoers who had been filing past his table began to thin out.

"It's not the end of the world," he muttered, furious with himself for such mouselike hesitancy. It was merely a look at the damn woman, after all. Not a commitment. Yet he felt nailed to the chair. He drew on his gloves and forced himself to his feet. The opera was about to begin.

* * *

The elaborately painted faces of soprano and contralto, Dorabella and Fiordiligi, stared out at the audience in artificial dismay as the curtain dropped on the first act.

During the lukewarm applause, Julie laid a hand on her husband's arm and drew his attention to the dark-haired man seated below them. "Do you know him?" she asked. "He keeps looking this way."

The man had entered at the end of the overture and had been shown to the last seat of the second row of the orchestra stalls, just a few feet away. He had not been the only latecomer but he had captured Julie's wandering attention for two reasons. He was unaccompanied, and men did not generally attend an opera alone. And he had an arresting appearance, a lean, powerful build that was more than pleasant to look on. Her gaze had involuntarily followed his swinging stride down the aisle. Seated, he was equally noticeable for the rich bronze of his complexion in that sea of white faces.

Guillaume shook his head and rose. "I've never seen the man before. If he has been looking our way, undoubtedly it is because he finds you more diverting than the prima donna, my dear, and one can hardly blame him. I must leave now. Let me accompany you to the Cassat box and have a chair brought in for you."

But Julie slipped her arm in his and walked with him to the front entrance. "I would like to stretch my legs before I sit again," she told him. "I will join them presently."

Guillaume glanced at her. Under his knitted brows his pale blue eyes showed concern. "Are you sure, Julie? Will you be comfortable making your own way?"

"Yes, truly. I shall be fine...thank you."

For a long time she had been terrified of crowded places, but she had left those irrational fears behind for good somewhere in the calm, uneventful domesticity of the past four years. She was touched at this evidence of Guillaume's lingering concern. And ashamed of her earlier restless thoughts.

As they rounded the corner into the large foyer, her hand tightened on his arm. He might not be the answer to a maiden's prayer, she thought, and he was certainly not the kind of hero who inhabited those illicit romance books that had circulated among the girls of Sainte-Martine des Anges, but he cared for her enough to be solicitous, and there was many a wife who could not say that much about her husband.

With a peck on the cheek, she bid Guillaume good-night and turned back into the concourse. The various doors of the auditorium were open wide and through them thronged the audience, intent on seeing and being seen, exchanging gossip and sharing witty critiques of the first act. Attendants bearing trays of wine, cordials and little cakes circulated among the strollers.

Julie felt a sudden chill on her arm. She looked down and with a gasp of dismay watched a dark stain spread over her long silk glove. Before she could utter a word, her hand was grasped, lifting her dripping arm away from her white skirt.

"Attention, *madame*, or the dress will be damaged, too. I have quite ruined your glove. A thousand pardons."

The voice was urgent and deep, the accent English. She looked up at the fine bronze features she had admired through much of the first act and could think of no reply.

One of his hands held hers out to the side as if they were dancing, the other held what was left of a blackberry cordial.

"Let me find you a towel," he said, leading her across the crowded foyer to the refreshment table in the far corner. She followed, unresisting.

Had he contrived the spill? she wondered. But his dismay seemed real enough, and when he asked for water, his command of the language seemed to fail him. His words became hopelessly garbled. She tried not to smile at his mistakes, but she saw the bartender's confusion. Unable to suppress her laughter, she pointed to her glove.

Puzzled, the Englishman glanced from the bartender's barely suppressed smile to her own open amusement.

"You asked for water to 'wash away this ruined lady's sins,'" she explained.

"Ah, thank God! You speak English." His laughter joined hers. "I mean ruined glove...lady's stains..."

"Yes, of course you did," she murmured in the tenderly indulgent tone she would have used to calm an upset child.

His face darkened with an embarrassed flush that turned his skin from bronze to rich mahogany. "I am laid low, *madame*. I have gone from clumsy to inept to positively half-witted in a matter of moments. Allow me to redeem myself."

"By all means! You may do so by kindly unclasping my bracelet so that I can remove the glove."

"The name of the oaf you see before you is Sebastian Ramlin," he said, removing her gold-and-onyx bracelet with great care.

His hair was dark and cut to shoulder length. It smelled faintly of chamomile and citron.

She felt his eyes on her as she peeled off the sticky glove and mopped her arm with a moistened towel. "Julie Farroux." Her face still sparkled with recent laughter as she replaced the bracelet on her bare arm. "Enchanted to meet you, Mr. Ramlin."

"I doubt that," he muttered, "but if you will give me your ruined glove and the name of your glover, you shall at least have a new pair tomorrow. Now, may I offer you some refreshment?"

A faint warning signal traced a quick light path from her breast to her throat. "Nothing, thank you. I'm very grateful that you were quick-witted enough to save my gown from the same fate. Please don't distress yourself, Mr. Ramlin. It's only a silly white glove. A mere trifle."

"But not to me," he insisted. "Come, I shall escort you back to your seat, and you shall give me the name of your glover."

"Oh, if you insist. It's Baton Frères in the Rue Saint-Honoré," she said, taking his arm and walking with him across the marble floor. "But it really isn't necessary."

"And where are they to be delivered?" he insisted.

"Baton does not deliver."

"Then I shall deliver them myself."

Julie hesitated. She had been so intent through the whole encounter on putting the poor man at ease that she had not been discountenanced until that moment. Now her own color began to rise from under her lace collar, up past her cheeks and temples, under the stylish bandeau and the feathery curls to the very roots of her hair.

She withdrew her hand from his arm and stood in the passageway just outside the Cassat box. "I am a married woman, Mr. Ramlin. I cannot entertain a gentleman caller."

"Then you must be the last married woman left in Paris who cannot. Is your husband a jealous man? Not that any man could blame him, laying eyes on you, *madame*, but—"

"I give him no cause to be, sir." Her voice became icy. "I fear you have been sadly misinformed about Paris."

His expression changed from frank admiration to chagrin. "I fear I have offended you, *madame*. I beg you to forget my words. I meant nothing ignoble. I was merely about to suggest that you present me to your husband. I shall explain the matter and ask his permission to— But no. Enough faux pas for one evening. If I may have your address, I will have a messenger deliver the parcel to the service entrance of your house."

His tone was so chastened that she instantly regretted her harshness. He had said nothing more forward than she had heard many times before. In fact she had rebuked much bolder proposals than his with a mere laugh and a light tap of her fan on the offender's wrist. "This is my box, Mr. Ramlin," she said, and reached into her reticule for one of her calling cards.

"In any event, you could not have asked my husband. He has left the theater to attend to some business. And— and—" At the stricken look on his face, she melted. "Oh, what a silly fuss about nothing! I overreacted and you must think me a harridan. Yes, of course you may deliver my gloves. We have a town house on the Ile Saint-Louis and I shall be at home at three o'clock. Here is my calling card."

He glanced at the engraved ivory card she handed him and bowed. "Your servant, Madame Farroux."

"And who was that, pray tell?" Anne-Marie had waited until the curtain had risen and the performance was in progress before she whispered the question under the cover of a loud quartet of voices from the stage.

"Who was who?" Julie asked in return.

"That divine creature you were with in the corridor. The curtains were open a bit, you know."

"Oh, him. He accidentally spilled some cordial on my glove and he's going to replace it with a new pair, that's all."

Anne-Marie rolled her eyes. "How wonderfully romantic."

"Far from it! It was simply messy for me and unfortunate for the poor fellow." She folded her fan and gave Anne-Marie's shoulder a playful little tap. "The opera, my dear, is taking place on that stage, not in the corridor. You're just a dewy-eyed bride who thinks everything is romantic. I couldn't be happier for you. Now do let's attend to the performance."

Chapter Four

Julie heard the voices before she opened her eyes, and knew it was morning. Remembering Ton-Ton, she felt across the sheets for his warm little body. He was gone. If Babette had come in and taken him for his walk, it must be late, she thought. Drowsily she turned over to look at the clock on the fruit-wood bureau, but the shutters were still tightly closed and she could not see what time it was.

Her eyes drooped closed again as if weighted. Whatever the time, she would happily have stolen another hour or two of sleep, but the sounds of the house grew intrusive. The steady brush of a broom on the stairs. The squeak of polishing rags on the hall windows. Drips dashing into a pail from a squeezed wet mop. And voices two floors below.

She was usually an early riser, but last night she had lain awake for hours—not for fear of nightmares, but simply because of the memory of Sebastian Ramlin.

She had cataloged every last detail of the man, each feature revisited with the same dangerous pleasure she had experienced at their meeting.... The eyes dark as a midnight sea, deep set and expressive. The clean line of his jaw when he laughed. The lean muscularity of his body under the casually fashionable clothes. The unruly black hair that fell, disdainful of the latest short mode, to the top of his cravat. Not so much a handsome face, she decided, as a compelling one. The unexpected contrast of Latin darkness with the accent and breeding of an English gentleman made him quite the most exciting man she had ever met.

At first it was pure delight just to dwell on their brief exchange, but far into the night, she had caught herself indulging addictively in the memory, and despaired. It was akin to the way she had briefly felt with General Bonaparte but a thousand times worse. What was happening to her? Was she becoming a simpering, sluttish half-wit at the mercy of every attractive man in Paris? She had tried to escape into sleep. But the more she sought it the more it eluded her. In the small hours of the morning she had tiptoed downstairs to the kitchen, taken the sleeping Ton-Ton from his basket and carried him off to her bed. Enfolding the silky little poodle to her bosom for comfort, she had finally fallen asleep at daybreak.

The voices were on the stairs now, and recognizable.

"But the citizeness is still sleeping and I cannot—"

"Then it's high time she awoke. Don't fuss so, Babette. You did your duty and I promise she won't be cross with you."

Her door flew open and Anne-Marie walked in. "Wake up, sleepyhead, it's noon," she trilled, sweeping past the foot of the bed and throwing the shutters wide.

Julie winced as the searing light streamed over her.

"I only have a few minutes and we have much ground to cover. Babette, bring your mistress a strong *café au lait*. She can scarcely keep her eyes open."

The bed heaved as Anne-Marie landed on it heavily. "You sly little thing," she hissed, dropping her voice to a discreet level. She glanced at the door through which Babette had disappeared, closing it behind her, then turned back to Julie.

"It was all prearranged, was it not, your rendezvous after we brought you home last night?" Anne-Marie wore a riding habit, and the skirts were tangling about her legs as she inched up the bed on her knees, babbling furiously all the while. Her broad-brimmed hat fell askew and her riding crop lay carelessly on the coverlet where she had thrown it down.

"You met and went off to some lovers' nest, and he brought you back here just before the servants were stirring, embraced you passionately in the shadows of the *porte cochère*, then rode off into the night while you stole up here just before daybreak and fell into an exhausted sleep after your tumultuous night of love. Oh, how marvelous! How absolutely splendid!''

Julie was hard put to keep a straight face. Anne-Marie's fantasies were wilder than her own. ''What on earth are you talking about?'' she said blandly.

''You know very well what! You and that divine man I saw last night. Your lover. No wonder you were so silent and mysterious in the carriage yesterday evening, you little minx! You were dreaming of the night ahead. And I think it most ungenerous of you not to have shared it with me. Do you not trust my discretion? Now hurry up! Admit it and let's get it over with, for heaven's sake. I have important news to share with you.''

''I admit nothing of the sort. I told you the truth last night. He was just someone who spilled cordial on my glove.'' Julie drew her knees up and hugged them, noting Anne-Marie's impatience. ''I'll admit he was attractive, though.'' She gave a silly grin. ''I spent half the night remembering just how attractive. Now what is your important news?''

Anne-Marie looked as disappointed as a child deprived of a new toy. ''I don't know if you even deserve to hear it now. Oh, very well. Bernard's sister Mireille has become a great friend of Hortense de Beauharnais, General Bonaparte's wife's daughter. They are both at Madame Campan's school and I'm sure it will—''

''Heavens, did you say noon?'' Julie pulled the bell cord and leaped out of bed. ''Mercy, I had no idea it was so late.''

''Julie, do pay attention. Do you not see what this means? I shall be invited to the Bonapartes' house, which means we shall reciprocate, and...''

''Please, Anne-Marie,'' Julie begged, ''not now. I have so much to accomplish and the whole morning has gone by.''

''Ah, so he's coming today, is he?'' Anne-Marie's nose for gossip was relentless. ''Bringing you a pair of gloves, no doubt?'' She climbed off the bed, straightened her hat in the mirror and collected her riding crop.

"Yes, yes, I told you that last night.''

"I shall expect a full report,'' she announced, but Julie was able to shoo Anne-Marie out of her bedroom without any further admissions and begin her day.

The hackney smelled faintly of tobacco, and Sebastian, who rarely smoked and never carried cigars about his person, yearned to light up as he rode through the heavy eastbound traffic on the Rue Saint-Honoré. The slender package resting on his knees trembled suddenly to the rhythm of a jumping nerve in the ball of his foot. He laid the package beside him on the seat and stretched out both legs, resting the heels of his boots on the facing banquette. Immediately his left knee locked and a tiny leaping, jittering nerve began to plague him. He was full of tics and cramps and odd sensations beneath the skin. His body seemed to be acting out a mocking version of his thoughts.

The phenomenon was not unknown to him, but it had never happened before except at sea. When storms had blown them days off course, when they were entering hostile waters, when they were so overdue at their next port of call that water was dangerously low, when he sensed a threatening truculence in the crew. Sea voyages were peppered with these prolonged tensions, and on rare occasions they were dire enough to produce the erratic sensations he could feel now.

There was no need for all this nervous apprehension, he told himself. Farroux was awaiting his answer, and he would have it soon enough. It had to be no! There had never been any question. It had been sheer idleness to procrastinate by agreeing to the opera. It had been mindless to contrive an incident just to see the lady up close. And now, on his way to present her with a new pair of gloves, his answer in all good conscience remained unchanged. No bribe on earth could tempt him to become Farroux's creature in this unnatural bargain. Curiosity alone had brought him thus far.

And he would have done well, he realized, to have suppressed that curiosity.

For now, dammit, he had been touched by the girl's youthful charm. If the circumstances had been different he might have pursued her single-mindedly, but the circumstances were what they were. He must not forget that—even momentarily—as he had last night. Now more than ever he could not bring himself to deceive her.

Of course, to undeceive her was equally out of the question. What could he say to her? Your husband has agreed to compensate me handsomely for seducing you? But now I have made your acquaintance, I have a mind to seduce you strictly for our mutual delight . . . ?

He cast off the absurdity and stared through the grimy side window. A pale mist lay over the Seine, and as the carriage lumbered across the Pont Saint-Louis toward the small cluster of houses on the island, he could see not the sharp edges of roof and masonry but only soft gray shadows, as blurred as his own resolve.

Changing his position once more, he heaved a great sigh. He had met every dilemma in his life with bold strokes. He had been decisive, risking failure if necessary. Why was his will suddenly so limp? His course of action was clear. If he was not prepared to take advantage of the situation, then he must turn back immediately. He would have the gloves delivered by messenger, give Farroux a firm negative and take the next packet to Dover.

But he let the driver continue across the bridge. He wanted to see Julie Farroux just once more. Perhaps she would be less enchanting by daylight, and he could leave with less regret, he told himself. He was behaving like a green boy, hopelessly distracted by a pretty face. But so be it. He would allow himself the brief diversion before he faced up to the realities of his shaky fortunes.

In the pocket of his greatcoat lay a slim letter from Percy Mayne, his agent in London. Percy had managed a compromise with the Carib Company. It hadn't saved Sebastian's share in the *Celestine*—that had been sold to pay off the crew—but someone else could worry about Lloyd's now.

On the next voyage he would be master for five hundred pounds plus 2 percent of the profit if there was one, but he couldn't count on that. The *Celestine* would not be ready to sail until the beginning of April, by which time he must have it refitted, provisioned and manned. And how would he stave off the remaining creditors? His stipend for the voyage was a fraction of what he now owed. And poor Cecil owed even more. Sebastian felt largely responsible for that.

He squared his shoulders and slapped his thigh briskly. "Scruples be damned, Ramlin," he muttered. "Stop palming off maudlin sentiment as honor. For the delicious task of bedding a beautiful woman, you can avoid debtors' prison. If you succeed in begetting a child, your fortune could be made. If you fling this god-sent opportunity away simply because the woman stirs your gallantry, you're an ass and debtors' prison is what you deserve!"

Julie felt considerably more at ease since she had told Guillaume about last night's incident. He had been home working in his study all day. His response had been brief and quite matter-of-fact.

"You were quite correct in letting him come to the house, my dear. It was only proper for him to suggest it after ruining your gloves. Indeed, you should offer him some refreshment for his pains to establish that he is forgiven and there are no hard feelings." He had resumed his writing immediately, implying that the matter was settled and of no great import.

Her feverish night had been sheer foolishness, she decided. Besides, France was officially still at war with England. Such few Englishmen who came on urgent business never tarried long. No doubt he would be gone in a day or two and she would not see him again. If she had sensed any romantic intention in his manner, it was probably her imagination, and if not, it could do little harm.

When Babette announced the caller, she had him shown into the salon. She wore a modest dress of deep blue with a white lace collar and a painting smock over it, because she had been at her watercolors. She removed the smock, and with the merest fleeting glimpse in the mirror, she headed slowly, deliberately, for the staircase.

Gracious, she thought. She would be serene and gracious, the perfectly contented wife who was simply putting a stranger at ease. There was nothing more to it than that.

"Good day to you, *madame*," he said, and held out the package. "Gloves from Baton Frères. I trust they are a satisfactory replacement and that I am forgiven."

"Good day to you, sir." Her serenity evaporated under the warmth of his smile. "Of course you're forgiven. Accidents will happen, Mr. Ramlin. I thank you for the gloves."

By daylight he was less exotically dark and more golden, tanned from the sun. His deep-set eyes were so dark a shade of blue they could be mistaken for black. "May I offer you some tea?"

"Thank you, no."

"I believe we have blackberry cordial, if you would prefer it."

"I do not care for cordials, thank you."

"But, Mr. Ramlin, it was surely blackberry cordial you were drinking last night?"

As soon as the words left her lips, she knew it was a mistake. A trace of a smile curved his mouth for a moment and she couldn't decide whether he was mocking himself or her. "I wasn't drinking it, *madame*, merely spilling it."

She tried to change the subject, ignoring the challenge in his eyes, but could think of nothing to say. After an awkward silence he continued, as if perhaps he had not made himself quite clear.

"I chose the drink not for my palate but for the damage it might do. . . . I had a mind to meet you at any cost."

"Well, you succeeded," she said, trying to make a reprimand but smiling in spite of herself. His rogue's grin was irresistible.

"Surely you guessed that the accident was contrived?"

"The thought did occur to me. However, you seemed so genuinely distressed that I quickly dismissed the idea." She laid the package on a side table and looked at him squarely. "Since you have decided to be honest with me, I must tell you in return that whatever may be true of most wives in Paris does not hold for me. If you are looking for romantic diversion, I would suggest you look elsewhere. With your engaging manner, I'm sure you won't have to look far."

This time he was not in the least discountenanced. He attempted no eloquent apologies. Indeed, he attempted nothing. He seemed quite content merely to stand there, fixing her with his intent gaze, a half-amused smile playing about his wide mouth. She felt oddly nervous under that silent gaze. She thought he would take his leave now, but the silence lengthened until she felt obliged to fill it.

"Flattering as your attention may be, I am not in the market for a dalliance, sir. I am a perfectly contented wife... which by no means implies that you are not welcome in my house, however. And now that we understand each other, you are still perfectly welcome to some tea and conversation."

He shook his head. "Thank you, but I think I shall return to my rooms and lick my wounds. I shall walk toward the river and disappear into the mist as befits a rejected suitor."

She could not help but laugh at his deliberately exaggerated gloom, and as he turned for the door, she found herself detaining him.

"Wait! I like to take my dog for a walk before dark. I'll fetch him and walk with you to the bridge."

Minutes later they were leaving the courtyard together, Ton-Ton on a leash, yapping at their heels. "Did you fear I was about to drown myself?" he asked her lightly.

"Not in the least. I was simply enjoying the conversation. I don't have too much occasion to speak English these days. And I always take Ton-Ton for a walk at this hour."

"Are you English?" he asked her.

"My mother was—she died giving birth to me. I was sent to my grandmother in Surrey every summer. Those visits are my happiest memories of childhood. That ended when I married."

"Your childhood," he asked, "or the happy memories?" But he knew it was both.

She paused before she answered and her words had a grave, sweet quality. "The summers in England were what I meant, Mr. Ramlin."

For a few moments they walked in companionable silence, their pace retarded by Ton-Ton's tiny stride. At the end of the block, they turned into an alley that went down to the embankment. It was bordered on either side by the wrought-iron fences of town houses, but the gardens were well planted and the overhanging evergreens gave it somewhat the air of a quiet country lane. The gray afternoon had discouraged casual strollers, and they shared the footpath with no one.

"Did you enjoy the opera?" she asked him.

"Only the intermission."

Julie hid her smile from him. "It was not terribly welldone, was it? Save for your performance, of course. Really, Mr. Ramlin, I believe you would have done better on the stage than in the audience. You are a talented actor."

He cast her a shrewd look. "We all play our parts in life."

"Not I. I am exactly as I have told you."

"A wife contented with constancy?"

"Yes."

Their pace had slowed. Ton-Ton was now ahead of them and tugging on the leash in Julie's hand. Sebastian looked down, as if he were absorbed in the dog. It was hard to believe that she had been married for three years to that desiccated old lawyer. Beneath the prim surface he sensed the dewy freshness of a child, untarnished and unsubdued. She attracted him more than physically, it occurred to him. She had qualities that touched him profoundly.

"Do you love your husband then, Madame Farroux?"

"Of course." The question surprised her and she answered it reflexively. She owed him no further explanation, she realized, but for some reason she wanted him to know. "Oh, not in the way you mean. I do not need to love him romantically to feel gratitude and loyalty and respect. Since my father's death, he is my closest kin."

He turned to face her, laying a hand on her shoulder and halting their progress for a moment. There was no trace of provocation in his dark gaze but something else, something she had not detected before, a deep sincerity, which belied the lightness of his tone. "You are very young to be content at the prospect of a life without romantic love."

They walked on to the end of the alley and turned the corner onto the busy embankment thoroughfare. "Mr. Ramlin, I am lucky to have a prospect of life at all," she said after a lengthy silence. "If it were not for the efforts of my father and my husband, I would have perished in the massacres."

His response was stopped by her sudden cry of dismay as Ton-Ton leaped into the street, wrenching the leash from her grasp. A great post chaise was thundering down from the bridge at frightening speed. The dog ran blindly into its path.

Julie darted after him but Sebastian overtook her and pushed her back with a force that sent her reeling. Then, with a dive that landed him prone on the paving stones nearly under the hooves of the cantering horses, he grasped the dog by the scruff and rolled into the ditch to safety not a moment too soon.

Julie hurried over to the muddy spot where, for a moment, Sebastian lay winded and motionless, the dog yelping and wriggling in his grasp. He held out the leash to her, released the dog and, with an odd spiraling movement, rose to his feet.

She stared at him, appalled. His nankeen breeches were streaked with mud. The cape of his greatcoat was ripped and filthy. "Oh, Mr. Ramlin, I am so sorry! Are you hurt?"

He shook his head, swaying slightly.

"My attachment to that dog is quite absurd. It was so stupid of me to lose the leash and then dart out like that when the horses were moving so fast. I didn't stop to think."

He looked down at the mud streaming from his clothes. He could not walk through the streets in this condition and even less could he hail a hackney. No driver in his right mind would accept him as a fare.

"Are you sure you're not hurt? Oh, your poor clothes! How stupid of me to let go of the leash!"

"If we are competing for the crown of fools, I believe I win," he said quite clearly, and folded at her feet in a dead faint.

Chapter Five

He awoke to a stinging odor in his nostrils. Countless heads swam before his eyes and he heard whispers he could not understand. His own head seemed to float disembodied, and the ones bobbing before him suddenly gave place to an astonishing display of fireworks followed by black velvet.

"Mr. Ramlin, please, do not close your eyes again. Please, please wake up. Oh, thank God, Doctor. I believe he is coming to again."

He forced his eyes open again and, with a considerable act of concentration, merged those innumerable heads into three distinct faces with features. One face came nose to nose with him and spoke.

"I am Dr. La Salle, sir. You have suffered a kick to the head from a horse, but only a glancing blow. I have dressed the wound and the damage is not grave, but you must lie still for a while and make every effort to keep awake.

"Now, with your eyes only, follow my finger.... Good, good! In a few days, you will be up and about again. Do not be disturbed. You are with the family Farroux and they will take good care of you according to my instructions."

Sebastian heard the words quite clearly, was able to follow the physician's instructions but understood little else until the face withdrew. Then the significance of what he had heard began to filter through, thick and slow as porridge through a sieve until at last he felt connected to the world again.

Full consciousness returned to him like a clap of thunder. His head throbbed mightily, and he realized that the two other faces leaning over him belonged to Farroux and his wife. One moment he didn't know why he knew their names, and the next, he did, all the missing parts flooding back. The deputy, the young wife, the wretched little dog . . . four hooves flashing above his face.

"My dear fellow, you had us quite worried!"

While his mind lumbered through the jumbled facts, making sense of them, Farroux spoke in an unctuous voice.

"My wife tells me you undertook a heroic rescue with no regard for your own safety. We are deeply indebted to you. No, no, do not try to sit up yet, sir. This room is yours—indeed my house is yours—until you are mended. Please do not hesitate to ask for anything you desire. The doctor will call again in the morning. Now I will leave you to the excellent care of my wife."

Alone with Julie, Sebastian sat up and was rewarded with cannon fire between his ears. Groaning, he let his head sag against the quilting.

"If you can bear to remain in that position for a moment, I have some medicine to ease the pain." She disappeared into the gloom beyond the lamplight, then returned bearing a spoon toward his mouth.

He swallowed some vicious-tasting liquid then washed it down with the tumbler of water she held out for that purpose. She took his hand and held it in both of hers. Her oval face was pale and taut with compassion. "You will feel better very soon. Lie still and do not try to speak yet. I know, it must be very bad."

Her voice was whisper-soft with sympathy, and she was right about the medicine. In a few minutes the cannon fire under his skull began to fade to a dull, tolerable roar, allowing him to take note of his surroundings. He lay in a large four-poster bed in a small bedroom, quite dark save for the lamp on a small table beside him and, at some distance to his right, the glow of a coal fire.

A bandage encircled his head at the temples. Aside from the dressing, he wore only his lawn shirt and his under-breeches. The rest of his attire was nowhere in sight. "How long have I lain here?"

"Less than an hour." Gingerly she sat on the edge of the bed. "You've been slipping in and out of consciousness. An occipital concussion, the doctor says."

"A what?"

"I believe it means you were knocked silly—only temporarily, of course...thank God!" She covered her face with her hands. "I have never known such fearful guilt and shame. It was all my fault. You could have...oh, Sebastian, you could have been killed."

Embarrassed at the outburst, she rose and moved to a boudoir armchair a few feet away and added belatedly, "Mr. Ramlin, I mean—forgive me."

The medicine began to seep through his blood. Laudanum, he guessed. He felt quite light-headed and carefree. "I prefer Sebastian," he said. "Honorifics are out of fashion in France, are they not?"

"Why, yes, but—"

"And I also preferred it when you were sitting on this bed." He patted the indentation on the down coverlet where she had briefly perched. She shook her head. "Come, I am in no condition to ravish you. Besides, what did your husband just say? 'Do not hesitate to ask for anything you desire.' I desire you to come closer. I cannot see you over there in the gloom. It is excruciating for me to turn my head and..."

"All right, all right," she broke in. She rose from the chair and went over to the hearth, poking the fire into a blaze and adding more coal from the scuttle. When she returned to the bed, her face was no longer pale. On the contrary, it appeared to be glowing with pleasure.

There was undisguised triumph in his voice. "So, you wanted to come closer!"

"Whatever makes you think that?"

"The pleasure in your face."

"What you see, Mr. Ramlin, is relief—the infinite relief of knowing that the accident has not robbed you of your wits ... or your impudence. In short, you remain unchanged."

He studied her features in the soft yellow light. Her beauty was not the languorous, calculated kind he was accustomed to. Her hair was artless, the long mahogany tresses brushed to a natural gloss and tied simply with a white velvet ribbon. Her wide amber eyes were innocent of kohl. There was nothing of the sophisticated coquette about her. She had just given him a provocative retort, and he sensed it was the first she had ever made. For that reason, he relished it with disproportionate pleasure.

"Where are my clothes?" he asked after a moment.

"The servants are cleaning them. Your greatcoat is quite beyond repair I'm afraid. Only the fur collar can be salvaged. Tomorrow it will be taken to my husband's tailor with orders to make another coat just like it."

He grinned. "Our acquaintanceship is costly on articles of apparel, don't you think? Perhaps God is telling us to take them off."

He watched the deep color suffuse her cheeks and feared he had offended her, but her answer was spirited. "You can hardly attribute the ruin of my gloves to the Almighty, sir. You were the sole architect of that scene ... and I begin to wonder if you did not also ..."

"Did not what?"

Laughter danced in her eyes. "An injured hero and a devoted nurse? A classic from a hundred romantic tales. Did you not perhaps engineer this scene, too?"

He shook his head and the pain of the vigorous movement made him wince. "I plead not guilty. If you could feel the distress behind my eyes, you would not ask that question. Besides, I am no reader of romantic tales." His eyes quickly scanned the room, the dim, cozy ambience of it. With the pain fading, he was beginning to feel decidedly better.

"But since you mention it, this circumstance is certainly ripe with possibilities. Shall we profit from them, Julie?"

Her folded hands tightened in her lap. "If you continue in that vein, I shall leave and send in a servant to tend you," she said, rising to go.

He caught her wrist and pulled her back. "Please, don't leave," he begged. "You must not hold me accountable for my indiscretions. You have given me opium and it makes my tongue wag, but my heart tells me that I need you close by."

The resistance in her body relented and she settled back on the bed. His hand slipped from her wrist to her palm and their fingers entwined. The distance between where she sat on the red silk quilting and where he lay between the sheets was far greater than it seemed. Perhaps that gap was unbridgeable, he thought. But for the moment, feeling her slender fingers laced in his, he felt no pressing need to find out, no need for anything except rest. With their hands locked together, drowsiness overcame him and he sank into a deep sleep.

In the morning, Sebastian requested a bath. "Provided someone stays with him throughout," the doctor pronounced on his return visit, "a soak in warm water would be beneficial." Victor Benoit, Guillaume's manservant, was charged with tending to Sebastian's toilette and reported to Julie when it was completed. She hastened to his room.

"Good morning. Do you feel a little better?"

"Well enough, thank you." Dressed in a clean white nightshirt and a brown velvet robe from Guillaume's press, Sebastian sat on a chaise longue. "I still have a dizziness when I stand up," he said impatiently. "Last night's medicine, I suppose. I'll take no more of that."

"It's not the medicine but the blow you took that makes you dizzy. That is why Dr. La Salle insisted you be watched while you bathed. You are not supposed to be standing up until that dizziness is gone. It is nothing to worry about. It will pass in a day or two."

"But I can't stay here forever!"

"Drink this chocolate while it's hot and don't fuss," she ordered, smiling broadly. "Three days is not forever."

But in a sense, it was. Over the next few days, Julie's normal perception of passing time seemed suspended. Victor took care of Sebastian's intimate needs, and Julie provided everything else. She was with him from dawn until he slept at night, and he acted the perfect gentleman most of the time. She would even steal from her room to his once or twice during the night to see if he slept well or needed anything. During his waking hours she read to him, ate with him, played chess and checkers with him and, through the long evenings of enforced idleness, they began to exchange increasingly important fragments of their respective personal histories.

He was Italian by birth, he told her one evening. Orphaned in infancy by a typhoid epidemic, he'd been raised by a relative. His guardian was a monsignor, sent to England on a long-term mission of a diplomatic nature. The priest had made England his home thereafter, and thus Sebastian had been raised as a native Englishman until he was sent to a Jesuit school in France.

"Domenico cherished the idea of me entering the priesthood," he told Julie, "and I was a dutiful child." He looked down at the checkerboard that lay on the counterpane and idly moved a black piece forward to a vulnerable position. "I attended a seminary in Douai, but I quickly discovered I had no taste for poverty or chastity."

He had run away to sea at sixteen and in nine years had worked himself up to master mariner and a trader in his own right.

Although he sat in bed, a bandaged, reluctant invalid, Julie sensed the essential vitality and drive of the man, the energy that surged through his veins…so very different from Guillaume. "Did you inherit your drive to succeed from your father, perhaps?" she asked him.

He shrugged. "I know very little about my parents except that they came from Genoa. Domenico finds it hard to discuss them. My suspicion is that he is himself my real father and I am the result of some venal lapse of his youth." Sebastian grinned, his teeth a sudden piratical brightness in the flickering shadows.

"Of course, as a professional celibate," he went on, "Domenico would never be able to admit that to me. But when we are together, I call him father, not monsignor. I am the only one who does and I believe he likes it." He spoke with deep affection and for a moment his eyes took on a distant look.

"At all events, he is the only father I have ever known, and as I grow older, whether he sired me or not seems less important than our mutual affection."

Julie felt her heart expand and go out to him. "How hard it must be for you, not knowing about your parents. I never knew my mother, of course, but I was very close to my maternal grandmother. I have seen my mother's portraits, and I know exactly how she was as a child. I know her well in fact. She is very real to me in most ways—perhaps even more real than my father. My memories of him are few, although he died only three years ago in the terror."

"Why are your memories few?" he asked.

She heard a disturbing tenderness in his voice. It was an intonation that warmed her with its implicit concern, but at the edges of her mind it troubled her with its intimacy. She brushed the disturbance away and answered his question.

"Papa was never at Marduquesnes when I was little. I was in the care of a nurse, servants, a governess. Then he sent me to Sainte-Martine des Anges to be schooled by the sisters. Summers in England..." She frowned, her fingers gripping a white checker counter but her mind elsewhere.

"It was almost as if he could not bear the sight of me—or so I thought. Now I know that he always had my best interests at heart. Perhaps he felt that without my mother at his side, he was not fit to raise me. He had several mistresses but never married again. But then he gave his life for my safety in the end." She sighed and turned her attention to the checkerboard. She moved her piece swiftly, capturing four of his. As she went to take them off the board, his hand reached out for hers.

"Any father who did not love you would have to be a freak of nature," he said hotly. "If I were your father I would dote on you, cherish you and find it hard to let you out of my sight. I would grant your every whim and be your slave.''

He felt the slight movement of her hand, first retreating from his clasp and then consenting to it. It drew his attention to the fact that his grasp was too eager. Reluctantly he released her hand and lay back against the pillows.

"It's your move," she said softly, but he seemed to have lost interest in the desultory game. His strong, attractive face was no longer pale from the accident, but the signs of stress and uncertainty were unmistakable.

"Your move," she repeated.

A small smile lifted the corners of his mouth. "I would probably have spoiled you terribly and turned you into a demanding, imperious shrew," he said, "if I'd been your father."

"Then it's just as well you are not," she said, giving up on the checkers and putting the pieces away carefully in their inlaid box. She began to busy herself tidying up the room, replacing the game set in a drawer, pouring him fresh drinking water and collecting used glasses on a tray.

She was busily straightening his bedcovers for the night when she paused and flashed him a smile that tripped his pulse rhythms. "You are much too young—by any stretch of the imagination—to be my father."

"And I'm heartily glad of that," he said fervently.

She gave him a chiding look as she took the tray. "Good night, Sebastian. I hope you sleep well." Her voice was firm and even, but her slight shiver of excitement was betrayed by the chink of crystal on the tray.

The next day he expressed a desire for fresh air.

"You're supposed to rest in bed until tomorrow," Julie said dubiously.

"Just the garden," he begged. "I'm not used to so much confinement. Besides, resting in bed is not so restful when you're in the room. You're far too pretty to make this a restful exercise."

"Should I perhaps appoint Victor as your companion," she suggested, "to make your convalescence more restful?"

"I am not in need of rest," he assured her, "merely fresh air, exercise—and the kind of restorative stimulation that Victor cannot supply."

By midmorning the sun was sparkling bright and she consented to a short airing. She brought him Guillaume's warmest alpaca dressing robe and a muffler, then, carefully holding his arm, walked him down the stairs and out into the small garden at the back of the house.

They strolled for a while under the bare branches of the cherry trees and soon she was chattering again, sharing with him her summers at Clarendon, her doting grandmother, her English friends and her years at Sainte-Martine des Anges, where she roomed with three other girls and sometimes giggled until the small hours of the morning.

He was an attentive, sympathetic listener and it occurred to her now as she spoke that Sebastian knew more about her than Guillaume did or had ever wanted to know.

After their walk, they were both reluctant to return to the house so soon. The day was beautiful, dry, still and filled with the crisp clean snap of winter. It was chill in the shade but pleasantly mild in the sun, so they sat for a while on the sun-warmed stone steps that led back up to the salon doors.

Julie hugged her knees and lifted her face up to the sun. "The physician will be back tomorrow," she said. "I think he will find you much recovered. Well enough to leave, perhaps," she said, and heard the regret in her voice.

"And it's all thanks to you," he answered. "This has been terribly dull for you, I'm afraid."

"Dull?" She laughed. "Sebastian, I think perhaps you have a distorted view of the life of a Parisian matron. My days are quite routine, and it has been a most welcome change to hear from someone who has traveled the world over. Tell me some more of your adventures."

Leaning his elbows on the steps, he stretched out and thought for a moment, then regaled her with a tale of an island peopled with dusky South Sea natives. As he spoke, his eyes focused on the white clouds above the cherry trees. She listened entranced, as much by the sheer closeness of his profile as by the seafaring adventure he narrated.

It was the sweetest of December days, but for Julie it was clouded by knowing it was probably the last day they would ever spend together. With his health restored, there was no way to prolong his stay.

On the fourth morning, when the doctor pronounced him well enough to leave, he asked for Guillaume.

"He has been called out to the provinces by the minister," Julie told him. "He cannot be here to bid you farewell, but he wishes you a fair trip back to England. He left early this morning and did not wish to disturb you."

"I wanted to thank him for his care and hospitality."

"I will tell him. He left you this," she said, holding out a large sealed envelope. "It contains your keys, money and personal items you had about you when you were brought here. Do you wish to open it and go through the contents before you leave?"

"I'm sure that's not necessary." He thrust the envelope into the deep pocket of his frock coat.

Julie was wearing her cape and her muff. "Our carriage will return you to your lodgings," she said. "It is waiting in the courtyard."

"Will you ride with me?"

"I shall indeed," she said, "and I will stay with you until you are safely up the stairs and in your rooms…just in case the dizziness returns."

If he saw through that remark, saw how she longed to postpone their final separation, his face betrayed nothing except pleasure and gratitude. They both knew that he was quite restored and able to make his way alone. Dressed in his new greatcoat, a fair duplicate of his old one, he looked much the same as he had when he'd arrived to present her with new gloves. The dressing that had bound his head had been removed the previous day.

Except for the shaved patch at the back of his head where his wound had been tended, he was the same man, she thought. But it wasn't so. That man had been a stranger. This man was a close companion. She knew that he hated oysters and parsnips, that he was fond of music but sang out of tune and refused to admit it. She was familiar with the way his body curled when he slept, with the sound of his laughter, with a dozen subtle and baffling expressions that informed his mobile face.

Of the countless little details she had gathered about this man, she cherished each one. And she knew, oh yes, she knew beyond a doubt that he found her desirable, and that with the very least hint of encouragement . . . She banished the fantasy before it captured her completely. It was out of the question.

Side by side in the carriage, they talked briefly of his immediate plans. His business in France was completed. He would pack his things, pay his reckoning at his lodging and take the first post chaise to Calais. The flurry of conversation prompted by her questions was brief, for she was soon left with the one question she could not voice.

How will I part with you? she wondered. A kiss on the cheek seemed the most appropriate, as if he were a very dear old friend. But it was only a partial answer, for the question had depths she was fearful to explore. Somewhere in her breast throbbed the question, how can I *bear* to part with you? How can I bear to pick up the busy, meaningless life I led before I met you?

This is nonsense, she told herself. It has been a diverting episode and it is over. There is nothing more to it than that. How could there be?

He turned to her, and she could feel the disturbing bulk of his arm against her shoulder. "Did you say something?"

She was startled to discover that she had spoken her thoughts half-aloud. "I was just wondering what the weather will be like for your journey," she said briskly. "The Channel crossing can be odious at this time of year."

He grinned. "It's a very small crossing. It won't bother me."

"No, of course not." She remembered that he had sailed distant seas, had braved the fury of tropical hurricanes, and she felt foolish, disconsolate and lost.

His lodgings were at the Relais Grenache, an inn just north of La Madeleine and one of the regular stations of the Calais post. Sebastian's rooms were on the third floor with a view of slate rooftops and spires. She mounted the stairs with him on the pretext that he might succumb to a dizzy spell. She entered his rooms to help him pack, but he insisted that she had pampered him enough. He made her sit in an armchair and rang for hot tea. "You will sit and rest while I pack," he said. "You've toiled ceaselessly over me for days."

He had become impersonal and very correct, as if the distance between them had already begun to widen. "I must learn to do without all your tender loving care. It won't be easy, Julie." With those words he turned, leaving the sitting room to enter the inner bedchamber.

It was a brief, insignificant departure, but as he turned away to leave one room for another, she felt a tugging beneath her ribs as if her heart would follow him, a foretaste of how she would feel when he left in earnest, forever. The chill desolation of that thought made her shiver and pull her cape tight about her shoulders.

For distraction she turned her attention to her surroundings, her eye registering each cornice, carpet and floorboard as if she were preparing an auction catalog. A daybed and armchairs covered in well-worn chintz...a sturdy oaken writing table. Plain country furniture and white-painted walls adorned with etchings of Paris and a traveler's map. A large stone hearth with a coal fire freshly laid and ready to kindle. A bell cord of braided silk hung to the right of the hearth.

It was not where the fashionable would lodge, but it was clean, carpeted with thick Turkey red carpets, and generous in size and comfort.

An apt place for a man of substance making a brief sojourn in the city, she thought. *Brief*. She found a cutting edge to the word. Her hands clenched into fists, pressing against her knees. She would not fall in love with this man. Absolutely and positively, she would not! How could she be so stupid as to let herself love a man who in a few hours would be nothing but a memory?

The boy who brought in the tea was no velvet-clad footman but a young city lad of perhaps twelve. He wore long trousers, a coarse linen smock and the short carmagnole jacket of the Paris working class, but he seemed passably clean. She asked him to kindle the fire and he obliged, lighting a taper from the wall sconce burning in the hallway. She was shivering, and it was a great comfort to see the flames leap up.

Sebastian emerged from the bedchamber in dark breeches and frock coat, his cravat hanging loose about his shirt. He was already dressed for traveling, she noted. He intended to waste no time. "When does the post chaise leave, boy?" he asked.

It had left an hour ago, but an express carrier leaving at noon could get him to Beauvais before nightfall. He could pick up the Paris to Calais post from there.

"Or you could wait until tomorrow morning, sir," the boy added. "The post leaves here at seven every morning." He waited for Sebastian to consider his alternatives. "Shall I reserve a place for you on this afternoon's express, then? Or will it be tomorrow?"

Instead of replying, Sebastian turned his gaze on Julie and raised one eyebrow, as if the answer lay with her.

"Tomorrow," she said without hesitation.

He nodded to the boy as he gave him a tip, and as soon as the door closed behind him, Sebastian pulled Julie up from the chair. "Thank you," he whispered, and there was such heavy meaning in that whisper that she felt a sudden awkwardness and wondered exactly what he had taken her to mean by that one unthinking word. She had spoken utterly without calculation, and to veil her nervousness, she began to babble.

"My coach is waiting below. Now we have the rest of the day, I will take you on a tour of Paris. I know you've visited before, but always on business, and I'm quite sure there are many things of great interest you have never had the opportu—"

He laid a finger on her lips, stopping her in midsentence, and tugged at her bonnet strings. "I have seen the city sights and had my fill of them." He lifted her bonnet and tossed it behind him while her hair tumbled loose and long about her shoulders. He stroked the tresses, then let his fingers trail lightly along her shoulder and down her arm, his eyes never leaving hers.

"There is only one tour I long to take..."

A riptide of longing surged through her blood, making her feel so naked that she looked down to avoid his gaze. He lifted her head and touched her lips briefly with his. Too briefly.

She was hardly aware of her actions as her lips sought his again, and this time his arms enfolded her and she clung to him. In the tight circumference of his arms her lips parted. She felt the soft kiss of his tongue, gentle and amorous on hers, and for a moment it was enough to receive its tentative caress. A brushing of her inner lip, a probing of the inner walls of her mouth, and suddenly the gentle play became an exploration, a bid for possession.

Julie responded eagerly, driven by an urge she had never known before. It was as if she were incomplete, as if she must for her very survival blend herself with him until from heart to outer skin their identities merged into one body and one soul, inseparable and complete.

When he released her, she stood trembling and rooted to the spot. Slowly her wits began to reassemble and she was appalled that in moments she had become so addicted to the warm pressure of his body, that without it, she shuddered at the coolness of the room. It was as though she were suddenly deprived of a life-sustaining warmth.

"I will send your driver home," he whispered, and taking her hand, he pressed his lips to the racing pulse at her wrist. "We shan't need him again."

It had begun to rain when he reached the courtyard. He sent the Farroux carriage home with a generous tip to the driver, who, happy enough to be released, asked no questions. Next he sought out his host, the bullnecked Georges Cavette.

The innkeeper was in his closet of an office behind the tavern room, working at his accounts. With his heavy chest and arms, Cavette seemed too massive to be at ease working with the small meticulous columns of figures.

"I may stay a day or two longer if the rooms are still available," Sebastian told him. "At any rate, don't hold a seat for me in the morning's post. I may not be ready to leave."

Cavette nodded, the gesture so reminiscent of a fighting bull about to charge that his words seemed at odds in their mildness.

"Happy to have you stay as long as it pleases you, sir. Your reckoning has been paid in advance for the next six nights in any case. I hope your head is mended."

Sebastian paused, digesting the news. "Who paid you?"

"Why, the messenger you sent. My wife and I, we were sorry to hear about your fall."

"Well, I— Yes, I'm quite mended now, thank you." He mounted the stairs with a distinct feeling of unease. He did not wish to become Farroux's creature. He had not yet made his decision known, and for some reason was reluctant to do so. But already he was beholden to the deputy. It irked him even though he could hardly blame the old man for assuming consent.

Reentering his rooms, he found Julie standing at the window, staring out at the rain. She cast a brief look over her shoulder at the sound of his entrance, then turned back again to the rain without a word, as though she could not face him. Her hesitance puzzled him. He was no ravisher of maidens; she had come with him freely enough. Surely she would not have stayed if she wished otherwise. And yet she gave him not the least encouragement. Although her bonnet still lay on the chair where it had fallen, she had yet to remove her cape.

It was not lack of desire, this reluctance; he knew that, at least. Over the past few days, he could recall a dozen indications, gestures, small kindnesses—and then there was her

passionate response to his kiss. She needed love as surely as
a flower needed the sun, and because she was artless, she
was easy to read. An easy conquest surely, and yet as he
stood looking at her slender vulnerable back, so rigid and
still in the gray winter light, ten years of success with women
seemed to fall away and he felt an uncertainty....

He joined her at the window. Standing behind her, he
breathed in the lavender fragrance of hair. Julie was very
young, even if she was four years' married. She believed she
was betraying her husband—a practice unremarkable
enough in these times, but not for Julie Farroux. With all
Paris cavorting in a veritable merry-go-round of fornica-
tion, this lovely creature actually found it hard to take that
first step into adultery. It was an aberration with a charm of
its own.

He would make it easy for her, he resolved, and reached
for her cape. "The room is warmer now, Julie," he said
softly. "May I take your cape?"

But she moved away from him and shook her head. He
did not insist but stood watching her, his expression vulnerable. It had not occurred to her that he might be less than
poised and confident in the act of seduction. But that of
course was all it was. Seduction.

During his absence she'd had time to reconsider. Reality
had now descended like a stone. He would be gone tomorrow, his real life calling him away. If she gave herself to him
now she would be no more than an interlude. She would bid
him adieu.

But neither of them made a sound and there was such a
palpable quiet in the room that for the first time she became aware of the rain, heard it splashing on the roadway
below the closed window.

She turned to the couch and picked up her bonnet. Her
arms felt leaden as she put it on. A few days of acquaintance, one kiss, and she had lost her heart, lost her independent ability to generate contentment. Could any human
being become essential to her happiness in so short a time?
It seemed so. But how much worse it would be if she surrendered to him now and tomorrow saw him leave. What

could she look forward to then? Even if they remained lovers, the most she could expect was endless months of longing and brief reunions, stolen in secret. Nothing would change the fact that his life lay in England and hers here.

No, it was not to be borne. The longer she stayed, the more wrenching it would be to part. She must do it now, while she still had strength. She could not trust herself to speak. He would have to know, to understand. He questioned her with his eyes, but all she could do was shake her head again.

Without a word she made for the door, and when he called her name, she paused, willing herself not to turn back. How she wanted to take one last look, to etch his dear features into her memory forever! No, I must not, she thought. It was better to forget how he looked than to torment herself for the rest of her days.

Chapter Six

Guillaume Farroux stepped down from the carriage at his usual corner of the Rue Saint-Antoine. As always when the weather permitted, he would finish the morning journey to his office on foot. The walk was good not only for his constitution but for his soul, passing as it did through the heart of the most civilized city in the most civilized nation on earth. It never failed to remind him of how far he had advanced in this, the greatest seat of power on earth.

Heading into a side street, he passed by the Café Duclos, where some of the minor government officials sometimes gathered for meals. At that moment Barras's senior clerk, Paul Voisin, sat alone at a window table taking breakfast. Guillaume acknowledged him with a smile, touching the brim of his beaver hat. The poor man's days were numbered. Barras had a new mistress whose ambitious young brother had a covetous eye on Voisin's position. Barras would "advance" Voisin to some post in the Weights and Measure Department and send him into the provinces to spread the gospel of centralization. What a waste of an able fellow! But then Director Barras himself would soon fall prey to another, stronger predator. Raw power was akin to raw nature.

Guillaume's taste ran to a quieter but more enduring power. To acquire it took certain qualities, which Guillaume had first observed in Talleyrand. Like Talleyrand, Guillaume had withstood the downfall of a monarchy, two indiscriminate massacres and three coups. But unlike the illustrious foreign minister, who was born to great position and wealth, Guillaume had been heir to little but wit. He was fifth in a line of humble country lawyers. But he was the first Farroux to come to Paris and the first to rise above virtual servitude to the masters of Marduquesnes.

It had not happened by chance. All his life he had courted power as other men courted wealth or women. Not the short-lived power that dressed itself in crown or toga or military braid, but the real power, flexible enough to meet all circumstances and exploit them. He liked to think of it as a gray unnoticeable current that ran so deep into the life-blood of a nation that it was all but indestructible. Each step in his climb was a tribute to his patience, his shrewd assessments, his lifelong study of human nature, both individually and en masse.

The Reign of Terror had been the culminating test of his arts, and he had passed it. Now Marduquesnes was his with all its fat meadows and grazing and villages and half of its income. Nothing lacked but an heir.

He had thought, when he had married young Juliette, that it would be only a matter of time before she took a lover and presented him with a son he could acknowledge as his own, but time was running out for him. Perhaps he should have made his intentions clear from the outset, but the girl had been numb with shock. His first concern had been to make her feel secure, and then let nature take its course. She was young, comely and leading a leisurely life in a society that was free to the point of licentiousness. Sooner or later she should have discovered temptation. How could he have anticipated such relentless chastity from the daughter of Charles Sainte Aube—a man of the grossest appetites and promiscuity? He would have bedded her himself if there had been the remotest chance of success, but he had relinquished the hope of a child from his own loins many years ago. There was no other reason to bed her; temptations of the flesh had long since yielded in him to temptations of the mind. His deepest satisfaction had always been the successful manipulation of lives; now it was his only satisfaction.

No, it could never be a blood child, but it would be his own brain child, accepted by the courts as his flesh and blood—that would be more than enough to circumvent the restitution clause Sainte Aube had insisted on placing in the contract.

Ramlin had dropped into his lap like a ripe plum, healthy, young, ambitious—and most convenient of all, a foreigner who could remain long enough to complete his task, then be gone for good.

The plan had its flaws of course. He might have overestimated Ramlin's chances of making a conquest. Julie might be slow to conceive and Ramlin could not remain in France much more than twenty days; then it would be months before he could return. But for four thousand louis, it was worth the gamble, especially if he gave it every chance to succeed.

He had absented himself from the house for a day or two, but it was unlikely that Juliette, obsessed as she was with duty, would succumb to a lover under her husband's roof. It did, however, give Guillaume some time to draw up his next step, now that Ramlin's cooperation was no longer in doubt.

Leisure and privacy were what was needed. Marduquesnes was the natural place for this romance to be consummated—far enough removed from Paris to be discreet, staffed by villagers who never left the region, and conducive to seduction with its gentle green slopes and sense of isolation. He could smell again the fragrance of wildflowers in their full summer profusion, feel the sweet shade of the woodlands on a hot day. But it was December. What plausible reason could he find for having her undertake a lengthy stay in the country in midwinter? Some problem to be solved . . . some matter of discretion, perhaps, that could not be handled by messenger or letter. Ah, he would devise something to be sure, for what could be more appropriate than to have the heir to Marduquesnes conceived in the château itself?

* * *

Sebastian found himself staring after Julie as she slipped away from his room, astonished that he could think of no way to stop her. He had not expected to be rendered speechless and powerless by her sudden change of mind, nor had he expected the stew of feelings that simmered in his breast. Hot desire, an almost paternal tenderness, shame and guilt all battled fiercely in him. It was unthinkable to let her slip out of his life now. He must do something, he decided, pacing the length and then the breadth of the rooms. But what? There was such an ambivalence in him that he seemed to have no judgment, no resourcefulness. Surely, surely there was *something* he could do.

On the coverlet of his bed he found the large envelope she had given him that morning from Farroux. He opened it and discovered a key to his rooms, his money purse and a bank draft promising to pay the bearer four thousand louis d'or.

If she should ever suspect he had agreed to seduce her for this paltry sum . . . He shuddered at the thought. But it was not so paltry that it could not buy him precious time, bring him that much closer to solvency. He took the draft in his hand, slid his thumb over the fine cambric weave of the paper. Over the penned words "four thousand louis d'or" a stamp embossed the paper. His guilt in receiving this sum was like a stamp embossing his soul, a disfigurement. All at once he felt so vile that he had a strong urge to throw the draft on the fire. Clutching the paper, he reached out his hand to the glowing coals, then drew it back.

To burn the paper would destroy only the evidence, not the base agreement he'd entered into. Only by returning the draft to Farroux or tearing it up in his presence could he truly clear his conscience and approach Julie as his own man.

But to reject Farroux's proposal was to reject his cooperation. Farroux would do everything in his power to make sure he never saw Julie again, and the man's power was not to be discounted. Then too, he might be bringing a host of other evils upon himself. He could count on Farroux's aid at present, but to some extent he could expect his ill will if he reneged on his end of the bargain, perhaps to the point of ruination. And worse, Farroux would seek some other swain for Julie, one even less scrupulous than himself. The thought of some ambitious Lothario seducing Julie, exploiting that young lissome body for material gain, sent bile into his throat. About one thing at least he had not lied to her. When he told her he desired her, it was the truth, and he knew the feeling was mutual.

Why, then, had she left? A change of heart while she was alone for those few minutes in his room? She had certainly not discovered what lay in the envelope; he had just broken the seal himself.

He was half in love with her already, he realized, and as wounded by her leaving as though he were in his teens under the spell of an infatuation. He must see her again. That alone he knew. And yet if he pursued her now, four thousand louis richer than he was this morning, he would be weighed down by this odious deception. He wanted to be worthy of her, but to purge his conscience would surely be to lose her. He would not risk that.

He felt trapped in a dilemma of his own making, and his thoughts were beginning to race in circles. To escape the mental treadmill, he hired a hack from the inn's stable and rode out through the cold wet city streets and byways until dark. He returned numb with cold and saddle sore but no wiser or easier in his mind.

It was not until after a turbulent sleepless night that he determined he would call on Julie and demand to know why she had so suddenly abandoned him. He had, he decided, a right to know.

Anne-Marie sat on the edge of a boudoir chair watching Julie plunge into the neat pile of wraps, robes and undergarments on her bed. She claimed to be assembling a traveling wardrobe, but she was clearly creating havoc. Why on earth was she not leaving it to Babette? What was more to the point, why was she going at all? Marduquesnes at this time of year? What could be more absurd? "I can't imagine what Guillaume is thinking of to ask this of you," she said crossly.

"He needs me there, obviously." Julie tossed a pair of lawn pantalets on top of a green cashmere shawl. In fact, it was a relief to immerse herself in some useful task, a relief to be leaving Paris for a while.

She had returned home the previous afternoon in a state of distraction, her emotions swinging wildly between remorse for letting herself come so near to compromise and sharp regret that she had lost the chance forever. She would never be in Sebastian's arms again.

When Guillaume had mentioned his concerns that evening, she had leaped at the opportunity to go to Marduquesnes and investigate. To Anne-Marie, however, it was an imposition, an outrage.

"What could possibly be so important in the country at the height of the Paris season? Guillaume has his brother taking care of estate matters, does he not? Besides, you'll be missing our next soiree!"

"That hardly matters."

"Not matter!" Anne-Marie stamped her foot in frustration. "You could have really become acquainted with Hortense de Beauharnais. She may even bring her stepfather with her, General Bonaparte, in case you've forgotten! He's at fearful loose ends waiting for his wife to return from Italy. Mama is keeping it deliberately intimate. You really are tiresome, Julie."

Julie shrugged. "It's something that must be resolved. There are discrepancies in the livestock accounts and Guillaume thinks his brother may be suffering lapses of memory and needs to be retired. Anyway, an estate always suffers from an absentee landlord. Guillaume cannot take the time. I really have no choice."

"Well it's a terrible shame—criminal! Oh, I completely forgot! Aside from everything else, were you not on the brink of an amour with that dark handsome man at the opera? How is that progressing?"

Julie turned her face away so that Anne-Marie would not see the tears that sprang suddenly to her eyes. She lifted a gray riding habit from the bed and laid it on the press, then reversed her decision in favor of a blue habit. She turned determinedly to a crisp pile of petticoats. Which ones would she take? But her tear-blurred vision made it hard to distinguish one from another.

Sensing something amiss, Anne-Marie rose and joined her at the foot of the bed. Julie attacked the petticoats, blindly tossing them about. The need to share her secret was a fierce ache at the base of her throat.

"My dear, dear friend, is something wrong?"

The sympathy in Anne-Marie's voice was too much. Julie drew breath to speak and promptly began to sob. Anne-Marie embraced her until the weeping subsided.

"There, there, my pet. You shan't leave Paris if you don't want to." Anne-Marie stroked her hair. "I shall speak to Guillaume myself. I don't think he has any idea what a hardship this is for you."

Julie pulled away, brushing the tears with the back of her hand and shaking her head. "It's not leaving Paris that saddens me, it's Sebastian leaving me. Oh, Anne-Marie, I never meant for this to happen.... But we grew so close in a matter of three days—and I never thought it could make me so unhappy. I love him so!"

Anne-Marie clutched her face in horror. "Oh, my dear, has he broken your heart already?"

"Yes. No. Oh, Anne-Marie, it's impossible," she blurted out, and described the events of the past few days.

Anne-Marie pinched her pert little chin and frowned. "But this could be a grand passion. You cannot simply walk away without a word. It is terrible luck that he has to leave, but it's not reason enough to destroy something of beauty. You can survive the separations. You'll find distractions. And you can look forward to his return."

Julie shook her head violently. "You don't understand how hard it was to part from him after just one kiss. If we become lovers...if I grow accustomed to him...if I let this love take root in my heart, it will be impossible to live without him. My only sane course is to nip it in the bud. To start this very day to forget him, and pray it will happen quickly."

At the sound of two raps, both heads turned toward the door. Babette entered. "Mr. Ramlin has called, Citizeness. He wishes to have a word with you. I have shown him into the drawing room."

Julie paused, willing her body to be still when every nerve and sinew vibrated with the urge to fly down the stairs and into Sebastian's arms. For a moment the effort was so great that she could not speak but merely shook her head. "No," she managed finally, "I will not see him."

"Of course she'll see him, Babette. Tell him to wait," Anne-Marie said quickly. She laid her hand on Julie's trembling arm. "Please, please," she begged in a whisper, "don't send him away without one word. At least wish him well and a fair journey home."

Julie looked at Babette, who was standing confused and irresolute by the door, and found herself nodding. As soon as the door closed Julie clutched her friend's hand. "If I am to do this, you must come with me."

"Well of course, I long to meet him, Julie, but now is surely not the time. You must have privacy."

"No! You do not know how he affects me. Privacy would be dangerous. I insist you stay."

Anne-Marie sighed. "Very well, I will accompany you, but I must say I find you quite perverse. You have a husband old enough to be your grandfather and a marriage that—it is clear to any fool—is little more than a business contract. Downstairs waits a man who could bring you joy and fulfillment and happiness—all that your marriage lacks. Why must you complicate everything so? Why do you not grasp the opportunity gladly?"

Tears threatened to gather again in Julie's eyes. "Because it would end in grief, Anne-Marie. Nothing but grief."

"Nonsense! If the separations seem long, we'll find some lesser amours to distract your heart while he's away."

Despite her internal agitation, Julie found herself laughing. "You should have lived in Louis XIV's reign, my friend. If you ever decide to behave as outrageously as you talk, I pity Bernard."

"I'll worry about Bernard, thank you," Anne-Marie said with great dignity. "You worry about the man downstairs." Taking Julie's arm, she led her out to the hallway.

At the top of the staircase, Julie held back. "My face! My coiffure! I've been weeping. I must freshen my toilette before I see him."

Anne-Marie drew her toward the tall window and scrutinized her face in the shaft of daylight. "You look deliciously pale and romantic. You need nothing more."

"But my eyes must be red."

"They are not red at all, merely somewhat bedewed. Besides, if you go back to your boudoir now, you will change your mind and I shall never get you out again."

Julie laughed again and realized that Anne-Marie's unfailing ability to raise laughter was one of her most lovable qualities. "Why am I allowing you to bully me in this fashion?"

Anne-Marie did not hesitate. "Because I am only making you do what you really want to do. And in this fashion, you can tell yourself you were strong, you were saintly. It was only because of your feckless friend that you were forced, yes, cruelly, brutally forced—"

Julie silenced her lips with two fingers. "Are you hinting that I am a hypocrite? A prude?"

Anne-Marie's mouth became a tight little rosebud as she took Julie by the arm and began to descend the stairs. "I was merely answering your question, Julie. As for your last inquiry, I can only reply, if the shoe fits, Citizeness Perfect, then it must be yours."

"Good day, Mr. Ramlin, what a pleasant surprise," Julie said as they entered the drawing room. "Anne-Marie, may I present Sebastian Ramlin. My dear friend, Anne-Marie Cassat."

She watched him exchange a brief salutation with Anne-Marie. He looks tired, she thought, as if he has slept as little as I. "I thought you were leaving for Calais this morning." Her voice emerged cool and colorless in her effort to remain unaffected by his nearness.

"Well, yes, I had planned to—but certain unexpected events have detained me for a while longer. I came to tell you that—" He broke off and glanced miserably at Anne-Marie, then turned back to Julie. "That I will remain in Paris for some time more. In fact as long as my commitments in England will allow. I was hoping to have a private word with you on an important matter."

Anne-Marie stirred herself. "I was in fact about to make my departure, sir. I am delighted to have met you, and trust we shall meet again. Now if you will forgive my haste, I simply must leave." She turned and kissed Julie's cheek, whispering into her ear, "Remember what I said."

Sebastian exhaled noisily as the door closed behind Anne-Marie, leaving them alone. His gaze fastened on Julie with a fierce intensity. "Why?"

"Because I had to protect myself."

"From me? But I thought . . ."

Julie gave a weak smile. "From loving a man who will be more absent from my life than present. From condemning myself to heartaches and longings that will seldom be fulfilled."

"Did you think I would run off this morning after what happened between us?"

"Nothing happened but a kiss, Mr. Ramlin."

"It was a good deal more than that. Do you think I failed to notice how your heart raced along with mine? Can you deny that your willing participation was a promise of much more?"

He took her silence for agreement and opened his arms to her. "Julie, Julie—"

"As it happens," she said, stepping back from his intended embrace, "it matters little whether or not you remain in Paris. I am leaving in the morning for my country estate."

He frowned, and as his expression changed, she could see the pallor of his cheeks and knew that his feelings were deeply engaged. "Your husband is a deputy. I cannot believe he would vacate Paris with the government in full session. Why do you—"

"It is not my husband who is leaving. It is I."

"For how long?"

She shook her head. "A few days, weeks perhaps."

"Then let me come with you." He grasped her wrists.

"No!" She tried to withdraw her wrists from his hands but his grasp was too strong.

"You can leave Paris, but you cannot run away from the fact that you are a flesh-and-blood woman. Oh, Julie, you know how much I want you! And I know that you have a heart as well as a mind. Don't ignore it. You say you are protecting yourself from grief. But if you protect yourself too much you will never live at all."

"I will do as I see fit . . ." she began.

He stopped her words with a kiss. She pressed him back with her arms, but he held her firmly until her resistance melted. All the sweetness of their first kiss came rushing back and it was too late. The cautious practicality that had brought her intact to that moment in her life, that precious talent for survival, seemed to fall away, crumbling to dust like ancient, brittle parchment . . . and a strange new recklessness took its place.

No matter what befell, she would not waste this happiness. She would gather it greedily and live for the moment. The future would have to take care of itself.

"Let me come with you," he whispered again, and this time she knew she would not deny him.

Chapter Seven

Château Marduquesnes, Loire

She had not brought Babette with her, and she had taken the post chaise rather than the family carriage so that none of the Paris household would know that Sebastian was her traveling companion.

Guillaume raised no protest when Julie announced her intention to travel unescorted in a public conveyance. His easy consent surprised her, but she knew he was distracted by his work at the time and more than grateful that she agreed to go at all. In fact it had all gone so smoothly, so easily, she thought as they approached their destination, that it confirmed what she had at first merely suspected: it was all meant to happen thus.

On the two-day journey south with Sebastian, she had shed every last misgiving, each mile put between herself and Paris increasing her confidence in the rightness of what she was doing.

Their overnight stay at Etampes offered no romantic opportunities. The *auberge* was crowded with travelers and she was obliged to share a room with two other women passengers on the post. By the time they were alone together, two days' proximity in the cramped post had intensified her desires until there was no room for second thoughts.

They arrived at Marduquesnes very late, and rather than rouse the servants up at the château, they used the guest lodge, where a bed was always made ready for visitors and log fires were laid in the grates.

It had begun to snow heavily and the stone lodge was cold. When the fires were kindled and the lamps lit, they stood in front of the sitting room hearth sipping brandy from Sebastian's travel flask. She gave a little shudder at the first swallow, not caring for the taste but welcoming its warmth.

"Cold?" he said, and gently rubbed her back. Even through the thickness of her heavy winter mantle her body responded to his touch with longing—and nervous anxiety.

"I found warming pans in the bedroom," she said, "but no coal. We shall have to—"

"We shan't need them," he said. Draining his brandy, he turned her to face him. He looked at her glass. "Drink up. You may not like the taste, but I promise it will feel good going down from here...to here." With his fingertip he traced a path as he spoke, starting at her lips and trailing down her throat.

She downed the remainder of her drink in one gulp, let him take the glass from her and draw her into his arms. His lips met hers in the lightest of caresses.

"I have a great desire to make love to you this very night," he whispered. "But you are cold and travel weary, and I will not press you."

"It is warm in your arms," she said, the brandy making her bold.

He kissed her again with more purpose. Then, with great delicacy, he explored her temples, the delicate wings of her nose, the round thrust of her chin. Whisper-light kisses roamed her face. Parting her mantle, he moved his mouth down to the base of her throat and lower.

She gave a light gasp and drew back to seek his mouth with hers, mingling velvet interiors, dark as wine. When he lifted her off her feet she made no protest.

The bedroom was small and already warm from the blazing logs. Setting her down beside the bed, he removed her mantle and the fichu at her throat.

A wave of shyness seized her when her feet touched the floor, but it quickly ebbed away. In the dormitory of Sainte-Martine they had discussed such occasions, speculating and giggling over the mysteries of seduction, bridal nights and the like. None of them was quite as ignorant as they were expected to be. Most had observed the mating of animals. Some girls had older sisters who were married.

But for all their shared knowledge, Julie had never been able to picture herself being unrobed by a man as anything but a humiliating ordeal. There were such scores of tiny hooks and closures, so many layers to overcome. But now she was seized by a desire that had been mounting for days. As he continued to caress her, she was aware of little but his touch, his voice and her growing need to be utterly consumed.

He drew down her loosened bodice, uncovering her breasts and exploring them with his hands. Then his lips fastened on her soft pale nipple and he began to suckle, drawing on the tiny dormant bud in a firm rhythm.

She began to murmur, wordless whimpering sounds of pleasure and excitement. When she lay naked on the sheet, she was too enraptured to feel how cold it struck on her bare skin.

Kneeling beside her, he took her hand and placed it on her breast, where his lips had been. She could feel the risen nipple under her palm, hot and moist from his mouth, and his breath was warm in her ear.

"Julie, oh, Julie! This tells me of your desire . . . just as this . . . tells you of mine."

She had heard of the hardness of a man, but never before had she felt it. The tension in her mounted to such a fever pitch of wanting that it crashed through every last barrier of her reserve, and she felt the deep centers of her body weep with a craving to receive him. She cried out to him to take her, but as if he had not heard, he continued his leisurely exploration of her body, caressing every curve and valley until she was opening to him in undisguisable lust and begging for release from the suffocating tensions that racked her body.

When at last he moved between her thighs, easing forward, she heard him exclaim in shock and draw back.

"No, please!" she protested. "Please don't stop."

"But you—"

"Yes, but tonight you will change that. Please!"

After a moment she felt his silken gentle probing, which only goaded her more with the need to possess him.

His voice was oddly thick. "I'll try not to hurt you."

"Don't spare me! I cannot bear it any longer. I must have you now!" And such was her pitch of excitement that she felt not the pain as he entered her but only tumultuous waves of tension followed by relief, as if she were a storm-tossed sea that could know no peace until its fury was utterly spent.

"Oh, Julie," he said when they lay entwined and at rest, "why in the name of God did you not tell me you were a virgin?"

"I was ashamed."

"Your husband—has he never even—"

"Never. I believe he is impotent, or just too old to desire me."

She was astonished at the ease with which she could lie nested with him and naked under the covers, awed at the bond of intimacy forged between them with one act of love. It was a bond she had never experienced with another human being. She could speak freely, tell him anything now. He had become her other self. It was a wondrous and intoxicating sense of freedom.

"Julie," he murmured, fondly caressing her shoulders, "no man is too old to desire you. Guillaume Farroux is either impotent, or..."

"Or what?"

"Nothing you should know about, my innocent love."

"A pederast? I don't think so."

Sebastian laughed, tightening his arms about her. "So my little virgin does have some knowledge of the world's corrupted ways and aberrations."

"Well, of course! Being a virgin does not make a woman an idiot or an ignoramus, my darling—nor does being a faithful wife."

"You are no one's wife. The marriage was never consummated."

"It's a contract in law nevertheless. Signed and sealed."

Sebastian slid his hand along her thigh and cupped her bent knee. "For that matter you're not a virgin, either.... Did I hurt you?"

"No. As a matter of fact it was surprisingly..." She stopped, realizing she knew no single word that could adequately describe what she felt at becoming one with him.

His hand tightened on her knee. "Surprisingly what?"

"Pleasant."

"*Pleasant?* I am damned with faint praise," he murmured in her ear.

"Enjoyable, then. Extremely enjoyable."

He raised himself on one elbow and looked down into her face with a lopsided grin. "Virgins aren't supposed to enjoy being deflowered. There is supposed to be vast room for improvement."

And wives were not supposed to be virgins after almost four years of marriage. What other rules have I broken? she wondered, not really caring. "I was a little anxious about what you would think. About what was expected of me. Perhaps," she added in a thoughtful voice, "perhaps there *is* room for improvement. Now I know what to expect."

This from a virgin, he thought, still quite shaken by that discovery. She looked up at him, her skin silken smooth and redolent of lavender. No erotic French perfumes that heated the blood with their sexual overtones—just innocent country lavender. Everything about her was an unexpected delight. The back of his fingers lingered on the curve of her cheek, then he turned his hand, lightly floating his palm down until it nestled between her breasts for a moment then slid up to cup one of them. "Perhaps," he said, smiling.

Jolted by the instant erotic pleasure of his hand, she gave an audible gasp. "We'll not know until we try," she breathed.

2, Nivose, VI (December 23, 1797)

Dear Husband,

You will be relieved to know that I arrived safely last night after an uneventful, if tedious, journey. As it turned out, the post chaise was a fortunate choice (five staging posts and fresh horses at every one!) Thanks to its speed, I was here before the snow began to settle. It snowed steadily throughout the night and everything here is covered in a soft white blanket—no carts or carriages on the road today. So peaceful!

This morning I had Bijou saddled and rode her out to Joseph's house. You will be pleased to hear that the matter of the flocks is already resolved!

There have been no severe losses in livestock. There are still some two thousand head of sheep in all. I have not personally counted heads of course, but I have consulted with Joseph and verified with the chief herdsman that each flock is accounted for. The discrepancy arises from a misreading of Joseph's last report. Last month Joseph's clerk caught the grippe, and although he was absent only one day, Joseph chose not to wait but to pen the report himself. Your brother's mind is vigorous as ever, but he grows frail of body, and he is too proud to admit that his palsy has made his writing shaky and often indecipherable. He still covers every inch of the estate on horseback, inspecting everything from winter seed to the state of the granaries. He knows down to the last bundle how much winter feed is stored for the Charolais cattle and how each case of sorefoot is healing in the various flocks.

As for the matter of his retiring from the stewardship of Marduquesnes, I did not raise the subject but I can see that he would be adamantly against it. He will never admit it, but the long hours in the saddle are becoming very hard on him. This is a delicate matter that is best discussed between brothers. Now to other news.

The shepherds anticipate an excellent spring lambing, and there will be some urgent decisions to make. As you know, the army will buy all that is for sale of the next wheat harvest, and since their demands are so enormous, Joseph wonders whether we should not sacrifice some grazing land in order to increase the arable hectares.

Joseph is off to take the waters at Menoyes tomorrow if the roads are passable. He did suggest postponing his journey for the duration of my stay, but it was only out of courtesy to me, and I insisted that he keep to his plans. His poor old bones really suffer and the hot springs are what he needs. I am content to remain here awhile, and I shall make myself comfortable enough until I hear that you have received this letter and have no other reason for me to stay longer.

The château is in good repair but was fiercely cold when I arrived. The Riettes, of course, did not expect me. Last night I stayed in the guest lodge as it was easier to heat, but my rooms have been opened and warmed today, there will be hot water for a bath tonight, and Auvergne has recalled three of the servants back from the village so that I shall be more than well provided for. I can assure you, Guillaume, it is no hardship for me to leave Paris for a while. It is peaceful here.

Indeed, with the countryside glistening white as far as the eye can see, I can think of nothing more delightful than to sit here in my boudoir by this roaring fire of fragrant cedar logs, read a good book and know that I need not stir until Auvergne sends up her steaming pot-au-feu.

May your days be as pleasant as mine are.

Your obedient wife,

Julie lifted her pen and tapped it on her chin. She was contemplating something far more delightful than a book beside the fire. She quickly scanned the letter and decided it would more than suffice.

"The absolute truth but not all of it," she murmured, and smiled as she signed her name.

With her wifely duties behind her, and Sebastian awaiting her in his room just a few steps away, she could enjoy the prospect of long unbroken days and nights devoted to the pleasures of love.

Everything was so perfect, so miraculously right. How blind she had been not to recognize that God, who had sent her tribulations to endure, could also send her joy. How very nearly she had spurned this heaven-sent gift! She had been a prude, a hypocrite, a coward, to run away from love. Anne-Marie, she realized with a flicker of surprise, was infinitely wiser in these matters for all her surface silliness.

For once in her life she would know the joys that other women knew. She would savor every moment, hoard the memory, and no matter what befell later, she would always have those glorious memories to sustain her, a precious album of keepsakes she could open at will.

She felt reborn, bold, lighthearted and brimming with vigor. She felt it in her movements, her gestures and every word she uttered.

With a flash of inspired inventiveness, she had introduced Sebastian to the housekeeping couple as an American architect. "Next summer we hope to modernize some of the château," she had explained that morning. "Mr. Ramlin is here to survey the interior and discuss the changes with me so that he may draw up some plans."

At the time, Sebastian's expression betrayed nothing beyond a slight movement of one eyebrow. "An American?" he had said mildly as soon as they were alone.

Her shoulders bobbed in a lighthearted shrug. "Of course American. To have chosen an Englishman for the commission would be most unpatriotic, Sebastian. France and England are at war."

Solemn faced, he had tapped her nose with his forefinger. "I would never have guessed from last night."

"Nor will you know it from tonight I hope, my dearest darling...*enemy*!"

Julie laughed out loud as she hurried along the gallery to Sebastian's room. He sat at ease in his shirtsleeves by the crackling hearth. "Put on your riding jacket," she told him. "You will need it."

"Are we going out?" he asked.

"No, but beyond this wing the house is chilly." Her smile brimmed with mischief as she took his hand and tugged him away from the fire. "There is just enough time for a brief tour before the light fails. Come. If you are to earn your architect's fee you must inspect the place.''

"Ah, the plans. And in what currency is my fee to be paid, *madame*?" he asked, obediently slipping into his jacket.

She tilted her head and regarded him obliquely under lowered eyelashes. "Why, sir, I thought we had already agreed on the currency. Did you not receive the first installment last night in the guest house? And a very generous installment it was! Could you have forgotten so soon? At any rate, there is another payment due after supper—in the same currency.''

His peel of laughter rang through the east-wing gallery as they made their way to the main staircase. "How wanton you have become! Whatever happened to that virtuous Roman matron who hovered by my sickbed for three full days without ever being tempted into it?''

Julie raced down the staircase ahead of him. "I did not invite her," she called up to him. "She would not have been good company.''

She was as changeable as quicksilver, he thought as he followed her into the dim reaches of the house. She was another creature entirely from the woman he had first laid eyes on. Was he the sole cause of this transformation? Or was it simply the result of leaving Paris and all the self-imposed restraints of that unnatural marriage? He had been attracted by the chaste young wife, but this light-as-air sprite, this blaze of fire and spirit and wantonness held him spellbound. He must curb his feelings or he would find himself blurting out the dangerous truth to her. With an effort, he tore his thoughts away from his predicament and directed his attention to the various chambers and galleries she was pointing out to him as they went.

"Slow down, for pity's sake, Julie," he called out, quickening his pace. "You may turn one corner too many too fast. Then you may mark my empty grave . . ." He paused, cupping his hands around his mouth, and his voice took on a hollow tone as he called out with pulpit solemnity, "He was lost in the bowels of Marduquesnes and left no trace."

Some ten paces ahead of him she turned back, her laughter belling out joyfully in the cavernous passageway. Her hand reached for his as they met. "Come, you silly goose, there is much to see."

Château Marduquesnes, its dependent village and its vast fertile holdings lay to the south of Orléans in the great northerly curve of the Loire. Its beginnings could be traced back to a fortress built more than three hundred years earlier and it was therefore listed as "château" in the property rolls of the province. But the sprawling house bore no resemblance to Sebastian's idea of a Norman castle. It reminded him more of a great Tudor palace with wings and expansions and staircases added on at the whim of successive generations until all logic and flow had disappeared.

Indeed, twenty minutes into the tour he felt he could more easily plot a course to the Indies than back to his room. They had arrived at a remote part of the structure, one that had not been used in Julie's memory. She took him to a window of an unfurnished room to look down on a diamond-shaped patch of snow, three sides of which were defined by the walls of the house.

"My mother's orangery," Julie said. "It was once a walled garden, but my mother found it in ruins when she came here as a bride. A few months before I was born she decided to build an orangery because it had just the right exposure. She never lived to complete the project. My father closed up this entire section of the house after her death and never used it again."

As they continued their progress through a tangle of sinuous passages she began to speak of her infancy. "I had two older brothers, but only the faintest of memories of them. When I was four, they both died of smallpox. I can't imagine why they both succumbed to the epidemic and I was spared—neither could Papa. That was when he stopped spending any time at all at Marduquesnes and abandoned me completely to my nurse and the servants."

She looked down and her voice became shaded with regret. "I felt guilty because I survived. I wasn't even sickly.... It was my childish notion that he blamed me for killing off the family. As a girl, I could never hope to console him for the loss of his sons. I knew that even then. I thought he hated me."

She turned her face up to him with a sad little smile, opened a concealed door and led him down a dark flight of stairs. At the bottom, she turned and waited for him. "It was nonsense, of course. If he came rarely to see me it was only because I looked so like my mother that it saddened him to lay eyes on me. But I wasted too many years believing I wasn't loved."

By some obscure route they had returned to the furnished wings of the house and the main reception rooms of the second floor. Julie led him into the great dining hall and gestured to the portraits on the walls.

"My Sainte Aube ancestors," she explained, and turned to dwell on one painting in particular.

It was a fair likeness of Charles Sainte Aube, a younger, leaner version of the man with whom he had played backgammon in a London club. It pleased Sebastian that he could detect no resemblance to Julie in his lineaments and he looked around for a portrait of her mother, but the walls were devoted exclusively to the male Sainte Aubes, a chronicle of inherited wealth and dominance unbroken for some seven generations. It was not the implications of power that impressed him but the unquestionable solidarity of kinship, and he tried to imagine what it was like to be so firmly rooted in the past. To know from whence one sprang. No amount of money, no powerful recommendations could secure membership in that club. If he was covetous, it was only for a moment. He looked at Charles Sainte Aube once more, posturing in lace and apple-green brocade within a gilded frame. Rather no kin at all than that.

Standing just behind her, he watched her commune with the portrait, her head tipped up, her slender shoulders suddenly tense and frail as she pulled the cashmere shawl tight about her. He sensed her bereavement welling up anew.

Don't waste your grief on him, he wanted to shout. He is alive. He risked your life and happiness to save his precious estate. You owe him not one tender thought.

The urge to speak out was so overwhelming that he stiffened with the effort to remain silent, the lies between them suddenly intolerable. But how could he afford the luxury of truth now? He was in too deep for that. Was this his punishment for making a pact with the devil? he wondered. To develop such a high regard for Julie that the very thought of deceiving her made him suffer the tortures of the damned?

"Your father?" he whispered, touching her elbows and gently turning her to face him.

Her cheeks were wet. "I never knew how much he loved me until it was too late."

Heartsick, he brushed her tears away with the back of his finger and enfolded her in his arms.

"I love you, Sebastian, and I need to know that you love me. I need to know it now while you are living and breathing and able to say it."

"Yes, Julie, yes. I love you with all my heart."

It was a moment when mere compassion would have prompted him to say it, to say anything she wanted to hear. He would not have begrudged that statement to any of his past mistresses, he realized. He had known affection before, and desire and strong attachments. But something different was happening here. As his words echoed off the hard surfaces of the room his heart responded, and with a leap of recognition he knew. This was no act of charity, no tender gesture made in the heat of the moment and as quickly forgotten.

"I love you with all my heart," he repeated. It was nothing less than the truth.

That night was like a priceless string of pearls, each moment with a precious value of its own. Her body became, by turns, an exquisite instrument for giving and receiving pleasure and a mere husk, a resting place for her soul. So acute was their delight in each other that neither slept till dawn but shared the stillness of the night together.

In the small hours, hot and passion spent, they rose and stood by her window, enjoying the blue luminescence of the moon on snow. She leaned against him, held fast by his arms and the coverlet they shared.

"How many mistresses have you had?" she asked him.

He bent to kiss her disheveled hair. "Hush. They are the past. None of them were virginal. And none of them matter anymore."

"I do not question that. It is just that I want to know everything about you."

"Three."

"So I am the fourth."

"You are not a mistress but a bride. I still wonder at the miracle of it."

"Miracle?"

"That you have been married for almost four years and yet I was your first lover. Many men must have desired you. Were you waiting for me? Or did you plan to remain a maiden wife forever?"

"I did not plan, my love. Mine was not a life where plans could be made." Safe in the circle of his arms, she could speak it, the terrors she had buried so deep that only in nightmares had they surfaced until now.

"I was very naive when I came to Paris," she began.

She had been not quite sixteen at the time and still boarding at the convent. There had been few students left in residence. Most of the girls had been of noble birth and had already been fetched. They had left for Austria, Switzerland, England—any country where an aristocrat's life was still safe.

Late one night Julie had been woken and summoned from her dormitory. A messenger from her father had thrust marriage papers under her nose. She must sign them and prepare to leave immediately—not for England but Paris. Her father awaited her in the city, and it was urgent. Paris, the very seat of the terror! The sisters had been fearful for her and argued with the messenger, but she had sensed that her father was in danger and only her obedience could help him.

"In any case," she added, "I would have insisted on going. It was such a rare privilege to be with him, I would have ridden into the jaws of hell just to see him. Just to prove my worth to him."

There had been five days of traveling before they had at last ridden safely through the Saint-Denis gate and entered the city.

"But it was a gendarme of the revolution who waited for me at the town house, not Papa. 'Where is my father?' I asked him.

"'Where you will be soon,' he replied, and marched me out of the house into a tumbril full of prisoners."

She began to tremble. Sebastian lifted her in his arms and carried her back to the bed. "Don't go on if it distresses you," he said. "You are safe now. No harm will come to you."

He pulled the quilt up to cover them both, then held her fast in his arms, sensing both her need and her fear to speak of it. It was some kind of rite, he thought. An exorcism. He willed her to feel the power of his love like a garment of protection. In a few moments she continued quite calmly.

"I was confused, exhausted from the long sleepless journey. I did not know what to think at first except that my father had been arrested and I was being taken to him. But I learned from the others that this was a death ride. I refused to believe it. Over and over I told myself it was all a bad dream. But it wasn't a dream, not when we stopped in the square. A prisoner said something to me, I remember, something about the guillotine being a quick and painless death. And then the executions began, and I resigned myself to an end that was swift and merciful.

"I do not remember what followed, but I remember riding in a carriage with a man who was about my grandmother's age. He told me he was my husband, but I seemed to know it already.

"What shocked me next was learning that my father was dead. He had been executed two days before my arrival."

She turned, quite calmly, and touched Sebastian's cheek with a light, caressing stroke. "When I was somewhat recovered, it was an enormous relief to discover that this husband of mine was not going to demand his marital rights. I was so grateful to cling to him, so grateful for my very life and breath, that I vowed I would be a good wife, dutiful, helpful and agreeable. In fact, everything that could be expected from the wife of a deputy... outside of the bedroom.

"So you see, my love, no matter how Parisians comport themselves in these times, I could never deliberately have planned to deceive him. He was the rock I clung to."

Sebastian gentled her in his arms, his heart so full that he could think of no response save to hold her wordlessly.

He was the first to wake, his eyes opening to a broad shaft of white light shining through the unshuttered window. Julie's cheek nested in the shallows of his breast, her loose hair spread randomly over his arms and shoulders. The clock on the mantelpiece told him it was past noon. She began to stir, and feeling the silken brush of her skin on his as she woke, he remembered something.

"Good morning, sweetheart," he whispered. "Do you know what day this is?"

Drowsily she moved her hand, tracing a slow path from his breast to his shoulder and on up to his mouth.

As he kissed her fingertips, she sighed. "I plan to forget the calendar, but I know yesterday was the second Nivose. Today is the third."

"Yes, here in France. What a dedicated Republican you have become! Do you not recall what the rest of Christendom calls this day?"

Suddenly she was wide awake, sitting up and laughing joyously. "Of course! It is Christmas Eve. Oh, Sebastian, I have not celebrated Christmas or the New Year for four years! Some continue the old ways, but we had to set an example." She began to recite the new holidays, marking them off on her fingers. "The Festival of the Supreme Being, the Festival of Liberty, the Festival of Reason, the Raising of the Liberty Tree—"

"Would you like to celebrate Christmas this year?"

"Oh, yes!" she murmured, as fervent as a child at the prospect of a rare treat.

"Is it treasonous?"

"Oh, yes," she repeated in the same tone. With a wide grin, she flung her arms around him. "No, my darling, not strictly treasonous. But, like our amorous embraces, like all things bright and beautiful, forbidden by law and yet still practiced in secret defiance."

They began their day by giving the servants a holiday, and they ended it by celebrating midnight mass in a small church in Orléans. Sebastian drove them in an open shay, neither of them discomforted by the frozen rutted roads or the crackling cold air.

"Thank you," Julie said as they bumped along between the dark hedgerows back to Marduquesnes. "Thank you for the most wonderful Christmas Eve I can ever remember. How wonderful to hear Christmas carols again! Sometimes I wonder what I would be doing now, where I would be if it weren't for the revolution. Certainly I wouldn't be married to Guillaume Farroux."

"Neither would you be with me," Sebastian added quickly. "We would never have met."

"Oh, but we would! We were destined to meet."

"Only as a result of—" He stopped short as though his breath had failed and she turned to him anxiously. "Only as a result of all that went before," he finished.

Her smile was more radiant than the moonlit snow. "Then I gladly accept everything that went before, because it has led me to you," she said, and vowed to herself that she would not think again of anything that came before this happy occasion or anything that might follow. She would allow nothing to spoil the joy of these perfect days and nights with Sebastian.

Chapter Eight

Floriscombe, Cornwall—May, 1798

Monsignor Domenico Tremonte smoothed out the week-old letter and read the news one more time. For the pure joy of it.

Sebastian was arriving before nightfall this very day. It was almost two years since his last visit. His room was ready. Mrs. Jenkins had found one last jar of raspberry preserves to make a syllabub for the evening meal, and the aroma of roast leg of lamb was already beginning to rise from the kitchen.

Domenico closed his eyes and breathed in the rich scents of meat and shallots and rosemary. "A fatted calf would be more apt," he would say as he began to carve, "but the good Mrs. Jenkins knows your preference for lamb."

No! No prodigal son jests or allusions to the boy's overly long absence; he must feel unconditionally welcome. Domenico's fingers drummed on the lacquered desk, lately cleared of papers and polished to a mirror shine. He had cleared his calendar for the occasion, too. There was nothing further to do but await Sebastian's arrival and look forward to a rare three days of his companionship.

Outside the study windows the gardener stooped over the last of the daffodils, pinching off dead blooms. Domenico looked out and for a few moments saw the daffodils of another spring, saw *il piccolo* taking his first steps. He sighed with remembered pleasure.

Sometimes a man could distinctly recognize the hand of God in his life. Domenico had not been at all sure at the time, but nearly thirty years was long enough to contemplate a truth and understand it.

He had once been guilty of pride, worldly ambition and sins of the flesh. As a monsignor of thirty-five, his service to the Curia was conspicuous, his sins discreet. His stock was rising; an archdiocese beckoned, his for the plucking. He was quite naturally reluctant to accept the responsibilities of an infant ward, albeit his own godchild. It could help neither his present office nor his future plans.

"It is out of the question for me to take him on personally," he explained to the mother, "but I will arrange something suitable." At that moment she was suddenly distracted by her firstborn. The child was tipping a heavy chest toward him as he scaled its open drawers like ladder rungs. She thrust the swaddled babe at him and ran to save the older child, an instinctive maternal act, completely unpremeditated.

Domenico had performed his share of baptisms and knew the feel of such small bundles, but the mute appeal of this sleeping infant in his arms was something he had not bargained for. It had changed the shape of his life.

It still astonished him that since the day he had accepted his ward, not once had he broken his priestly vows, neither had he advanced in the eyes of the church. He felt no loss. How often after all did God grant to an ordained priest all the simple pleasures of a parent?

Turning his back on the archdiocese, he had begged for some humble position where he could serve God in obscurity—some remote Calabrian village perhaps, where a priest raising an orphan would be considered a harmless eccentricity. The Curia had its own moral agenda. How would the church look, suddenly demoting one of its own for no good reason? And one so prominent, a monsignor of brilliant persuasive powers, fluent in five languages? No, no and no! It would smack of impropriety.

For pity's sake, come to your senses, Domenico, he had been implored. The church has orphanages for such cases. God has more important work for a priest of your talents.

But *il piccolo* was not a case, he was a living soul in need of love. What more important work could God have for anyone? Domenico knew the intricate machinery of the Curia, knew when to persist and when to compromise. And so it was to England they sent him, to represent the jurisdiction of Rome for a disenfranchised minority of the faithful. It was the perfect compromise, an acceptable office for a monsignor but only marginally so. There were fewer than sixty thousand Roman Catholics in all the country, and Domenico's brief was confined to the counties south of London—in charge of a handful of overworked priests who traveled constantly to serve the far-flung parishes. A little encouragement to the itinerant pastors, the odd dispensation, an occasional recommendation for a would-be seminarian.

His duties were far from arduous. All the dedication and zeal he had once used for personal advancement he poured into nurturing the child, and each day had brought its own trials, its own rewards—like those first steps toward the daffodils.

The gardener was trimming the hedges now, and Domenico's chest lurched as he heard footsteps on the gravel path leading to the front door. I must remember not to call him *piccolo*, he thought as Sebastian came into view. He is a grown man, this son of mine.

He opened the French windows and went down the steps to the gravel, his arms flung wide. He saw the crumpled sheepish grin, which hadn't changed since adolescence.

"Father!" In two long strides, Sebastian was in his arms.

"Mio piccolo," he whispered, then louder. *"Finalmente,* Sebastiano! Did you forget how to navigate overland that it took you so long to find your way home?"

As always, Sebastian had brought gifts. As always, the housekeeper dined with them on his first night home and he held back the gifts until the meal was over. Cognac, cigars, a new Wordsworth volume and a cashmere robe for the Monsignor; for Mrs. Jenkins a Paris bonnet, some lengths of Ceylon silk and the finest Egyptian cotton; silver trinkets and sweetmeats for the housemaids.

Domenico was animated, but throughout the long festive ritual, Sebastian could not help but mark the change in him. On his last visit Domenico had turned sixty but looked and acted in his vigorous prime. Now under the handsome silver hair the face had become thin, and in repose it sagged. The black silk soutane, always flawlessly tailored to his elegant proportions, hung too loose. To Sebastian, the garment had always radiated the wearer's princely authority. Now it suggested a sudden frailty.

And what was the gardener doing trimming daffodils? The spring bulbs had always been sacrosanct; nobody but the Monsignor was allowed to touch them. Sebastian remembered thinking as a child that those particular flowers had some profound religious significance like the sacrificial Host. He's had many good years. Everyone gets old, he thought, but it was no consolation. He needed this man in his life, more now than ever. Would he ever stop needing Domenico?

"Are you feeling quite well, Father?" he asked when they sat alone by the parlor fire sampling the cognac. "You look a trifle peaked."

"Nonsense, my boy. When you're an old codger of sixty-two, you will be lucky if you are in such splendid shape as I am."

"I saw Penworth at the daffodils, and I wondered."

"There's no law that says I have to break my back every spring. It's been a busy season." Domenico held his brandy glass to the firelight, admiring the color. "Convents and seminaries popping up like mushrooms these days to accommodate the French immigrants. And now with the papal states occupied by the French atheists, I travel more—to shore up the Holy Father's authority with my presence. Do you not read my letters? There is little time to tend the garden."

He looked across the hearth at Sebastian, his faded blue eyes full of memories. "Do you remember asking me if you had to be ordained before you could touch the daffodils?"

"You told me yes."

"I lied."

Thou shalt not touch the daffodils. They exchanged smiles, traveling back together to happier times. Innocent times, when Sebastian had tried to heed all God's injunctions. He swallowed a mouthful of cognac, letting the mellow heat flare a path down his throat. When had he stopped trying? he wondered.

It was Domenico who broke the silence. "I'm old enough, Sebastiano. I won't feel cheated if God should shortly call me," he said, smiling. "But I think I have a few minutes left! Long enough for you to tell me what it is that weighs on your mind so heavily. It's not just the state of my health, is it?"

Sebastian started. "Am I that easy to read?"

"Yes."

"I can bluff as well as any. A trading competitor once described me as inscrutable. As a matter of fact, in Portsmouth last week, when I told the shipmaster that his—"

"Sebastiano, I said I have a few minutes left. If you don't come to the point soon, they may not be enough."

"Don't jest about such things, Father."

Domenico's thin tilt of a smile straightened and widened. He lifted his palms toward the ceiling in a well-remembered coaxing gesture, the spirited shoulders raised almost to his ears. The pose never failed to ignite a host of youthful memories.

There is the broken window, Sebastiano, and there is the ball. *Vieni!* You must never be afraid to speak the truth.

Lots of seminarians doubt their calling before ordination. I'm not saying you should continue, I'm just asking you to talk it over with me. Must we have this stiff-lipped silence about it?

Domenico's voice brought him back to the present with a crisp tone. "*Basta!* I have done with my jesting. Out with it, *mio figlio*, before you choke on it!"

"I am in love," Sebastian said.

"Good. Since you'll never be a priest, you should marry. Is she a Catholic? *Bravo, bravo!* You have my blessing. What? Why the long face?"

"She is married already, but her marriage is only—"

The Italian eloquence of Domenico's hands stopped him. This time the palms were rigid, fending off what he did not choose to hear. "You cannot use me as your confessor, Sebastiano. Father Hennessy will gladly hear you, but I am too close to have any spiritual detachment."

Sebastian shook his head. "I know that. I'm not looking for 'ten-novenas-and-sin-no-more, my son.' Just hear me out. I'm looking for practical solutions not spiritual absolution."

Domenico raised his eyebrows and nodded. "Very well."

"My last voyage was not profitable," Sebastian began. "I came back to many problems. It was the reason I went straight to London instead of visiting you first." He drained his brandy glass and reached for the bottle, replenishing both their glasses. "There were days of meetings in the city—partners, shipping agents, creditors, Lloyd's. Then one evening at my club I became acquainted with a Frenchman. He had contacts in Paris he thought might be useful. His connection was through his daughter's husband, and his story was quite bizarre. . . ."

The fire had burned low by the time he finished with his parting from Julie at Orléans, she heading back to Paris and he bound for England. "It is as though we never parted," he added. "There has been a whole month's delay on the *Celestine*'s departure. You know how costly that is. Yet all I could think of was that it gave us another month of daily correspondence, that when I am at sea it will be weeks between letters. She does not leave my mind or my heart."

Domenico rose, threw another log on the fire, then looked down at Sebastian. "Did you get her with child?"

"I don't know. No. She would have told me in her letters."

There was no criticism in Domenico's face, he was merely pondering. After a long silence he gave Sebastian's shoulder an affectionate squeeze and settled back in his chair. He drew a breath to speak, then exhaled in a long sigh and reached for a cigar in the box beside him.

"Give back the money. Such a marriage could be annulled," he said. "Your fortunes will mend without this Farroux. I am not totally without resources. You should have come to me for money. There is still the trust your parents provided."

Sebastian smiled and shook his head. He no longer believed in that mythical trust; Domenico was offering money from his own pocket. "Farroux holds a good deal more sway in France than the church," he said. "He could block an annulment or a divorce. And if he knew I was not honoring our agreement, he would tell her the truth about me."

"No, *you* must tell her the truth. She must not hear it from him."

"Either way I would lose her."

"It is the risk you take, yes."

"Oh, it's not a risk but a certainty. I have toyed with her affections, I have seduced her for my own flagrantly self-serving reasons. How can I ask her now to believe that I do truly love her, to give up her life of ease for a husband encumbered with debts and an uncertain future?"

Domenico watched the column of gray smoke curl up from his cigar. "Did you seduce her solely for the prospect of material gain?"

Sebastian was silent for a while before he answered. "There was desire present, certainly. Mutual desire. I never gave Farroux another thought in Marduquesnes."

Domenico smiled. "No doubt. Perhaps this mutual desire will die a natural death. She is beautiful, I assume—with an old and impotent husband who longs for a son and will encourage her infidelity. There will surely be other suitors before you return. You will be at sea for many months."

"I could not bear the thought—"

"Aaaaah!" The soft intonation registered a whole octave of divine justice. "But you will be obliged to bear the thought. You have already decided what you will do—nothing. So do nothing. I cannot condone it, but since you are not in the confessional, neither do I condemn you for it. Perhaps at your age I would have done the same had the occasion arisen. But I was devious by nature. You never were. It will be hard on you.''

It was as close as Domenico had ever come to confessing an intimate knowledge of women. Sebastian was moved and strangely comforted.

Affection and empathy shone in the old man's eyes as he leaned forward and patted Sebastian's hand. ''In Tuscany we have a saying, 'If you spice your meat with gall, don't complain of bitterness when you eat it!' ''

He raised his shoulders again and sighed. ''At least some things have simple solutions. I made a killing on cotton last year. Now how much did you say is still outstanding to your creditors?''

Yellow and white irises bloomed in the Tuileries gardens. The lime trees and sycamores were a tender green. At the town house, late tulips blazed red and yellow in the courtyard planters. Paris had never been more beautiful, Julie thought, or so full of wonderful things to do. Since returning to Paris she had danced every dance at Anne-Marie's wedding reception, had accepted almost every social invitation that came. She was filled with zest for whatever presented itself every waking moment. Gone was the pale watercolor Paris viewed from her boudoir window. Every chattering passer-by, every noisy carriage, every weed that intruded itself between the cobblestones was a thing of beauty now. Even the dullest dinner party yielded amusing material for her letters, her prodigious letters, which filled the hours when she was neither hostess nor guest.

It was almost three months since she had parted from Sebastian in Orléans, but her life was bright with the promise of his return. She did not know when but did not need to know; she had his precious letters to sustain her, and more precious yet, the glorious knowledge that she was loved. *No matter where I am, I can never leave you,* he had written, *for I find that you are grafted onto my very soul.* Such sentiments could sustain her forever if need be, or at least for the months and months that lay before her. Meantime, there were fresh distractions each day, every one keenly observed through her love-heightened senses and poured into her daily letters.

That morning it was a small breakfast hosted by Citizeness Bonaparte in the delightful little house on the Rue de la Victoire. Anne-Marie had been working on it for weeks. "They are virtually newlyweds," she had said. "The general left for the Italian campaign just three days after their wedding. She joined him there after he took Milan, but they had almost no time together, and since their return they have shunned society. But with Hortense and Mireille such fast friends, I knew that sooner or later this invitation would come."

Paris had opened its heart to Marie-Joseph-Rose Bonaparte, and Julie could now see why. Upon being presented, Julie addressed her hostess formally as Citizeness Bonaparte.

"Oh, let's have none of that dreary citizen stuff, Madame Farroux," she said in her sweet soft accent. "We Creoles do not stand on ceremony." Impulsively she grasped both Julie's hands. "Heavens, even *Madame* sounds ponderous for such a pretty young thing. Anne-Marie calls you Julie. May I not, too?"

"With pleasure, *madame*."

"Splendid! And you shall call me by the name my husband prefers, Josephine."

"No doubt he prefers it," Madame Cassat whispered to Julie the moment their hostess turned away. "As Marie-Rose she has too much of a past."

"Come, ladies, to the table," Josephine called, clapping her hands. "We shall have a Martinique breakfast—at least as close as my cook can come to it this far away from the islands."

There were eight of them in the sunny yellow dining room, and with the three schoolgirls, Hortense, her cousin Emilie, and her friend Mireille, there was much giggling and byplay on that side of the table. Julie sat between Anne-Marie and Justine. At the head of the table, Josephine presided, explaining the exotic items set before them and eating almost nothing herself. At the foot of the table was her glamorous friend Theresia.

Julie had heard that Josephine was irresistible, but she was no great beauty like Theresia. She was dressed and coiffed exquisitely, but it was her grace and unpretentious charm that melted hearts.

While they sampled fresh-fried *beignets* filled with guava jelly, and mango preserves with sharp cheese, Josephine's eye scanned the table, noticing whose coffee cup needed refilling even before the servant. She kept them amused with her adventures in Milan and unburdened herself on the subject of her in-laws. She began by describing her first encounter with her sister-in-law Pauline. She had come to Milan to visit her favorite brother. "But unfortunately Bonaparte was gone most of the time and it was I who was obliged to entertain her. She is sixteen, and quite the prettiest of all the girls. Since I missed my Hortense so while I was away, I looked forward to the girl's company. But she hated me on sight, simply hated me. I was so relieved when my husband announced she was to marry General LeClerc, but it was to get worse before it got better—I had yet to meet the rest of the family.

"They all came up from Marseilles for Pauline's wedding." She laughed, ducking her head mischievously. "And lo and behold, they *all* hated me on sight. If I'd thought about it more, I would not have been so shocked. I cannot really blame them. For their darling Nabullione to marry a widow with two children when he could have his pick of fresh young things! Well, it was unthinkable. Letizia hated me before she ever laid eyes on me, but when she saw how her son adored me she was positively glacial."

Hortense leaned across the table, laughing and ducking her head with her mother's gesture. "Letizia the Terrible, Mama calls her," she said in a whisper audible to everyone.

Josephine turned to her daughter with an indulgent smile. "Hush, my darling," she said by way of reproach, then continued her story.

"Bonaparte was so naughty—I mean truly outrageous! He took to caressing me—fondling me shamelessly in her sight just to goad her. Just to make clear to her that he was not to be swayed by her opinion of me. Of course, it only worsened matters, and as for her brood, they closed ranks behind her like little hussars. Louis tried to make peace between us—rather halfheartedly—but it was hopeless.

"I can't tell you what a relief it was to see them all ride off back to Marseilles," she said, again with that dipping gesture of her head as she laughed. "I threw an impromptu dinner party the very next night just to celebrate their departure."

Josephine laid a hand to her throat and exhaled soulfully. "Oh, such a treat, ladies, to be able to say it. My inlaws despise me. But there are consolations. Bonaparte adores me and his mother does not live in Paris. Will you not have another *beignet*, Anne-Marie? Well, I see you have all had your fill—of breakfast and my tales of woe. Come, would you like to see what I've done to the house? It's all been redecorated."

Just as Paris had renamed the street in honor of the general's victory, so Josephine had redone the entire house for his return. Their bedroom was turned into a circular tent with striped awnings and wallpaper. The little tables looked like military drums, and the two beds, also covered in striped fabric, slid together at the touch of a hidden spring. That evening Julie wrote:

The general returned from wherever it was he had gone, just as she was leading us back to the salon. She rushed out to the terrace when she heard the carriage, and we were all able to see their most passionate embrace on the steps before he came into the house. I can see now what she meant by "shameless embrace." After kissing her on the lips he buried his face in her bosom and began to devour her, his hands kneading her buttocks.

When he came in with Josephine and saw us, he nodded cordially, muttered, *"Mesdames,"* and strode past us into his study. It was obviously time for us to

leave, and leave we did. He is jealous of every moment
he can spend with her. Oh, I should feel exactly the
same, my beloved, were you with me now. But until
you are, my greatest joy is in reading your letters and
in sharing with you the moments I spend in waiting.

P.S. Anne-Marie has explained Josephine's little
head dip when she laughs. She has bad teeth. Justine
says they look like a bunch of cloves—but Justine can
be rather unkind. Anyway, the trick is effective, for I
never did glimpse her teeth, although she was gracious
and smiling throughout.

Chapter Nine

Croissy—March, 1802

Julie was always a welcome visitor at Anne-Marie's country house. It was less than an hour from Paris and she had visited faithfully during Anne-Marie's tedious pregnancy. Two miscarriages had prompted the doctor to confine Anne-Marie to bed from the third month on. She had become quite melancholy and dreadfully bored. But Julie always raised her spirits; she would come from the city laden with sweetmeats and the latest romantic novels from the book shop on Rue Parnelle.

Now with the baby safely delivered three weeks ago, Julie thought the new mother would be anxiously counting the days left before she could return to the social whirl of Paris, but motherhood seemed to have made her quite placid.

"What an angel he is," Julie said, returning from a visit to the nursery. "When he purses his lips he looks a little like Mireille. You did a splendid job."

Anne-Marie was on the daybed in her boudoir, massaging her swollen breasts with oil.

Julie bent to kiss her cheek and wrinkled her nose as she caught a strange whiff of fish laced with lavender. "Phew! What is that?"

Anne-Marie turned her attention to her left breast, fondling the slippery globe with tender care. "I know. It doesn't matter what I do to the stuff, that fishy smell lingers. But there's nothing like it for keeping the skin elastic. You get used to the smell after a while. It's better than going through life with stretch marks.''

She glanced up for an instant, gave Julie a brief distracted smile, then returned to her task. The table beside her was laden with paraphernalia, various small linen cloths and madras handkerchiefs, a small porcelain bowl and a shallow chafing dish of oil kept warm with a candle. She seemed to find the task soothing.

''Josephine gave me the receipt. It came from her mother—handed down for generations, I daresay. Those Creole women really know how to take care of their looks. Of course, there can't be much else to do in Martinique.''

Julie looked on in frank fascination. Under the oily sheen, Anne-Marie's breasts were heavy with milk, the skin stretched tight as a sausage and showing ropy blue veins. ''I thought if you didn't nurse you were supposed to bind your breasts to stop the milk coming in,'' she said humbly.

''Ah, but that wrinkles the skin dreadfully. If you want to remain unblemished, you let them breathe. They shrink back quite naturally and the milk dries up if you don't—'' she winced ''—don't use it.''

Julie grimaced in sympathy. ''Does it hurt?''

''Yes, when they get too full. Then I have to relieve the pressure a little. But only when I absolutely can't bear it any more, and only after they've been freshly oiled.'' She wiped her hands on a clean cloth, reached for the bowl and held it at her breast. At the mere touch of a finger, the plum-colored nipple spurted milk at such high pressure that it overshot the basin and landed on the rose carpet in a foaming little puddle.

Julie took a cloth and dabbed at the carpet. ''Josephine told you all this?'' she asked dubiously.

''She's got two children and you don't see marks on her breasts, do you? Goodness knows there's enough showing in those gauzy white gowns of hers.''

Julie laughed. ''Come, Anne-Marie, you know she's much more modest these days—ever since she became Madame First Consul.''

"Have you heard the rumors?" Anne-Marie asked, her voice muffled in the loose cotton bodice she slipped over her head. "Our sweet little Josephine may end up queen of France!"

"Oh, yes," Julie murmured, "I've heard." There were always wild rumors in the city, but now one really wondered.... How life had changed!

Napoleon had gone from war hero to head of the army to head of state. And now, if there was a grain of truth to the rumors, he might become king and establish the royal line of Bonaparte. Noble titles were being used again quite openly, and the term *citoyen* had been all but abandoned, along with the revolutionary calendar. Only government documents bore those baffling dates anymore.

France had survived the bitter hardships of war and revolution to find a new prosperity under Napoleon, First Consul of the Republic. And Madame First Consul had survived a terrible scandal. She had taken a lover while her husband was fighting in Egypt. He had resolved to divorce her, but she had begged forgiveness and he had melted under her tears. Ever since, she had become the model of propriety, reducing her social circle to the few intimate friends who passed her husband's standards of behavior. Julie and Anne-Marie were still counted among the few. Would they still count, Julie wondered, if Josephine became queen?

"There's no fear of that," Josephine had confided. "I shall never be queen. He'll need a young queen to give him an heir to the throne. He'll divorce me. I pray it will not come to that."

Anne-Marie laid her head back drowsily and closed her eyes. "There are those who oppose the idea, of course. Those who say Napoleon is power hungry and dangerous, in spite of all he's done for the country. What do you think?"

Julie was silent for a moment. Napoleon power hungry and dangerous? Restless, yes, brilliant and intensely passionate, but dangerous...?

She shrugged. "Who can tell? In any event, I do think he's a very forgiving man to have reconciled with Josephine after her Captain Charles affair."

Anne-Marie gave a snort. "She was alone for a year and a half! What *Parisienne* wouldn't have taken a lover after all that time!"

"But he's not a Parisian. He's from Corsica and they're very straitlaced. There are Corsican husbands who would have killed her for that. You know how passionately he loves her, how heartbroken he must have been. She wasn't even discreet about it. Imagine how he felt, learning about it in Egypt and just when the fleet was destroyed."

Anne-Marie looked up with a knowing smile on her lips. "You'd never do that to Sebastian, would you?"

Julie removed her shawl and folded it, combing the tangled silk fringe with her fingers. Never, she thought. For all the long separations, for all the terrible anxiety she endured knowing his unarmed British clipper braved a hostile blockade and a thousand dangers, she would always remain faithful to him. His brief visits to France between voyages had become the pivot of her life.

"No, I would never betray Sebastian," she said softly, but Anne-Marie did not hear. She was lightly dozing.

Julie looked out the window at the slender cypresses dancing in the breeze like overgrown children. She'd been an overgrown child herself when she first fell in love with Sebastian. All that guilt and self-examination at the thought of adultery! She knew now that Guillaume had been engineering a lover for her from the beginning of their marriage. It was so obvious to her now that she wondered how she could have ever been so ignorant.

She had brought him the Sainte Aube estates but no heir. All his efforts to surround her with young men, his emphasis on her amusing herself, her freedom to pursue whatever distractions pleased her "so long as it is discreet." It was excruciatingly clear now, although he had never stated it out loud. He wanted her pregnant in the only way possible, by a lover. He would claim the child as his legal heir.

Did he know Sebastian was her lover and the only one? If so, he could hardly be satisfied. Their reunions had been rare and fleeting over the past four years, and she had not conceived a child. She still went through the motions of careful discretion, joining him secretly at his lodgings whenever he came to Paris. Guillaume still subtly maneuvered her toward other likely men without ever putting it in so many words.

Anne-Marie stirred and stretched her arms lazily after her brief catnap. "When is Sebastian coming again?" she asked drowsily.

"I never know for sure. Next month, I think. Perhaps we'll go to the Tivoli Gardens and have our fortunes read."

"If there's ever enough time," Anne-Marie said. "For heaven's sake, when are you going to get another lover to take up the slack? This dark and dashing pirate of yours is all very well, but he just breezes into town for three, four days, then he's off again for months and all you have is Guillaume. And he can't be much in bed after the pirate!"

Tea arrived with a platter of tiny *gâteaux aux framboises*. The maid set the tray on the carpet for want of a free surface.

"You can take all this away, Lisette. I'm finished with it," Anne-Marie said.

Lisette set to work clearing the table, snuffing out the chafing candle and piling soiled dishes and cloths onto a salver.

"He's not a pirate," Julie said quietly, "he's a merchant mariner." And she had survived thus far on his brief visits, making up in intensity what they lacked in duration. And his letters, sent by any messenger or any means available in these uncertain times. Letters that came irregularly but were always full of passion and intimacy. Such a love never had time to stale; it was still breathlessly exciting but its urgency tormented her when he was gone. Oh, it wasn't easy to remain content with so little. He had aroused such longings in her. It would be so easy to succumb to lust in the long arid weeks of waiting when he was at sea and in mortal danger, when anxiety nipped cruelly at her nerves. Guillaume never

stopped hinting. *I demand only your discretion, my dear.*
Anne-Marie pressed and goaded at every turn.

Nothing would be simpler than to find brief distraction
in some philanderer's bed. She was such an obvious target,
walking into salons on the arm of an old man. But all her
feelings were engaged, not just the hunger of her body. She
was blessed with the love of a man who was kind and gentle,
of high courage and, above all, honor. She knew Sebastian
was true to her, and no lapse of faith on her part, not one
meaningless night of infidelity, would ever taint that flawless meeting of hearts. She meant to remain worthy of him
always.

Lisette placed the tea tray on the table and her reclining
mistress dismissed her from the room with an indolent wave
of her arm. Anne-Marie seemed disinclined to stir herself
and serve tea, so Julie reached for the silver pot. "When I'm
ready to take another lover, you'll be the first to know," she
said lightly, and tried to picture Sebastian on the *Celestine.*
Where was he at this very moment? And was he thinking of
her?

The first eight bells always woke him, but now he rarely
got back to sleep. He took to relieving the officer of the
second watch. In the dark hours they made their best head-
way and the second watch could be strenuous. But on a fair
night with the wind steady, Sebastian would fall to brooding. After he'd circled the deck, nodded to the watch crew,
verified the helmsman's setting, he needed only to check the
reassuring rustles and creaks of the rigging, the slap-crack
of well-trimmed sail at fore, main and mizzen. He could
hear the least sound above the licking of the waves.

He would lean over the gunwales and inevitably it would
happen; a starlit sea always filled him with wonder at the
beauty of the universe. He would be overwhelmed by the
yearning to share it—with the one woman he had deceived.

Julie, Julie! Could you love me still if you knew what I
was capable of? Often he would decide to risk it, to tell her
the truth. His tongue would curl around the words.

I had a bargain with your husband before ever I laid eyes on you.

He would utter the words on the damp air and let the wind carry them out to sea. He would taste the residue of salt on his lips.

On a night pricked with stars all things seemed possible. But then he would hold her in his arms again, knowing how little time they had, and his courage always failed him.

He would feel the smooth planes of that perfect heart-shaped face under his palms, see the trust, the unconcealed admiration in her eyes, and he would know he could not say it.

Perhaps she could be reconciled, forgive him even. But she would never feel the same toward him, never again shower him with that utterly unguarded love. He was deadlocked. It was like trying to make way with a dragging anchor.

His fortunes at least were progressing untrammeled. In the gossipy London world of merchant shipping, word of a certain vessel's exploits circulated. She was a ship destined to draw notice. For one thing, most of the English merchantmen afloat were of an older design, armed frigates who heaved to at night and played it safe. The *Celestine* sailed around the clock unarmed, a sleek lady shockingly ahead of her time. She brought the dashing Yankee term "clipper" into the city coffeehouses. After the fourth lightning trip, the shipping trade was buzzing from Blackfriars to the Temple with the *Celestine*'s successes. Each voyage was brief and the profits quickly realized, and each venture more successful than the last.

At first, London merchants vied for spare cargo space in the *Celestine*'s hold, but after the first two successes, the craft had only space for its own cargo to be traded for rare foreign luxuries. Then the brokers who crowded the loading docks came only to welcome home the plucky clipper and bid for her foreign goods at war-inflated prices.

Spices and tobacco. Silks and eastern perfumes. Dates and Smyrna figs. And even that prized goat wool, brought by caravan through snowy passes and over deserts to Alexandretta all the way from Kashmir—a substance that would hold dye in soft mysterious colors, cloud-soft and so light that it was worth its weight in gold.

The clipper's fame spread to the general public when some wag wrote a letter to the *Times*. It was a poor piece of doggerel, but a compliment nevertheless.

Here's to the clipper braving
French-infested waters
And sailing back with dainties
So beloved of our daughters.
A saucy little lady,
Heart of oak and copper coaming,
She's never heard the warning words:
"We'll go no more a-roaming."
So raise your glasses, gentlemen,
To feats of bold seafaring.
Britannia yet may rule the waves
But one clipper wins for daring.

In a matter of four years, Sebastian had more than discharged his debts; he had grown wealthy beyond all expectation. It did indeed seem to him that the *Celestine* must be charmed. The French blockade was impenetrable for most British vessels but not for her. The clipper was welcomed wherever she dropped anchor and every docking somehow turned a profit.

It was, to Sebastian's pragmatic mind, far too good to be true. He might have concluded that Farroux was behind it, but two arguments convinced him otherwise. Even Farroux's clout was not that extensive, and he was not a man to give more than he bargained for. He had bargained for an heir, and for all their passionate couplings, Julie was not yet pregnant.

Sebastian longed for a child by Julie almost as much as he feared it. If he were to get her with child he could never honor his end of the bargain; he would as soon give up his soul to Farroux as that child. It would force the truth out. And then he stood to lose both child and mother.

His life seemed dappled with ironies. With his partner, Edward Cecil, he now owned the *Celestine* and had commissioned the building of two more clippers. Soon he would no longer be sailing, his time could be more profitably spent ashore with Cecil. He was rich enough to retire. His dream was achieved, but he found it wanting... wanting Julie.

Most of his waking hours were caught up in the intricate tasks of his trade, and what leave he allowed himself he spent on his brief trips to France. He was living a frenzied pace and thanked God for the toll it took, for when his thoughts were idle, he was racked by his need for this woman, his desire to possess her body and soul, to be always within the sound of her voice, the sight and scent of her.

Domenico had said it would be hard on him. Could he have imagined just how hard? If Farroux would only die! The problem would die with him. There was, thank God, nothing in writing. Farroux was old. He could not last forever.

Meanwhile Sebastian plied his trade, invested in a terrace house in Park Lane and an estate with a few acres near Epping Forest. And he followed the progress of the war. Napoleon had managed to subdue or align all the European monarchies. Britain alone was still at war with France.

Chapter Ten

The Tuileries Palace, April, 1802

Letizia sat before the opulent mirror table. She brushed her long dark hair with those dashing, almost angry strokes she had learned from her mother. It is as sinful to waste time as it is to waste food.

Lucien lolled against the *secrétaire*, his square face passive. "Mama, didn't Josephine offer you a *femme de chambre* for your stay? You shouldn't have to coif yourself anymore."

Femme de chambre, indeed! She'd raised five children on the Via Malerba and never needed more than four servants.

"Yes, she sent in some woman who asked me if I wouldn't like to try curls *à la grecque*." She pursed her lips and made a dry spitting sound. "She would have turned me out with a nest of worms on my head like her mistress. Look at this place, Luciano!" Still plying the boar bristles, she lifted her chin in disdain at the ornate furnishings.

The room was a vast size for a boudoir, all white and gold, with graceful *bibelots*, a dainty velvet chaise and silken stools and chairs. It was the guest suite of the largest private quarters in the palace. The furniture was courtesy of the late Marie Antoinette, but the hostess touches were pure Josephine. Every surface bore a peace offering, urns of forced roses, porcelain bowls filled with fresh fruit, tiny silver dishes of sugared almonds and nougat.

"What do you want, Mother? A barn? This was a Bourbon palace."

"It looks like a brothel. She thinks she can shower me with her excesses and buy her way into the family. Never! Madame First Consul, my eye! Just because she fooled Nabullione into a mayor's office one morning and dragged some witnesses off the street, it still does not make her a Buonaparte. She is still the whore she always was."

It was a perfectly legal marriage, but Lucien was not about to rub salt in Mama's wounds. He simply nodded agreeably and watched her morning toilette.

With a few deft twists she gathered her hair, shaped it into a long chignon and anchored it with an ivory comb. "Six years with the whore and it's still not enough for him!"

She withdrew a fine netted snood from a silk case and began to pin it in position over the chignon. "And how he's made the family suffer from her! Marrying his own brother to her daughter. And poor Caroline, breaking her head at that ridiculous academy, Madame Campone's."

"Madame Campan."

"Yes, and just because the whore's daughter attended it. For what? Did he want to turn his youngest sister into another French whore?"

Lucien sighed. "Mama, it didn't hurt Caro to learn to write properly before she married. Father would not have liked to hear you say such things."

Your father betrayed Corsica, she thought, stained our name. Nabu could restore our honor if it wasn't for that whore. But all she said was, "I never thought my cleverest son could be such a fool. But it will end soon, this madness. You'll see. He plans to ascend the throne of France, so he'll have to do something about her. She's pushing forty. She won't keep him infatuated much longer."

Letizia removed her white *robe de chambre*. Underneath she was dressed for the day, her perennial black gown with its thirty-five small buttons, a plain white fichu at her throat. Her blue shawl, the one touch of color she permitted herself, lay neatly over the back of her chair.

Lucien took the shawl and draped it over her shoulders. "We got you out of Corsica, Mama, but shall we ever get you out of black?"

She smiled and patted his cheek. "When Nabullione gets married."

He grinned. "I'll tell him not to expect you at table anymore. You can have all your meals on a tray in here. Then you won't have to see her at all. Huh? It's not for much longer. Another two days and you can move into your own house and we can all come to dinner at your table."

"The house should have been ready weeks ago," she said, sounding mollified. "I shall drive over there this morning and find out why it takes a hundred years to hang ten rolls of wallpaper."

"A good idea, Mama. I would go with you if there was time, but the Committee convenes in less than an hour, and I need a private word with Nabu before the session."

"Then what are you doing here, Luciano! Don't waste time here. *Andiamo!* Go to your brother. He needs you."

"I just came to wish you good-morning, what else?" Lucien enjoyed his mother's company, but here, under the same roof as Josephine, she had become a harridan, *una vecchiaccia*! This morning he had lingered merely to kill time. He had arrived to find Nabu still in bed with the whore. He bent to kiss Letizia's cheek and left, hoping Nabu was in his study by now.

At the door, he met a girl carrying Letizia's breakfast, the same repast she always took: bread, goat cheese, coffee and dried fruit.

"Breakfast, Mama," he called back into the room, and nodded as the girl waited at the door to let him pass. She had a pretty smile; she was one of Josephine's mulattoes. He hoped his mother would not blame her for that.

"You have a visitor, *Madame*, a General Diderot," the girl said. "He is waiting in the vestibule."

His calling card lay on the tray. *General Jean-Paul Bertrand Diderot*. Letizia ran her finger over the words, startled. So he was still alive. And a general.

She rarely thought of it anymore; it was more than thirty years ago, but she had never forgotten how it was...feeling the fire of righteous rebellion coursing in her veins. Locking her door against Carlo every night.

She had only two sons then. Guiseppe was two years old and the baby, Nabullione, was already trying to walk at eight months. Her two little men, she called them. From now on they would be the only men in her life.

Amorosa mia, please! No more silly games, I beg you. I want to sleep in my bed. Let me in, will you?

Games, you call it? You betrayed us, Carlo. You betrayed your sons to the French. Our forefathers will turn in their graves.

Enough with the forefathers, Letizia. The French have won. Even Paoli admitted that. Can I fight alone? There's been enough bloodshed. Would you want to spend another pregnancy hiding in the mountains? Seeing Corsicans torn apart by cannon fire? God forbid! Let's get on with living.

There will be no more pregnancies, Carlo. Save your breath and go away. I will not sleep with a turncoat.

She had been married to Carlo four years, but it was the first time she felt her strength. She was twenty, a woman with two little sons she would kill for. Carlo was twenty-four and still a boy. General Paoli had fled to England and would return to free Corsica from enslavement. But Carlo had surrendered his sword and his musket and given in to the French. They rewarded him with an office in the colonial government. She would never forgive him.

Each morning he left for the *bureau,* an important man, a slave master. Each night when he came home and embraced his sons, she winced and turned away.

After two weeks she packed up the children and their nurse and went to stay with Cousin Udolpho and Anna-Bettina.

Yes, of course you can stay until this foolishness is over, but...you wrong him, Letizia. He is only doing what must be done to survive.

You are lucky he is so gentle, Tizzi. Most husbands would beat you for this.

"Madame?
"Madame Bonaparte?"

Letizia came out of her reverie and saw the mulatto with the empty tray under her arm. The food was set out on a small gaming table by the east window. "What shall I tell the general, *Madame*? Will you see him? Do you wish to eat first? I brought a second cup in case."

He would be a stranger after all these years. An old man. But Jean-Paul Diderot was the cause of her reconciliation with Carlo. After a fashion.

"Send him in," she said. "I will see him, just for a few minutes."

He was still a striking figure, but not the one she knew. His hair was pure white and the cane he used was no mere fashion accessory; he leaned on it heavily as he limped toward her. She would not have recognized him. Too many years in his face.

"Jean-Paul?" she said uncertainly.

"Maria Letizia," he said, and kissed her hand.

She had forgotten he used to call her that.

"You are very kind to see me."

"Just very curious, Jean-Paul—to know why *you* want to see *me*. Come to the table. There is coffee."

He seated himself opposite her. His hooded eyes were still blue, but shades paler than the dark midnight blue she remembered. More like the color of her shawl, she thought.

He watched her pour coffee into Sevres cups painted with butterflies. "I heard you were in Paris and looking for a house. This is not Ajaccio, you know. In Ajaccio you couldn't throw a pebble without hitting a cousin's home. Here . . . you will need friends."

Letizia set the coffeepot down with a thump. "It's been a long time since I saw Ajaccio. Didn't you hear about the troubles? My son tried to liberate the island, but they turned on him. They had learned to like slavery. We heard they were going to raid the house."

"Your house on Malerba?"

Letizia nodded. "We were lucky to get away with our skins."

"Only your son behind the coup, not his mother?" he asked, half-teasing.

She laughed. "Don't be a fool, Jean-Paul. I was a widow of forty-three with three daughters and a boy still at home. Nabu and Guiseppe got us off the island and to Marseilles. It's old history now. I've been away from Corsica nine years."

"I never knew you were in Marseilles."

"Why would you? We weren't news for the *Moniteur* in those days." She saw the lines deepen between his frosty eyebrows, a look of genuine distress. "Never mind, Jean-Paul. You wouldn't have wanted to know us. The girls had to work in a laundry to help pay the rent. I took in sewing." She shook her head, still smiling. "Survival was far more pressing than the sovereignty of Corsica."

He reached out and squeezed her hand. "Maria, my *dear*! I wish I'd known. I could have helped you."

She drew her hand back sharply and reached for the crusty round loaf. She broke off a wedge, spread it with soft white cheese, then waved it in the air. "Jean-Paul, *my dear*," she said, mocking his tone, "I managed very well for thirty-two years without your help—and half of them without Carlo's help, too."

His face lifted in admiration. "Only your politics change! You are still the same exciting, impossible woman. I look at you and I can't believe it's been that long."

She laughed again, flushing with pleasure. "I believe it. You, my friend, are much changed. Then you were a young fool. Now you're an old fool."

His grin showed good teeth still, and the same provocative imperturbability that used to pique her so. He was not in the least offended. He joined in her laughter and immediately looked younger. When the laughter subsided she realized she could actually discern the young captain behind the softened jawline and crinkled cheeks. The marks of age were like stage makeup worn by an unskilled actor.

"So you've lived in Marseilles, and now you will live in Paris. Napoleon is making a French family of the di Buonapartes."

"Hah! He is making a Corsican colony out of France."

They shared laughter again, then subsided, drinking coffee together and quietly enjoying the astonishing novelty of the occasion.

"When did Carlo die?" he asked.

"Seventeen years ago. A bad stomach. He was thirty-nine."

Diderot nodded sympathetically. "That's a long time to be a widow. My wife died two years ago and the time passes too slowly." He turned his eyes to the ebony cane resting against the table. "My leg has put me out to pasture. A soldier shouldn't die in his bed but it's all I can expect now. Unfortunately the rest of me is in excellent health."

"Unfortunately? Most men of your age would consider themselves blessed."

He stood up, took his cane and limped to the window. "My children are married and well placed. My work is done. I tend my rose garden and I write my memoirs. But it's not enough. I want a wife again—something to fuss over besides my roses." He glanced at her over his shoulder and smiled. "I'd be a better husband this time."

What he wanted was not a wife but an army commission again, Letizia thought. That's what all this gallantry was about. Retirement bored him. Naturally he would come to the mother of the First Consul. There was nothing Nabu would not do for his mother except get rid of that Creole whore.

When she realized why he was here, she was disappointed for a moment. What a foolish old woman she was becoming! She put down her cup, wiped her lips and stood up.

"I won't marry you, Jean-Paul, but I will let you ride with me to the new house. Would you like to see it?"

"Of course."

"It's on the Place Poivre near Les Halles," she said, buttoning up her redingote.

"An apt address for a woman of your temperament," he said dryly.

So he still found her peppery, did he? She supposed it was a compliment. He had once had a great taste for pepper.

The driver took Rue Saint-Jacques and headed north. The thoroughfare was clogged with rain-slowed traffic that ground to a halt for twenty minutes on the bridge. A cartload of barley had overturned; one sack split wide open was spilling grain over the wet paving stones. A frisky pair of horses, barely broken in, were upset by the commotion and slewing a post chaise across the path in an effort to turn back.

Letizia lowered her window to look. Trapped drivers shouted in frustration and shook their fists. Passing pedestrians yelled helpful hints as they picked their way across the bridge. There was nothing to be done but wait while men righted the cart, recovered the barley sacks and calmed the horses.

Icy rain drove against her shoulder and she closed the window, returning the view to a slate-colored blur. "The bridge is turning into barley soup," she said.

Diderot grinned, indifferent to the delay. Inside the carriage heat rose from the pan of hot bricks at their feet; he was warm, he was dry, and he was seated beside Letizia. "The winters seem to get worse every year in Paris. How you must miss the lemon trees, the golden hillsides baking in the sunshine."

"You never saw a Corsican winter," Letizia said, but thought of those summer-gilded hills nevertheless, and of one summer in particular.

She was ill at ease at her cousin's house, but she was still too angry to go back to Carlo.

At siesta time she would drive a shay through the elm-lined streets until she was free of the bustling town and climbing into the foothills. She would find a tree to which she could hitch the tired old roan and begin climbing on foot through the *macchia* up toward the cool pine forests of Monte Rotondo.

She would look up to where eagles nested, to where they had camped when the French invaded. Carlo had taken her and Guiseppe up there for safety. For his own safety he cared nothing. He was fighting to free Corsica or die in the attempt. "One of my noblest," General Paoli had told her. Her eyes would grow wet when she thought of those weeks.

La Resistenza! She had never loved Carlo more passionately, never been a prouder wife. She had told him so, over and over up there in the guerrilla camp, while Nabullione kicked and danced in her womb.

Now she felt only shame for Carlo.

Captain Diderot was a guest at Udolpho's while his quarters were being painted. He was part of the army of occupation and she avoided him as much as possible, but Udolpho's house was not that big and she could not stay on the hillside all day.

"Your husband asks after you," the French captain told her one night at dinner. "Shall I tell him that you are well?"

"Camilla takes the children to see him every day," she said, biting off her words. "She can tell him."

"He is lonely for you. And you, *madame*? You walk alone in the uplands every afternoon. I think perhaps you are less than content."

"How dare you! Are you not satisfied with enslaving Corsica that you must pry into the personal patterns of my life? Carlo sent you to plead with me! What good friends you must be," she said scornfully.

The captain merely smiled his patronizing smile. "Udolpho is a good friend, too. How is it you can tolerate this house, when you can no longer abide your own home?"

Letizia clenched her teeth. "Udolpho is not the father of my children!" she said in a fierce whisper.

Captain Diderot was a persistent man with a gift for diplomacy. He smiled frequently. Letizia couldn't decide whether it was for the pleasure he took in harassing her or whether he was simply vain about his white, even teeth.

"Your husband is a lawyer, *madame*, a good administrator. Corsica will be virtually self-governing if there are enough reasonable men like him. Cool heads are rare among

Corsicans, but your husband has one. He understands that cooperation is best for the people." Again he smiled.

"As for you, Signora Buonaparte, you do not see beyond that noble Italian nose of yours. The war is over. The work of peace and prosperity must begin."

Blood rushed to her cheeks and she jumped up, overturning her chair. "Freedom is over. It is the slavery of our people that begins," she cried, and stormed out of the room.

Every dinner after that precipitated an argument. Always she had the last word, but he never gave up.

One afternoon he startled her. She was laying a posy of wildflowers at a lonely mountainside shrine when he appeared from nowhere.

"Praying for the souls of dead heroes, *signora*?" His tone was mild and reasonable as always.

She was furious that he had seen her moment of fear. "Yes," she told him, "and for the advent of new heroes who will break our shackles."

He put his hand over his heart and murmured, "A second coming. Bravely said!"

The sarcasm made her want to slap him. Her fingers clenched and she raised her arm. But he bowed his head with obvious sincerity, crossed himself and said a brief prayer for the fallen on both sides.

Letizia felt cheated. She had discovered she enjoyed their altercations.

She began to look for him to appear from behind a stone whenever she was out walking. She missed him when he did not come. By the end of the summer they were lovers. It was not the same painful love she had for her husband; it was youth, it was loneliness and vengeance. A betrayal to avenge a betrayal. She had always been sure they would beat back the French and Carlo would be a hero. She would never be sure of anything again, ever.

In September Diderot was ordered back to France. Her anger against Carlo had burned itself out. She returned to the bed they had shared for four years, and he welcomed her back with tears.

* * *

The house on the Place Poivre smelled of sizing. Letizia led Diderot through the empty rooms, stepping over thick rolls of wallpaper and raising her skirts off a floor strewn with wood dust and splinters and pans of glue. At past fifty her ankles were still as trim as Pauline's. She inspected the completed walls, particularly the corners, and complained fiercely to the carpenter about the molding around one door. She took Diderot up the first flight of stairs. Three bedrooms were finished, the oak floor swept clean but in need of polishing. The small fourth bedroom had not been started. An old brass bedstead stood in the middle of the room, a paint-spattered cloth covering the base.

Letizia stamped her foot. *"Maledetto!"* she said, glaring at the tarnished brass poles. "They haven't even thrown out the junk yet. Two more days, they told me."

He caught her hand as she started to leave. "We never did make love in a bed, did we?"

She went to the bed and ripped off the cloth. Must rose from a ruined mattress stained with mildew. "You want to use that, General Diderot?"

He lifted the cloth from her hand, tossed it on the bed and put his arms around her. "Your skin still glows when you blush."

She thrust him away with both hands. "Don't try to fool a Corsican, Diderot. It doesn't become you. If you want me to ask Nabullione for a position in the army, then come out and say it."

"I want nothing from him, Maria Letizia. Don't you believe me?"

"Then what do you want?"

"At least, the privilege of your friendship. At most, your hand in marriage. Is seven years alone not enough?"

She was silent. Perhaps he was serious.

"Have you had lovers? No, I'm sure you have not. I was the only sin you ever allowed yourself, was I not? Are you still doing penance for that?" He smiled dazzlingly and waited for some small response, but there was none.

"You were always such an extremist. I loved you for it, Maria. I loved your stupid, stubborn bravery. I could love you still if you let me."

"My wifehood is over," she said. "I have my children. I am content to be their mother."

He cupped her face and drew it up to his. "You cannot use that for an excuse with me. I read the newspapers. What else do I have to do? The youngest is Jerome. He's eighteen and a bit of a scamp, but he's in the Consular guard and he's Nabu's problem now, not yours. As for the others, they are all married and scattered over Europe as Napoleon sees fit.... Content to be their mother?" He echoed her last words softly, turning them into a teasing question.

He has studied us well, she thought. How lonely he must be!

"For once in your life, Maria Letizia, you will not have the last word. If you don't wish to marry, fine. But at least be honest. There's not a child left who needs your mothering."

"Oh, but there is, Jean-Paul," she heard herself say with a quiet calm she hadn't expected. "You want honesty? Very well. I have not eight children, but nine."

His eyes became wary at her tone of voice. "Nine? But I— Which child have I missed?"

"Ours."

Chapter Eleven

March, 1802—London

Sebastian had been eighteen and a seasoned midshipman when Edward Cecil entered his life. Cecil was a green apprentice on his maiden voyage and much in need of an ally. His upbringing had not prepared him for the trials of a schooner crew bound for Cape Horn, or for a diet of ship's biscuit, salt junk and burgoo. As the third son of a modestly endowed earl, Cecil's prospects were limited; he had no taste for the church or the army. At twenty-one he had ignored his family's urgings to marry a widow whose money could have launched him into politics. But when he had married a penniless actress who had taken the name of Flora May Passion, he solved his family's problem; they promptly disowned him—and as a consequence, Flora May did the same. At that point, Cecil discovered he was not entirely without inner resources. He ducked his creditors, rolled up his sleeves and went to sea to learn a trade. He was not a natural sailor, but he worked hard and discovered in small ventures with Sebastian a gift for private enterprise.

Over twelve years the two had joined forces on several speculative enterprises. Together they had scrimped and saved, lost and learned, won, then won again. Two years before the turn of the century, they had joined forces for good, buying out the other part-owners of the *Celestine*, and forming a private company.

The Daffodil Trading Company had started as an object of derision in the city trading houses, but with Cecil in charge of domestic transactions and Sebastian responsible for all foreign trading, that raffish name had come to earn profound respect. The war was over now, and the partners owned full title to three clippers. With an excellent line of credit and an embarrassment of money in the bank, the Daffodil Trading Company was branching out into marine insurance.

Far from being branded war profiteers, the two partners, still sole principals of the company, had been roundly applauded for their "splendid efforts in bringing comfort to England during difficult and dangerous years."

The Admiralty had just appointed Sebastian civilian consultant on marine matters in the Mediterranean, with an honorarium of two thousand pounds a year.

The stipend was modest, but to counsel the Lords of the Admiralty was a singular honor, and Cecil had taken him to dinner at the Cheshire Cheese that gusty March evening to mark the occasion.

Cecil eyed Sebastian's formal cutaway coat, the spotless lawn shirt and frothy cravat. They were both still decked out for the Admiralty House ceremony.

"What a far cry from the Ramlin I once knew," Cecil said, remembering his first sight of Sebastian. "He of the moth-eaten stocking cap and patched jerkin. Look at you! You're quite the nob. By God, we're both nobs! It'll be a knighthood next, mark my words, Seb."

"For you, perhaps," Sebastian said. "I don't think a Roman like me could ever make the list."

Cecil reached over the remains of his rack of lamb for the claret bottle and replenished both their glasses. "At any rate, it's time both of us married. Peace with Bonaparte can only increase our profits. By the time we're forty we shall be men of great substance—and no one to leave it to."

"Forty!" Sebastian exclaimed. "Ease up, Ned. You've still two years, and I have eight to go."

Cecil grasped his partner's forearm and cast him one of those earnest, man-to-man looks. "Give her up, Seb. That old frog in Paris could go on forever. I've never known you to shilly-shally except in this affair. But if you're not going to make a clean breast of it and take your chances with Julie Farroux, you might as well look elsewhere. Lizzie Carlsmere would have you in a moment. And what a peach! Besides the fact that she'll come into quite a fortune one of these days."

Sometimes Sebastian wished he'd never mentioned Julie, but he'd had to account somehow for rushing off to catch the Dover packet every time they docked. With war raging between England and France, Ned had become very unhappy about those mysterious side trips, then downright suspicious. The minute he learned it was a woman, a serious attachment, he was all cooperation.

Is that all! For God's sake, Seb, why didn't you tell me before? I've been imagining all kinds of foul cloak-and-dagger stuff.

Over the course of three years the whole story had come out.

"Lizzie Carlsmere is not for me," Sebastian said. "Anyway, you're the one who's hot to marry, and I'm sure she is, too. Why don't you press your suit, Ned?"

"Don't think I wouldn't, my lad, but it's not at *my* feet she drops her fan." Cecil raked the blond curls from his brow with an impatient hand. "She won't look at me while she thinks you're still on the market."

Sebastian threw back his head and laughed, breaking some of the tension he felt. "Cracker-hash! You're just the thing for her, a tall blond Cecil with a noble pedigree and more money than the rest of the Cecils put together. Lady Lizzie likes to flirt, but she'd never in a million years consent to marry a Catholic orphan of foreign descent."

"But the daughter of a French marquis would, is that it? Look at you, Ramlin! All dressed up in Savile Row's finest. A man who just came from hobnobbing with Lord Nelson. What woman would not have died to be the wife on your arm at that reception, busting her buttons with pride?"

Sebastian shrugged and began to survey the dining room. He didn't care to discuss it anymore. He was leaving for

Dover tonight and taking tomorrow morning's packet boat to Calais. The intense anticipation of seeing Julie again after so long made him touchy. "There's Dennis Packer," he said, and looked beyond Cecil's left shoulder.

The aging wool broker turned from his cronies and caught Sebastian's eye; the men exchanged amiable nods.

It was a fairly sparse dinner crowd, Monday being a slow night even for the Cheshire Cheese, the most popular eating house in Fleet Street. Three booths were empty, but the sound of clinking glasses and raucous laughter could be heard from a curtained alcove into which waiters disappeared bearing prodigious amounts of food and drink.

Sebastian saw one of the guests emerge from behind the curtain, apparently in search of a waiter.

"Garçon," he called out. "You 'ave brott mee ze wrong deesh."

Cecil slewed in his chair at the sound. "Good heavens, Robert! Another French *aristo* who lost everything," he told Sebastian. "Things must be looking up for him—the poor fellow was working as a draper's assistant last time I saw him." Cecil waved a hand and called out.

The Frenchman approached their table, a small neatlimbed man dressed in outmoded and rather shabby finery. His smile was radiant as his eyes lit on Cecil. *"Edvard, mon cher ami!"*

Cecil rose and offered his hand but received instead an ecstatic back-thumping hug. "My partner, Sebastian Ramlin," he said when he was released. "Robert Chaumaille, count of Seligne."

"You muzz bofe join us for a cup, my friends. We celebrate tonight. Tomorrow we leave for France." He slapped his thigh, spilling over with joy, and announced by way of explanation, "We 'ave been erased!"

Chaumaille's invitation was not to be denied. Sebastian and Ned found themselves pressed into the boisterous celebration of some dozen French men and women all well into their cups. Chaumaille's introduction was barely heard above the laughter and toasts and snatches of song. Cecil, who had forgotten what little French he had once learned, was none the wiser when he emerged from the private room. Sebastian had picked up the gist of an explanation. The erasures, he learned, were Bonaparte's token of goodwill to appease his new allies.

Of the thousands of royalist names blacklisted in the Republican rolls as *émigrés*, Bonaparte had ordered a few erased. Those few were being allowed to return and reclaim whatever remained of their property as fully restored citizens of France.

Sebastian learned even more the following morning, when he met the Chaumailles again as fellow passengers on the packet boat. The *comte* dozed in the salon throughout the crossing, suffering the effects of the previous night's celebration, but the Comtesse de Seligne was bursting with excitement and much in need of a deck companion to share it with. She attached herself to Sebastian's arm and paced the small passengers' deck treating him to a nonstop recital in fluent English.

The erasures were few, she explained, "Only four families we know of in London besides our own. Saint Fleury, Valere, Sainte Aube and Baudret. We are most blessed to have been chosen, and we have no idea on what basis the—"

"Sainte Aube, did you say?" Sebastian cut in, for the first time interrupting her flow.

"Ah, you know him? Then you will agree, *monsieur*, it was a great tragedy!"

Charles Sainte Aube had choked to death on a fish bone the same day that he received his official invitation to return to France.

Sebastian was still digesting the news as his coach rattled its way south on the road to Paris. He had not seen Sainte Aube since that first meeting at Benson's. Four years ago he had discharged his obligation to the marquis with a brief note:

Sir, Your son-in-law has received me in Paris and I thank you for your introduction. Your daughter is apparently in good health and, as of this writing, still childless.

Ever since, he had avoided Benson's like the plague and considered himself fortunate not to have encountered the man again.

His sudden death could mean nothing to Julie, of course; she had mourned her father eight years ago. But to Farroux it meant one less provision in his entitlement to Marduquesnes. Sainte Aube could no longer challenge it. With a clear title, Farroux would be more anxious than ever for an heir, hardly disposed to leave it to chance and Sebastian's brief visits.

The press of business had kept Sebastian away from Julie almost five months this time. Her letters were as regular as ever, but he fancied a change of tone, a dampening of her enthusiasm to see him. Was it only his imagination? Perhaps not. Much had happened in those five months. Peace for the first time in years. Bonaparte turned from soldier to statesman. Emigrés returning to France. Sainte Aube dead.

And much could have happened to Julie that she had not chosen to share in her letters. Cecil's remarks about shilly-shallying had left Sebastian more disconcerted than he had shown. The public characterized him as a man who would dare all and never count the cost. But in the private ambition of his heart he was all weakness and dread. He had let four years slip away, always craving Julie, always shying away from the risk involved in claiming her. Had love made him so pusillanimous? He was obliged to face it, and the likely rewards of such cowardice.

A half dozen possibilities darted about in his troubled mind, all of them odious, and by the time he reached Paris he was half-convinced that Julie would no longer rush into his arms, that Farroux had already exposed him as a cad, that perhaps at this very moment she was carrying another man's child.

After depositing his luggage at the new Hôtel de la Concorde, his first stop was not at the Farroux town house but at the Hôtel de Ville. He would confront Farroux in his office and persuade him that he still had hopes of fulfilling his agreement. He must buy himself more time with Julie if there was still a chance.

In a different setting, away from Paris and the shadow of Farroux, he would find a way to tell her the truth and make it palatable.

It was the first time Sebastian had visited Farroux in an official setting since their very first encounter, and it took a morning of inquiries to locate him. He had moved and his new office was in the Luxembourg on the other side of the river.

Farroux was on a judicial panel now, heavily involved in the work of writing a new constitution for France, and his time, Sebastian was told by three levels of protective officials, was very limited. After a morning of dogged persistence and then a wait of five hours, Sebastian was granted a few minutes. It would take no more, he decided. He was well rehearsed, prepared with arguments to counter every possible obstruction that might be thrown in his path. Every nerve and fiber beneath his skin pulsed with determination.

Farroux's manner showed none of the cordial hospitality he always assumed in Julie's presence. It was a reminder, if such was needed, that nothing had drawn them together beyond mutual self-interest—in an alliance that had so far failed to bear fruit.

"I do not know what you can possibly expect of me," Farroux announced by way of greeting. "You appear to have surmounted your own difficulties. But for me you have accomplished nothing save to engender in my wife a reluctance to take a lover who could give us a child."

"Your wife has a lover," Sebastian answered, giving a silent prayer of thanksgiving that he had not yet been supplanted.

"A lover, but no child. After more than four years. I do not—"

"That is why I am here," Sebastian put in. "Four years, but very little opportunity to spend them with your wife."

"Precisely. I did not anticipate so long an association. An error of judgment on my part," Farroux said. "I counted on you to accomplish the task before you left Paris the first time. Failing that, I assumed the liaison would die a natural death. Obviously it has not. You do me no favor by continuing your visitations. Our agreement is terminated."

Sebastian looked squarely into those cool, pale eyes with a look he hoped was equally shrewd and dispassionate. "And if it is terminated, *monsieur*, then what? Will you tell her in the language of the stable what you want of her? Will you pick out the stud to cover her and order her to breed? Or do you propose to start again with another intrigue and throw out an investment of four years? That would only be a further error of judgment. She is a woman, Farroux, not a bargaining chip. And she is in love with me. You will find it hard to dupe her into another such affair. I have a far more practical plan."

Farroux made no answer except to raise his brows.

"Circumstances have changed for me. I can afford some leisure now and our countries are at peace. Let me take her to England for an extended stay. She has family there, does she not? Surely a visit would be timely?"

"Perhaps so, but what possible benefit could I reap from that?"

"Why, the one you seek, sir. An heir. Your wife does not take adultery lightly. Even after all these years in Paris she has not abandoned the morals of her childhood. She is under constraint whenever we share a bed, be it Paris or Marduquesnes, for she knows that she will be facing her legal husband across the breakfast table. She knows—or at least guesses—your compliance in this matter but, nonetheless, deception is hard on her."

Farroux's thin lips curled in disgust. "Does a body of water between us legitimize adultery?"

Sebastian took a deep breath, trying to ignore the cold trickles of sweat that coursed down his ribs. "It is common knowledge that a woman ill at ease is not likely to conceive. And I have rarely tarried with her more than three or four days at a time. It would be far more conducive for her to return to the England of her childhood, to know leisure in my company... I believe we could both benefit.''

Farroux's eyes bored through him as he spoke. The argument sounded thinner spoken in this room than it had in his imagination, pathetically thin. And if Farroux asked what Sebastian still had to gain, his answer to that was weaker still. But he had spoken his piece and could only wait for a response.

Outside the window behind Farroux's desk a crow cawed derisively. After a day smothered in clouds the westering sun broke through with a blinding shaft of light, adding to Sebastian's discomfiture. In the sudden brightness he could no longer watch Farroux's facial expression, while his own face, beaded with sweat, was brightly lit. His shirt was sodden and cleaving to his back as he sat through an interminable wait. He had forgotten how shrewd an adversary this was. He would not break the silence. An inscrutable face and a calm, confident silence. There was nothing else left in his armory.

Farroux frowned and let his chin sink into the soft white folds of his cravat. All Juliette had conceived over the past four years was an immovable passion for this man. He was well aware of her feelings. He had tried often enough to divert her interest toward a more accessible sire for their heir, but she had become stubborn and single-minded. And what could Ramlin possibly have to gain?

He glanced across the desk at the man sitting frozen in his chair. There was an air of urgency about him, almost desperation. Why? He was no longer in need; he had apparently become quite a successful buccaneer. And now Europe was at peace, he had little to gain by seeking favor here. Could Ramlin's own romantic passion for her be that pressing? Could he be cherishing the idea of carrying off Juliette for good? A strong possibility, but Farroux need have no serious qualms on that score. He smiled to himself. Marduquesnes was secured by law. And as for his wife, he need only expose this Romeo's motives in pursuing Juliette and her romantic delusions would be shattered. But a simple letter of agreement was in order, just to protect himself.

"Very well, Ramlin," he said at last in his deliberate advocate's tone. "Three months and no more. If she does return pregnant, our agreement is terminated. She may visit her English relatives. The suggestion will come from you, of course. When she proposes it to me, I shall give my consent."

Sebastian Ramlin leaped to his feet like a man reprieved.

"And you shall have my consent in writing," Farroux added, "before you leave this room. Please be seated. This will take but a moment."

He drew out a sheet of paper, reached for a pen and paused only slightly before he dipped it into the ink pot.

On this second day of Germinal in the Year X, I, Guillaume Farroux, hereby set forth the terms of my agreement with Sebastian Ramlin.

In consideration of the sum from me of four thousand louis d'or in the form of a banker's draft dated 19, Frimaire, Year VI, and my undertaking to extend my efforts in the furtherance of the said Sebastian Ramlin's shipping ventures, Sebastian Ramlin offers his services for the purpose of siring a child by my wife, Marie-Louise Juliette, their joint issue to be recognized by me as my legal heir.

To this end and no other, I sanction his departure to England in the company of my wife for a period of three months, to terminate on the third day of Messidor, Year X, also known as 23 July, 1802.

Signed, sealed and accepted by both parties in the presence of both parties.

Farroux scanned his handiwork and nodded. There was little legal validity to the paper without witnesses, but it was adequate insurance against treachery. Judging from Ramlin's loss of facial color as he read those words, it was a precaution long overdue.

Chapter Twelve

I'm so glad the rain stopped," Julie said as she tugged Sebastian's hand and threaded through the pleasure seekers. "I've always wanted to bring you here. Anne-Marie said there'd never be time. She's always encouraging me to take a second lover." She cast him a sly look. "To amuse me when you are gone."

He squeezed her hand hard. "Don't," he said.

"Won't," she replied.

Anne-Marie was not infallible after all. She had not, at least, foreseen this delicious turn of events, a whole summer with Sebastian! At this very moment Babette was packing her trunks for the journey she would take tomorrow. England again, after all these years...and with Sebastian. For two days now she had been so deliriously happy that she could neither eat nor sleep.

Matching her mood, the Tivoli Gardens wore a festive air in the late-morning sunshine. Early showers had left a glistening residue on the greenery and flower beds. There was a new spring planting on the grassy slope at the entrance: massed tulips and irises in red, white and blue stripes forming a great tricolor shimmering in the breeze. The living flag of the Republic drew smiles of approval from tourist and Parisian alike.

In the north circle children rode the carousel horses, some in the protective arms of mothers or nurses, others solo in the saddle, their boisterous cries drowning out the mechanical music that accompanied the ride.

Like hundreds of other lovers, Sebastian and Julie ambled through the paths hand in hand, admiring the floral displays and lingering at the attractions. They paused to watch the first balloonist of the day ascending toward a sky strewn with spun sugar clouds.

"That's just how I feel," Julie said, flinging both arms skyward, "light as air."

"Don't float away from me now," Sebastian said, and drew her close again. "Not just when—"

"Not a chance!" she cut in. "Not when Guillaume is bringing me my passport home tonight. Three whole months together! Oh, Sebastian, I am so happy I feel dizzy!"

She opened her parasol, held it rigid in front of her and spun round and round, faster and faster, until the condition was real and she tottered against him, light-headed and laughing. "Guillaume has absolutely no idea that you are here in Paris. I will have to watch my tongue tonight lest I let it slip out. God forbid he should change his mind."

With a hand at her throat as though she were restraining her heart from leaping wildly out of her body, she resumed her progress with him around the central square. "You can't imagine how easy it all was. When I proposed a summer visit to England, he took it as the most natural, the most reasonable suggestion he had ever heard."

"It is," Sebastian said.

"But my grandmother died five years ago." Only her maiden aunt, Emma Allingham, and the Thomas Allinghams were left, she explained. "Uncle and Aunt Allingham were always jealous of my place in Grandmama's affections," she said, "and their three horrid sons always took great delight in bullying me and conspiring to get me into trouble. They used to say the most dreadful things about my father, too. Just to pain me. We haven't corresponded for years. I think we all used the difficulty of wartime postal communications as an excuse. But you and I managed, did we not? And I do occasionally receive news from Elizabeth Margrave. She is a very dear friend—truly my only credible pretext for a trip to England. I was relieved that Guillaume accepted that I was actually pining to see my surviving relatives.''

''I am so grateful,'' Sebastian said, squeezing her waist. ''To Guillaume for his consent?''

''To you, for remaining true all these trying years to such a neglectful lover. I'll never neglect you again, I swear it, Julie.''

She lapsed into a long silence before she dared utter the words. ''Are you saying there'll be no more separation?''

''Yes. If that is your wish.''

The ambiguity of it distressed her, and so did the possibilities that immediately came to mind. Bigamy? Desertion? ''A common-law marriage?'' she asked him.

''A lawful one.'' Sebastian's tone was unequivocal.

''Then why are we going off tomorrow without a word to Guillaume? I must start divorce proceedings. I must tell him that—''

''No!''

''But why?''

''I want you to know me better. There are things about me you may not accept so easily.''

Julie had often sensed a darkness floating beneath the surface of Sebastian's contentment; she saw it clearly now in his eyes. She forced a smile, making light of it.

''My darling, I know you have been a gambler, a womanizer, but it is past history. You have told me so often enough. It is the truth, is it not?''

''The truth.''

''You have no wife?''

''No, I've never had a wife.''

''And you are true to me?''

''I swear it.''

''Have you ... have you committed some foul crime for which you are being hunted down?''

''It is nothing like that, my love. Just trust me. Come to know me better in my own surroundings in England, and then I will tell you.''

''But why do you not trust me and tell me now?'' Julie persisted.

"Because I cannot bear the thought of losing you."

She gave up. She had known him adamant before and there was no profit in pursuing it. There was nothing on earth for which she could not forgive him and she would be content to wait until he chose to speak of it. She only longed to relieve him of the pain it caused him.

"Please don't," she said, stroking the angle of his jaw and feeling the grinding tension beneath her fingertips. "I will always love you. Whatever it is, please be happy."

His face lightened, but she thought it was more an act of sheer will than conviction. He turned to cup her face in his hands. "Here is all I will ever need to make me happy," he said, and smiled.

It was the saddest smile she had ever seen.

"In England we shall have time to speak of the future," he said. "And the past."

She took his arm and, with her own act of will, turned her thoughts to the pleasures surrounding them.

In the central square a grenadier band was playing a rousing march. Lining the square were little shops, bistros and cafés. Most of the boutiques were crowded with eager shoppers seeking gifts, toys and mementos of the day. At the cafés, waiters were carrying out chairs and tables, anticipating a sunny afternoon and a brisk outdoor luncheon business. At the southeast corner, a golden pavilion greeted them, covering most of the width of the walkway. It was covered with shiny satin and shaped like a pyramid. A large pennant flew from the apex. It bore some hieroglyphics and the words, Madame Hatshepsut Descendant of the Pharaohs.

Beneath the sign stood two men decked in turbans, baggy trousers and Turkish slippers. One played a plaintive Oriental tune on a silver flute; the other addressed the passersby.

"The future foretold through the ancient art of the pharaohs, handed down to Madame Hatshepsut from her ancestor, the queen of Egypt. Visit Madame Hatshepsut and know your destiny."

Julie looked up at Sebastian. "Shall we?"

He grinned, quite himself again. "A fortune-teller? You don't believe in such things, do you?"

"Of course not, but it will be fun."

Inside was a dim windowless vestibule lit with perfumed candles. Three veiled women greeted them, salaaming and undulating across the tiled floor in harem costumes of flimsy gauze, their spangles, sequins, and finger bells clacking and jingling. As their eyes grew accustomed to the gloom, Sebastian and Julie took in a splendiferous jumble of Egyptian and Turkish culture. Cushioned divans had been placed below murals depicting Pharaohs and their handmaids. Plaster heads of Isis and Osiris and brass censers adorned low, inlaid tables. Pungent sandalwood and myrrh permeated the air.

"She used to be Madame Iphigenie," Julie whispered, sinking into the cushions, "but since the Egyptian campaign, the Orient is all the rage in Paris."

"Have you been here before?" Sebastian asked.

"No, but Anne-Marie has used her. She is in great demand at soirees and dinner parties. Her real name is Louise Créche. She's one of the servants Josephine brought here from Martinique. But she couldn't afford to keep her household during the revolution—most of them had to fend for themselves."

"Well, Louise seems to have landed on her feet," Sebastian said. "This is quite a theatrical troupe she's supporting."

"Anne-Marie believes she truly has a gift. At all events, everyone finds her amusing at the soirees."

One of the houris approached. "Five francs each, *monsieur*," she said. As she took the money a gong sounded. She bowed low and intoned, "May the gods of the Nile shower you with good fortune throughout the long river of your life."

"I didn't think the Egyptian venture would be so popular in Paris," Sebastian said.

"It cost France a fortune, yes. But there were those initial victories. And Bonaparte is so loved here. And although it brought little political advantage, it's considered a great coup for France culturally."

"In what way?"

"Well, the Rosetta stone, for one. The savants at the institute say it is the key to the language of the Pharaohs. With time they will be able to read those hieroglyphics and unlock the mysteries of the entire civilization."

At that point a gong sounded, and Julie was led into the fortune-teller's presence.

Madame Hatshepsut herself was veiled, but her eyes were visible, heavily painted to give her a somewhat ferocious feline look. She sat at a table over a bowl of burning incense that occasionally sent up eerie flashes of yellow light through the smoke.

"Breathe deeply, my child." Her voice sounded as if it came from a bottomless pit lined with gravel. "Deep breaths so that we may both be filled with the spirit of my ancestor."

Madame Hatshepsut offered up an imposing but unintelligible incantation, then, rolling her eyes back in her head, she began to intone in a mystic litany.

"Hear me, Khepera, in the morning. Hear me, Ra, at noon. Here me, Tum, at eve."

Her breathing quickened with each repetition of the words. She began to gasp and labor, the words becoming distorted until she could say no more. She shuddered, her arms flailed the air in tortured spastic movements, and then a heart-stopping howl rent the air. She slumped backward against her chair, her head lolling sideways.

"I see waaater," she said in the high-pitched tones of a young girl. "Oceans of waaater."

They always see water, Julie thought. It could symbolize so many different things. But she *was* taking a boat tomorrow. She tensed and waited to hear more.

"There is a man. A strong man, fair to behold, who pleases your eye. In his right hand he holds the fruits of light, and in his left, the fruits of darkness. You will eat— Ah, alas, you will eat from the wrong hand. You will spurn him and cause him great grief."

Julie became irritated and stopped listening. She was no more likely to spurn him than to sprout wings. It was hard enough to convince Sebastian of that. Was she now going to have to argue with the gods of the morning, noon and night? She reminded herself that this was just theatrical nonsense after all. *You will spurn him and cause him great grief!* Pure coincidence, of course. Madame Hatshepsut was canny, certainly, but she was no visionary. She was simply exploiting the fact that most young women liked to think of themselves as heartbreakers. The high voice wailed on for another ten minutes with its arcane messages but Julie shut them out. She needed no more clouds on this perfectly glorious spring day.

"What did she tell you?" Sebastian asked, squinting as they emerged into the bright sunshine.

"Just a lot of mumbo jumbo." Julie laughed. "I'm going to eat from the wrong hand and cause grief. All kinds of mysterious nonsense like that. I simply stopped listening after a while. I've decided Louise's talents have been vastly overrated."

"She puts on a good show, you must admit."

"Not bad," Julie admitted grudgingly. "And how was your session? Do you know your destiny now?"

"Someone waaatches over you and brings you good fortune," he wailed in a poor imitation of the fortune-teller. "You shall know happiness in your life, and aaah, alas, also grieeef. A good five francs' worth of wisdom, don't you think? How did I ever manage to conduct my affairs before this profound enlightenment?"

Julie laughed. "Is that all she told you?"

"No."

"Well, do tell."

Sebastian's teeth flashed in the sun. "She told me I would take my beloved to lunch at Tortoni's. So please oblige me by not eating from the wrong hand."

The journey to Calais was unusually long. Four hours out of Paris and midway between two staging posts one of the horses stumbled into a pothole, laming itself and damaging one wheel. They waited three hours for a replacement and, as a consequence, spent an uncomfortable night in a wretched little town that did not expect travelers and was ill-equipped to lodge them.

On the packet boat a capricious wind lengthened the channel crossing to a grueling ten hours, through which Julie, exhausted and still distressed by the shooting of the lamed horse, suffered in queasy silence.

Sebastian had planned London as their first stop, for Julie had never seen the city. But after the bone rattling on those atrocious road surfaces and a day of seasickness, she was in no mood for sight-seeing. Instead, he hired a well-sprung coach and headed directly to Bryony for a restful few days in the peace of the Essex countryside.

Pale with fatigue, Julie laid her head in his lap and slept through most of the ride.

Sebastian had purchased Bryony Manor in a rare mood of optimism, envisaging Julie as the mistress of the house. It was an old manor house, much changed from its original plan, but from the front the outer walls retained their integrity. They were built of rose-colored brick and of local stone, weathered by four hundred years to a frosty gold. The interior had been gutted and modernized by successive owners but had escaped the imposition of Corinthian columns, marble cherubs, fountains and the other pretensions that were currently spreading through the country estates like a bad case of the pox.

The sprawling three stories sat squarely in the center of the estate, a dwelling not a showplace but, to Sebastian's mind a thing of beauty, suggesting enduring substance rather than great wealth. The estate yielded a modest income from a small tenant farm, a dairy and sixteen tenant cottages.

"You could have found something much more profitable for that price," Cecil had pointed out, but Sebastian begged to differ. Cecil saw only land and livestock, upkeep and income, and "damn it all, Seb, the roof leaks!" Sebastian saw permanence, tradition. Family. He didn't mind fixing the roof.

Here he could bring a wife. Here he could see daughters trailing dolls across the wide lawns and sons who would roll about with the dogs, climb the spreading elderberry and beech trees and swim in the clear stream that ran through the meadow. They would learn the secret paths through Epping Forest and ride like the wind on stout ponies. They would say, "This is my home. This is where I come from."

Much to Cecil's dismay, Sebastian had not negotiated for the property but instantly agreed to the asking price, an act of faith. And since it was Julie he had in mind when he made the purchase, he had commissioned the improvements accordingly—a north-facing study with a great wall of windows where she could sketch and paint, a bathroom on the second floor with a second boiler in the kitchens that served no other purpose than to provide hot water. He purchased a pianoforte, turning the salon adjacent to the drawing room into a music room. A cozy morning room not far from the back stairs would be the place where they gathered for meals hot from the kitchen. They could avoid the vast dining hall except for banquets.

The reconstruction had been completed more than a year ago, and he had not slept there once since, neither had he mentioned the work to Julie except to say casually that he had acquired a property near Epping Forest.

As the coach left paved highway for dirt road and cart path, penetrating deeper and deeper into the gently undulating wheat fields, Julie awoke and watched their approach to Bryony.

The hedgerows on either side of them were scarcely more than an arm's length away. She opened the window and smelled hawthorn in bloom and began to remember the wildflowers of her childhood.

Grandmama had known them all. Names she had not thought of for years occurred to her, and with them came a lightness of heart she had not enjoyed since the day she left Clarendon.

The hackney drew up at a pair of tall wrought-iron gates, and Sebastian jumped down to open them.

"We are not expected," he said, climbing back beside Julie, "but I promise we'll eat well tonight. You can never starve on a farm."

Julie barely heard him. Her eyes were glued to the window, admiring the rugged stands of chestnut, beech and oak that graced the carriageway, subsiding at odd unmeasured intervals to massive clumps of rhododendron. The fine gravel path curved around a copse, descended into a shallow decline, then began to climb. At the top of the rise, beyond the emerald reaches of lawns, sat the manor house.

As soon as she laid eyes on it, she knew why he had chosen it. "Oh, my dearest," she said, reached for his hand and pressed it. "I shan't ever want to leave."

Three days of rest, they agreed, before they ventured further. But a week went by, then another, the days spilling through their fingers like barley grains.

Such peace seemed to descend on Julie that she was content with the gentle rhythm of unambitious days. They neither visited nor entertained. They spoke to no one but the members of the household and the cottagers on the estate.

Rising each morning from Sebastian's bed, she would return to her room to bathe and don a riding habit. She ate the first meal of the day with him in the sunny morning room with its bright yellow curtains and white walls. After breakfast they would ride out through the estate, each day exchanging a few words with the tenants. One morning he showed her the dairy; on another, she saw a foal just six hours old. She met Buttercup, a huge Jersey just days away from dropping her first calf. Or they would explore one of the innumerable shady paths of Epping Forest, just a strip of common land away from the northeast border of the estate.

The smells of simmering meat and buttery vegetables would greet her return to the manor house and follow her up the stairs to her room so that by the time she arrived at the table, changed into a day dress, she was ravenous for luncheon.

Sebastian took delight in seeing her eat so well. In France she had had such a small appetite, and although he would not have her change one whit, sometimes when he held her in his arms, the fragility of her body made him fear he would crush it.

Sometimes the sating of one appetite would provoke another. Over coffee he might be answering a question she had just posed about the crossbreeding plans for the Jersey herd. He would stop in midsentence because he read the clear hot message of her eyes and knew she had suddenly lost interest in the livestock.

He would rise from the table and extend his hand to her. "Come," he would say softly. "I'll tell you about the Jerseys later." And for the space of an hour or so, their horizons would shrink to the confines of a four-poster bed and yet contain all they asked of the universe.

Time was a luxury they had never had before. It altered the nature of their lovemaking into a contemplative act, a lingering giving and taking of pleasure, with little of the greed and desperation they had known previously. They became spendthrifts of the hours, consuming them extravagantly, soaking in hot baths, dawdling over breakfasts, over indolent games of backgammon that were never finished.

Most afternoons were spent idling in the meadows. The weather was golden, and the outdoors beckoned. With Sebastian at her side Julie would watch the lambs frisk, inspect the brambles for ripening blackberries, collect watercress then leave it to wilt in the sun. She would point out wildflowers, make daisy chains to hang about their necks. He would watch her, sometimes stretched out in the long grasses, chewing on a stalk or trailing his hand in one of the streams. He was at ease here, the occasional frowns and darknesses she had come to dread quite banished from his face. Seeing him at peace, she was utterly content to idle away the remaining daylight hours simply being with him.

It was on such an afternoon that she stood staring at a clump of delicate pink blossoms. She remembered the plant from Clarendon, from that summer when she learned to ride. Cracker, the little Welsh pony, had liked those flowers better than sugar and would never pass a patch of them without stopping to graze. But she could not put a name to them. Sebastian was no help. From his childhood with the priest he knew daffodils and roses, but as for the flowers of hedgerow and meadow, he scarcely knew buttercups from clover. She racked her brain, amused that the problem should consume her so.

Of such was the small currency of her days. The name of Cracker's passion! More important than affairs of the world, more crucial even than the larger issues of her life. In the balmy indolence of that summer afternoon, only the name of a wildflower was of any consequence. And when it came to her, her happiness was complete. *Eyebright!*

"Eyebright," she cried, sending a curious lamb skittering back to its dam. And in a wave of elation she began to gather wildflowers of every description, darting from hedgerow to knoll to stream bank until her arms were full and she had to gather her skirts to hold them so that she could pluck yet more.

On the other side of the tiny rill, Sebastian reclined against a gentle bank of moss. A book of humorous essays lay at his side. They always brought that book, planning to read to each other. They had yet to open it.

He watched her butterflying about in the sun. How she had blossomed in the gentle country air. The pallor of her skin had yielded to satiny peach, her thin fragility had softened, and the feverish vivacity that drove her in Paris had mellowed into an even-tempered contentment. It was as if the place had nurtured her. *His* place, he thought, with pride, *his* garden vegetables that she loved so much, *his* dappled meadows where she could play for hours. His instincts about this place had been right. Julie belonged here.

She ran to him laughing, breathless, and emptied her skirts at her feet. Her dark hair flashed the color of burgundy as it caught the sunlight; it had tumbled from its combs and dark wisps clung moistly to her brow.

"Eyebright," she said, and dropped down beside him. "It was the only one I couldn't recall. But I have it now."

She reached into the tumble of flowers and picked out a sprig dotted with spiky blue blossoms. "You shall see how I improved the shining hours of my childhood," she said.

She wore no fichu at her throat and her breasts nestled like doves in the scant bodice of her fashionable Paris chemise. Her skirt was stained with crushed petals and she wore all the green smells of summer about her.

"Chicory," she said, waving the sprig under Sebastian's nose. "The dried petals make a good potion for darkening gray hair."

He reached up and smoothed the dark wisps on her brow. "Then you are much too young for chicory," he murmured.

"Forget-me-not." She squinted at him through a spray of tiny flowers the color of a summer sky. "It will blacken no hair but is much used by lovesick poets."

"Lovesick I may be," he said, "but alas, no poet." Pollen clung to her upper arm and he brushed it away. Her skin felt like warm down to his fingertips and he let them linger.

"Meadow saffron, the flavor not as potent as the Spanish variety but the color of the stamen is the same."

The tops of her breasts bore witness to that with their light dusting of reddish gold. He smoothed it away then licked his finger and tasted the sharp flavor.

"Let me see...pennycress and, of course, sorrel for salads. Lady's fingers. Are you listening?"

He reached for her hand and kissed her fingers. "Lady's fingers," he repeated.

"Vetch. Saxifrage. Self-heal...the last a deceptive name, for it will in fact heal nothing, according to my grandmother."

He returned his attention to her bosom as if he were seeing it for the first time. With the outer edge of his little finger he stroked the curves that rose above her dress. With each stroke a new word sprang to mind. Full. Taut. Smooth.

Warm. Sleek. She was still naming flowers, allowing his caresses but not aroused by them, as rapt in her recital as he was in his tender fondling.

"Heartsease," she continued. "Corn marigolds. Red hemp nettle."

Sweet ripe peaches, he thought.

"Blue pimpernel."

The light rise and fall each time she drew breath could engage him for hours.

"Bindweed."

She had turned to him upon waking that morning, pinpoints of flame in her eyes and her hand sliding down his belly. They had made love, long lingering love, and yet his hunger was mounting again. He could not love her here. Any farmhand could pass by and—

"Wild chamomile."

At this moment their only company was the flock of sheep in the enclosure. It was tempting, but he would not offend her sensibilities.

"Field madder. Dainty, is it not?"

He contented himself with thoughts of later.

Her voice continued, bright as a child's. Overhead a lark sang.

"Pheasant's eye."

He seemed unable to draw his hand away from her breast.

"Celandine. Tansy. Woody...night...shade." Her voice faltered and she lifted his hand away.

He took it for a protest; she had seemed so intent on her nature lesson. But she ignored the remaining flowers and moved to cradle his head on her arm. Then with a slow, deliberate movement, she dipped her hand into her bodice and drew out her breast, offering it to him on the palm of her hand.

He cupped his hands around it, astonished that in the broad light of day she would so publicly declare that the delights of her body were his for the taking. He closed his mouth around her nipple and found it sweeter, more full-bodied to his lips than he could ever remember.

She stroked his face and combed her fingers through his hair while he suckled her. Suddenly her fingers tightened and grasped fiercely, wrenching his head up.

"Take me," she said.

"Not here."

"Yes, here," she insisted. "The house is too far."

He laughed, covering her breast and lifting her in his arms. "Not that far. I will carry you up to the house and then I will take you to the stars."

"Hurry, then."

He ran up the bank and climbed a stile and raced across the upper meadow. She clung to his neck, spurring him on with hot messages in his ear. He cut through the double row of cottages to shorten their route. He ran through the orchards, past the stables and across the banks of lawn, which seemed wider and steeper than they ever had before. He ran up the steps, through the front doors, and took the wide staircase two steps at a time.

The maid who was making up the bed in his room looked up, startled. Another maid polishing the windows turned, dropped her cleaning rag, then covered her mouth with her hand and turned back to the window.

Backing out, he moved on down the gallery, Julie's weight increasing with every step. Her bedroom was clean and deserted. Awkwardly he fumbled for the lock to secure the door, then, with a sigh, dropped her down on the bed.

She rolled on her side, bent double with laughter. Laughing so hard that tears flowed down her cheeks. Laughing so hard she was groaning.

"And what is so uproariously amusing?" he said, fumbling with his shirtsleeve buttons. He was grinning because her laughter was infectious, but he was acutely embarrassed for her sake as well as his own. Before servants they'd been caught acting like a lickerish plowman and his doxy.

"What is so funny?" he demanded, rearing over her and pinning her shaking shoulders flat against the coverlet.

"Nothing, nothing," she gasped, slowly recovering the powers of speech. "It is just that— Well! Now at least three cottage wives, the gardener, one stable boy, the housekeeper and two parlormaids know exactly what we are about to do. We would have done better to have stayed in plain view of the sheep,'' she said, and another gale of mirth shook her. ''Sheep can't talk!''

He had never seen her laugh so robustly. He stretched out above her and rolled over on his side, pressing her to him and feeling the ripples of her happiness flow over him.

After dinner that night, she played for him. Some light-hearted Scarlatti. Then a somber Bach fugue. Too somber.

''It's beautiful, but it's very sad,'' he said as the last dark chord faded. ''Can we not have some more happy pieces? A dance suite, maybe?''

''I can't play any more from memory,'' she said. ''It's been so long. I should have brought some sheet music.''

It was something he had planned to do in London, he remembered. There was a shop next to Hatchard's with the best selection of music in England. She could have shopped for piano music to her heart's delight.

''Then play whatever you wish,'' he said, and went to her. Standing behind the piano stool he laid his cheek on hers and encircled her with his arms. ''When we are married you shall have a library of music. You shall fill this house with sound, you shall sketch and paint and put a name to every growing thing in the meadow.... And if you are not too busy, dear heart, I want you to be the mother of my children.''

Julie had a growing suspicion that she was already granting him that wish. She woke briefly at first light the next morning, hugging the private thought to herself as she watched Sebastian's sleeping face on the pillow. She fancied that she knew the very occasion she had conceived, on his second day in Paris. Was that possible? She recalled the tall windows of his suite in that splendid new hotel, the sweet desperation of his body and the dark burden in his eyes. What was it that intruded on his peace of mind? she wondered.

He had tried to tell her in the Tivoli Gardens and failed. It had alarmed her then, threatening to blot out the joy of the day, but it no longer held any threat. Whatever that burden was, he seemed to have laid it down here at Bryony.

She had never known him to sleep this soundly. He lay half-turned toward her, one arm flung out, his hand at rest under the curve of her breast. His head had sunk in the pillow so that only his profile was visible, as still as the head on a coin. Sun crinkles marked his eyes, but the Roman nose, the brow, the wide mouth, the planes from cheekbone to chin were free of every trace of tension. Would it perhaps return if he knew she was carrying his child?

She let her eyes close, drifting off again. She had blissfully forgotten how to worry. And she would not tell him anyway unless she was sure. Perhaps she had miscalculated. It was so hard to keep track of the days in this paradise. But it was less the cycles of her body that informed her than the intimations of her soul. She had the sense that she was somehow possessed of a special dignity, a sort of self-sufficiency of spirit, and that nothing, no fortunes of war or love, no contract or custom, could ever dispossess her.

The sun was warm on her cheek when she woke again, and Sebastian was gone. She stretched luxuriously and wandered into his dressing room. He was gone from there too, and no wonder! The small carriage clock on his tall-boy showed almost eleven.

Smiling to herself, she hurried down the gallery to her own dressing room. He had probably waited for her until his stomach protested. Breakfast was his heartiest meal of the day. It was a habit acquired at sea, he'd once told her, when he was master of the second watch.

She dressed hurriedly in her riding habit, hoping Mrs. Pettersley would have left at least some morsels on the table. She brushed her hair in haste; she always coiled it into a cadogan for riding, but this morning, begrudging the time it took, she left it free. She even left her riding coat on the bed and headed downstairs. She was still tying the shirt ribbons about her neck as she took the stairs.

The door to the morning room was ajar and she heard Sebastian's voice as she approached, telling Megan to leave the food on the table.

"Sebastian," she called out, "you should have woken me at—"

The presence of a stranger at the table stopped her short. Sebastian rose and pulled out her chair, but there was an odd silence in the room, and a long pause before the stranger rose to his feet. Megan felt something, too. About to collect the used plates, she suddenly changed her mind, whisked past Julie with a silent bob of a curtsy and hurried out the door.

"I'm sorry," Julie said. "I didn't know you had a visitor. Am I interrupting something?"

"No, of course not. This is my partner, Edward Cecil. Ned, Julie Farroux."

"Mrs. Farroux." Cecil gave a brief bow and did not resume his seat.

He was a tall, elegant figure in impeccable city clothes. His blond hair was dressed *en brosse*, a startling contrast to Sebastian's dark shag. Julie found his appraising glance somewhat offensive. She regretted now that she was coatless, her shirt poorly tied and her hair adrift about her shoulders.

"I'm the intruder, I fear," he said with a rather strained politeness. "Sebastian's holiday is long overdue and I should not have disturbed it but for..." He shrugged and left the sentence hanging with a cool smile of apology, as if Julie's presence was an understandable constraint.

For the first time since she had arrived in Bryony, Julie began to feel the delicate vulnerability of her position. The tenants and domestics treated her with affectionate respect. But Edward Cecil was her and Sebastian's peer, and his appraising glance made her wonder what she was doing here, since he was obviously wondering, too. Had she merely progressed from Sebastian's lover to his kept woman? Certainly she could not regard herself as his betrothed. He had been deliberately vague about marriage and she had been endlessly patient. Too patient.

"I shall wait in Sebastian's study until you've had something to eat, Mrs. Farroux," Cecil added with a condescending nod. "Then perhaps you will spare me a few minutes with him to talk business." He bowed again and walked stiffly to the door.

"Damn your eyes, Ned—come back here!" Sebastian called to Cecil's retreating back. "Sit down and get it off your chest. I know you're still vexed with me, but there's no need to start mincing words like a dancing master. There is nothing Julie cannot hear." He turned to her. "It seems, my dear, that a certain meeting slipped my mind. Nothing crucial, but Ned has never known me—"

"Nothing crucial," Cecil protested, bearing down on Sebastian and leaning over the table. "When did the captain of a clipper become less than crucial?"

"I made the selection before I left London," Sebastian said in a cool, quiet voice, "and I drew up the papers."

Cecil dropped back into the chair facing his partner. "Sebastian! You were to be there! You were to brief him personally and hand him his commission."

Julie glanced from one to the other. Sebastian too was without benefit of coat or cravat, his shirt open in a deep V. To Julie it seemed to put him at a distinct disadvantage, but apparently he did not feel it.

He tipped his chair back from the table in a deliberate gesture of ease and grinned. "Did you have such trouble briefing Captain Chatsworth?" he asked jovially. "A man who's run that course five times before and has more charts than a dog has hairs? Come, Ned, don't make a tragedy of this. Briefing the man was no more than a formality. Or was your arm too short to reach across the desk and hand him his papers?"

Cecil's voice was ominously low. "That's hardly the point. The crews have always been your concern, not mine."

Sebastian grinned and threw up his hands. "You're right, Ned. Right and right again. What's done is done and I have already apologized for that. What else can I say?"

Cecil's fingers were suddenly busy with some bread crumbs on the tablecloth. He swept them together, then kneaded them into a soft lump. "Just convince me it's not a taste of things to come. We've done well, Sebastian, and mostly thanks to you. But it's as easy to lose a fortune as to make it. I just hope that while you're country squiring it around here, you won't let the money go to your head."

"Ned, Ned, don't you know me better than that?" Sebastian rocked on the rear legs of his chair, unruffled.

Cecil's eyes closed for a moment. "Yes, yes, I do. Of course I do!" His gaze left the tablecloth and turned to rest on Julie, chill and deliberate. "It's not the *money* that's gone to your head, is it?"

Sebastian leaned forward, slamming his chair upright with a crack on the parquet. For the first time, his expression looked thunderously dark. "You meddling son of—"

"Mr. Cecil," Julie cut in, rising from her chair. "I have no wish to cause dissension between two partners."

"Julie, oblige me by—" Sebastian growled, but her voice overrode his.

"If Sebastian neglected a responsibility in London, I suspect it was my—"

"Stay out of this, woman!"

"—fault, but I promise you, wherever his duty calls him next, he will not fail again." Her eyes turned angrily from one to the other. "Not on my account at least," she said as she hurried out of the room.

Sebastian bellowed after her for all the servants to hear. "Julie, come back here!" She only quickened her pace up the stairs. He caught up with her at the door of her room with a fierce grip on her elbow. "I will not be treated like a child, do you hear me? Not by Cecil and not by you."

She shook off his hand as if it were loathsome. "And I will not be treated like your—your weakness! Your little toy to play with and put away like a good boy when it's time to do your homework. Oh, I saw what you were trying to imply to Cecil. 'She's just my little piece of summer recreation. Don't take it so seriously, you'll spoil my fun.'" She leaned against the door, rage stiffening her back as she remembered. "How *dare* you call me *woman*! How *dare* you?"

Sebastian's eyes widened in astonishment. "I believe you had too much sun yesterday. You've eaten nothing. I'll have your breakfast brought up." He glanced at her riding skirt.

"And you might as well change out of that. There'll be no riding today. Why don't you rest for a while and compose yourself," he said, and made for the stairs. "We'll discuss this later."

Compose yourself! Stay out of this, woman! There'll be no riding today. Julie lashed herself into a fury with those insults as she headed the sorrel toward the woods. She spurred her mount into a canter over the common land, her unbound hair flying in the wind.

Oh, there would be riding today, all right. As fast and as far from this house as the sorrel would take her. What gall! What audacity! To reprimand her in front of a stranger. How dare he tell her what to do! How to behave! What to say!

After a while she slowed the mare to a walk, somewhat calmer now the house was lost from view. It was cool and soothing to move through the dappled shade and she began to reason out her anger. The mare was a good listener.

"I don't suppose he meant anything by it, Cora. He just saw red. It was Mr. Cecil who slighted me, don't you think!"

Cora's head dipped in agreement.

"Still, it was not the act of a gentleman to shout at me so. I believe a heartfelt apology is in order.

"On the other hand, perhaps I spoke out of turn? No, it was quite obvious that *I alone* was the bone of contention. What was I to do? Sit there mum with a permanent smile on my face like the china doll they think I am?"

Ah, but had she not always been his china doll? Always there for his pleasure at his convenience? Waiting patient and uncomplaining when he threw her aside for more important matters? Waiting endlessly until he had a mind to play with her again?

"No, Cora! That's simply not true. I mean all the world to him. I know it. It is Mr. Cecil who regards me as a regrettable distraction. Surely that alone provoked Sebastian to shout."

After two hours of arguing with herself she was diverted by her gnawing hunger. She regretted now that she hadn't waited for her breakfast tray. Now there was surely luncheon on the table. She decided to return to the house. But when she emerged from the forest she was in an unfamiliar place, where fields stretched ahead as far as the eye could see and a small village lay to her right.

In the village she watered the horse and received directions. The road that skirted the forest would take her back to Bryony, but it was almost a day's ride. Cutting through the forest was quicker and cooler, and "you can't rightly miss the road," the farrier pointed out.

She had thought she had it right. The farrier's instructions were quite clear. Back to the path she had just left and straight on. A clearing, then a left turn where two paths crossed. She would pass the charcoal burners' huts on her right. "Then Babblin' Brooks Corner where the new highway cuts right through. Cross over and go 'alf a mile then take the right fork. I can walk it in 'alf an 'our, miss. You'll do it in less, riding."

But she never found Babblin' Brooks Corner or the charcoal burners' huts, and it was early evening before she led Cora back to the Bryony stables. The hostler was gone and it was his young helper who took the reins from Julie as she slid from the saddle.

Tom was no more than twelve, a cottager's son, and he'd never had sole charge of the nags before. His excitement was hard to contain. "Yer back, mum! Yer back," he kept announcing.

"Where are they, Tom?" she asked, pointing to the empty stalls.

He batted back his sandy forelock with his wrist, delighted to take part in the drama. "Out looking for yer. Master thought yer got lost, ma'am."

"I did for a while, but as you see, I managed quite well on my own."

"Been out looking for hours, 'e 'as. Came back twice to see if you made it by yerself. Then 'e sent Mr. Pim out on the gelding over to Frimley in case you were over that way. So now they're both out looking."

"Thank you, Tom." The idea of Sebastian worried frantic about her was rather satisfying. It was time he knew how that felt.

Mrs. Pettersley opened the front door with an obvious look of relief. "Lor', Mistress Farroux, you look fair done in! And you've not eaten all day. Shall I send Lily up with a tray?"

"Oh, please! Anything you have in the kitchen," she said, "and lots of it. I'm famished."

"She's back, sir," Tom called out from the door as Sebastian rode into the stable yard.

"Thank God," he breathed, easing himself wearily from the saddle. "When did she get back?"

"An hour or more. She lost her way for a while."

"For a while?" Sebastian's voice rose indignantly. "Is that what she told you? She's all right, isn't she, Tom? I mean she didn't come a cropper or anything?"

"Fer as I could tell, she's right as rain," Tom said.

Sebastian closed his eyes for a moment.

"I've rubbed Cora down, sir, and she's had a feed."

"Good boy. If you'd do the same for Dexter, I'd appreciate it." He patted the stallion's rump as Tom reached for the cinch buckles. "Then you must run along home. Don't wait for Pim. It's late and you've missed your supper."

"Mrs. P. sent over some bread and cheese to keep me going. Me mum'll keep me supper for me. Not to worry."

"Good, good," Sebastian said, and turned toward the house, trying to empty his mind of gruesome images...Julie enraging some cutpurse because she carried no money, the thief exacting his price on her body. Julie spirited away by Gypsies. Julie lying helpless and injured at the foot of an oak tree. Now that he knew she was back, his fears abated, but the sick pulsing in the pit of his stomach continued. How could she *do* this to him?

The last rays of the sun turned the rose brick to apricot as he approached the front door. Another hour and she'd have been wandering around in the dark. His heart lurched.

Standing outside her door he was enveloped in a cloud of lavender-scented steam that wafted from the open bathroom. He took a deep breath, the physical evidence of her presence in the house easing him. He knocked hesitantly.

"Come in," she sang out in a good-natured tone. Evidently a hot soak had restored her humor.

She sat in the middle of the bed, gnawing hungrily on a chicken leg. Under her white chemise, her skin glowed like a softly burning lamp, but her voice held no warmth. "Oh, it's you," she said. "I thought it was Megan. She's bringing up some rice pudding."

Sebastian stood at the foot of her bed. He felt conflicting urges to shake her till her teeth rattled for putting him through such anguish and to wrap her in his arms and thank God she was safe. Both urges exerted about the same pull, canceling each other out. He stood rooted.

"You thought it was Megan," he said carefully. "If you had known it was I, you would not have invited me in? Is that it?"

She looked at him without expression and tore off more meat with her teeth. He couldn't tell if she were completely ignoring him or merely making him wait upon her hunger.

"Invite you?" she said at last, and gave a heavy shrug. "This is *your* house, these are *your* rooms." She waved the chicken leg in the air then pointed it at her breast. "This is *your* mistress. It's not *my* place to keep you out."

Sebastian's stomach churned. "If that was a joke, I don't find it particularly funny."

She slammed the chicken bone down on the plate. "Well, a thousand pardons, your highness—"

"Julie, please—" he cut in, moving to the bed.

"—if I failed to amuse and distract. How thoroughly remiss of me not to please my lord and master—"

"Julie, stop—"

"After all, what am I but—"

"Goddammit, woman, give me a—"

"Don't you *dare* call me woman!"

They glared at each other. If you're not a woman, my darling, your disguise is flawless, he wanted to say, but choked the words back. But why are we clawing each other when all I want to do is— Damn you, Cecil. Damn you! He breathed in deeply, letting his fists uncurl.

"I apologize," he said. "Please forgive me."

She turned her face from him.

"I lost my temper this morning," he said, and walked around the bed so that he could see her face. Seeing the gleam of unshed tears in her eyes, the last shreds of his anger evaporated. "I was furious and ashamed this morning, because Cecil was right."

He took her hand. It lay limp in his. "You *have* gone to my head, and here, to my heart, too."

"You are ashamed to love me?" she asked dully.

"No! I am only ashamed to have offered you nothing all these years but a few nights of passion in rented beds—when I want so much to share my life with you. I was angry at myself, Julie, so angry that it spilled over to you and I behaved like a clod. I never meant to offend you. Never."

It was time to tell her, he thought. The bubble was pricked, the spell broken.

"Oh, my love," she said. Slipping into his arms, she let the tears fall. "You gave me everything you had to give. It was not your fault that I had a husband, that the sea was your livelihood, that the war raged for so long."

He held her against him, luxuriating in the pressure of her warm soft body against his breast while he silently rehearsed the words. Those were all convenient excuses for my despicable procrastination. The truth lies elsewhere. I was paid to seduce you....

"We've never had harsh words between us before," she whispered against his cheek. "It was horrible, as if all the beauty of our love had turned to ugliness. Let us never quarrel again, love. I could not bear it." She leaned back and looked into his eyes. "Promise?"

"I will try," he said, "but if we marry—"

"If...?"

The change in her face was too painful to watch. "When!" he amended hastily. "When we marry and have children, there will be times when we disagree."

"Then we'll do it lovingly," she said, recovering instantly. She reached across the bed to the night table and took a strip of chicken breast, offering it to his lips with her fingers. "It will be easy for me, at least. If we should ever disagree, I shall always know that your motives are honest and kind and well intended. It's one of the things I love best about you."

He accepted the meat from her fingers because he did not have the heart to refuse. "My motives have not always been irreproachable, Julie," he said, chewing reluctantly. "I would not want to deceive you about that."

She smiled. "Don't make such heavy weather of it, my darling. Let me put you out of your misery. I *know* you're not a saint. I know for instance that your motives were very base when first we met."

He swallowed with difficulty, the muscles of his throat suddenly constricted. "You do?"

"Of course. I faced that long ago. When a handsome foreigner comes to Paris and seduces a married woman, he never has honorable intentions. He is moved only by lust. But I was obliged to forgive you that because I felt it, too." She rested her face against his. Her voice dropped to a confessional whisper and her lashes swept down, brushing his cheek. "I led you on. I really did."

Moved by lust, he thought, and wished to God his intentions had been at least that honorable.

She yawned, and her voice became drowsy. "I fell for you madly when I first laid eyes on you at the opera. Long before the intermission. When you left our house and I thought we would say goodbye forever, then I knew I loved you with all my heart."

She slipped out of his arms and lay back upon the pillows with another yawn. "Oh, what an exhausting day! I must get up and wash but I'm too drained to move."

He took her hand, still greasy from the chicken. "Don't move," he said. "I'll bring you hot water and a cloth."

"And you still smell of horse sweat, my darling. When you've bathed, will you come and sleep with me here?"

"Of course." He covered her tenderly with the sheet, kissed her lips and tasted chicken.

"Never sleep on angry words," she said. "Now I know what Grandmama meant. I'm so glad we forgave each other tonight. I don't think I could have borne another moment of this."

That look of utter trust and admiration was back in her eyes. Here in Bryony he had believed it would be easier to confess. In this place where he could enfold her with his love and attention, she could accept that he had feet of clay. She would hear what he had to say, show a moment's astonishment, then laugh and forget about it.

But he had never counted on this Eden of contentment. Ever since the coach had deposited them on the carriage sweep, he had felt enclosed in a bubble of enchantment.... Such an iridescent, delicate membrane. It had been threatened today—enough to warn him just how much he had to lose. How could he prick it now?

When they could take their happiness for granted, then he would tell her. When boredom set in and these horizons grew too small to satisfy. When she was so convinced of his devotion that he could confess what he must without diminishing in her eyes. Then, God help him, he would tell her. But not a moment earlier.

Chapter Thirteen

Julie stirred in the night and awoke groaning as her legs and back protested.

"What is it, Julie?" Sebastian said, turning toward her instantly.

"Oh, I did not mean to wake you. I'm just stiff from too many hours of riding."

"You didn't wake me," he said. He rose to his knees and his hands sought for her right leg, the one that suffered most from confinement in a sidesaddle. Tenderly he began to massage the sore muscles in her thigh and her calf. "Here?" he murmured, "and here?"

"Mmm."

"You will not wish to ride in the morning. Perhaps it's for the best."

She closed her eyes again, her muscles warming and easing under the gentle pressure of his hands. "You've been awake all this time?" she said presently. "What were you thinking?"

"We have let two months slip by here. I have not thought of business. You have not thought of visiting your family."

"Two months," she repeated drowsily. "Has it really been so long? Never mind. My family can wait, but judging from Cecil's demeanor yesterday, I suppose your business cannot. Should we go to London now?"

"Yes," he said quietly.

Two months, she thought, and as the significance of it dawned she was instantly wide awake, her hands spreading over her stomach. *Two months*. There was no evidence there yet, but she could no longer pretend to doubt her condition.

Sebastian rolled her facedown on the bed and his palms pressed warm circles of relief into the knotted muscles of her lower back. "If you have no urge to visit your family, then I'll take you to London, and then Cornwall for a few days. You will love Domenico."

"Is he not a priest?" she said cautiously.

Sebastian laughed. "Yes, my darling. You *know* very well he is a priest. But he's also my father. Do you not wish to meet my father?" His hands stopped.

"Yes, but not—" She broke off and turned on her side with her back to him. "I'm a married woman and your mistress," she said into the darkness. "No, it is too— I simply cannot. We should both be ill at ease. You go to Domenico. I'll shop in London while you're gone."

"He's very worldly, Julie," Sebastian said. "He will not judge you. But if you insist, I shan't go, either. I shall simply stay in London with you." He drew her into his arms, letting her back rest against his breast. "Is that better? Or shall I fetch you a draft of something to help you sleep?"

"No," she said quickly. "I don't need it. Sebastian, I'm carrying your child."

She felt the tremor in his arms and the quick intake of his breath at her back. "Can you be sure?"

"Yes."

His hand slid across her smooth flat stomach and she smiled. "No, you cannot feel the child's body yet, my darling, but you can feel the changes in mine." She covered his hand with hers and guided it up to the heavy fullness of her breasts.

The miracle of what was occurring made him feel stupid. He had seen the changes in her and had attributed them to the country air, the serenity, the sun, the food—to anything and everything except the most obvious cause of all. Pregnancy. The very reason he had presented to Farroux for bringing Julie to England. His seed, he thought. His child, not Farroux's. The child that would force his hand.

"When?" he asked distractedly. "I mean, how long?"

"I should have had the flux when we crossed the Channel," she told him. "Instead I was seasick and in the excitement of our plans, I didn't count—" She broke off and turned to face him. "Sebastian, this means I conceived before we left Paris. Over two months ago."

"My child," he whispered. "You are carrying my child."

There was a muffled rumbling in the air like distant thunder.

"Guillaume must not know," she said, suddenly very assertive. "I should have returned to sue for divorce as soon as I suspected. If he should guess, he will not be willing to free me. It is the one thing he still has to gain from our marriage. An heir." She became agitated. "If I wait another month, there will be no disguising it. Sebastian, I must leave tomorrow."

"Then you shall not go back to him at all. Oh, I could curse myself for wasting all this time! You can sue for divorce from here. I will deal with Guillaume." Sebastian heard the thunder once more, louder than before, but he gave more heed to the wayward leap of a nerve in his thigh, the erratic pulse in his biceps. He had not felt such a dance of nerves under his skin for years...not since that first time he had ridden over the Seine to the Ile Saint-Louis, a pair of ladies' gloves on the seat beside him.

But this time he welcomed the discomfort gratefully; he knew now that he was about to tell her the truth, that nothing could stop him. His moral fiber had at last returned and she would know now before they slept. The jumping nerves stilled instantly and he was filled with a sense of purpose.

His voice crackled with decision. "You shall not go through that ordeal, Julie. This is my task and I will confront Guillaume alone," he said. "I will go directly from London and you shall stay here—or in London. Or pass the time with friends, family, whatever you choose."

"But I am not afraid to face him," she said calmly. "I should be the one—"

"No! Let's not gamble with our future, our child. The journey might be strenuous for you. And if he should look

at you and guess... You are right. He could make it that
much more difficult.''

"Let him, then!" Her chin came up stubbornly, and he
heard a flash of hard determination in her voice that was
new to him. "He cannot keep me in chains. This is 1802, my
love, not the Middle Ages. If he will not grant a divorce, I
will live with you as your common-law—''

"Julie, no! There is something I must tell you. I *know*
how much he wants an heir. I have *always known* that—''
He fought against the distracting rumble. "Right from the
start, I knew—I knew because he *told* me, Julie— He *asked*
me to— What the devil?''

The thunder was fighting his words with a nerve-racking
persistency he could no longer ignore. It dawned on him that
the sound came not from the sky but from the front doors
of the house. He fancied he could hear a voice calling out in
desperation. A fire, he thought, rising instantly and turning up the wick on the night lamp. The weather had been too
dry. He had talked of wetting down the thatch on the cottages if it didn't rain this week....

"I'd better go before they break down the door," he said
calmly, not wanting to alarm her, and grabbing a wool robe,
he hurried out of the room.

Julie's thoughts were still on the subject of divorce. As she
waited for Sebastian to return, she wondered if perhaps he
was right. She would be in Paris in three days at the most.
It wasn't long, but her body was changing so fast. Could she
state her case to Guillaume without his guessing that she hid
in her womb what he most wanted from her? She could trust
Sebastian, she reminded herself. He wanted only the best for
their future together. And yet she had expected more exultation from him. Had he not told her he wanted her to be the
mother of his children? Why then did he seem at a loss when
she told him? And why was he so fierce and desperate about
facing Guillaume alone?

When he returned he was dressed for riding and his face
was ashen in the yellow circle of lamplight. His voice shook.
"Domenico. He is ill. Asking for me," he said. "He would

not do that if... Mrs. Jenkins sent to London for me and Cecil sent Jared from our office.''

A wave of compassion engulfed her at the anguish she heard in his voice. Suddenly her reluctance to meet the monsignor vanished. "I will go with you," she said, and rose from the bed.

He shook his head. "There is no time. I'll ride horseback, starting with Jared's mount—it's a stage hack. I must be there as fast as— I should be there now! Oh God, how I've neglected him!''

"What can I do to help you?" she asked.

He came toward her distractedly and took both her hands. "Jared is our office courier. He's staying the night in the attic. Tell Mrs. Pettersley what happened and see that he gets breakfast and that Pim drives him back to London in the morning. Then wait here for me. Please. I will send word as soon as I reach Cornwall. Just—just wish me Godspeed."

She felt the painful thudding of his heart as she slipped into his open arms.

"Please wait for me," he said, his voice pleading. "Do nothing before I return." He paused at the door and turned back to her with a ghost of a smile. "Take care of my child," he whispered.

Time hung heavy at Bryony after Sebastian's departure. Julie felt alone, abandoned, as if all the rich pleasures of these past weeks had been just a dream from which she had been rudely awakened. It was just a mood, she told herself sternly, but it seemed to her that at one stroke all the brightness of her present and future happiness had slipped beyond reach, that she was once again cast back into that state of endless waiting-to-hear. She had thought that torture behind her forever, but it had taken just one ill-fated messenger in the night. Nothing was certain, nothing was safe to assume... except the child in her womb. There was no circumstance or mood or turn of events that could change that fact or postpone its fruition.

Sebastian had begged her to do nothing but wait, and wait she would, but she found each day longer than the last and harder to get through. She wandered disconsolately through the grounds of the park. She browsed through the books in Sebastian's study, but none of them held her attention. Texts on theology from his seminary days. A grammar of New Testament Greek. Volumes on navigation and astronomy. No novels that could offer her a few hours of escape.

At Bryony she knew no one. Here there were no social rounds to fill the days and nights, no Anne-Marie and no Josephine. Without Sebastian, even the wildflowers and the lambs in the meadow had lost their fascination.

She thought the hours would pass more quickly if she wrote those much-belated letters to friends and family. She spent hours with a pen in her hand but came to the conclusion that if she could not tell them what was in her heart, she had nothing to say. She could not admit that she was with child until she could openly acknowledge the father, and so she abandoned the attempt to write at all. She walked the meadows and visited the new calf, but this small peaceful world had lost all its enchantment.

After nine endless days of fretting, Sebastian's promised letter was scant reward when she read it.

My dearest,
Domenico is dying and I will not leave his side until the end. The doctor says it cannot be long, and seeing him in such pain, I can but pray for his speedy release, but it is so hard to let him go. I have had a cot brought into his bedroom so that he can see me whenever he opens his eyes and speak when he has the strength. Most of the time he sleeps and I hold his hands so that he knows I have not left him.

I write here at his bedside, and I hope this is not too hard to decipher. From his breathing I know that he will sleep now for an hour or more, and my thoughts turn to all I have left in suspension. I must try to make some sense of things and make a list of priorities. I must inform Ned Cecil of my whereabouts. I must go to London and tend my neglected affairs as soon as I am able, but I shall be needed back in Cornwall to settle this estate. When I next send you word, it will be to join me in London. Then we can return here together and your presence will comfort me in this sad task. Pim will take you to my town house.

    Meanwhile, write to me here. Just the sight of your handwriting will bring me cheer.

Your own Sebastian

In a wave of frustration, Julie took the hastily scrawled letter and crumpled it in her hand. There was no mention of going to Paris. Apparently confronting Guillaume was no longer of prime urgency to him. She remembered the look in Sebastian's eyes when he left and knew that, for the moment, nothing counted except his final leave-taking of his father. It was as it should be, she thought, feeling ashamed that her immediate reaction was to find the letter vexing. She wished now that she had gone with him. But it was natural that he would choose the fastest means of travel, and how could she in her condition have spent seventy, perhaps eighty hours in the saddle on rented hacks? No, there was no way to avoid this separation, but how much longer would she be able to hide her condition? Her restlessness spilled over.

How long could an old man take to die? she wondered. Days? Perhaps weeks? But the new life she carried would not slow down to accommodate the dying. She could wait no longer.

She hurried out of the house and made for the stables, the letter still clutched in her fist.

"Pim," she told the hostler, "I want you to take me to London tomorrow. I must take the first possible packet back to France."

She wrote back to him that night, her trunk already packed and sitting in the front hall.

My dearest,

I find it impossible to wait here and do nothing. I leave for London in the morning and thence to Paris.

My heart and my sympathy are with you in Cornwall, but I cannot leave to chance so important a matter as the future of my child. Rest assured that I will tell Guillaume nothing of my condition. (To keep him in ignorance, it is essential that I do not waste another day.) Thus he will have little reason to contest my suit. I will make it quite clear that I have chosen to spend the rest of my days with you, divorce or no. Why, then, would he choose to impede me?

By the time this reaches you, I shall, God willing, already have broken the news to Guillaume. You may reach me care of Anne-Marie Bernard, 9 Rue Temoins, Croissy, as I will most certainly leave Guillaume's house as soon as I have announced my intentions.

Do not worry on my account. I am in the best of health, and Pim will take me to London. I have missed you more than words can say this past week, but I feel better now that I have taken matters into my own hands. I should have done it a week ago, but things happened so fast, I did not stop to think. You have more than enough to be concerned about, so please do not concern yourself about me. I am not a child, but a woman—and perfectly capable of handling this procedure now that I am borne up by the assurances of your love and the token of it that rests secretly deep within my body. I will write you as soon as I have spoken to Guillaume. Believe me, it is better this way. I owe Guillaume much, and the least I can do is break this to him myself.

Until then, my love, my husband-to-be, I embrace you with all my heart.

The pain had struck on a fine summer morning, the pressure bearing down upon his breast with all the relentless weight of mortality. It was the third attack, and although Adam Bolan talked of resting in bed, of light nourishment and recovery, Domenico knew it would be the last. Each day he weakened but fought off the final sleep until *il piccolo* should come.

Death hung about his face, pulling his sparse flesh earthward, stretching his candle-wax skin taut over the fine bones of his nose and cheeks. But he would not surrender. Not yet. When he was tempted, he would elude the pain for a spell, slipping back to younger, healthier days. Then the closed eyelids were pale as cracked parchment, but beneath them his eyes were busy. He saw, he heard, he spoke...

Lit tapers flickering in the drafts of a chapel; the widow's face across the bier, stony with grief.

"God be with you, Tizzi," he said as they left the graveyard. "Forgive me—I cannot stay for the funeral meats. The tide is turning."

She nodded, her face still frozen. "But you came for the mass. I am grateful." She walked beside him down to the pier where his launch waited, their only private moments. "How is he?" she asked. "Does he look like any of my sons?"

"Any of your *other* sons," he said, but the correction was lost on her. "As a child he resembled no one in particular. Now he's fourteen, he has a look of you, Tizzi. And he has something of your iron will."

Her face showed less emotion than one of the plaster saints in the chapel. She had borne fourteen children but had raised only eight past infancy. Sebastiano was just another lost infant to her, he decided.

She looked back to where the group of mourners proceeded from the graveyard, going down the hill toward the black-draped house. "There is no reason he shouldn't be told now."

Domenico took his time before he answered. "He believes his parents are dead. If he learns that you chose to abandon him, he will hate you."

She dipped her head in stoic resignation. "So be it. His hatred will be my punishment."

He gripped her arm, raising his voice above the waves that slapped at the pilings. "And what of the child's punishment? Would you have me inflict a pain he does not deserve?"

"You are the priest, Domenico," she said flatly. "You have raised him, loved him. You know what is best for the child. I will accept whatever you see fit to do. It must be your decision."

The rhythmic sounds of the tide gave way to meaningless noises. Startling. Close at hand. His eyes flew open and he found himself bedridden again, forced back to the pain, to the grueling labor of staying alive. He could close his eyes and so easily leave it all behind for good, but *il piccolo* had not come yet, and Ida Jenkins leaned over him with fear behind her smile.

He sipped at the broth she held out, but it was hard to swallow. His need for food was over. If only the boy would come, that's all he needed now.

I still have a few minutes left. When had he said that? Had he said it or dreamed it a moment ago?

He'd had eighteen years to give the boy his true heritage but there had seemed little point to it at the time. Now it would be his final gift. Years and years of lies, omissions, prevarications....

He was shriven, he remembered. It was as well that God's forgiveness knew no bounds, but he wanted Sebastian's forgiveness, too. Will he forgive? Will he come while I can still say the words?

"He will be here soon, Monsignor," Mrs. Jenkins said, wiping broth from his lips with a towel. The announcement startled him; he had not realized he had spoken aloud.

She smoothed the sheet and grasped his hand briefly. "It's been five days. He won't waste a minute now he knows you want to see him. He must be on his way by now. Perhaps tonight we'll hear him knocking on our door. Surely tomorrow at the latest. And you'll want to have your strength then. Will you not take another sip?"

But it was not broth that would keep him alive until the boy got here, it was God. Surely in His mercy He would grant this sinner one more sight of the boy? But because his faith in God varied according to his mood, he had one assurance, a letter he had written after the first attack, when he knew he might go without warning. If he went before Sebastian arrived, the boy would learn it all from the letter.

Ah, but it would be so much better coming from his own lips.

Father? *Padre mio*!

Domenico had traveled the years of his life so exhaustively in the space of the past few days that he had no way of judging the passage of present time. At times he opened his eyes to daylight, at times to darkness and flickering shadows. He simply knew at some point that the boy was with him. But it had happened so many times already in his dreams.

"Father, I am here."

He opened his eyes reluctantly, fearing it was another dream, but he could hear the bubbling in his lungs; the smell of horse and sweat was real enough as the shadowy figure loomed above him. The face was swimming, and he had to wait such a long time before he could see it clearly, but— Ah! It was not fading. Under the matted hair and heavy stubble, the gaunt face was no dream child. *Grazie a Dio!* Sebastiano had come home.

A slow grin spread over Domenico's features and for a moment his chest lightened. "You look as if you rode all the way posthaste like a king's courier."

"I did." Sebastian grinned back although he was stricken to the heart by the sight of the old man lying helpless.

"*Pazzo!* Hope you carried a pistol at least. Help me up, boy, so I can see your dirty face."

Sebastian was appalled at the feathery lightness that was Domenico as he moved him up closer to the head of the bed and propped him up on the bolster. After they kissed, he took one gnarled hand and let it rest in his palm, fearful of squeezing such brittle bones.

Domenico began to speak in short bursts, floating as many words on each shallow breath as it could carry. "This house—I wish I could leave it to you but...it belongs to

Rome. Everything else is yours. Not much. It's all in my will.''

"Then let's not speak of it, Father. Rest. I won't leave you."

"But the truth of your birth . . . worth more than all the rest . . . I must tell you now. Should never have waited so long . . ."

He was forced to stop, closing his eyes for a moment to master the pain of breathing.

"Will you take some of the draft Dr. Bolan left?" Sebastian pleaded. "Mrs. Jenkins said you refuse it, but it will ease your pain."

Domenico's hand fluttered in a gesture of dismissal. It was hard enough to stay lucid. They could fog his mind with opiates all they wanted later—after he performed this last duty. He must do that. "I have deceived you, son."

Sebastian had to bend his ear to Domenico's lips to hear.

"Your mother did not die. You never had the truth. She is my cousin and a close friend." He paused for a moment to form the words. All his life he'd had a diplomat's gift for words. Now the subtleties fled. It was all he could manage to choke out the harsh facts.

"You were born out of wedlock. She asked me to take you. She could not tell her husband you were not his. No, not mine, either. Your father doesn't know you exist. You bear her family's name. Ramolino. Her husband died eighteen years ago. I was free to tell you then. Should have. Procrastinated. Each year it became harder. It didn't matter. But it did. The truth always matters."

Sebastian had always known his name was Anglicized from Ramolino. The fact that his mother lived could hardly matter now. She had been dead to him all his life. What mattered was Domenico spending himself, tearing the words from his breast at such terrible cost.

"You are the only father I need," he said fiercely. "The details don't matter. Rest now. We'll talk later."

"Your mother—not a detail! The reason for your prosperity. Letizia Ramolino . . . Carlo's wife! Will you forgive me?"

"There is nothing to forgive." Sebastian stared at the infinite relief and—yes—triumph in Domenico's face. It was a look that seemed to demand a dramatic response, as if he had just heard a great revelation. "There is nothing to forgive," he repeated. "I love you, Father."

"Carlo's wife," Domenico insisted. "Go to her. Paris. Instructions with my will. Your father...she can tell you. Never met him. French. He doesn't matter."

"Nor does she," Sebastian declared. He took the old man in his arms. "Don't waste your breath on her, Father."

Domenico's thoughts cleared. Of course! These names meant nothing to the boy. He forced himself to deeper breaths, to speak in sentences. He must understand. *Must!*

"Carlo di Buonaparte," he said slowly, then lay back gasping.

But Sebastian made no reply, no sign of recognition, no sound of any kind.

"*Mio figlio*, hear me," Domenico said. He took a deep breath that cost him such pain he thought it might be his last. "You have eight brothers and sisters. The one closest to you in age is called Napoleon."

Chapter Fourteen

Babette's brown eyes widened in delighted surprise when they settled on her mistress standing at the front door. "*Madame!* Welcome home. I thought you were..."

"Thank you, Babette." Julie slipped past the girl and Jacques, who stood behind her. She headed for the stairs. "Yes, yes, I know I am early. Two months in England was more than—" She broke off. She had given no thought to what she would tell the servants. "Is the master home? Not until seven? Well in that case, please start me a bath and— No, no, Jacques! Leave the trunk. After that journey, I just want some peace and quiet in my room. Leave the trunk exactly where it is and help Babette with water for a bath. I'm simply pining for a long soak and a rest."

She removed her bonnet and her gloves as she mounted the stairs, knowing that at her back were two very disconcerted servants who must be looking at her rather oddly. Unpacking was always the first order of the day upon returning home. But this was not home any longer. She was anxious to begin removing all her possessions from the house; for that she would need Babette's help. But she could not decently inform the servants until she had spoken to Guillaume. "Let me know as soon as the master arrives," she called down to them, and hurried along the upper corridor to her boudoir. "And wake me if I am asleep."

The room was stuffy and already looked abandoned, the furniture covered with dust sheets, the windows and shutters closed. She threw them all wide open and looked out at the familiar view of Paris from the left bank. It had a certain charm, she thought, and it had comforted the last eight years of her life, but she felt no sadness at leaving it. She had never looked at it with a light heart except when she'd been on her way to Sebastian. Now she was on her way to him for good. She should be all smiles; she should be rejoicing, not queasy with apprehension. She was not afraid of Guillaume. Perhaps the queasiness was simply her condition, the nervousness no more than the weariness of travel.

She sank onto the chaise longue by the window, listening to the sounds in the hall and her adjacent bedroom. Babette and Jacques were carrying in the bath. Hot water could be pumped upstairs but not directly into the bath, as it could in Bryony. She grinned suddenly. How spoiled and impatient she'd become! It would be ages before they carted enough cauldrons from the little first-floor closet to the tub placed at the foot of her bed. What an absurdly tedious procedure it was after the modern plumbing of Bryony.

She closed her eyes and tried to doze. Three days of travel and two fitful nights in hotel beds at Dover and Amiens. Perhaps she could take one of those little catnaps she'd indulged in quite often in Bryony. But tension drove all hope of sleep away.

"Thank you, I will bathe myself, Babette," she said when at last the girl announced the water ready. "You can go on with whatever you were doing and I'll ring when I'm finished."

Babette said nothing, but the shrewd brown eyes were full of questions and disappointment. She had looked forward to hearing about her mistress's adventures. They chatted like friends when she was in the bath. Besides, how would she scrub her own back and wash her long hair properly? Who would hold the towel for her as she stepped out?

"Don't take it amiss, girl," Julie said in a gentler voice. "I'm not cross with you—just a little out of sorts from the coach ride. I took the first post from Amiens and we were packed like herrings in a barrel. I need to be by myself for a little while. I'll manage well enough...and if I can't, I promise I'll ring for you."

But she wouldn't, of course, not until she was dried and dressed. She couldn't run the risk of the girl seeing her naked. She might guess.

"You will find the towels on the stand, *madame*," Babette said with a hurt little curtsy, and left.

In her bedroom, Julie cast a grateful eye at the fragrant steaming bath and with a sense of relief began to shed her clothes. Her breasts felt confined in her tight bodice and then sore when she loosened it . . . and so heavy that it made her think of Anne-Marie during her lying-in.

"Imagination," she mumbled to herself. "You couldn't possibly look like that in your third month!"

For three days she'd had no access to a decent full-length mirror. Was it possible that in so short a time her pregnancy had gone beyond disguising? She took a hand towel from the folded pile of linen on the brass stand and wiped the light coating of steam from her pier glass. A little nervously she slipped her chemise down from her shoulders and let it slide to the floor, leaving her naked to the waist. Unbound, her breasts did not look unduly large, but they felt hard and full, and the skin was so taut, she knew they were swollen.

Her nipples were no longer pale and soft but rich brown buds springing sturdily from a circle only slightly paler in color. She pinched one of the buds, astonished at the firm, springy feel of it. Instantly she felt again the hungry pull of Sebastian's mouth, the crisp black mass of his hair between her fingers and the touch of his strong hands caressing, claiming. She shuddered as desire clutched at the dark paths of her body and left her aching for him. And wondering. She had not thought that a pregnant woman could have such intense longings. . . .

"It is permissible up until the fifth month," she heard Anne-Marie saying. They had been sipping tea together at the Café de Foy. "Sometimes longer, but it varies with each pregnancy, my physician says." Julie remembered how mixed her feelings had been—excitement and happiness for Anne-Marie, and a sadness touched with envy for herself. There was no longer cause for envy. . . .

"You are an unrepentant hussy," she told her brazen mirror image. "You are *enceinte.* Swelling with the fruits of sin and still hungry for more of the same."

And it would continue to be sin until she set things to rights. She must put an end to this meaningless contract with Guillaume. Just a contract, she thought, not a marriage. She knew now what a marriage should be, and although property had changed hands, although Guillaume had given her his name and his protection, they had never known a true marriage.

She peeled off her pantalets and turned sideways to examine her body in profile. There was no telltale protrusion below the waist yet. With relief, she realized that her pregnancy was obvious only to her. It was in the ripe feel of her body, not in the way she looked. With a careful choice of dress, the right fichu . . . her secret would be safe. It would be all right. Guillaume would merely assume she had plumped a little from a restful two months in England. After all, she had not been so markedly thin when he first laid eyes on her.

Floral essences enveloped her as she sank into the water and let its warmth seep deliciously into her tired muscles. She closed her eyes and tried to decide what to wear. A dark color would of course help minimize her bosom, but anything darker than sky blue had long been out of fashion. All her new summer gowns were still packed in her trunk and she was not about to have it opened. In her dressing-room press were some things left over from the previous summer.

She soaped her body with long, lazy strokes. "It's hardly gowns you should be thinking of," she whispered into the fragrant steam. "You should be preparing your serious talk with Guillaume. This calls for much tact and delicacy." But she knew what she would say—the simple truth. Exactly how she would say it, well, that would come to her at the appropriate time. While scented water lapped at her thighs, it was infinitely more restful to think of nothing more complicated than the gowns that hung in her press.

By half-past six, the bath had been removed and Julie lay on her bed clad in a loose white wrapper. She should get dressed now, should have started long before this, but the long hot soak had made her feel indolent.

Reluctantly she forced herself to rise and go to her dressing room. She settled on a blue lawn dress and a broad fichu of heavy ivory lace. It was rather bulky to top a summer dress, but it would certainly disguise the swelling bosom beneath. She was fastening the lace with a pearl pin when she heard Guillaume's voice in the hall below.

Her body stiffened at the sound. A sudden extreme carefulness settled on her, and in a flash of recognition, she knew it as a familiar feeling. It was exactly the way she always felt with Guillaume. It had become a habit so ingrained by the years that she'd never been aware of it until that very moment. This was not a marriage, it was a harness. It had taken her two months with Sebastian and the sound of Guillaume's voice again to find out who she really was.... She was not this constrained creature who always moved sedately, who always thought with caution, who never spoke without considering and selecting every word. She had grown up imprisoned in that contrived creature as a means of survival, but it was not her. She was the woman who had gamboled in the meadows and made passionate love to Sebastian; she was the woman who was here solely by her own decision, and the time had come to act.

Her hair was still damp and caught back with a ribbon. She would not fuss with it now. She heard Guillaume's footsteps on the stairs. She would not waste another minute.

Courage, Julie. You are about to throw off your shackles. Taking a deep breath, she went into the hall to meet him.

"Juliette!" He paused halfway up the stairs. "I saw your trunk in the hall.... Is anything amiss?"

She shook her head, and when he reached the landing where she stood, she greeted him with a gingerly peck on the cheek. He did not look pleased to see her, for his face had taken on a look of self-controlled consideration. Although he seemed unchanged, she was struck afresh by his age.

She gave a small smile. "Nothing is amiss, Guillaume, except . . . I need to talk to you. Without delay. May we go into your study?"

Guillaume ushered her into the small, rather gloomy chamber and seated himself behind his dark walnut desk. She stood looking down at him while he leaned his elbows on the lacquered surface and made a steeple of his thin hands. "Will you not sit, my dear?"

She would have preferred to stand, but she took the tall-backed chair on the other side of the desk knowing it would make her feel defensive, rather as if she were back in Mother Superior's office for a disciplining.

"I trust you are well," he said cordially. "Indeed I believe the trip has agreed with you. I see roses in your cheeks and some flesh on your bones."

Heat rose into her cheeks, and she plunged into her announcement. "Guillaume, I have a lover. I'm sorry. I should not have deceived you but the plain fact is—"

"Sebastian Ramlin?"

Julie dipped her head. He knew. He must have guessed long ago, but she was grateful to him for bringing it out. It was a relief, and it made it so much easier to go on. "We love each other, Guillaume, and we want to marry. I'm sorry, and I shall not forget all you've done for me, but I plan to put an end to our marriage so that I will be free to—"

"There is no need to apologize, Juliette. And there is no need to end this marriage. Whatever it lacks, I have always tried to make it clear to you that you are at liberty to compensate for it as you wish, so long as it is discreet. You *do* understand that, my dear?"

"Yes, I've understood that for some time. But this is beyond mere dalliance for my amusement, Guillaume. We are determined to marry. I have found the man with whom I wish to spend all my days."

"I see." His demeanor remained unchanged, his voice calm and reasonable. "Well, my dear, I cannot prevent you from exercising your rights under the law. I presume you are already aware that you do have recourse."

Julie frowned, aware of a faint sense of alarm. She had assured herself repeatedly that he would have no choice but to accept her decision, but she had nevertheless prepared for some resistance. Could it possibly be this easy?

Guillaume's eyes narrowed as he scrutinized this young woman of his. There was a marked fullness about her face and her figure that suggested fruitfulness. He hoped so. If not, Ramlin was due for the coup de grace anyway.

"You will live in England, then," he said, staring at his fingertips. "I suppose France will always hold dreadful memories for you. Yes, I can appreciate that the prospect of a proposal from Ramlin is very attractive from every point of view. I respect your decision and I will put no obstacles in your way."

"Thank you, Guillaume," she said, weak with relief.

"But I will always be keenly interested in your welfare, therefore I want to assure myself that you know all you should about your future husband before you take this serious step."

"Oh, but I do! I have known him for more than four years. I have seen him in—"

"Yes, I'm quite aware. But I have known him slightly longer than that, my dear."

"You?"

He nodded. "It was through me that you came to meet him."

Julie rose, pressed her palms on the desk and leaned toward him. "That simply isn't true," she said hotly. "I met him quite by chance one night at the opera when—"

"No," he broke in. His words fell precisely, deliberately spaced for emphasis. "Not...quite...by chance." He leaned back in his chair with a sigh and shrugged, raising his hands then letting them drop into his lap in sad resignation. "My dear Juliette, I hoped you would always be spared this knowledge. But for your own good I must tell you, no matter how painful."

"Tell me what?" Her eyes challenged him, her posture, even the rise of her chin had turned hostile.

"Sebastian Ramlin agreed to meet you at my request. You see, my dear, we both had pressing needs. He needed money and political favors to aid his shipping ventures. I could help him. I needed an heir. He could help me."

Guillaume waited for a stronger reaction. But she only shook her head slowly from side to side. "I don't understand," she said flatly. "The circumstances of our first meeting are neither here nor there. We love each other."

"We had an agreement," he said, impatience making him brisk. He had already made it clear enough. She simply did not want to understand. Ah, well, he'd expected something of the sort. He did not want to shock her more than necessary—particularly if her condition was as delicate as he hoped—but it had to be done.

"He agreed to court you—to get you with child—in return for what I could do for him. Nothing came of it the first time, but he kept trying. In fact your summer trip was his suggestion."

In the long silence that followed he could see the truth sinking in. She gasped and held a hand to her lips while every trace of color left her cheeks. "I don't believe a word of this," she said softly.

"I'm afraid you will be obliged to, my dear," he said, pausing for a moment. "Ramlin had some time on his hands," he continued evenly. "He persuaded me that after four years of failed attempts, an extended spell in England might get the job done."

"Lies! Lies! Lies!" she cried, and covered her ears as her voice rose to a scream. "I won't listen to this. I won't hear another word!"

Guillaume rose and went to her. He took her wrists, prying her hands away from her ears. "And I believe he succeeded, didn't he?"

Julie wrenched her hands free of him. At first she'd been merely hurt at Guillaume's sudden viciousness. Now that hurt was burning into a pounding, flaming rage beyond her experience. She couldn't express it in words. She merely stood rigid, fists raised, eyes glowing like amber coals.

"I asked you if he succeeded," he said, his own anger only slightly more contained. "Are you pregnant?"

"Yes!" The sound was an explosion of defiance that loosened her tongue. "Yes! But it will never be your child. It's mine. Sebastian's. And no cheap lawyer's trick will keep that child from his rightful parents. There's nothing you can do about it. Nothing!"

He backed away, instantly regretting the ugly scene. The girl's rage had been so unusual that it had infected him for a moment, but he had no need for pyrotechnics. He must calm her down. He returned to his desk chair, retreating back to his sober and reasonable manner as if he were slipping on a more comfortable suit of clothes.

"You are quite right, my dear. There is nothing I can do about it. But please remember, I am quite prepared to raise this child as my own. As my principal heir. Are *you* prepared to trust your future to a man who has deliberately deceived you for years? A professional womanizer who seduced you for money?"

"Certainly not," she said, cooling slightly now she had vented her anger. "But I am quite prepared to trust my future to Sebastian Ramlin, and I will not listen to these preposterous lies about him."

He smiled. Although she protested that she would not listen, she remained standing by his desk, listening. The worst was over.

"I can understand your reluctance to believe what I say, and I'm sorry it had to come to this. I never thought such a serious attachment would develop. But I have told you no lies. I can show the proof."

Guillaume unlocked a drawer in his desk and drew out a sealed envelope. "I wish I could have protected you from this," he said, "but you owe it to yourself and your child to read this before you do anything you may regret."

He tapped the envelope against the palm of one hand as if of two minds whether to give it to her, then he placed it carefully on the desk. "I will give you some time alone. Peruse this at your leisure. Then, when you've had time to consider, I will accept whatever decision you make."

Julie seemed unable to move. She stared after him as he left the room. Then because her knees failed, she found herself sitting again, the document before her. It was an innocent enough piece; she had seen a thousand similar envelopes. It lay facedown bearing Guillaume's red seal of office. She turned it over. There was no name or address, no instructions at all except for one word—*Confidential*.

She drew her hands away and clasped them in her lap, staring at the envelope as if a coiled serpent might spring from inside. The room was so still that she could hear the quick thudding of her heart. Sebastian loved her. He had far too much honor to have ever been guilty of such horrors. Guillaume was to be pitied, in fact. He had guessed her condition, and in his desperation...

Her fingers entwined in ever-changing knots. She had always known Guillaume was a clever manipulator. He had never tried his fiendishly clever tricks on her before—but he wanted this child and he would do anything... Yes, that's all it was. A trick. It was absurd to be afraid, she thought, reaching out her hand to the document.

The words took up less than half a page. She did not bother to read them but went straight to the signatures at the bottom. There was no question of forgery. She knew Sebastian's streak of a signature better than she knew Guillaume's. As she read what lay above it she neither flinched nor wept. A mere sheet of paper could not alter the course of her life; she must hear what Sebastian had to say. And above all, she must keep calm—there was a baby to consider. "We'll see," she murmured soothingly, slipping the sheet back into the envelope. "We'll see." But crouching deep in her heart was the fear that she had seen too much already.

She rose with the letter in her hand and left the study. On the floor below, the dining room doors were open. She could hear the clink of china and silver and Babette humming as she set the table. Tonight she could not bring herself to eat, not even for the sake of the child, but it was a busy hour for the servants. She would wait until after dinner to have the trunk brought up.

Chapter Fifteen

Cornwall

He died with the same grace he had shown in life, this handsome, gifted man who could have been a prince of the church. He smiled, he pressed Sebastian's hand, and then, as quietly as the sun sliding behind the downs on that long July evening, he slipped away for good.

He was sixty-six years old, but Sebastian had never prepared himself. Never able to face the inevitability of Domenico's death, he now felt disconnected and heavy with remorse. He had been a careless son, neglectful these past few years. He needed space and time and privacy to come to terms with this loss, but the world rushed relentlessly back, pressing him on all sides.

Julie waited at Bryony, carrying his child, still ignorant of the truth. Cecil waited in London. And a household full of servants looking like lost sheep waited for his instructions regarding the funeral.

"He wrote how he wanted it," Mrs. Jenkins said, rivulets of tears bathing her tired cheeks. "It's with his papers, Master Seb."

The news that he shared a mother with Napoleon Bonaparte scarcely touched his thoughts until the following day. He had set the funeral preparations in motion and was riding toward London.

So his mother was the reason for his shipping success. He was too numb to react to anything but the irony of it and his mouth crooked in bitter amusement. Her one acknowledgment of a blood connection. A cold one, but magnanimous to be sure. He was rich because of it. Set for life. He should be grateful, he supposed, but he felt no more connected to this Letizia woman than he did to the fat midwife who pressed against him in the fast mail coach and talked all the way through Somerset.

On the journey, he penned a note to Julie to join him in London directly. He sent Jared up to Bryony with it as soon as he reached the offices in Blackfriars.

"Good God, Seb, you look awful," Cecil said, rising from his desk as Sebastian entered the inner chamber. "Here, sit down and let me get you some brandy."

But Sebastian only leaned against the doorpost, not bothering to mention that he hadn't slept for days, that while his mind was overburdened, he felt spiritless and empty and almost disembodied, that only the thought of seeing Julie kept him moving. He spoke of essentials in a flat, exhausted voice.

"Domenico's gone. I'll catch up with things here tomorrow. No brandy. I need a bath, a shave. Bed."

Cecil laid a hand on Sebastian's shoulder. "I'm sorry. I'll go down with you for the funeral. You didn't have to return before the service. Nothing is that urgent."

"I'll be detained for some time after the funeral," he said in the same monotone. "I'm the executor. I'd better put in an appearance while I can."

"Seb." Cecil's hands gripped Sebastian's arms warmly. "I'm sorry I caused such a rumpus at Bryony. Chatsworth was just an excuse, of course. Things are running like clockwork here. Don't concern yourself. Mrs. Farroux's a fine woman and I can see you—well . . . I shouldn't have interfered, but I was worried about you. You, um, haven't told her yet, have you?"

"No."

"Well, go get yourself some rest, boy, and set your personal life to rights."

Sebastian nodded and made for home, so exhausted that for once George Farnham, his valet, would earn his keep. In the hackney, his thoughts ran ahead to Julie and the evening. It would take Jared less than an hour to get to Bryony. Pim would have her to the town house before seven, even if she took two hours to pack. But she expected his message hourly; she'd be prepared.

He would be bathed and shaved and looking human again before she arrived. He might even have time for an hour's sleep.

But he heard the sharp rap of the door knocker at five o'clock and reached it before Farnham. Jared stood there, sweaty and a little nonplussed by the fool's errand he'd just completed. Julie had left Bryony two days ago.

It was another three days before he read the letter she had sent to Cornwall.

"By the time this reaches you, I shall, God willing, already have broken the news..."

God was most certainly willing. By now, he thought, she would know everything there was to know. The confession that had stuck in his craw like heartburn for so long was suddenly gone, leaving him as empty and hollow as a blown ostrich egg. He wrote, telling her everything, trying neither to spare himself nor justify his actions, but finished by begging her forgiveness.

Mea culpa, mea maxima culpa. I bore this secret for far too long. A thousand times I meant to tell you, but at the thought of your disgust, of losing you, my courage always failed. It was wrong to have entered into a bargain with Farroux, but had I not, I would never have met you. It was wrong not to have confessed it to you when I realized how much you meant to me. I will always love you more than words can say, and I beg you to forgive me. I shall come to you as soon as my duties here are discharged. Meanwhile, I shall pray to God for your forbearance.

Somewhere in his dismay was a slight relief. Either she would forgive him or she would not. He wouldn't know for some time, but at least there was no longer any shocking news to break to her.

There were, however, bills to pay on Domenico's estate, servants to pension off, recommendations to write for new positions, a few bequests, a small house in Bath to dispose of, and all the monsignor's personal possessions. For three weeks following the funeral Sebastian discharged his duties with the tireless efficiency of a milling machine. His grief remained buried, his concerns for Julie suspended. He was doing Domenico's last bidding with minute attention to every detail. A thousand tasks large and small filled the empty spaces in his breast as he went about his last filial duties.

Paris

"I am not prepared to give you my final decision until I hear Sebastian's side of it," Julie told Guillaume with an icy calm, as if yesterday's scene had left her unmoved, as if the very idea did not sicken her to the heart.

Unless Sebastian could convince her it was a pack of lies, she would never want to lay eyes on him again. As for Guillaume, that he could have gone so far as to act the procurer disgusted her. But at least she did not have to share his bed, hardly needed to see him at all if she chose not to. All he wanted was to be the legal father—and if she did not marry Sebastian, she would have to grant him that.

She remembered an old rocking chair stored in the basement and had it cleaned up and brought to her boudoir. It was dark-stained chestnut wood and had once sat in the servants' hall. Babette made a face when she saw it by the window. It hardly blended with the upholstery of rose and ivory silk, but Julie found it a comfort. It was there by the window, gently rocking herself, that she composed what was surely the tersest note she had ever penned: "Did you seduce me for profit? Come and explain yourself." And it was there that she was able to reason with herself when panic welled up inside her. There had to be some perfectly acceptable explanation, of course. The two men formally agreeing to use her body for their respective purposes? It was unthinkable, and she tried her utmost to leave it that way until it was resolved. For if she dwelt on it she would not eat, she would become ill, and there was more than her own health to consider now. The child—no matter under what circumstances it was conceived—was hers and she would not fail it.

If she had wanted company, she could have sent word to Anne-Marie or even Josephine. But she let none of her friends know she was back in Paris, nor would she until she knew where she would make her home. It might be a month before Sebastian was free to seek her out, but mercifully the unborn child kept her thoughts occupied.

Within the week, Dr. La Salle formally confirmed her condition and recommended an excellent midwife. "No hot baths and no riding, but a daily walk is beneficial, weather permitting," he said jovially. "If you have any questions, ask Marie Soubire. If you have any severe problems, send for me. But you're in prime health and I doubt you'll talk to me again for some time."

The following week Julie met the midwife, who predicted a late-November delivery. Marie Soubire was a gray-haired giant of a woman who, despite a respectful manner, inspired instant obedience. "The first, is it? My felicitations, *madame*. Will you be needing a wet nurse?"

"Ah, I'm not sure where I'll—I'm not ready to book one yet because—I may decide to nurse the child myself."

"That's always a good idea, at least for the first few weeks. But sometimes delicately formed ladies like yourself have trouble giving suck. We'd better start toughening up your nipples right away. I'll write you a receipt to use daily."

Her body also demanded new clothes. Claudine was delighted to oblige. Together they pored over magazine sketches, discussed gores, gathering, draping, crosshatched ribbons and a dozen other dressmaker tricks to disguise a swelling belly.

"You shall have a well-dressed mama, Charles," she told the tiny mound that was emerging at her waist. It would be either Charles Louis or Charlotte Louise, in memory of her parents. At least some things she could resolve by herself.

In spite of her intentions, the hideous subject drew her irresistibly. Sometimes she feared Sebastian would never come and dispel this black cloud. If what Guillaume claimed was true, then Sebastian had already fulfilled his part of the bargain and all the talk of love and marriage was false, just a string to bind her to him until his seed caught. He would have no reason at all to come back. Indeed, he would never have the gall to face her again....

There was the Tivoli Gardens, of course. He had wanted to tell her something then, something very grave. And it was true that his business was suffering severe setbacks when they first met. He had shared his concerns with her at Marduquesnes. Certainly his fortunes had made great strides since then... miraculous strides, one might say, in the four and a half years of their love affair. Perhaps it was no miracle, but— "No, no, you mustn't think those awful things!" She would retreat to the rocking chair and promise herself this would be over soon. She would give him six weeks. If she'd heard nothing by then, she would stop waiting. If he came, she would know instantly, before he even opened his mouth, that he was the innocent victim of Guillaume's monstrous calumny.

As August approached, Guillaume spoke of their summer stay in Marduquesnes, but she announced that she was staying in Paris. Four weeks had come and gone, but she must wait two more. Sebastian would come straight to Paris first. She wanted to be here waiting for him.

"But it's August in four days, my dear." Guillaume's manner toward her had become very tentative, rather as if he were handling gunpowder. Most of the time he avoided her, and they spoke only over the dinner table, constrained to do so by the presence of the servants.

"We don't *have* August, Guillaume. We have the last part of Thermidor and the first part of Fructidor." Her voice was loud and truculent, heedless of the presence of Babette removing the soup plates and Monique serving the fish.

Guillaume gave a thin smile. "Well, let's not quibble. It is the season when we always go, and if I leave you here alone in Paris—in your present condition—people will . . . What will they think?"

"Whatever they choose. Perhaps the same as they have always thought when the press of your work has left me unescorted on countless social occasions. Only this time our roles are reversed. Mine is the pressing business and I cannot leave Paris."

With minute concentration, Guillaume flicked blanched almond slivers from his trout, pushing them neatly to the rim of his plate. "I understand that your condition makes you testy, my dear Juliette. It also indicates to me that a month in the country would be most beneficial. Perhaps we could postpone this discussion until after dinner."

"There is nothing to discuss," she declared with absolute finality, and he did not attempt to stop her when she marched off from the table and closeted herself in her quarters for the rest of the evening.

"How little he understands," she said, rocking rather vigorously as she watched a luminous sunset with little appreciation. "He thinks my condition makes me testy. But it's you, little one, and only you that prevents me from quite losing my wits."

The discussion about Marduquesnes was never resumed. At four the following afternoon when she returned from her walk along the embankment, Babette announced that Mr. Ramlin was waiting in the salon and should she serve sherry or tea and *gâteaux*?

In reply, Julie merely dropped Ton-Ton's leash at the girl's feet and flew into the room.

He looked so drained and sad that without a word she slipped into his arms and hugged him. He had lost his entire family in that one priest, and she'd scarcely given a thought to his grief, his deathbed vigil and the heartbreaking duties that followed.

"Oh, dear heart," he whispered into her hair, "I came as soon as I could."

To be safe again in his arms, to feel the pressure of his body against hers. It was all the reassurance she needed. She could admit it now; these past four weeks had been purgatory. Without warning, the tears she had not shed spilled over in an uncontrollable flood, and he held her while she gasped and shook with racking sobs.

When the storm subsided, she drew back, smiling through her tears and brushing her fingers across her face ineffectually. "I don't have a handkerchief," she said. He produced one, mopping her cheeks and kissing the last drops that still pearled her lashes.

"I'm sorry," she whispered.

"For what?"

"For weeping," she said, smiling as she touched the soggy lapels of his coat, his sodden shirtfront. "For doubting you. For suspecting for a moment that any of it could have been true."

He felt a chill pricking beneath the skin. His letter, his full confession explaining all and begging her forgiveness. She hadn't received it. She still thought . . .

"Oh, my darling, you can't imagine what it's been like here. Guillaume even produced a filthy, trumped-up document that said you accepted money from him to get me with child. And it bore your—it was *so like* your signature."

She buried her face in her hands for a moment, unable to continue. When she looked up, her smile pleaded with him. "But of course you would never—You wouldn't even be here if that were true. Would you? I must hear you say it, Sebastian. *Say it!* All I need is that you swear to me there's not a word of—"

"It is true. I wrote to you. Everything."

"Sebastian?"

For a moment he could not look at her. Her face bore the look of a waif being abandoned by its parents and unable to comprehend what was happening. What had he said in the letter? It was as persuasive as he could make it. He could never be that persuasive at a moment's notice. Not when she was looking at him like that.

"It *was* true," he said desperately, "but I never knew then that I would love you. And I do love you, Julie. I could never lie about that. You are my life."

She recoiled from his arms as if they were serpents and stared at him, the smile, the pleading, the pathetic childlike confusion gone. Her eyes held no more emotion than chilled amber glass.

"I regretted that damned agreement the moment I met you. You must believe me."

"Believe you?" Her voice was incredulous. "How could I ever believe you again?"

"Julie! I tried to tell you so many times, but my courage failed. I loved you too much to risk losing you. But I've never lied to you. Never."

She laughed, a shrill, brittle sound that devastated him. "You have lied to me for four years."

"Sweet Jesus, no! Without you, I— What you are to me—"

"Four thousand louis d'or is what I am to you. Huge profits in the Mediterranean. That's what I am to you. Much more profitable than your prize Jerseys. But of course the cows, they're just a hobby."

She had become an avenging angel, as formidable and relentless as an iceberg. He was silent, helpless under her lashing accusations.

"Little wonder you made time for me in your busy shipping schedule. Even if you only had six days' leave or less, you always made time for a visit. All that desperate thrashing about in hotel beds, at Marduquesnes. At Bryony! It was a part of your business agenda, was it not? A vital part. How hard you worked at it! Well, you got your deserts and it was well worth the effort, was it not? Don't think I haven't marked the miraculous rise in your circumstances."

"For the love of God, Julie, it wasn't like that," he protested. "None of it was like that. My rise in fortunes had nothing to do with this. Loving you as I do, do you think I could possibly do anything like—"

"You cannot possibly do *anything* to change the truth. Please go now."

He closed his eyes, groping for some way to redeem himself. His heritage—the Bonapartes— No, he could not violate that confidence; he could give only the vaguest hints and it would sound preposterous. He could not bear to hear her laugh that way again. When he looked at her again she was clasping her hands beneath her breasts, almost as though she were protecting the new life within her from further indignity.

There was a sudden imposing stature about her. She seemed taller in the silver-gray gown that flowed unbroken from her shoulders to the floor. He had seen her grow from an innocent adoring girl to a woman of such beauty, poise and determination that he was awed. He himself had taken her on that journey to womanhood and motherhood. By all that made sense she was his, as much as the child was his. But he would not beg. He had gone violently against his conscience and he had always known there would be a price to pay.

I wrote to you, he wanted to say. I explained it all. Guillaume never gave me anything but that one bankers' draft. I wish to God I'd burned it; I almost did. But I'll pay it back a thousandfold if you will forgive me. Don't I merit a second chance?

But he'd had a thousand chances to make it right, failed a thousand times. It was futile to argue. His gaze went to where her hands lay clasped.

"You carry my child, Julie," he heard himself say, and he felt his heart swelling, pressing against his ribs as though it might burst through with another pair of arms to reach out and hold her.

"No, not your child," she said quietly. There was no rage left in her voice, no resentment, not even regret. "Guillaume has paid for his heir. You have been well rewarded for your services. They are no longer required."

Sebastian left the house with a slow, cautious tread, as if his body had turned into thin crystal and might shatter with a sudden movement. He walked toward the embankment. A stiff breeze blew over the river. A torn sheet of newsprint fluttered up from the wheels of a passing carriage and flew like a tattered street sparrow before it came to rest on his shoe. He kicked it into the gutter, noticing that his fists were clenched tight. He looked at them curiously and uncurled them. It was all right; he would talk it out with Domenico and— His lungs deflated as he remembered that he would never do that again.

He had nothing left to lose. He was a husk. Tomorrow, he thought, approaching the first of a row of hackneys waiting for a fare. Tomorrow I will meet my mother. It would do nothing to fill the husk. It was merely a last obedience to Domenico.

On the right bank, the street was alive with hawkers and vendors, drays and carriages, children playing in the gutter, women shouting from second-floor windows. But as his hackney moved west on the noisy Rue Saint Antoine, Sebastian heard only Domenico's voice.

If you spice your meat with gall, don't complain when you eat.... I was devious by nature. You never were.... It will be hard on you.

Chapter Sixteen

The two-story house on Place Poivre was squat and unpretentious, flanked as it was by newer, more elegant five-story terraces. But it was the only detached house in the square, and with its wide plot of land, its side access leading to stable and coach house, it was probably worth a fortune.

Sebastian wondered how he might feel at this moment if he'd had any feelings left. Certainly he wouldn't be coolly appraising the real estate. There was one thing to be said for being a walking husk, he thought as he lifted the brass eagle on the door and slammed it down twice; it made one impervious to fear, to nervous apprehension.

For the first time in his remembered life he was about to meet the woman who gave birth to him, and her name was Letizia Bonaparte. Yes, there was a certain sangfroid about having nothing left to care about.

The servant who let him in was an olive-skinned woman who spoke no French and whose Italian was such a deep south dialect that he caught only a few words. But when he announced his name and gave her his card, her smile made it clear he was expected. She showed him into a salon furnished with a mixture of carved cherry wood and primrose silk chairs and couches. At one end stood a large harpsichord. The open French windows beyond it gave on to a narrow stone terrace and the rear garden. Sebastian went to the windows and looked out.

A tall man, white-haired but with a youthful military posture, stood in the garden examining a bush of scarlet roses. After a moment he seemed to sense a presence behind him; he turned, looked across the lawn at Sebastian, then came limping into the room.

"You must be Monsieur Ramlin," he said, and smiled broadly. "Jean-Paul Diderot, at your service. I am an old friend of Madame Bonaparte's. Please, won't you join me?" he added, making for the nearest chair by the hearth and resting one leg on a footstool. "Madame will be here in a moment. She is never tardy."

Sebastian took the opposite chair. An inlaid chess table stood between them. "Does my visit interrupt your game, sir?" he asked, glancing at the disposition of the ivory and ebony pieces.

"No, no. This one she started with one of her sons days ago." He flashed his smile again, showing remarkably white teeth. "She had a feverish cold and was ordered to rest until it cleared up. Joseph came to see her and thought a game might divert her. But as you can see, it was abandoned after a couple of moves. She has a somewhat fleeting interest in salon games. 'A pointless way to fritter away one's time,' she calls it." There was the fondness of an aging lover in his voice.

"A serious-minded lady, then," Sebastian responded, merely for something to say.

"My dear fellow, don't misunderstand me." Diderot leaned forward to a white bishop and fingered the exquisite carving of the miter with obvious appreciation. "She is no killjoy. She takes much pleasure in dancing, opera, gardening and soirees. She's passionate on the subject of politics, and she's even been known to read a light novel. She simply has no patience with—"

"What is it I have no patience with, Jean-Paul?"

At the sound of the heavily accented French, Sebastian rose to his feet and turned.

"Chess, Letizia." Diderot reached for his cane and stood up. "I have been amusing the boy while he waits. And now, if you permit, I will leave you two to your private discussion." He kissed her hand lightly and limped toward the door.

Sebastian found himself looking down into large brown eyes set in a long pale oval. She was not tall, but her regal carriage seemed to suggest both height and enduring strength.

"Madame," he said with a stiff bow.

"Sebastiano," she said, and he half expected some rush of feeling, but there was nothing. Only detached curiosity as she took both his hands in a grasp that was powerful.

"It was good of you to write. And to come and see me."

"It was the least I could do," he said, "for Domenico."

"Ah, yes, poor Domenico. All those years in England. And to be buried there." Her eyes closed for a moment.

"He loved England." The words came out cold and defiant. "He was buried exactly according to his wishes."

"Yes, yes, of course. It is hard for me to understand. Do you love England, too?"

He shrugged. It was a difficult question to answer when he felt cut off from love so utterly. "England was always the place I came home to. I loved Domenico."

"He was very beloved of me, too," she said, stung by his tone. "I have had requiems sung for his soul. You know there is worship again in France? It was terrible here—a country without a church. But my son has made a concordat with the pope."

He nodded and gave a wintry smile. My son, he thought, as though she were addressing a stranger. But she was, of course.

A shadow crossed her face as though she were appalled at her own thoughtlessness, then she recovered, gathering herself together and smiling a little uncertainly.

"Come, it's delightful in the garden. Let me show you my flowers. Rosalia can bring our refreshments out on the terrace."

Together they walked down the terrace steps and along a paved footpath that roughly bisected the lawn. In a low voice she began to speak of Domenico. "He was a distant cousin who grew up in Siena. An only child." She paused to finger the petals of a perfect yellow rose, then sighed. "With Domenico's passing, all the Tremontes are gone...but when we were children, he came every summer to Ajaccio. I loved him like a brother—better than my brothers. He was more fun to be with and he was never cruel."

"No, he was never cruel," Sebastian echoed.

A bee flew up from the yellow roses and hovered around his face. She chased it away with a fierce flick of her hand, then drew him on beyond the rosebushes and dense shrubs to a stand of slender birch trees at the end of the garden. "I had no choice, you see. My husband never suspected my adultery. Had he known, he would have died of shame. You cannot imagine how it was to be a Corsican then." She began to tell him how it was.

In the dappled shade of the birches they sat on a wooden bench, hidden from the house, and she forced out the memories in a quick painful monologue, head bent, fingers laced in her lap.

Then she turned toward him, reached out and traced his fine straight nose with her finger, almost overcome by her feelings. It was not easy to say these things. It was harder even than telling Nabullione four years ago.

He was so cold, so grim with her, but how could she complain? He was much taller than the others. And so handsome. His long legs and lean body favored Jean-Paul, she thought. But the eyes, the nose—it was like looking at her favorite, at Nabu.

"You were a strong baby," she went on, "but Carlo thought you were premature because I had returned to him only seven months earlier. He was sent to Paris when you were four weeks old. I had to do something then, before he returned. No one but Domenico knew. He came all the way from Rome and left with you and your nurse." He was like ice, this one. What could she expect? She was telling him how she abandoned him. He had a right to know the truth.

"Two of my babies were born dead. Three died in their first year. When Carlo returned in the autumn, he thought that you too had died. It was the only way...."

"How ingenious," Sebastian said, and she slapped him hard with the flat of her palm. It was sudden as lightning, but he did not flinch or raise his hand to his stinging cheek.

"It was *desperation*." She raked her fingers down her face, shutting her eyes. "Why should you understand?" The solemn eyes turned to him again, then she looked at her hand. "Forgive me, I have a sharp hand as well as a sharp tongue. That's what I used to do to Nabullione when he pushed me too far. He was the worst of the boys, but not as bad as Pauline."

Silence fell between them. He could feel the imprint of her fingers fading on his cheek and something deep within him shifted like a sleeping creature in a burrow. Presently she spoke again.

"When my husband died—"

"And your French lover— My father," he cut in. His tongue was thick and slothful, barely under his control. "Did he die, too?"

She looked at him strangely. "Your father is General Diderot, the man you were speaking with when I came into the salon. He did not tell you?"

Your father is General Diderot. Another meaningless entry in his logbook, he thought. A polite stranger, too polite to find the words. He thought of his own child, asleep in Julie's womb. Did he carry some icy inheritance in his blood to be handed down the generations? Was it possible that twenty or thirty years from now, Julie would stand beside their grown child and repeat this scene? Your father is Sebastian Ramlin. He shuddered, and the forest creature under his ribs stirred again.

"I wanted Domenico to tell you everything when Carlo died. You were fourteen then and I longed to see the last of your boyhood while there was still a chance. Domenico said you would hate me for abandoning you. He was right of course. It was too late, but oh, *dio mio*, how I wanted to see you and... Enough!" Her back stiffened. "If you hate me, that is justice. But do not hate your father. He did not know. Not until a little while ago."

"I do not hate you, *madame*. I feel . . . nothing at all. I thank you for your intercession with the First Consul. I have profited much from it. That is all I came to say."

But she saw painful longing in his eyes where before there had been only a hard emptiness. He was bereft, grieving for Domenico. So it was true, and the hardest thing of all to bear. All those years he had loved Domenico as much as Domenico loved him. She was nothing to him. A month ago she had not existed. What right did she have to touch him?

Nabullione was coming to dinner especially to meet him. But she couldn't bring herself to ask him to stay. His look said he wanted to leave as soon as it was decent.

Rising, she resumed the warm voice of a hostess making a stranger welcome. "You need some refreshments. There is *citron pressé*, a little plum cake. I'll have Rosalia make tea."

Sebastian rose mechanically but did not follow her. Something had risen like a monstrous tide, flooding the hollow spaces in him, threatening to drown him. He wrestled with the stifling rush in his breast, the pressure in his throat.

Letizia turned back and saw him struggle. If she embraced him now, they would both weep. He was proud, as proud as Nabu, she thought. He would die rather than shed a tear in her presence. She averted her eyes, looking instead at the small acacia tree growing alien among the birches, and she chatted impersonally to give him time to master his feelings.

"Your trading, it goes well, I hope? My son looks forward to meeting you. He has just raised the tariffs in the Rhineland for foreign goods, but rest assured that it will not in the least affect your—"

"Your son? Your son?" he broke in. "And what am I, *madame*? Merely your *sin*?"

His voice caught and his despairing eyes were so like Nabu's that it pierced her heart. With a gasp she put her arms around him.

"*Mio figlio*," she sobbed. "*Mio figlio!*"

Sebastian clung to her, mourning at last for all that was precious to him, and bitterly aware that he was weeping in the arms of a stranger.

Chapter Seventeen

Charles Louis Jules Farroux was born on a wet October evening, a tiny wisp of a thing who struggled for air and turned blue. Julie expected no labor pains for at least a month, and when she gasped and doubled over with pain as she came down the stairs for dinner, Guillaume quickly summoned both a midwife and doctor.

Marie Soubire was at home when Jacques went to fetch her, and it was fortunate indeed, for the labor was short and violent. When La Salle arrived almost an hour after the delivery, the midwife was working desperately to keep the baby breathing.

Julie lay spent in her bed, drifting from ether and loss of blood. The physician took one look at the pathetic infant and turned to its mother. Her pulse was good and she had no fever; he judged her strong enough to sustain the news.

He took the ether bottle from her night table and sprinkled a fresh linen towel. "He is too early, *madame*, and far too small. I fear you must prepare yourself for the worst, but at least we can relieve your pain. Breathe deeply," he said, pressing the ether-soaked cloth to her face.

She wrenched it away, instantly alert and furious. Prepare for the worst? Marie had made no such prediction. "It's a boy, *madame*. You shall see him presently," she had said. How dare this doctor condemn her son to death!

"Bring him to me," she demanded.

"It will be easier for you not to see him. Now please, my dear, for your own good—"

"Marie," she called with all the remaining strength in her lungs. "Marie, bring him to me this instant."

"Yes, *madame*, in a moment. Let me clear the phlegm in his throat again, then you shall have him."

Somewhere in the dim shadows beyond her bed she could hear Guillaume's voice. "Good God, don't just shake your head at me, La Salle, *do* something!"

"My dear Farroux, I can't tell you how sorry I am, but there is nothing to be done. His lungs are not fully developed."

"Rubbish! He has little fingernails, hair on his head. He is small, granted, but he will grow."

"I doubt it. He is at least five weeks premature and—"

"I know that!" For the first time in Julie's memory, Guillaume's rage was uncontained. He was shouting at the top of his lungs. "That is why I sent for you, La Salle! To save him, not pronounce a death sentence!"

"I perform medicine, my friend, not miracles. Be grateful your wife is so strong. She'll give you another. Do not upset her at this critical time. As for the child, if he lives through the night, there is a faint chance he may survive, but he is already failing. The midwife means well, but I fear she is only prolonging your distress. She should wrap the child warmly and leave him in the cradle. All this puffing and poking and chafing is useless. It would be cruel of me to raise your expectations. There is nothing to be done."

"Then get out! Get out!"

The child was so thoroughly swaddled that when he lay in Julie's arms all she could see was a purple gnome face with eyes scrunched shut and tiny lips working furiously. She bared her breast and guided her nipple into the little mouth, but Marie pulled her arm away.

"No, *madame*, no! He will choke. He needs all his strength to take in air, and even then . . ."

"But how shall he feed, Marie?"

"Drops, *madame*. You'll see. But first we must help him get through the next few hours. Do not listen to the doctor," she said disgustedly. "The boy is not dead yet. We will try."

The eyes fluttered open then shut again, the face convulsed and darkened like a squashed plum.

"Marie, help me, he's choking—" she screamed.

But before the words were out Marie had snatched the child from her and turned him upside down. She patted his back, then fished in his mouth with her finger. After a moment she puckered her mouth against the infant's, forcing him to breathe. It was some time before she handed him back to Julie, but she was smiling reassuringly.

"It's only mucus. There is still perhaps more to come up. I will show you how to do it. Hold him upright, and don't take your eyes off him."

"Stay with her, Marie Soubire," Guillaume said. "Stay with her and you shall be paid handsomely."

"I shall stay the night, sir." Marie frowned. "But I have another delivery to attend—it may be very soon. They will not know where to fetch me unless I send word."

"Is there someone else who could go in your place? Another midwife?"

"There is . . . yes, it is possible, but—"

"You shall not lose the fee, I promise. I will provide messengers, whatever you need. Just stay, Madame Soubire, I beg you. Save my son, and I shall pay you for your time, not a midwife's fee but a physician's."

The cradle was taken from the nursery and placed by Julie's bed, and next to the cradle a cot for Marie Soubire. Three times in the night Charles Louis stopped breathing, but the women kept watch and forced him to start again, and when the sun rose, his tiny lungs struggled painfully on.

They fed him sugared water and Julie's milk, not straight from her breast but from her little finger, one drop at a time.

When Julie held him, his body felt as light and tremulous to her as a newborn chick. Fiercely she willed life and strength into him and despaired when the nourishment she fed him drop by painful drop all dribbled out again. "Swallow, my love. Oh, please swallow," she begged.

"It's not all coming out," Marie assured her. "He's getting some of it and he doesn't need much."

"How can you tell?" she wailed, mopping up the trickles from a chin no bigger than a strawberry and very like in color.

Marie grinned. "Because his little bladder is working. I've changed him three times."

Julie stared at her in astonishment. "When?"

"You were dozing."

"Oh, you shouldn't have let me close my eyes, Marie. You haven't slept, either. What if we both—"

"That won't happen. Babette is bringing me coffee all the time. Don't worry, *madame*. I've done this before. My success rate is as high as any midwife in Paris. This one is going to live."

But there seemed no sign of improvement. Julie was beginning to fear that La Salle was right. "How do you know?" she asked, her hope and strength leaking away.

Because I lost the Grenache child, Marie thought. That means the next four will survive—five, if God is good. "I just know," she said firmly. "Try to sleep a little. You have a long road ahead of you."

The long road seemed more like a tunnel. Julie had no time, no strength for visitors but focused her being hour after hour, day after day, on keeping that tiny creature alive. Days and nights merged in a blur of meals on trays, changed linens, glass droppers, expressing the milk that flooded her breasts and the constant oiling of tiny limbs that were changing color from blotchy purple and angry red to an almost uniform pink.

She was still confined to her bed, but on the fifth day, Julie allowed herself the distraction of scanning the pile of cards and letters that arrived by postman and by messenger in a steady stream. Babette, always methodical, had them in wicker baskets chronologically arranged in the order of arrival.

Anne-Marie was the first. "Babette tells me you can see no one and that the child is in mortal danger. I will call every day and I will pray for you, dearest Julie. I attach a copy of Josephine's receipt."

She had not expected to hear from Josephine; she had seen little of her since the family had moved from the Luxembourg to the much grander royal palace of the Tuileries. In fact her husband had been extremely suspicious of all her personal friends since the Captain Charles affair, and now that she was the wife of the head of state, her entertaining was no longer spontaneous. But Josephine never forgot a friend, and her letter was by far the most encouraging.

The stationery was engraved in gold with just two words. *Les Tuileries.* And as Julie unfolded the fine linen something slipped out. It was a minute copper pipette, so slender that nothing much bigger than a toothpick could have passed through it.

Courage, my dearest Julie, and my fondest felicitations on the birth of your first son. My beautiful soldier son was a seven-month baby. Tomorrow we celebrate his twenty-first birthday. (Doctors are rarely to be trusted with newborns and hate to be called to a birthing.)

Here is one of the droppers with which we used to feed Eugene. I have kept them all these years. I am a sentimental mother, am I not? I know these days there are glass droppers that are much easier to use, and I would like this back for my collection sometime. But I wanted you to see it. I miss our little breakfasts.

I embrace you and I wish you as much joy from your son as I have known from Eugene.

The glass droppers were far less messy than a finger, and more controllable, but occasionally Julie still gave him her finger, enjoying the feel of his pink mouth. The evening after Josephine's letter came she was doing just that when she noticed something new. The warm velvet of Charles Louis's mouth clamped on her little finger with a tiny rhythmic pressure.

"Marie! Marie!" she called out. "I think he is sucking."

Marie was on her cot, sleeping for the first time. At the sound of Julie's voice she tensed her muscles, ready to leap to the rescue. Then the words trickled down through her addled senses and she grinned.

"He's sucking on my finger! Truly!"

"Then put him to your breast, girl, and give him some encouragement." As she spoke, she heard the sound she'd been listening for these past five days, the high, thin wail of a hungry baby.

Chapter Eighteen

1803

Sebastian had left the house on Place Poivre vowing to put Paris behind him forever. Julie, the child they had made together, that was his family. He had lost them irretrievably, and a thousand Bonapartes could not compensate for that. Letizia had been a duty discharged, a shoulder to weep on. But an exchange of tears did not make her his kin. He learned only that the numb emptiness he had felt had been a brief respite to the pain of loss he was to suffer. The only anodyne was work.

He would have returned to the sea but the trading company had grown too big to spare his presence in London for long stretches of time. His work lay in London—unremitting work to meet the ever-growing payroll and capital expenses, work that brought mounting profits. But the principal reward of his grueling schedule was the exhaustion it brought at the end of each day, a mindless fatigue that drained all desire save for sleep. Letizia wrote to him of family ties, but he never responded.

He dreaded Sundays. He would ride or walk for miles. He often set out from Hyde Park on foot and did not stop until he was deep in the country common lands. By the time he returned to his town house and bathed, it was evening. He would dine at a club, drink and gamble until Sunday was put thoroughly to death for another week.

Thus he passed the autumn, the winter and inched his dour way through the following spring without ever turning his face to Paris.

It took an international incident to bring him back and face-to-face with his brother.

On May 20, the *Celestine* called at Le Havre. Captain Chatsworth had broken his leg and needed medical attention. He was carried ashore and promptly arrested as an enemy alien along with two midshipmen. The gendarme was acting under instructions from the highest source. The clipper crew, back from an eighty-day voyage, had no way of knowing that England and France were once more at war, that Napoleon had ordered all British subjects arrested.

The clipper, however, was allowed to sail for home without its captain and two crew members after a rigorous inspection of its hold. Sebastian learned the news in London from Chatsworth's second-in-command. It seemed the magic spell that had safeguarded the Daffodil ships and all who sailed in them had finally collapsed.

Sebastian was at Letizia's house by the following Tuesday morning—a *décadi* in France, a day of rest. But messages were exchanged, and before sunset Sebastian found himself being escorted into the study of Malmaison, the First Consul's weekend retreat. It was their very first meeting.

"It is already done," Napoleon said by way of greeting, as if they were resuming a conversation momentarily suspended. He sat at a vast desk, his shoulders squared, head up. He could have been debriefing a colonel just returned from the front. "I learned of it last night before we left the Tuileries. The two sailors are already on their way to England. Nothing detains your captain but the break in his shinbone. It's mending. He is receiving excellent medical attention.

"It's all right, Creuse," he said to the military aide who hovered by the open door. "You can leave us now."

As the doors closed soundlessly behind the aide, Napoleon hunched his shoulders in a shrug reminiscent of Domenico. He began to speak in short sharp bursts as if words were a form of ammunition.

"A new sergeant at arms! Only following my orders! There have been several attempts on my life! Can't be helped. I cannot personally oversee every last official in the country when it comes...when it comes to your diplomatic immunity."

Sebastian stood by the desk stiffly. "I do not expect that, sir. I never asked for it. But I am deeply grateful for your prompt action."

The crisp martial behavior vanished abruptly. Napoleon stood and skirted the desk with a wide grin, his entire manner instantly transformed. A disarming expression of affection, amusement, mischief and welcome mingled in his mobile face.

"But it wasn't such a terrible thing, uh? Sebastiano!"

Sebastian was captured in a powerful hug, a fist thumping heartily on his back.

Napoleon was still grinning when he drew back. "You didn't wait for me at Mother's last summer. How else was I to meet my hardheaded brother—except if he needed something?"

Sebastian's mission had been dispensed with before he opened his mouth. He was left at a loss, and with the sensation that his reserve was melting. Reflexively he tried to resist the warmth that radiated from the man, but he could not repress a smile. "Are you telling me that you *contrived* the arrest, sir? Just in order to bring me here?"

Napoleon merely closed one eye and made little jabbing gestures with a forefinger pointed toward Sebastian. "Sit, sit," he said, returning to his chair behind the desk. "You shall call me Napoleon—or Nabu when you are in a hurry." His tone became serious once more. "The time has come for you to have a French passport. You have all the privileges of a full French citizen—have had for four years now. The passport is long overdue."

He reached for pen and paper and wrote, saying, "I shall set this in motion tomorrow when I return to Paris. Call for it at the Tuileries anytime after one o'clock. Ask for Captain Valois of the Consular guard."

It was easier to remain aloof with the desk between them. "I am a British subject," Sebastian pointed out rather coolly.

Napoleon's eyes widened in formidable displeasure, but he mastered the reaction before he spoke. "Then you have more than I, brother. Dual citizenship," he said brusquely, dismissing the subject. Leaping from his chair and prowling the length of the room, he launched into the matter of tariffs, shipping routes, blockades, the problems of civilian trade in times of war.

Sebastian was awed at the man's grasp of the knotty economics of Europe, and once more he was overwhelmed by the complex conspiracy that for years had allowed his clippers to reap enormous profits yet had kept him unaware of the source of his protection.

"How in God's name did you manage it?" Sebastian asked. "You weren't First Consul then."

"Your stupid daffodil helped. That bizarre pennant your vessels fly. As a soldier I had more power than you imagine." Napoleon's mouth turned down grimly. "Then I knew who my enemies were—and everyone else obeyed my orders."

"Why?" Sebastian asked. "Why did you go to such enormous lengths for me? We'd never even met!"

"Famiglia," he said, as if nothing could be more obvious.

Family. In Italian, how much more weight the word carried, Sebastian thought. "You leave me monumentally beholden. How shall I repay you?"

Another Domenico shrug that set the fine hairs rising on the back of Sebastian's neck. "Be my brother," he commanded. "And of course, always protect Mother's name."

Protecting Mother's name meant he was to hold the truth of his birth in strictest secrecy. That was simple, and he would anyway, because it was a request in Domenico's posthumous letter. Be my brother.... That was an altogether different matter. The thawing inside him was a painful distraction. It made him remember long icy struggles in the topgallant yards and how his frozen fingers and face burned when feeling began to return. He knew he should be wary. Those penetrating eyes had a strange seductive power.

"I will be your brother," he found himself saying, "so long as it does not affect politics."

"Huh! Do you think your success came innocent of politics?"

"I never carried arms, only peaceful merchandise." His words sounded much firmer than he felt.

Napoleon stopped his pacing and perched on the desk corner, appraising the strange, yet familiar, face turned to his. "Our family tends to soldiering and to statecraft. It amazes me that one of us should have taken to the sea like a fish."

Sebastian smiled. "More like a lemming," he said, and found himself speaking of his flight from the seminary. Three words echoed in his head all the while he spoke. One of us. No one had ever said that to him before.

The air between them lightened as they began to trade boyhood reminiscences—almost with the ease of real siblings just reunited after a long summer apart. For minutes on end, Sebastian forgot that he was in private audience with the most powerful man in Europe.

At the sound of a bell, Napoleon ushered him in to dinner. He'd been told he would dine here tonight, but he hadn't expected such an intimate setting, just an informal room adjacent to the study, a table set only for three. It was staggering simplicity after all he'd heard.

The consulate had become very grand, positively imperial in its protocol. Josephine had four ladies-in-waiting, he'd heard. Napoleon was surrounded by velvet-robed ministers and aides.

"He thinks he's an emperor," Cecil had remarked last week, looking up from his London *Times*. "He wrote not to Pitt but King George direct and referred—good God!—referred to the French as his subjects!"

But Sebastian had found a short man in shirtsleeves, blunt and earthy and likable. He had not wanted to like him. They stood at an open terrace door, Napoleon watching Josephine cross the lawn in the early summer dusk, Sebastian watching only his brother, struggling to adjust to this strange feeling of kinship.

With the appeal and the power of his presence, Napoleon gave that same short-but-tall impression as Letizia. They shared the same burning eyes, the same passionate intensity. He'd not been able to summon much feeling for Letizia, but he could not look at Napoleon without feeling something; he doubted that anyone could.

"Come, angel, meet Sebastiano, my long-lost brother," Napoleon said to his wife as she joined them.

He could see from the quickly covered surprise on her face that she'd had no warning at all. She held out her hand and smiled while she examined the visitor's features. "My dear Sebastiano! I never know when my husband is joking, but looking at you closely, I would say he means brother in a quite literal sense."

Her poise was magnificent. She simply linked arms with both men and walked them to the table. "Bonaparte," she protested, "why have you never told me?"

"Never fear, he is no Bonaparte but a Ramolino." There was not a servant in the room. Napoleon seated his wife and kissed the top of her head.

If that left her little wiser, she did not press the point. "We like the privacy of not having the servants hovering constantly," she explained to Sebastian concerning the lack of attendants. "Some bread? I'll ring for the soup in a moment. Bonaparte, do pour the man some wine."

"Ramolino is Mother's family name, as you may or may not remember," Napoleon said, reaching for a bottle of Rhenish and filling their glasses. "The rest of the family will meet him in due time, I suppose, but only as my friend and trusted companion. You, dear heart, shall be the only one entrusted with the truth. It is a delicate matter, my mother's indiscretion, but he is in fact my half brother."

Josephine dipped her head and turned pink. She looked as if she had been given a priceless gift. Sebastian remembered what Julie had written of Letizia's hostility and instantly understood. Napoleon was in some way compensating Josephine for all the insults she suffered from her mother-in-law. Sebastian was charmed by the sweet and gentle intimacy between this couple as he broke bread with them, and a wave of longing for Julie swept through him.

"Sebastiano," Napoleon barked, drowning his wine with water and swirling it around in the crystal goblet, "do you want to be useful? The damned English navy is a thorn in my side. I need a good admiral. Will you consider it?"

"I will not!" He thought they had laid that subject to rest in the study and was startled at the new tactic. "My talent is in avoiding battles at sea, not engaging in them."

Napoleon blinked slowly, deliberately. "You're honest at least. Do you truly think yourself an Englishman, then?"

Sebastian grinned, amused at this preoccupation of the Bonapartes. Letizia had asked him much the same question, he remembered. "Well! Not by blood, of course, and not by birth. I count myself a citizen of the world. But England cradled me. I've reaped honors and rewards there, and—"

"You can't thank England for your rewards, man. Many an English privateer has gone to the bottom! You have just two men to thank, and they are both in this room. I paved the way, and you had the courage to take it—with unarmed ships to boot!"

"Yes, it was mostly your courtesies and I'm grateful for that. But I never asked for that protection and I expect nothing further from you. I'll be your—"

"Expect nothing further?" Napoleon growled. "Have you forgotten already why you came today?"

Touché, Sebastian thought, and put down his wine. He had not hesitated to use this powerful blood connection to free the crew members of the *Celestine*. He'd taken it for granted. But the war between them put family ties and national ties at cross-purposes. He needed no further protection for his business in order to make a living and he would ask for none. He had discovered what only the very rich know. After a certain point, money seems to be self-perpetuating, invulnerable to the fortunes of war and politics.

Then it struck him that something astonishing had happened in the past hour. He had found a man who called him brother and meant it. He wanted neither to lose that gift nor to abuse it.

"You're right," he said ruefully. "How quickly one takes privilege for granted! I'll not do that again. I expect nothing from you that is against the best interest of your country. In fact, I look for nothing further at all. In return for all you've done in the past, I'll be your brother gladly, a personal friend you can trust. I'll do nothing to contribute to England's side, but neither will I betray England or spy for you."

"What can you do for me, then?" Napoleon's eyes brimmed with affectionate teasing.

But beneath the jesting, the man was calling in his markers, Sebastian thought. He had a right to. "Money for personal use?" he asked, embarrassed to say it.

Napoleon laughed. "You'll have to do better than that! If you believe your London *Times*, there is currently more gold in my personal coffers than in the treasury. Well? What can you do for me, brother?"

Sebastian shrugged, then looked squarely into the challenging eyes. "Damn little, I must admit."

Napoleon grinned from ear to ear and looked at Josephine. "I like this one. He tells the truth! I suppose I'm stuck with you," he told Sebastian. "A half-French, half-Corsican half brother with the touchy honor of an English gentleman!"

Josephine dipped her head in a swanlike movement and laughed as she rang for the soup.

How well he seemed to know that little gesture of hers from Julie's letters! Again he suffered that longing, the feeling piercing his senses as painfully as if Julie herself had just entered the room and joined them at the table. Had she safely given birth? The child would be several months old by now. It seemed incredible that an hour's ride from where they sat there might live and breathe a child who was flesh of his flesh, and with that child a woman he could not excise from his heart.

And at arm's length from him sat her friend Josephine, who could surely tell him. Before he left this table, he promised himself, he would know.

Chapter Nineteen

1803, Ile Saint-Louis

At four months the frail newborn had become a sturdy, rambunctious little boy, the apple of his father's eye and heir to all his possessions. Guillaume seemed to manifest a second blooming of youthful enthusiasm and a warmth of feeling that Julie had not seen before. He expressed his profound gratitude to her in touching ways, and what had once been a hollow contract between them was forged into a bond; they shared a common passion, Charles Louis Farroux.

But Guillaume was seventy-nine, and his new burst of vigor was not to last. Just five days before Charles's first birthday, Guillaume died in his sleep.

A state funeral, letters to be written, official condolence visits and all the duties incumbent on a government widow left Julie little time for introspection.

But the night before her meeting with the estate lawyer, Pascal Hiver, she lay in bed and quietly, dry-eyed, mourned Guillaume's passing. She had put away her resentment for the sake of a tolerable life under his roof. But now he was gone, she realized her forgiveness was quite genuine.

Guillaume had provided for her generously. He had even made her the sole trustee of his estate, a rare token of trust. If the estate was largely property that she herself had brought him as a Sainte Aube, well, that was simply the way most marriages were. He had asked nothing of her except a child. He had used her, of course, but then Guillaume was simply a man who used others for his purposes. It was his way. The way of the world, she decided.

Nevertheless, he had saved her from the guillotine and had tried his best to save her father. She could never forget that.

Guillaume might have been penurious, cruel and jealous, but he was none of those things. And although she would have left him for Sebastian without hesitation if Sebastian's love had been genuine, she bore her departed husband no ill will.

Sebastian was another matter entirely. He had broken her heart, shattered her dreams beyond repair. Last summer he had had the temerity to call on her, demanding to see her and the child. She had avoided the polite euphemism that she was "not at home." Instead, she penned a message, brief and to the point.

"Do not attempt to approach me or my son again either in person or by letter."

She would never be able to love him again, and worse, she was robbed of the capacity to love another. At twenty-five her life held no prospects beyond raising a fatherless boy. As the rage and bitterness began to well up in her, she consoled herself as she always did by turning her thoughts to the baby. Maternal love, thank God, was indestructible.

How fortunate that, with her mother's bright blond hair and green eyes, he bore no resemblance to the man who begot him. She could look upon the child at least with unqualified joy. He was not Sebastian's and not Guillaume's. He was hers.

Pascal Hiver was her own appointee, a skilled and level-headed lawyer who had once been Guillaume's aide. He seemed rather young when she first saw him, but then most men did compared to Guillaume. Anne-Marie's father had assured her that Hiver was brilliant and had been dedicated to estate law these past twelve years. Since the recent massive changes in civil law, few were more current than Monsieur Hiver on what a trustee could and could not do. Furthermore, his wife was a pamphleteer who wrote powerfully on the injustice of the law to women.

He was bound to be sympathetic and helpful, she decided as he carefully stacked nine leather-bound ledgers on the dining room table. He had been examining them all week to acquaint himself with the principal accounts of the estate.

"Have you read the will yet, *madame*?"

"I read it last night in preparation for this meeting," she told him, handing him the document.

He read through it quickly, gave a summary glance at the codicils, then turned to her, adjusting his spectacles.

"Essentially you have an annual income of three hundred thousand francs for life. There are no conditions," he added, pausing to smile at her over the spectacles, which had slid down to rest on the bulbous end of his nose. "That means the income will not stop if you remarry."

She nodded.

"There are various small properties and parcels of land with descriptions in the first codicil, but the bulk of the estate comprises Marduquesnes, and of course this house. Everything is willed to your son, but it is all yours to administer for his benefit until he reaches the age of twenty-one. In the event—" he coughed discreetly behind his hand "—if your son should die before he reaches his majority, the estate is entailed to the family Farroux, as set out in the second codicil."

If your son should die… Yesterday, when she had glanced at the will, that provision disturbed her. She hesitated, remembering Guillaume's avaricious family. His brothers and one sister, their children and grandchildren…they were a formidable clan. None of them lived in Paris fortunately, but she was obliged to entertain them every summer at Marduquesnes. She was always the interloper. The oldest generation treated her with an edgy kind of deference, never forgetting she was a Sainte Aube.

The progeny made no effort to hide their contempt for her. They had all prospered since the revolution, but none as spectacularly as Guillaume. The grandeur of Marduquesnes inflamed them with envy, and she had always been the focus of it, a despised aristocrat who stood between them and the opulence they somehow seemed to feel was theirs by right. She winced at the thought of all that malice directed at little Charles Louis. If the family knew of that provision, she would never know a moment's peace.

"Is it necessary for the family to see the will or know of that clause, Monsieur Hiver?" she asked.

"No, *madame*, all that is required is that you are faithful to its instructions."

"And if I should die before my son reaches his majority?"

"Trusteeship reverts to the Farroux family."

Julie frowned. "Then I had better survive until he is one-and-twenty, *monsieur*. I do not exactly trust my late husband's family."

"Quite, *madame*. I trust you will take good care of your health for your son's sake, then. Now, to pleasanter matters. You will want to hire a financial adviser, someone you can trust. You will have substantial funds at your discretion. From Marduquesnes alone, an average yield of three million francs, and—"

"No, Monsieur Hiver, that cannot be right. Perhaps in combination with the other properties, but I have some idea at least of Marduquesnes. In the best of years it was never more than two million."

"Could I be mistaken?" Hiver frowned and rose to attack the ledgers, a minute accounting of Marduquesnes for each year Guillaume had held title. For some time he leafed through them. "No mistake, I'm happy to say. For the past five years, the rentals alone have amounted to a little over two million.... Ah, I see. You have discounted the sums sent out of the country."

"Out of the country?" she echoed blankly.

"They have discontinued now. A hundred thousand a month to the account of Charles Sainte Aube, transferred to a Dutch bank and thence to England. Your father, *madame*?"

"Impossible! My father died in the revolution."

Hiver knew that was false. He had seen Sainte Aube on the one occasion when Farroux had charged him personally with a courier pouch filled with gold to take to London. He knew from certain clients returned from exile that the man had died shortly before he was due to return to France. That was less than two years ago.

Before he said another word, he took off his spectacles and rubbed the bridge of his nose. This was an unexpected turn. Either the woman was suffering from some insane delusion or... But she looked quite composed. And he doubted Farroux would have placed so great a responsibility on an hysteric. But if, for whatever impenetrable reason, she was in ignorance of the facts, it was definitely his duty to enlighten her—a delicate duty at that.

He would not blurt it out if he could avoid it, but let her discover the truth herself. "Did your husband keep any personal correspondence outside of this house, *madame*?" he asked in a quiet voice.

"Yes, he had a bank vault of papers. It has all been opened, inspected by functionaries and returned to the house. It is in the study."

"I think perhaps we should look at it, together."

One did not lose a cherished conviction in a moment, even when it was proved false beyond a doubt. She had been unable to continue the meeting and had requested an adjournment. She needed a little time alone to study the documents that stripped away her last delusion. It was pitifully easy to piece it all together. What a fool she'd been!

Papa had never feared for her life. Indeed, he had quite deliberately put her at risk to keep a claim on his property; he had gambled that the Bourbons would be restored and he would be master again, with the reasonable expectation that Guillaume would never sire a child. And Guillaume had gambled that royalty would not return, that he could outwit Papa by claiming a love child as the issue of their marriage.

The lie about Papa's death was simply to shock her into docility. Indeed, it was boldly discussed in their correspondence. And he stayed dead because it was...logical. The dead did not return. What did he care for her grief? What did he care if he never saw her again? He was living safely in England on a million francs a year. And Guillaume had known it all along.

Her annual income, which had seemed generous enough on her first reading of the will, now seemed paltry. Aside from that allowance she had nothing; not even the roof over her head was in her name. To live here was a privilege she owed to an infant. It was insupportable. She would fight these men with their own weapons, she decided, and prepared herself carefully.

"I have been reading some of your wife's writings, Monsieur Hiver," she said when they resumed their meeting some days later. "I can personally vouch for their veracity. I myself have been a brood mare and a legal pawn for the acquiring and disposing of wealth. I have been used outrageously by the men in my life for just those purposes, and I will not tolerate another day of it."

Hiver's smile was compassionate. "I understand your need for independence, *madame*. Until your son is twenty-one, your living expenses can all be drawn from the estate. Your personal allowance, wisely invested for the next twenty years, should—"

"I had in mind contesting the will," she cut in harshly.

"Upon what grounds?"

"What if Marduquesnes and this town house were not my husband's to dispose of, *monsieur*, but had remained the property of my father?"

"Then of course we could contest. But I have seen the title deeds."

"This, you have not seen." Julie placed her marriage contract before him. "I believe one phrase offers hope."

She pointed to the words "If an issue results from the consummation of this marriage..." He read the paragraph that followed, then glanced at her.

"I do not follow your thinking."

"My marriage was never consummated. Monsieur Farroux was nearing seventy when I married him. The child is—"

"Yes, of course, *madame*, I understand," he broke in, wishing to spare her from divulging more of her indiscretion than was necessary. "But Monsieur Farroux recognized the boy as his heir. Any judge would uphold the—"

"Wait," she cut in once more. "Does it not state clearly here that if there be no issue from consummation, the titles revert to Charles Sainte Aube and his heirs?"

Hiver paused. He could see where the lady was heading, and he could also see the hazards of the journey as she could not. "Did your father die intestate, *madame*?" he asked, to buy himself a little more time.

"Possibly. But, as you have seen, he took exquisite care to keep me in ignorance. He might have remarried in England for all I know. To the best of my knowledge I am his sole surviving child. Monsieur Hiver, can I afford to have the matter investigated?"

The lawyer frowned. "Financially, yes. But I urge you to question the wisdom or the value of contesting the will upon these grounds. To prove posthumously that a marriage of some nine years' duration was never consummated would be difficult. And I must point out that such a case would subject you to the most insufferable indignities of cross-examination. Your husband was a respected public servant. The most intimate details of your life would be publicly—"

"Monsieur Hiver!"

The look of implacable vengeance on her face froze him.

"I care nothing for the cost or the ill repute. And as for the burden of proof... I can offer some evidence that you will find most apropos."

With a triumphant smile, she thrust a short document under his nose.

Hiver read it with astonishment. An actual agreement between husband and lover to sire a surrogate child with this woman. Taken at face value, it gave the lady an extraordinary case. There were problems, of course. One signatory was the deceased; the other, judging from the name, was an

Englishman—inaccessible for subpoena. A sworn statement from him, perhaps? And there were no witnessing signatures. Given the nature of the document, could a sympathetic judge perhaps find that understandable?

He cleared his throat softly to disguise his growing excitement. "May I consider this for a few days?" he said. "If I may take all the documents, I will read them again carefully. And I will need some time to search out some precedents."

"You may take whatever you wish, *monsieur*," Julie said, and noticed a gleam of elation in Hiver's eyes.

He began to gather up the documents with a rare eagerness. "I don't care to be hasty, *madame*, but I believe we may have a case."

Chapter Twenty

1804

Even though his first attempt to see Julie was thwarted, Sebastian returned to England heartened by his brief sojourn in France. He had at last connected with a kinsman in a way that meant infinitely more to him than having a friend in high places. And although honor demanded secrecy, a narrow sea kept them apart and politics made them circumspect, nothing could destroy that precious hot filament of brotherhood now it was forged. For Sebastian it transcended borders and politics and power. He did not know if they would ever meet again, but letters kept the link alive.

And more precious even than this was the knowledge he took home with him from Malmaison. He had a son.

If hope could revive in him, then love would revive in Julie. He could think of their separation now as a temporary estrangement. Eventually he would win her back and his child, too. And he would not wait until he was an aging stranger like Diderot, too embarrassed to announce the words "I am your father," to a grown man. He would not let that happen to him. *Famiglia*. He had learned what that meant at Malmaison. True family was composed of passions, loves and hatreds and seething jealousies, perhaps. But that precious bond was indestructible.

When he'd hurried from Malmaison straight to Julie, he had acted too hastily, he was ill-prepared. Once she had refused him admission, his only recourse would have been to force his way into the house, and that was unthinkable. Next time, he decided, he would move with subtlety. Guillaume Farroux, old as he was, could not be underestimated. He'd never give up the child unless forced to it and until then, Julie would never leave him.

Sebastian consulted solicitors. Was the lady not his wife by English common law? he asked. Did he have no rights to a child he could prove was his?

Their answers were not helpful: "A contract, you say? Ah, in France! That is altogether a different matter, Mr. Ramlin."

His case was complicated, and no London solicitor, no periwigged King's Counsel could offer much more than ambivalence and the opinion that, if he was patient, thorough research might uncover certain precedents that might aid in the preparation of a brief. The law was a slow-moving animal, and patience was not Sebastian's strong suit. Meanwhile he wrote—sweet persuasive words of love, remorse, loneliness, passionate appeals for her forgiveness. But in the absence of a single reply, he was beset with frustrations. It was uncertain enough these days to get letters delivered to Paris. And if they arrived, Guillaume was probably intercepting them. He tried sending letters to Anne-Marie's address and still earned no response. Julie might even be discarding them unopened. Why couldn't the old devil have died in his sixties like any decent human being?

After months of fruitless consultations, legal opinions ranging from dubious to ambiguous, his thoughts turned to trickery, abduction, any means fair or foul that would allow him a hearing with her, a chance to start afresh.

It was, in the end, a lawyer in Paris, quite unknown to Sebastian, who provided that opportunity.

Pascal Hiver's letter was couched in sonorous French formalities, but it brought him news that quickened his pulses.

Guillaume Farroux had died at last, in fact months ago. His widow was contesting the will upon the basis of her son's paternity. A sworn statement was requested, properly notarized . . .

Sworn statement be damned! He would do better than that, he replied to Hiver. He would appear in person and testify.

Babette's face lit up when she saw him. "Monsieur Ramlin, what a stranger you've been," she said, standing at the door. "Please come in. Madame has spent the morning with Madame Seurat, but she will be back any moment. I'm sure she will be delighted to see you."

Sebastian was not so sure and decided to wait in the courtyard. He would not enter Julie's house without her personal invitation, but he was pleased that his timing was auspicious. It was a good sign. She could not avoid the sight of him this time. The driver would stop at the end of the carriageway. He paced the gravel, his excitement mounting until her carriage pulled in a few minutes later.

It had been two years since he had laid eyes on Julie. Her anger would surely have cooled. Guillaume was gone. She would be ready to forgive, to be reasonable. After all, she needed something from him. The very fact that she had appealed to him through her lawyer was surely an oblique olive branch.

He was stunned by his first sight of her as she stepped out of the carriage. It struck him first that he had exchanged one formidable opponent for another. The avenging fury he had last seen in her eyes seemed to have chilled into an icy indifference. She nodded, as if he were a stranger passing by on the Rue Saint-Honoré, to be acknowledged but nothing more, then she turned back to where a nursemaid was stepping down with a child in her arms.

"Bonjour, monsieur," the girl said, setting the child down on the path and taking his hand to help him up the steps. But the child's eyes were lively with curiosity and he pulled back to stare up at the tall visitor who stood very erect and silent.

A blond head thrust back at a sharp angle, a shy smile and a sharp tug at the hem of his frock coat and Sebastian forgot all about adversaries. He bent to the boy, grinning from ear to ear and sitting on his heels for a face-to-face greeting.

"Take him into the house, Betty," Julie said in English. "This instant!" Her voice cut him like a horse whip.

Obediently the girl half coaxed and half pulled the child up the steps. Sebastian looked after the boy with a clutch in the pit of his stomach, then straightened up.

Julie stood on the top step, barring the open door against his entrance.

The pressure in his throat made his words thick. "He's beautiful," he said. "A perfect little boy."

"I don't need you to tell me that," she said.

"I am here," he reminded her, "because your lawyer, Pascal Hiver, needs my testimony."

"Then you have come to the wrong address," she said, backing into the house with the obvious intention of slamming the door in his face.

Sebastian's patience snapped.

He stood across the threshold, holding the door open with the flat of one hand. He towered over her, granite-faced, eyes black with anger. Julie had never seen him in a rage before. His face was so close that she saw the knotted muscles in his jaw and the generous mouth straighten into a dark slash. She smelled the sweet-sharp citron of his shaving soap. *And wildflowers wilting in a sun-glazed meadow.*

When she had caught sight of him from the carriage window, all the humiliation, disappointment and rejection that had devastated her on first learning the truth exploded anew. How dare he intrude upon her again! By the time she had stepped down from the carriage, seething with resentment, only the presence of the child and the nursemaid had prevented her from battering him with her fists.

Now, to her horror, she was shot with a physical longing that she had not felt for two years. She denied it. It was impossible to desire a man she hated so. It was only lust, her own body betraying her. She would not be used again. Not ever, she resolved, thrusting with all her strength against the door in a vain attempt to shut him out.

"You cannot have it both ways, Julie. If you want my cooperation, you had better treat me civilly." His voice was low and menacing. "I have already met with Hiver. Your case rests solely on proving that the child is mine."

That was true enough. Without him the will could not be broken. She would have to let him in. But only to use him, she decided, as ruthlessly as he had used her.

She relaxed her arm and stepped back so that he could enter. "What is it you want?" she said.

He glanced around the tiled vestibule where she had planted herself, truculent and stiff-shouldered under her cape. Somewhere beyond the staircase he heard voices. A kitchen boy scuttled down the hallway and disappeared into the salon with a basket of logs for the fire. "First I want a good deal more privacy than the front hall affords. I am not a housebreaker," he added grimly.

She took him to the study, still the spartan cell Guillaume had used for years. The old desk, the chairs, the massive walnut cabinets held only one memory for Julie that dwarfed all others. It was here that she had first learned of Sebastian's treachery.

"Well?" she prompted him. The air of the study was close and she removed her cape and bonnet, throwing them over the chair.

She did not invite him to sit, so he stood, watching her emerge from the loose cloak. Under the fall of her gray skirts, her frame was still lithe and dainty, but the fragility was gone, replaced by voluptuous curves of bosom and hips that seduced his eye and threatened to distract him. Gray, he thought. The second stage of mourning. Would she affect the grieving widow with him? He was not about to offer condolences.

"First I must give you this," he said, reaching into his waistcoat pocket for a slim key and holding it out to her. She seemed unwilling to take it, so he laid it on the desk. "It opens a deposit box in your name at Bruni Marhouac, my Paris banker. In the box is the sum of ten thousand louis."

"My son and I are not for sale."

He sighed. It was clear she had not read his letters. He forced his voice to a reasonable pitch. "I am merely repaying a debt. Guillaume gave me four thousand to cement an agreement between us. I repudiate the agreement. My intention was never to furnish him with an heir but only to steal his wife. I therefore return the money with six years' interest at—"

"Very glib," she cut in. "But you cannot repudiate an agreement by which you gained millions over the course—"

"Stop!" he roared. "Your husband gave me four thousand and nothing else. He never lifted a finger to help my ventures. It was for you that I came repeatedly to Paris, not for the furtherance of my livelihood."

Her smile was not encouraging. "Spare me your pathetic lies. I am not the guileless little girl I used to be."

"I can see that. Then perhaps you are mature enough to hear the truth. Guillaume played no part in my success. My aid came from family connections of which I was ignorant until my guardian's death." Her expression was as unmoving as marble. He could see she believed not a word. "I am distantly connected to the Bonapartes," he added reluctantly.

All his words brought was a harsh laugh, mirthless, cynical. "Of course," she said, still smiling. "Who isn't, these days? And no matter how distant the connection, I'm sure you managed to take advantage of it. Just as you profited from your bargain with Guillaume. You are a shameless, unconscionable liar driven only by your own greed."

It was too much. She had baited him into violating a confidence and now she was laughing in his face. His rage spilled over and he gripped her upper arms. "Vicious witch! You are as quick now to profit from that cursed document as you once were to judge me for it."

She struggled to free herself but he held fast, shaking her as his frustration and anger spilled from his lips, shaking her until the combs in her hair loosened and fell. "I could have lied then. You *begged* me to deny it. It would have been my word against Farroux's and it's me you would have believed. I told you the truth because I loved you and I thought your love was large enough to forgive. I was wrong! By God, if you press me too far I will lie now. I'll swear that my signature is a forgery.''

''Take your hands off me,'' she shouted.

''The devil I will! Not before . . .''

''What? For God's sake, what is it you want?''

I want you, he thought. Your good opinion, your love. All the things that made sense of my life. ''I want my son,'' he said aloud, and it flashed upon him that his grip on her arms was viselike, that he had never before touched a woman in anger. Before, their differences had always melted when their bodies met. If he could just once touch her with love again, then he could surely reach her heart; she would remember all they had meant to each other. He released her arms, shocked at the red imprint he had left on her soft white flesh. With a light fingertip, he brushed the angry marks in a mute apology.

She stepped back from him into a shaft of light from the window. The sun caught on dust motes floating in the still air. It gleamed on her smooth shoulders, caught fire in her tumbled dark hair and lit the quick rise and fall of her breasts.

Her breath was labored. She was as angry as he, but he knew at once that no matter how relentless she acted, the streaking desire he had once kindled in her lay just beneath that implacable surface.

Oh God, how I've missed her, he thought. ''I want many things,'' he said gruffly, closing the distance between them. He did not reach for her. ''But first, I want to make love to you. Now.''

He wants to make love to me. She fought against the melting effect of his closeness, his words, and her voice was brittle with the effort to hide it from him. ''Why not?'' she said, and glanced at the small brass key lying on the desk. With a slight tremor, her lip curled. ''For ten thousand louis, it's a small enough thing.''

His hand itched to slap her for that, but he clenched his fist instead and kept it at his side. He said nothing as she led him to her bedroom.

She needed no urging to undress but began to remove her clothes with such quick economy of movement that he found himself turning away. It reminded him of a whore. His heart plummeted. He shed his clothes with his back to her and wondered. Every word, every action seemed calculated to hurt him. Where had she perfected such piercing deadly aim? Where had all the sweetness gone?

When he turned back and saw her lying naked on the bed, his breath caught in his throat. Childbearing had not marred her beauty but enhanced it. The planes of her face were more sculpted than before, and her eyes were lit with desire. Her once girlish breasts were sumptuous, ripe fruit, upthrust like an offering, their rose tips already risen. His fading desire stirred again at the feel of her smooth, rounded thigh, the long delicate curve of her calf below one bent knee.

As he reared above her, he forgot the biting shrew who had goaded him to rage. He saw only the promise of her womanly curves, only the tenderness, the nurture, the deep fulfillment for which he'd pined so long. It was all there still, he told himself, buried under her fierce savagery. The alchemy of their bodies would surely burn clear through to the truth. Tenderly he covered her breasts with his hands and lowered his mouth to hers.

He could taste no acrimony in those dark velvet recesses, only her sweet hungry answer to his leaping tongue. And when he entered her only moments later, she was drenched in the juices of her own desire.

Julie surrendered herself up to sensations. I am using him for my pleasure, she thought, sealing up all access to her heart and unleashing only the tightly coiled energies that clawed at the walls of her body for escape.

When they were spent, he lay motionless beside her, purged of all passion and all rage. She loved him still. Perhaps somewhere there was a woman who could dissemble such consummate desire, such whimpers and gasps of exultation and joy, but not this one. Her fierce responses were the answer he'd sought, the truth she could not hide from him.

It was a moment to savor, their hands lightly entwined, their hearts slowing to a peaceful rhythm. It was a long time before he spoke, before he turned to her tenderly and swept the moist locks away from her cheek.

"Marry me, Julie. The law takes forever—and I don't think I could stand another year like this one—not even another month! Leave the lawyers to do what must be done and come back with me. Bring our son home to England. You are all I ever wanted."

She unlaced her fingers and rose from the bed, covering herself with a wrap. "Marry you?" Her voice was still lazy with love. Indolently she combed her fingers through her tangled hair and frowned, as if the suggestion were bizarre. "Why, I have no desire to marry any man, least of all you. And as for my son, he shall live with me, of course. If you swear you are his father, well, then you may be entitled . . . No, I am no jurist. I will not hazard a guess. You must ask Hiver about such matters."

Pascal Hiver listened attentively, his plain, intelligent face a blend of regret for the world's follies and compassion for the distraught, ashen-faced speaker. When the recital was over, the lawyer placed two fingers over his pursed lips and blew through them in a drawn-out sigh.

"My dear fellow, with the best of intentions, I can do no more than advise my client on estate matters. I do sympathize, but the fact is that Madame Farroux has little to gain from marriage—particularly if we are successful in breaking the will. As for your alleged son, if you refuse to verify your signature on the document now—well, it would be tantamount to disclaiming paternity. I'm afraid that would serve you ill in any court of law if you still wish to establish a father's rights."

Sebastian sat very still, only his fingers working, his nails biting deep into the curled palm of each hand. "And if I do verify my signature, I lose my only means of persuading her into a reconciliation," he said. "It is my only weapon."

Hiver shrugged. Weapon, he thought. Such a strange word to use. He heard it often enough in similar contexts, but he never got over the irony of it. "You speak of affairs of the heart, *monsieur*. That is beyond my expertise."

His own marriage was not romantic, but it was a pleasant, fond partnership nonetheless, and he had no regrets. Romantic passion could do terrible things to perfectly good people. It could make them vindictive, deceptive, ruthless. Dangerous even. He was not in the habit of divulging a client's confidence, but there was something compelling about this man, and his testimony was crucial to Madame's case. He would be as helpful as he could.

"Madame Farroux has good reason to feel ill-used," he began. "But it is more than revenge that motivates her. The terms of the will could put the boy's inheritance in question. If he should die before he comes of age, the Farroux family are the beneficiaries. If his mother dies before that time, they are the trustees. And they are, she tells me, a rapacious tribe."

"And if she breaks the will?"

"She will have sole title to everything. In which case, her intentions are to liquidate and leave the country for England."

He paused to watch the play of emotions on Ramlin's face. Astonishment. Interest. A flicker of hope. Disbelief.

"With Madame and the child settled in England, I believe your paternal rights will be more accessible. Maybe even your chance to regain the lady's affections will increase."

"Mr. Hiver," Sebastian said skeptically, "how could she possibly accomplish such a move to England? There is a war on."

"At present, yes. I have considered the complications, but there are European banks who can circumvent the difficulties of transferring assets. In Madame's case, I will recommend a certain Herr Rothschild in Frankfurt who has a family connection in London. He has successfully managed much larger transactions than this in adverse conditions."

Sebastian rose. "In any event, my testimony is not needed until a date is fixed on the court calendar."

Hiver frowned. It would be unwise to let this witness slip away. "With the court calendars, it is impossible to say when that might be, but as I explained, your sworn statement, taken now in this office before the proper witnesses, is more than sufficient for our purpose."

Sebastian stiffened. "Before I give you that, I want a written guarantee. I must at least be free to see my child. At least as often as I can come to France."

"I will recommend to Madame that she comply," Hiver said, already evaluating silently some specifics that might be acceptable to both parties. "I will suggest. I can do no more than that."

"She'd better comply," he said, "if she wants my testimony. When can I expect to know?"

"A few weeks, perhaps. There will be details to be agreed upon. May I have the name of your advocate?"

"I prefer you write to me," Sebastian said coolly. He was not about to turn his child into a legal battleground. But it was obvious he would receive no satisfaction before he left France. He had dropped everything to come, but nothing had been resolved. Sebastian turned toward the door then paused, combing his fingers through his hair. "You say she will settle in England?"

"If she succeeds with her suit, yes." Hiver sighed. "A somewhat dubious decision in view of the war, I grant you, but she has given much thought to it. And of course, this case could take years, and there could be peace before winter."

Sebastian left Paris in the spring of 1804. The case could take a year or more to be brought before a judge. Until then his testimony was not needed. And Julie would not grant him access to his son a moment before she was forced to.

So be it, he decided as his carriage rattled toward London on the last leg of his brooding journey. The boy would be three at the most. He could wait, if Julie chose to be cruel. Three was still a small child. He conjured up that perky little face again, bright with insatiable curiosity. He felt that insistent tug at his coattails as if they had been his heartstrings. Such a fleeting glimpse that he couldn't remember the color of his son's eyes. He would keep up his journal, he decided.

"Every literate person keeps a journal," Ned Cecil always insisted, but Sebastian's had been sketchy. During his later years at sea, the captain's log was all the journalizing he could tolerate. Since Domenico's death he'd made one terse entry: "Met N. and J. at Malmaison. Chatsworth and crew are free."

He must put down everything about his boy before it was lost forever. Already he'd missed so much.

He began to make a series of resolutions. He would busy himself with the company, but not as before. The journal would keep things in proportion. And he would no longer nail himself to this hermit's cross of brooding and longing and regret. He would return to society after his long hibernation, once again let Lizzie Carlsmere bat those china-blue eyes at him. Perhaps he would be stirred by them this time; Julie Farroux was not the only woman in the world.

At twenty-seven Lizzie Carlsmere still shunned marriage in favor of reaping a scandalous reputation for short-lived lovers. In less than three weeks, Sebastian became the latest, but he chose Lizzie only as the line of least resistance— she had made her eager availability quite clear. His lack of ardor made it a wearisome exercise. His former longing still tinged his every thought and action, and social diversions, even business affairs, failed to distract him.

In August he was briefly able to forget about Julie when he received a letter by special messenger informing him about a world event before it was generally known. It was a letter that stirred profoundly mixed emotions.

Napoleon wrote:

I know what they say about me in England but France needs a monarchy. I have brought the people as many freedoms as they can handle, and prosperity, order and glory such as they have not known since Charlemagne. But if my life is taken, the factions here would soon reduce the country to chaos. In weeks there would be another bloodbath. Only as monarch can I ensure the orderly transmission of hereditary power upon my death, and only as monarch can I achieve peace.

So it is arranged. The pope will anoint me. The powers of Europe will attend my coronation in December. Only Sweden, Russia and your damned little island across the ditch refuse to recognize me as emperor. I have tried to make peace with England, but they demand too many concessions.

So, my prickly Sebastiano, this is not the power-mad lunatic they lampoon in your newspapers but your sane and much-burdened brother. If it were not so public an occasion, and if you were not so "English," I would openly invite you to see me crowned at Notre-Dame. But I will not put you to the embarrassment of refusing an emperor. If you can find it in your heart to come, you have only to say yes to the courier who brings this and a personal invitation will be delivered. If not, I love you no less.

N.

Sebastian replied:

I find many things in my heart including family pride, and my fervent wishes for your well-being and for peace in Europe. But as you say, Nabu, it is a very public occasion, and sentiment here runs high against you. You are gracious to understand so well.

He read Napoleon's letter once again after the courier had left. He was tied in blood to this man, and by that bond he was rooted in history, too. Emperor! Surely such overweening pride would be doomed. But he was touched by the fondness of the words, the approval sought. He folded the paper carefully and locked it in a drawer. He would cherish this always, he thought, and one day he would pass it down to his son. Pulling out his journal, he tried to capture the feelings of this moment before they escaped him forever.

Chapter Twenty-one

1806

Julie stood on the passenger deck of the *Gut Zeelander*, tightly clutching her son's hand. She had given Dora some respite to explore the ship. As the seething Dutch port shrank to a pale gray streak and the sea wind slapped her cheeks, she began to relax a little. It was really happening! It had not been easy to secure passage to England—impossible from any French port. And even in Holland there were more special licences to acquire, endless forms to fill. But she had an English-born mother, she had wealth, and she had learned how to use her wide amber eyes to charm bureaucrats. After six weeks, the final government stamp was granted, and they were crossing the North Sea at last, leaving Haarlem behind them and bound for Ipswich. They would dock by tomorrow noon if the weather stayed fair.

"Look, Mama! Look," Louis squealed for the hundredth time, pointing to where two sailors climbed the foremast and began to scramble along the yards of the topgallant. "What are they doing?"

"Yes, darling, I see them. Aren't they brave? They are trimming the sail to catch the wind. They must do it every time it changes. So the boat will go to England."

Now, much to the child's delight, the wind turned capricious, and for a while he was content to watch the spectacle performed high above the deck where no one could block his view.

Unconsciously she squeezed his hand, her thoughts drifting backward. She had first arrived in Paris at fifteen, a naive child, dependent on Guillaume for her very survival. Now she was leaving at nobody's bidding, a rich woman, dependent on no man...and with a little dependent of her own.

How handsome he is in his tailored pantaloons and little blue greatcoat, she thought, looking down at Louis. He was already dressed *à l'Anglais*. His head was thrust back, his firm little chin pointed at the sky.

"We'll have to call you Lewis from now on," she said, replacing the muffler over his ears, but he was too absorbed to notice.

Julie shivered. It didn't feel like June at all in the North Sea. She hoped they weren't heading into a summer squall. But it was a large ship and only a small journey, really. Sebastian had always made it seem as casual as crossing the street. But Julie could not feel casual today even if the journey had not been so complicated by the war. She was crossing to a new life, and so much sooner than she had expected. Was she ready for it?

Pascal Hiver, so shrewd about everything else, had proved quite wrong in his predictions about how long it would be before this day came. The case had not taken the years and years he had prepared her for but scarcely eighteen months. It had been December, with France celebrating the first anniversary of the coronation. Prices had stopped outrunning wages, and the powerful new empire was prosperous, its administration functioning with more effectiveness and less corruption than had ever been known. Even the judiciary seemed spurred to new speed and efficiency.

In the following January, France openly celebrated the Christian New Year of 1806. After fourteen years the empire officially reverted to the Gregorian calendar. And in the same month, just four weeks after the preliminary hearing, Julie privately celebrated the judge's ruling. There would be no further hearings, no open court, no newspaper scandal.

The will was declared void and the entire legal procedure was behind her. But the war with England was not.

Monsieur Hiver had openly aired his concerns. "Are you quite sure, *Madame*, that you are still of a mind to go? You will be obliged to liquidate everything, you understand. You will lose your rights of ownership in France if you emigrate to a hostile country. The economy bodes better here than in England."

Julie's answer was decisive. "You have directed me to sound advisers, *monsieur*, and I thank you. I have already ascertained that nothing prevents me from ownership there. I can afford to buy a piece of England. Their economy is threatened, but by the same token, land prices are depressed, and I am told this is heavily in my favor at the present time."

She had not felt as confident as she sounded at the time, but she knew she would not be happy until she left France and all its memories behind her.

A fine white spray flew up from the prow. Julie stared out but saw the white cherry blossoms in the Bois de Boulogne. Last spring, she and Anne-Marie had driven through the Bois for a long afternoon together, both of them sadly aware that their almost daily intimacy would soon be coming to an end....

In the open calèche, Anne-Marie's new spring bonnet had been dazzling. She was all sunny-yellow organdy, but her face was somber. "I do not understand you at all," she said. "There are a thousand reasons not to leave France and only one I can think of to go to England. We both know what that is—and yet you protest that you hate Sebastian."

Julie pressed her lips into a thin white line. "I don't hate him anymore. I simply feel nothing for him. Let's not discuss it. The man is out of my life completely."

"How can you say that? He comes to Paris every month now!"

"Only to see Louis. I was forced to grant him that in order to break the will. But I never see him. I leave the house before he arrives or I stay in my rooms. I shall do the same thing in England. I don't ever have to see him again.''

"Then why go at all?" Anne-Marie clutched Julie's arm with a touch of desperation, then paraded her arguments like a quick cannonade. "Why take Charles Louis to a Protestant country? He'll grow up a nonentity. He won't even be able to vote.''

"Then I'll bring him up Protestant. And please don't call him Charles anymore. His name is Louis.''

"But I thought—"

"Lewis, when we live in England," Julie said firmly.

Tears glistened in Anne-Marie's eyes. "Marduquesnes has been in your family for generations," she persisted. "Don't you feel dreadfully guilty robbing your son of his birthright?''

"No!" Julie's voice rose with deliberate enthusiasm to counter the negative gloom. "Anne-Marie, you wouldn't *believe* the offers I've had for the place. I'll be selling high and buying low. Land is cheap now in England. He'll inherit something bigger than Marduquesnes, I can promise you that.''

"I don't care! How *can* you, Julie?" Anne-Marie wailed. "What's happened to you? All you ever talk about is money and property these days. It . . . it will be *dreadful* without you! I hardly ever see Josephine anymore except at those stiff receptions where nobody has any fun. I shall never have another confidante.'' She stopped to dab the wet corners of her eyes. "Besides, Julie, this is your home!''

But France had never been a happy home. Now it held only the bitterest of memories. The only sweet memories she took from France sprang from Louis's infancy, and Louis would be with her wherever she went.

She patted Anne-Marie's back, kissed her cheek and mumbled that it would still be months before she left in any case. "And we'll write copious letters. And as soon as the war is over, you'll come and visit.''

It had taken six months to arrange her affairs. During that time Julie had revived her correspondence with English friends, informing them of her hopes and plans. The regular post was hopeless these days, but private messenger services were doing a brisk trade, and for the clients of Herr Rothschild, there were all kinds of luxurious amenities. If she sent her private correspondence in care of his bank in Frankfurt, it was astonishing how quickly it arrived at its ultimate destination. She had managed to reach the people who mattered to her.

Her dearest school friend, Elizabeth Margrave, was now Lady Perry, and Sir William Perry, she learned, was making a fortune buying up country estates. Mill owners and manufacturers were in financial distress, Elizabeth wrote, "mortgaging their magnificent homes with vast parks or scrambling to sell at any price." The war, it seemed, had closed off most of their foreign markets.

Could Elizabeth, when the time came, perhaps rent a small London town house for them? Julie inquired. A short lease, just to give her time to look about her and decide where to settle?

"Nothing," Elizabeth wrote joyfully, "could be easier. Just say the word when you are ready to come."

Julie would have dearly liked to purchase Clarendon, the scene of all the childhood she could remember, her only home before returning to France in the Terror. Accordingly she wrote to Uncle Allingham, keeping him abreast of her plans. She knew that Clarendon had been rented since the death of her grandparents. Uncle had once mentioned that he had earmarked the small farm for his younger son, John. But perhaps things had changed for the Allinghams, too, after so many years of war; she had heard that John had become the family reprobate who would probably mortgage Clarendon up to the hilt then lose it unless his father bought it back. The Allinghams might just welcome an infusion of French gold into the family coffers. And she was, after all, family on her mother's side.

Clarendon, Uncle Allingham wrote in no uncertain terms, was not for sale—although as Louise's daughter, Juliet was quite welcome to come to England to live. He had no doubt a suitable residence could be found in view of the fact that money was not a problem. "Something small and tempo-rary until you find yourself a suitable husband—which shouldn't be difficult now you are sole heiress of both your late father and your late husband. You won't want to exert yourself with the tasks of an estate, at any event. It would be extremely inappropriate for any woman to do so."

Uncle hadn't changed a bit, she discovered. Quite wel-come to come to England, indeed. As if he were King George granting her asylum! And as for estate affairs being inappropriate for a woman, it was amazing how fast she had learned once she needed to . . . once she was sole mistress of all she surveyed. She would hire men, certainly, but she would watch them closely, never absent herself for long pe-riods and keep herself apprised of every decision. Al-though Pascal Hiver, Herr Rothschild and various skilled agents had served her brilliantly, they had been well paid, and it no way changed the opinion she had formed after so many bitter experiences. Men were never to be trusted com-pletely. Relax the reins an inch and they would cheat and lie to whatever extent they could get away with. Larceny was in their very nature.

Dora came running back to the forward deck, streamers of blond hair whipping out from her gray bonnet and her round face reddened with wind. The sky had darkened with blue-black clouds and the dank air was beginning to pene-trate. "Time to go in from the cold, I think," Julie said, and led them down the companionway.

After a supper in the dining salon, they were ready to re-tire to their cabin, except for Louis.

But although he had chattered nonstop during the meal and protested loudly at the thought of retiring, he was soon asleep in the double bed, blissfully calmed by the constant rocking motion, which Julie suspected would keep her wide awake for hours.

"If you want to go into the salon again, Dora, I'll stay with him," Julie said.

"Thank you, ma'am," she said, glancing at the soft white counterpane. "But I think I'm ready for bed myself. He was a little cracker today! Up before dawn and running ever since."

"Yes, I can see you're exhausted. Good night, then. Perhaps he'll sleep later tomorrow."

Julie returned to her adjacent cabin and sank down on the bed, glad of the quiet after a day of crowds and hurry and the perpetual curiosity of her overexcited child. She was so glad she had Dora. The girl was wonderful with him. Julie had hired her just a few months before war was declared and the supply of English servants vanished. She had wanted an English nurse because she had fond memories of her own Miss Annie. Now, of course, with the war threatening to go on forever, Dora was relieved to be returning to her country. Thanks to that bright and tireless young woman, Louis could chatter away with equal ease in French and English. I must remember to call him Lewis, she thought.

Slipping between the unwarmed sheets, Julie shivered as she closed her eyes. It was only for one night. Tomorrow she would be sleeping in a London house with open fires and warming pans.

It had all been worth the effort. It had cost her much, of course. The court procedure had been expensive, and if she had failed to break the will she would be severely in debt now. But the real cost couldn't be counted in money; the real cost was in having to share Lewis with Sebastian. It was a high price to pay for independence…the only thing that had caused her a moment's hesitation. Could he really care for the child as he claimed? Or was it just another way to torment her?

Sebastian would continue to visit on a regular basis, she had no doubt of that. And each visit was a fresh knife in her gut. She didn't have to lay eyes on him or even hear his voice; just the thought of his proximity sent her stomach into an uproar of agitation. And Lewis was already so fond of him, chattering about him for days after each visit.

Papa, he had called him once, but she had carefully explained that he was never to call Mr. Ramlin that. She sighed. What control could she hope to have over the child when Sebastian had him alone?

Her jaw began to ache and she realized she was grinding her teeth. She lay on her back, massaging the angles of her jaw with her fingers. How easy it was to charm a little child! But then, why shouldn't it be? Sebastian had charmed her easily enough and she was a grown woman.

For a long time, caught up in the daily details of a court case, busy with the management and the dissolution of a complex estate, diverted and delighted by her son, Julie had convinced herself that her life was now everything she could possibly want. But what did her future hold?

Lewis was three, and already he showed signs of fierce independence, of the grown man who would no longer run to her for hugs and kisses or clutch her hand so needfully. Indeed, in seven years or so he would probably be away at school. Then what would be left in her life? Paid companions? Shallow lovers? A husband who, as Uncle Allingham had pointed out, would be easy to procure for a wealthy heiress?

As she lay alone in that wide bed with nothing to occupy her mind, despair began to rise from some buried cache like a hand reaching up to pull her spirits down and drown them. She turned facedown and wept into the pillow as she had not wept since she first learned that Sebastian was false. Now, at last, in this damp, chill darkness, she was forced to admit what she had denied even to herself. She had lied to Anne-Marie.

Yes, she could turn her mind against Sebastian forever; he was nothing but an adventurer by his own confession! But her heart was still a hopeless fool; it seemed to have an obstinate memory of its own.

By the following noon there was a smile on her face. She descended the gangway into a cool summer day, Lewis's hand clutching hers on one side, Dora's on the other.

"Mama! Dora! Look, look!"

They waited for the trunks to be unloaded and brought to the customs shed.

"Mama, why...?"

"Mama, where...?"

"Mama, what . . . ?"

Julie answered as best she could as she led her little party to the customs shed. They could not enter yet. In a swelling cluster of passengers, they waited in a windy open court.

Crowds seemed to spill from gangways and gates to fill every empty space.

"Mama, who . . . ?"

The area bustled with port officials in black caps, well-dressed folk greeting returning travelers, porters, hackney drivers waiting for fares.

Julie opened her pouch of precious papers. Their passports, travel exemption certificates, emigration licences, customs declarations. A sudden panic overtook her. If any one of them was missing or judged unsatisfactory, she might be turned away. All her assets now lay in an English bank. If she were denied entry, if she were forced to return to France, she would be penniless. Homeless and—

She saw him as he was shouldering his way through the crowd, his dark hair lifted in the wind. Dora was holding Lewis in her arms for fear he would get lost. He gave a sudden yelp and wrenched himself free, shouting, "Papa! Papa, you came!"

It was so unexpected that her heart gave a somersault that made her gasp out loud. How could he possibly have discovered what ship, what port they would arrive at? Until three days ago, she hadn't been sure herself. She wrestled for composure, but her face was drained of color and her knees shook. Lewis was clinging to his neck, bouncing around like an organ-grinder's monkey and already launching into the saga of his adventures.

"What are you doing here?" she said, her voice shaking uncontrollably.

"I should have thought it was obvious," Sebastian said, tightening his arms possessively around the excited child. "I'm meeting my son."

Chapter Twenty-two

Pocket Hathaway, Berkshire—June, 1814

Julie sat in her first-floor study, thumbing through the household bills. Forty pounds to the tailor for Lewis...fifty to Clement of London for her Paris wardrobe alone. She had never spent so extravagantly as she had that spring. But then it was the first time since coming to England that there was peace with France, an opportunity to visit.

Lewis was to start Eton in September; his entrance examinations were behind him. Anne-Marie had written, begging her to visit. Paris, Croissy and then the Loire. Reunions with old friends. Showing Lewis the seat of his forefathers... It had seemed the perfect answer to her growing restlessness.

Julie sighed as she sorted the bills into orderly piles. France hadn't been the answer to anything.

Ten years of Napoleon had changed Paris so that she hardly knew it. Too much had happened since she'd left. Now there was a Bourbon on the throne, Napoleon exiled, soldiers milling through the boulevards of Paris, Prussian and English, Russian and Austrian uniforms everywhere. It hadn't felt like coming home at all; it had only made her nostalgic for a past that was irretrievable.

Seeing Anne-Marie again with her five children—plump, effervescent and still an incorrigible romantic—had only raised all the painful self-doubts she thought she'd resolved years ago.

She had tried to make a new life in England. She had reached out to her childhood friend, Elizabeth Perry, and had put down roots on a neighboring estate. The Perrys' second son, Tom, had become Lewis's bosom companion. Mostly she had centered herself on Lewis and her responsibilities as a woman of substance. It was a tolerable enough life, she supposed, but it would never feel exactly like home for her—and neither did France.

Julie had cut short the trip to France after Josephine's sudden death. She had visited Malmaison only days before and the visit still haunted her. Gazing out of the window, she tried to shake free of the memory.

This was Pocket Hathaway, with its black-nosed sheep and rolling park, its house, which she had tried so hard to make their home. They had returned so soon that even the lilacs still bloomed. The air was laden with their scent and she took a deep breath, but the vision of Josephine persisted.

Josephine as she looked less than a month ago, reclining on her chaise longue in the Malmaison boudoir, her cheeks flushed with fever.

The former empress had been in a precarious position, penniless and relying on the victors of the war to be generous. Anxious and ill, she had insisted on spending her strength to entertain her guest. She had shown Julie the art gallery, the treasures, the vast greenhouse vibrant with rare tropical blooms. Only at Julie's insistence had she returned to her boudoir to rest.

Drooping with fatigue, she'd stared into her tall glass. "Orange flower water," she whispered. "Bonaparte believes it will cure anything." Her spirits had visibly fallen with her waning energy, and for the first time she spoke of her misfortunes, the cruelty of the divorce. "Even so, I was happy for him that his new empress gave him a son. Now, of course, he may not even see the boy.

"Forgive me, friend. I have made you sad," she said, and made a visible effort to brighten. "You must come again and bring your son…when I am more myself. When I know what our position is to be, why, then I may be allowed to visit Bonaparte. Who knows? Perhaps the happiest years are still to come for both of us."

The empress forced herself to sit up and reached for a tiny cup of broth. "And you, Julie. You have spoken of your life in England as a mother, as the mistress of a sheep farm, but you have not spoken of happiness. I knew you before as a girl radiantly in love."

"That is over," Julie said softly. "A long time ago. He deceived me."

"Bonaparte had many mistresses during our marriage, but he always came back to me. Perhaps…"

"It was not another woman, Josephine. It was—something beyond forgiveness."

"Nothing is beyond forgiveness if there is love between you."

Nothing is beyond forgiveness if there is love between you.

Julie knew that for the rest of her life she would never smell orange flower water without hearing those words, but it was not orange flower but the scent of lilac that filled the air of the study, great white and purple spears of lilac standing in the brass urn. From the open doorway she heard the creaks on the landing. Lewis's trunk going downstairs.

She sighed. They would not be spending the whole summer together after all. At twelve, Lewis was no longer the short, chubby little elf who needed her so; he was growing independent and lanky. Yesterday she noticed that the top of his head reached her nose. And he seemed just as eager for this unexpected trip with his father as he had been about France.

He would be up in a moment to say goodbye before he left. She heard his feet climbing the stairs at a run and he burst into the room, hot and excited.

"I'm off now," he said, laying his cheek beside hers as she sat at her desk. "Won't you come down and wave me off? Papa's come in his new phaeton with four of the most splendid grays. Come and see! We're taking it all the way to Liverpool to catch the packet to Ireland. Mama?''

Julie rose and hugged him to her. "Such a long trip! I'll wave from the nursery window," she said. "If I come down I might cry."

A tiny movement of his eyes, a small spasm in his lower lip were his only reactions, but they were enough. He was as hurt as if she'd slapped him. "It's not the nursery anymore," he said after a moment. "And it hasn't been for years. It's the schoolroom."

And it wouldn't even be that anymore once he left for Eton in the autumn, she thought, just a big empty space.

"It's because of Father, isn't it? Why do you always hide yourself away when he comes? Do you hate him?"

"No, no, darling, I don't hate him. It's just that he upsets me. We don't agree about so many things."

"Never mind," he said, and turned for the door. And she knew she could never let him go like that. He was off to see Sebastian's horse farm in Wicklow, a tour of the Lake District, then sailing on the Solent. He'd be gone for weeks!

"All right, Lewis," she said, following him down the stairs. "I'm sorry—of course I'll come down."

Sebastian stood by the carriage door with Cook. "Your box is strapped down, Lewis," he said, then caught sight of Julie, lingering on the steps. "Good morning," he called out in a careful voice, then looked toward the cook. "Mrs. Dorritt believes I'm going to starve the boy. Look at all this!"

At Cook's feet stood an array of boxes and baskets. She gave a running commentary as she set them one by one on the floor of the phaeton. "There's a nice bit of Wensleydale cheese, a few apples and a loaf of this morning's bread. The tin box is shortbread and what's left of the treacle tart, Master Lewis's favorite pudding. The veal pies just came out of the oven. I've packed them in straw so they'll stay hot."

Sebastian winked at Lewis and shot Mrs. Dorritt a teasing smile as she straightened up. "Do you think two teams can pull all this?"

"Mr. Ramlin," she said with a little giggle, "there's not a decent luncheon to be had this side of Stroud. You'll be glad enough of this in a few hours."

"I'm sure we will. Bless you, Mrs. D. I wish you were my cook," he said, and planted a kiss on her cheek.

Julie ran down the steps and caught Lewis to her again, just as he turned to climb into the phaeton. "Yes," she whispered in his ear, "they're beautiful horses. Have a splendid holiday."

His arms tightened about her neck. "I love you, Mother. I'll write."

She turned to Sebastian and found herself speaking like a child who'd just been prompted by a conscientious governess. "I hope you have a very pleasant trip."

Lewis's departures had become commonplace over the years; she had learned to accept them. But this time he would be away so much longer, and when he returned, there would be just a few days before he left for school.

By evening she was grateful that Matthew hadn't left yet. Matthew Cullen had been a welcome addition to the household as Lewis's tutor. She had hired him six years ago, an aspiring writer who needed the post to support his ambitions. He'd done a wonderful job of preparing Lewis for Eton, and he was beginning to make a name for himself as a novelist.

He had accompanied them to France, and Anne-Marie had even suggested he was a likely lover for Julie. But he was a tutor not a suitor—and six years her junior. It was an absurd idea, and she had made that clear to Anne-Marie.

"Not as absurd as you remaining faithful to a man who you insist is out of your life for good," Anne-Marie had shot back.

There had been no quick answer for that one. She wasn't remaining faithful to Sebastian; it was simply that no one had replaced him in her affections. Anne-Marie would never have accepted that.

Admittedly, Matthew was a splendid-looking fellow, but Julie valued him for his teaching skill and no less for his informed conversation at the dinner table. He was one of the few educated Englishmen she knew who did not treat her as a simpering, fragile featherhead.

She brushed the thought away as she joined Matthew at the dinner table. "What will happen in the event that Lewis doesn't pass the exams?" Julie asked him.

"Then we should cram like mad and petition for him to take the exams again in February." Matthew's face broke into a wide smile. "But there's no danger of that! I'm quite sure he did well. He's streaks ahead of his peers. Tom Perry has only the flimsiest knowledge of Latin grammar, and as for mathematics, he thinks long division refers to the part in his hair."

She laughed. "Tom Perry didn't have the benefit of a genius for a tutor."

Matthew became intent on patterning his whipped potatoes with his fork. "Come, Mrs. Farroux, you don't have to be a genius to teach a bright boy the three Rs and a bit of Latin."

Yes, Lewis was bright, and she was enormously proud of him, but his whipping physical energy might have made him a poor scholar without this man's inspiration. Anne-Marie was right about one thing: Matthew Cullen was far more than a competent tutor, and she was lucky not to have lost him when his books began to sell.

"It was really very good of you to have stayed on, Matthew. I know you haven't needed this position for some time. Lewis would have missed you dreadfully if you'd left earlier."

"We plan to correspond," he said. "I've promised to visit him at school." He was looking down into his plate, his light brown hair falling forward and glinting red under the glow of the chandelier. His earlobes were reddening, too. Compliments always made him blush like a boy. He really wasn't much more than a boy, she decided, charmed by his shyness.

He waited until the blush faded before he looked across the table at her and smiled. She had always liked his blue eyes. They were so kind, and full of the sweet vagueness of

the nearsighted. It occurred to her that he never wore his
spectacles at dinner.

"I shall be sad to leave," he said.

"Oh, for heaven's sake don't be, Matthew. There's been
enough sadness this season. I hope you'll come back to visit,
and that you'll never become too grand and famous to remember us. But please, please don't be sad. You have such
a gift! You'll be so much happier doing what you were born
to do. Why, writing is your passion. Clearly you were meant
to devote yourself to it."

"I have other passions," he said slowly.

It was probably quite innocent, but Julie attacked her
breast of veal and decided not to pursue the remark. "He
clearly adores you," Anne-Marie had said. Well, she wasn't
always right.

"You are a very fascinating woman, Mrs. Farroux."

Julie chewed slowly. It was bolder, more personal than
anything he'd ever said to her. Bordering on the insolent?
she wondered. Not exactly; he wasn't a servant, after all. It
was probably just the writer speaking. To him, all women
were interesting. She thought of some of his fictional char-
acters, subtle, memorable women. One would swear they
sprang from vast experience of the female sex, which was
odd, somehow. He always seemed such an innocent. He'd
been part of the household for six years now, and if he had
some liaison in the village, she certainly wasn't aware of it.
It was just a writer's gift, perhaps. Keen insight. She decided to laugh off his remark.

"I'm not fascinating in the least, Matthew, just an ordinary widow and doting mother."

"There is nothing ordinary about a woman of beauty and
wealth shunning society the way you do."

Julie struggled with the angry heat that swept up suddenly from her throat. "I live exactly as I choose," she said,
and pushed back her chair and sprang to her feet. "I do *not*
shun society. I am *not* one of your fictional women nursing
some ancient wound. And it's *not* your affair!"

With that she fled from the room, through the salon and
into the garden, gulping the night air as if it could douse the

fiery turmoil inside her that had just exploded without warning.

It was that dusky time after a summer sunset when the coolness of the night began to rise from the earth with faint scents of mown grasses and honeysuckle and spicy sweet william. She hurried to the end of the formal garden and stopped by a slender aspen tree. Her face was still hot and she rested her forehead against the smooth trunk, grateful for the cool, damp touch of it. He had not exactly insulted her. Why the outburst? She felt frighteningly out of control suddenly.

She heard his footsteps on the gravel path behind her and the sharp intake of his breath. "Please forgive me, Mrs. Farroux. I did not mean to criticize or to pry. I would not offend you for all the world."

She shook her head and retraced her steps back into the house. His voice followed her, fading as she quickened her pace, then audible again as he hastened to catch up with her.

"There is nothing wrong with shunning society...silly and shallow most of the time...you are to be respected for..."

She hurried upstairs, along the corridor to her suite. She had intended to shut herself in her room, but his passionate entreaties gradually slackened her pace, and outside her door she relented. She would hear him out if he was so desperate to make amends.

"Please say you'll accept my apology," he pleaded. "I'm an oaf, I suppose. Scratch my thin veneer of education and there's still a country bumpkin underneath."

That wasn't true. He was demeaning himself because he came from country stock, but he was as much a gentleman as anyone she knew. Julie knew she was behaving badly. She had overreacted. Soon he would be gone. Lewis would be gone. Even Sebastian would have no reason to come. Yes, it was that feeling of everything coming to an end that made her so touchy tonight. She tried to say something gracious, but his voice continued, abject with apology.

"I did not mean you were—good Lord!—I did not mean to imply you were fascinating as a specimen. I only meant you fascinate *me*. I mean, I admire you so, Mrs. Farroux. I—I me-mean that I—"

"I know what you mean, Matthew," she said, turning to face him. He was a little in love with her after all. Fond feelings of tenderness poured through her, drowning out all her agitation. She touched his face as lovingly as if it were her son's. "Hush, Matthew. It's all right, it really is all right," she whispered, and lightly kissed his cheek.

He turned his head until their lips met with a sweet, fleeting touch that was over as soon as it began. When he drew back, she could not help smiling at his awkward stance. He was standing very straight, his arms pressed to his sides and his hands curled, his wide blue eyes uncertain, infinitely vulnerable. Only their lips had touched.

The tutor needs a tutor, she thought, suppressing her laughter. "Your arms are meant to hold me in such circumstances," she said gently.

His face was earnest. "If they do, you might regret it. You treat me like a child, but I am not as new to such circumstances as you might suppose."

"Is that a fact?" she said, touched and amused. Her lips still radiated the feather-light warmth of his. He was so unsure, but she saw the tremor in his arms, heard the rusty quality in his voice and felt herself responding. After such a long sleep, she did not immediately recognize desire awakening, hunger stirring up the dormant channels in her body.

"Dear Matthew," she said soothingly, "you are no oaf, no country bumpkin. The only thing that separates you from the upper classes is your honesty."

It had been too many years since she had felt a man's arms around her, she thought as she slipped into his embrace and gave herself up to his kisses.

"Come," she said, leading him into her room. She took off her fichu, then helped him remove his coat and cravat. As she opened his shirt buttons he grew impatient and caught her to him again. She felt the rhythms of his body quicken as his mouth explored hers, no longer childlike but with a man's frank intent to inflame and possess.

It was the hands of a deft man who bared her shoulders and kissed them as he pressed her to the bed. A passionate man, the wrong man, she thought, her longings sweeping her forward.

She would not stop him now, but she knew. Behind her closed lids it was Sebastian's touch she rose to, Sebastian's weight she welcomed.

Later, he lay still and peaceful, facedown beside her on the bed. Only the backs of their hands touched. She knew he had no thought of leaving. He was silent, blissfully content with the least contact of their skin. Her discomfort grew until it became intolerable. She broke the long silence and said something about the servants...the morning...suggesting he should leave now.

"It's hours till morning," he said with the lazy intimacy that follows spent passion.

"But we could fall asleep and—"

"Not a chance," he said, reaching out his palm. He touched her mouth then let his hand nestle between her breasts. "Not as long as I have you within arm's reach."

She stiffened at his touch and her voice became insistent. "Please, Matthew. I think you should leave now."

He withdrew his hand and lay still for a long moment, but the quality of his silence had shifted irrevocably. Without a word he rose, put on his trousers and shirt, gathered the rest of his clothes in a careless bundle and clutched it to his breast before he turned to look at her.

It was dark in the room, one lamp turned down to a faint flicker, but something made her pull up the sheet to cover her nakedness.

"This was unkind," he said quietly, standing by the bed. "Unworthy of you."

"Matthew, you're just a boy. You have a life of your own to live."

"No, Mrs. Farroux. Lewis is a boy. I am thirty years old and I *am* leading my own life. Tonight you have allowed me to hope that you might have some part in it. I have loved you for a long time. Lewis and I share a lasting affection. My writing is in demand. Of course I will never have wealth like yours, but tonight..." His voice held a quiet reproach. "You encouraged me to think that it was a reasonable expectation..." He shrugged and left the sentence unfinished. "Well, never mind. I know now. I'm not a complete fool. It's Sebastian Ramlin, isn't it?"

Julie closed her eyes, appalled. "Did I call out his name?"

He sighed heavily. "No, Mrs. Farroux, you didn't do that."

But he would know, of course. She had never meant to be so cruel. "I'm so sorry, Matthew. So very sorry."

His voice was edged with pain. "Oh, I'll get over it," he said, and thrusting his bundle of clothing under one arm with a jaunty movement, he made for the door. "But I'm not so sure that you will."

For a moment, in her distress and confusion, she wasn't certain what he meant, but from the moment the door closed behind him, his parting shot became clear.

She would never get over Sebastian.

"But I have!" she protested aloud, hugging herself fiercely. She was too canny a survivor to erode her life with a grudge. The bitterness was long gone. All she felt was a pervading regret. Regret that she was still susceptible to his presence; regret that he loomed so large in Lewis's life that she had no hope of forgetting him; regret that he could never be the man she had once believed him to be... but neither was she the woman he once...

Nothing is beyond forgiveness if there is love between you.

She sat up swiftly, astonished with a truth that pierced her like a swift dart from somewhere in the night. She *had* forgiven him. She didn't even know when. It had been an involuntary, unnoticed act, an attrition. She had merely hung on to a pattern of prideful resentment that would not allow her to express forgiveness, or even admit it to herself until now, when she had become so painfully aware of her own fallibility.

He had toyed with her affections and used her body for material gain. A wave of disgust went through her like an old habit. But his original intentions had gone awry when he fell in love with her. Yes, there was no question in her mind that he did love her. *Had* loved her.

Sebastian had learned too well to live without her. He was no longer affected by her presence. Since he had sold his shipping business and become a man of property, he was perfectly happy leading the life of a wealthy bachelor. He had his friends, his mistresses, his times with Lewis, his estates and building projects to occupy him. There were no empty spaces in his life.

But he had remained single.... There could be a dozen explanations for that besides the one she wished for.

Perhaps there was still a chance. At the end of the summer, she promised herself, somehow, there would be a way to find out.

Chapter Twenty-three

Italy—September, 1814

Sebastian had rented a jolly boat at Piombino for he needed a vessel he could man alone. He'd never traveled with fifty thousand pounds of his own gold before and he did not want to risk a crew of strangers. He used two old, disreputable satchels and waited until midnight to return to the port. Once the boat was loaded he sat in it, hoping the wind would rise soon.

He kept the lantern shaded and waited quietly. The small boat bobbed against the pilings, unnoticeable in the shadows of a brig. In the quietness, he could hear the squeak and groan of timbers and hawsers. It made him think of the cracks and slides in Lewis's voice, no longer a pure soprano.

He had been filled with bittersweet nostalgia this summer, watching adulthood bear down on the child so soon.

They'd grown especially close in Lymington, sailing together in the Solent every day, just the two of them. They even circled the Isle of Wight, Lewis loving every minute of it, Sebastian enjoying the boy's expressions as he tried out his new skill.

His face was hinting of the man he would be ten years from now. He was fairer than Julie, but his green eyes tilted like hers, like almonds. And the jut of his brow, the set of his ears, the way his hair sprang up at the crown—a dozen subtle reminders of Letizia and even Domenico.

They would come back to the cottage after a day on the water, ready to do little else but eat dinner and talk.

"Mother's not herself lately," Lewis had said on their last night. "I thought the trip would cheer her up, but it only made it worse, I think. She broods about me going away to school. I don't know why she doesn't marry again. She could, you know."

"Yes, I know." Sebastian was both touched and resentful. The boy was already becoming his mother's protector. "Did you ever ask her why she wouldn't marry me?"

"When I was little I used to. Then I learned that it only upset her, so I stopped. I never did get an answer I could understand. She never says 'your father,' just 'Mr. Ramlin.'" For just a moment Lewis looked like a small boy again, in desperate need of reassurance. "Are you quite sure? I mean, sure you're my father."

Sebastian dipped his finger in a jar of salve and put a blob on the boy's windburned nose. They sat in the small parlor, sated with food and a day of fighting capricious winds, both content just to laze by the coal fire and warm their tired muscles.

"Lewis," he said, "do you remember when I told you the facts of life?"

The boy nodded.

"Well, now I think you should hear the facts of *your* life, so you'll never wonder again who your real father is."

Sebastian wiped his hand on a napkin and placed the salve jar on the mantelpiece. Then he sat down cross-legged on the floor where the boy sat gingerly working the salve into his tender skin.

"This doesn't put me in a very good light, Lewis. I did something wrong, something your mother does not forgive. I hope you can."

Lewis listened closely, but when it was over, he was neither angry nor satisfied, merely confused.

"Don't understand this at all, Pater," he said, attempting a kind of detached sophistication. "I can see my *adop-*

tive father not forgiving you. You broke your word to him.
But you never broke your word to Mama. What does she
have to forgive?''

Sebastian smiled ruefully, wondering how you explained
sins of omission to a Protestant youth.

''I should have told her the truth about how we first met,
Lewis. I was always going to tell her, but I never did. And
then it was too late. She learned it from Guillaume Farroux.''

''Is that all?''

''She felt that I only romanced her for profit. That my
caring for her was all a massive pretense. I did get rather rich
rather fast.''

''But you *weren't* pretending and the money had nothing
to do with it. You just said so. Family connections in
France. Didn't you explain it all to her?''

''Yes, as much as I could. I couldn't go into certain details about my relatives. You see, that would mean breaking my word again, and I'll never do that.''

Lewis's eyes widened. ''You mean you've been sworn to
secrecy?''

''Yes. But in general terms, your mother's known the
truth for a long time. It's been twelve years.'' He stood up
and jabbed at the dying coals with the poker. It was almost
time for bed.

''Well, it doesn't matter now,'' he said. ''I don't suppose
she cares much anymore. People do get over things like
that.''

Lewis crossed his eyes in an effort to see his peeling nose.
''She still loves you, if that's what you're fishing for, Pater.''

''What makes you say that?''

''Mr. Cullen told me, and he's a clever man. I think he
used to be rather keen on her himself. Anyway, she dis-
courages any man who takes a fancy to her. Perhaps you're
not trying hard enough.''

Sebastian laughed. ''Lewis, do you know how often I've
been to Pocket Hathaway to fetch you and take you back?
More times than I can count. And what happens? She runs

and hides. It used to be Dora who brought you to the door, then it was Matthew. I didn't have to come, you know. I could have sent a carriage to fetch you. So don't think I haven't tried. But there comes a time when one wearies of trying."

Lewis uncrossed his legs and stretched out on the faded carpet, folding his hands behind his head. It didn't bother him anymore that his parents lived separately. He wasn't in the least envious of Tom Perry now. Tom never got to stay up this late talking with his father. At times he thought he was luckier than most of the chaps he knew. Their holidays were boring compared to his. Their parents went off somewhere together and left the boys at home—often with the younger children's governess. But sometimes he still wished longingly that they all live together.

"Mr. Cullen says that when I'm up to bat on the Eton eleven, I'll be told, if at first you don't succeed—"

"Lewis!" Sebastian's voice was sharp. "We are not on the playing fields of Eton, and in any case, I think the subject's been done to death."

He had taken to treating the boy like an equal and that was wrong, he thought, watching the white sickle moon slip behind clouds. But with no rule book and no wife to guide him, he was doing the best he could. His occasional mistresses—those who lasted long enough to hear about Lewis—always claimed that he was spoiling the boy.

Perhaps you're not trying hard enough. What did a child of twelve know about rejection and the slow erosion of hope?

Letting the problem yield to more immediate matters, he took off his gloves and flexed his cold hands. There was a good blow coming from the east. It was time to cast off for Elba.

The great powers of Europe were meeting in Vienna, dividing up the map again. Russia, Prussia, Austria and Great Britain.

"He needs you," Letizia had written. "They promised him a million francs a year, but the money never came. I have given him all my savings, but by the end of the year he will have nothing left. The island costs him far more than it yields in income. His wife and his son were not permitted to join him. After all he has done, they will let him die in exile, forgotten and destitute. If you cannot offer him money, offer him at least the comforts of his family. He is a broken man."

She had continued the letter with a lengthy diatribe listing betrayals, injustices, losses, sorrow. But she could have saved all that paper. Her first three words were enough.

He needs you. Sebastian would have come sooner, but there was no way of knowing he was welcome. Nabu's letters had stopped coming before the Moscow retreat. To be forced to abdicate, to have fallen from such heights…it was hard to know exactly what he was feeling. Sebastian had tried to imagine himself in such circumstances and had thought he would want solitude.

The victors had let Nabu keep his imperial title, but his "empire" had shrunk to one small island, so insignificant that Sebastian, familiar as he was with the Mediterranean, had to look on the charts to remember its exact location. A tiny ink blot flicked carelessly into the sea between the Tuscany coast and Corsica.

There were less than fifteen miles of open sea to cross from Piombino and a stiff easterly all the way. He crossed it, thinking of the last time they'd met in the walled Tuileries garden, the emperor's private sanctuary. It was after Sebastian had divested his interest in the Daffodil Trading Company.

"But why?" Nabu had wanted to know. "Blockade be damned—I would have protected your ships."

"That is why. I wanted to spare you that conflict of interests."

Nabu had followed the flight of two wrens with his great sad eyes. "I believe you are beginning to love me," he said, and began to speak of Josephine.

"I've had to divorce her, Sebastiano. And it kills me. *It kills me!* But I must have an heir." Tears coursed down his cheeks, and Sebastian knew now why he'd been summoned.

"My family rejoices. They've hated her from the day we married. They feign sympathy for me and say I am only doing what I must. And I *am*!" He pounded his breast with a tight fist. "But here, here—" His voice seemed to shatter into fragments.

"Do you know what it's like to love one woman to distraction? To feel so bound that you cannot—you cannot bear to hurt her? Cannot bear to lose her? And yet you must?"

Sebastian had laid a hand on Napoleon's arm. Under the fine sleeve he'd felt the hard muscles trembling with emotion. "Yes I do, Nabu. I know exactly what it's like."

He saw the port lights after an hour's sailing. Furling the jib, he rowed ashore at a tiny cove east of Portoferraio and waited for daybreak to enter the harbor.

At precisely eight o'clock, a courteous port official led him to a chaise, and under an escort of two mounted soldiers, still wearing the double eagle insignia of the imperial guard, he was driven to the governor's mansion on the hill, which now served as the emperor's palace.

Nabu was a shade stouter than the last time they'd met. Sebastian found him in a stark chamber leaning over a table covered with architectural plans. Plumpness had smoothed out the lines on his face, but his skin was very sallow. He straightened up stiffly as if his back muscles hurt.

He grinned at the two guards and said, "What's this? What filthy scalawag have you brought me? Sebastian! Put those things down, will you? You don't have to clutch your possessions like a refugee. I may have lost an empire, but I haven't lost my servants yet and my faithful little band."

Nabu was flanked at the table by two civilians. A footman stood at the door. The two guards hovered, waiting for dismissal.

"My luggage contains confidential material," Sebastian said. "For the emperor's eyes only."

Nabu quickly cleared the room with a series of orders.

"Signor Manza, Signor Di Lorico, I'll consider the harbor plans later today. Leave them with me, if you please.

"You can return to your posts now, gentlemen.

"Order this man a good breakfast, Paolo, and send it in here with some coffee for both of us. He will be staying here. Have a hot bath prepared—he could use it." Laughing, he stared at the stubble on Sebastian's jaw. "And warn my barber he has a new customer."

Only when they were alone did Sebastian swing the two satchels off his back and place them on the tiled floor. Napoleon looked at them, then turned to Sebastian with eyebrows raised in a question.

"Fifty thousand pounds in assorted currency," Sebastian said. "Mostly gold. Some silver."

"That's more than twelve million francs," Napoleon said, his voice thin with shock. "You're offering me this? But I'll never be able to pay it back! No, you must not pay for my mistakes, Sebastian. I'm not destitute—but you will be, if you part with this."

"It's not a loan, it's a gift," Sebastian said. "This is the first time I have been able to offer you anything, Nabu. Do not deprive me of that. I assure you, I can well afford it."

It was a long time before Napoleon spoke again, and when he did, he had to clear his throat. "Four hundred of my guards chose to come with me. Hortense gave me her diamond necklace... Mother, her savings. But you—" He shook his head slowly. "I can't tell you how moved I am."

"It's only money," Sebastian said. "It's all I could liquidate at short notice, but—"

"No! No more. I will never forget this, Sebastian. Never. I will use it in memory of Josephine. She always liked you."

For a moment he thought Nabu had some lunatic whim in mind, some extravagant monument to his dead love. Perhaps it was to be expected. Alexander had built the grandiose city of Bucephala to memorialize his horse. One didn't question the whims of great men.

"The money is yours now," he said. "Use it however you will."

"I will use it to clear her debts."

"Debts?" Sebastian echoed. "Josephine? But surely Malmaison supported all her living expenses. And you gave her three million a year for spending money."

"She spent four million. The bills started arriving here early this summer. I think they've all found me now. Dressmakers, glovers, caterers, florists, musicians, art dealers—and some substantial personal loans made by old friends."

"Nabu, surely here…in these circumstances…you could ignore the bills. What more can they do to you?"

"Nothing, I suppose. But I want her to be remembered fondly. Paris adored her, you know. They called her Our Lady of the Victories from the earliest days of our marriage. They never did take to Marie-Louise."

When breakfast arrived, it was laid on a sturdy writing table by a window that looked out to the harbor. Eggs and goat cheese, crusty bread and little red Corsican pears. Sebastian ate off the tray while Nabu stood staring out at the rain. The harbor was lost from view.

"My Josephine had only two faults," he said. "She couldn't resist spending more money than she had, and she couldn't remain chaste if I was away for more than a month. God, how we used to fight about it! But I could never resist her tears. I always forgave her in the end. And I always honored her debts." He leaned against the table and drank some coffee, watching Sebastian over the rim of his cup.

"Fourteen years of marriage," he said softly, setting down the empty cup without a sound. "I've regretted much that I've done—you can't amount to anything without making mistakes—but I'll never regret those years. Even if I should spend the rest of my life on this little patch of dirt, I'll always have that to treasure."

He leaned forward and rubbed Sebastian's head in a fond, playful gesture. "And you, little brother, what will you have to treasure?"

What indeed? It was a question that pricked him throughout the long journey home from Elba. It was like asking himself what his life amounted to.

On board the *Serenata* for six days, Sebastian had shunned company and mostly kept to his cabin.

If it were not for Lewis, he thought, what memories would he have to treasure that were pure and unsullied?

He would treasure his rare private times with Nabu. And that surely was no small thing.

It was certainly an extraordinary friendship—the most powerful emperor France had ever known and a bastard who'd made of himself an English squire. Our countries have fought for twenty years, he thought, and yet when we are together, so strong is our affinity that we create for ourselves a neutral territory where we meet as brothers, untouched by politics and disparity. Nabu had no comparable bond with his other brothers.

Sebastian had even shared with Nabu the darkness at the very center of his soul, his loss of Julie. "Never count her lost," he said. "If she is truly the woman unalterably locked in your heart, you must keep trying." But how did one persist with a woman who winced at the very sight of you, who found you contemptible?

"Don't take no for an answer," Nabu would say. "Take her by storm."

Sebastian watched the gray waters of the Thames as they steamed toward London. He shook his head. Nabu just didn't understand defeat.

Even if I should spend the rest of my life on this little patch of dirt . . . As if there were still other possibilities.

He looked through the porthole toward the wake, still thinking fondly of the man he had left behind on that tiny speck of land. A shaft of light turned the porthole to flashing silver for a blinding moment, and an odd thought came to him, as if borne on wings of light.

Could it be that Nabu really did understand defeat? Perhaps he understood that it was only a state of mind.

Chapter Twenty-four

Throughout the summer, Julie had tended the tiny germ of hope she had discovered through the words of Matthew Cullen. He had left immediately, formally handing in his resignation after the night that "I am sure you will agree, Mrs. Farroux, has made my further employment here out of the question." She had accepted his decision, regretful that she had spoiled such a good friendship but agreeing that his action was only proper.

She could not afford to look back, she had decided. The stretch of time ahead was like a steep mountain she must climb with its summit promising Lewis's return—and the prospect of Sebastian.

Outwardly she had followed familiar routines—supervising the purchase of winter feed and farm supplies, spending two weeks in Brighton with the Perrys, attending and giving dinner parties and card games. Inwardly she had lived only for the end of August, for the possibility of happiness renewed.

But Lewis had returned to Pocket Hathaway alone, sent home in his father's carriage because Sebastian planned an imminent trip to Europe. She tried to hide her disappointment but she felt this unexpected defection as sharply as a body blow. She had shed some hard protective skin over the summer and was left with a raw vulnerability.

"It's only thirteen weeks till the Christmas holidays, Mother," Lewis said, sensing her pain as he left for school. "And you'll come up for parents' day, won't you?"

"Yes, of course, darling. Of course I will," she answered brightly, but the effort was enormous.

I have shunned Sebastian for all of Lewis's life, she reminded herself. What right have I to think that my private relenting should bring him running to my door? I should write to him of my change of heart. But her pride was too fragile to initiate some gesture that might meet with rejection.

It was more than a month before she heard from Sebastian, and by then she was too wary to put much store by it. He wrote from London. He was considering changes to his will that would affect Lewis and needed to discuss the document with her.

"Unless I hear from you to the contrary," he wrote, "I shall call on Thursday morning of next week at eleven."

Julie was sleepless on the eve of his arrival, racked with unanswerable questions. There was only the faintest hope, and if it were dashed, what then? For weeks now it had seemed so. She began to pluck at memories that might define her, identify her purpose and position in the universe.

"How naughty of you not to have changed at all," poor Josephine had said, seeing her for the first time in nine years.

Matthew Cullen thought her fascinating, a woman to be admired. For what? she asked herself.

Anne-Marie had said she still looked in her twenties, but she was, after all, thirty-six. Surely a woman should know by then exactly how to define herself, should have achieved a measure of contentment. But nothing seemed to make sense anymore without Sebastian. It was as if he were all she ever wanted and she could not accept that.

In the small hours she abandoned hope of sleep and tried to center herself by looking at her private journal entries over the summer; there were very few. What had once been a meticulous record of her innermost thoughts and feelings had shrunk to little more than an appointment book. It seemed she could no longer articulate her feelings.

She leafed through July, August, September, searching.

Mr. Fortescue at ten to discuss the Consolidated Securities.

The vicar and his wife to tea. Dinner at the Perrys'.

Exam results. Lewis passed.

The Fortescues and Perrys for dinner.

To London for school uniforms.

Lewis left this morning. Didn't cry until he was out of sight.

She had written nothing since that day, five weeks ago. She took her pen, thought for a moment, then began to write aimlessly, just to occupy her hands.

Behind me lies the wreck I have made of my bed, hot twisted sheets and tortured pillows scattered like corpses on a battlefield. I cannot sleep because Sebastian will be here tomorrow, the very time when I should look my best! I shall wear my primrose cashmere dress and use rouge. Yes, I'll have to wear rouge or I'll be as white as a sheet on no sleep at all. I am making far too much of this visit, but I cannot seem to stop myself.

Courage, Julie! I have faced worse than this. I have managed well enough without him now for more than a decade. I have *chosen* to live thus. Now I choose differently.

She laid down her pen and stared at the last words. *Now I choose differently.* They had a calming effect. The outcome, she understood now, was less important than the fact of her choosing.

It was not given to her to govern the course of Sebastian's feelings, but she would deal with her life within the borders of whatever options offered themselves.

At eleven, a little pale but exquisitely coiffed and dressed, she was informed that Mr. Ramlin had arrived.

He was standing by the window when she entered the parlor, a powerfully elegant figure in narrow pantaloons caught with a strap under each shoe. His hair was cut short now in the favored London style; for the first time she noticed there were fine traces of silver at the temples, although the rest of his hair was still profoundly, luxuriantly dark, with the same bottomless quality as his eyes.

"It's good of you to see me," he said gently, and she invited him to sit.

He took a chair by the hearth and glanced into the coals from time to time as they exchanged the amenities, as though he were not quite settled.

"Lewis is getting accustomed to school?" he asked.

As she glimpsed his profile, lit by the glow of the fire, tiny winged creatures fluttered high in her stomach. "Yes," she said, "from his letters it would seem so. Was your trip enjoyable?"

"Very."

They sat a few more moments in silence.

"And you, Julie? I trust you are well."

Age only enhances him, she thought. Faint lines flared out from his nose to the corners of his mouth. His face was a shade thinner, highlighting the chiseled bones beneath, emphasizing the depth of his eyes. It was so long since she'd had more than the most fleeting glimpse of him that there was something she hadn't noticed. The dashing pirate look had yielded to something more noble, something almost heroic. He was not the man she had fallen in love with so long ago, not the man who had committed an unforgivable act. Neither of them was the same person. She felt herself adrift for a moment. He seemed to be waiting for her. He had asked her something....

"Yes," she said, remembering. "Yes, I am very well, thank you." And she remembered the purpose of his visit. She looked for a legal pouch, a dispatch box at his feet, but he had come empty-handed. "You have some papers you wish to discuss?" she asked.

"No papers." He looked distractedly into the coals again. "Bryony. It's about Bryony."

She knew he had been acquiring property for seven years. With the sum total of his estate grown so large, Bryony Manor must have become a rather insignificant part of it. But the very sound of the name inundated her with memories.

"Julie, will you come there with me?" He rose abruptly and looked with longing toward the door. "Now?"

Why? she wondered, but her throat was too constricted to let the word pass.

"Please, Julie." He seemed overwrought, incapable of explaining.

It was perhaps the most painful thing he could ask of her, but yes, she would go. For answer she merely dipped her head in a nod, drew her silk wrap about her shoulders and, without benefit of cape or mantle, followed him out to his carriage.

October mists shrouded the countryside and clung to the windows; they might have been traveling in a cotton cloud. After a while she found it soothing, this thick cocoon that lulled the sound of the wheels and blurred the middle distance.

"Why are we going to Bryony?" she asked him softly.

He simply shook his head. "You have borne with me thus far. I beg you to bear with me just a little longer. Bryony was meant to be— It means so many things to me. It will be easier to say when we are there."

It was several hours' drive but Sebastian would speak only of the smallest currency of his life, of his summer weeks with Lewis, of an offer he'd received for the Wicklow farm, the renovations he'd started on his London house, what a wet July they'd had in Ireland.

It is enough, she thought. A discussion of his will did not demand a change of venue. He wanted only a pretext to reach out to her; that knowledge gave her courage and hope.

"I have forgiven you the past," she almost said. "I have never stopped loving you, though I tried." But only of late had she breached that wall; she had yet to step through it to the other side. It was not, she discovered, as easy as it had seemed in her summer fantasies.

At Bryony the fog was so dense that from the carriage-way the house was no more than a huge dark shadow against a field of white. But inside, the stained glass windows in the hall, the warm colors of the Turkish carpet on the dark oak floor were like old friends. Instead of a great bowl of roses on the hall table there was a thin layer of dust. She almost made a mental note to tell the housekeeper—it felt so much like coming home.

She followed Sebastian to the south wing of the house, past the main staircase, the closed door to the music room. The memory of undiluted joy made her feel light and dizzy. She had tried to prepare and brace herself throughout the drive, but she had forgotten just how happy it was once possible to be.

He led her silently to the breakfast room, kindled the fire, rang for coffee.

The breakfast room. It wrung her heart to see that small round table again, the window bay. The tender indolence of their bodies leaning toward each other across the small circle of food and china and napery. Breaking bread with him like a morning affirmation of the love they had shared in the night.

"Julie, so much has happened this year that makes me rethink my life," he said. "And so much of it is already behind me."

Not so much that we can't make amends. She hugged the thought to herself, knowing that all he wanted from her now was a willing ear.

They sat at the table, a bowl of golden pears between them. He wrapped his hands around the warm coffee cup and fixed his eyes on her, but they were unfocused, as if they saw another woman.

"I got what I deserved, no question. I designed a hell for myself by falling in love with a woman I had agreed to use."

His voice, too, was slightly removed, as if he were telling a story of long ago. It occurred to her that he had rehearsed this many times, as she had rehearsed a dozen possible scenarios.

"At first I thought it was a passing passion, but it grew stronger. And it was a love flawed by my own deceit. I wanted only truth between the two of us, yet I put off my confession for fear of losing her. There was the danger of her despising me, the danger of retribution from her husband, who was powerful enough to keep us apart and ruin me." He sighed and shook his head.

"So I simply lived with it for four years, burdened with my guilt for the sake of the precious feeling we bore for each other and the fleeting hours we could sometimes spend together.

"Sometimes I thought, perhaps she'll never have to know. Her husband is old and cannot live forever. Sometimes I feared that Guillaume Farroux had defeated mortality itself. I lived in fragments, bright starbursts of joy in a dark night."

He put down his cup and glanced about the room, then stared through the leaded windows. Little was visible through the fog—just tall distant smudges.

Julie's memory pierced the haze and she saw those blurred markings as apple trees, heavy with fruit beginning to ripen under a hot sun. Meadowlarks...wildflowers...her own body ripening with motherhood...

The past hurtled toward her like a stampede of wild horses and she felt it would destroy her if she did not leap aside. Her fingers curled into her palms and something stirred under her ribs, something hard and protective.

His eyes returned to hers. "Bryony became a symbol of hope for me," he went on. "Here I poured out my love for her, making the home I dreamed we would share one day.

"When I knew I could no longer abide the waiting and the deceit, I deceived her husband into letting me bring her here. In England, I told him, I would have a chance to beget the child he wanted so badly. It was the last lie I would ever tell....

"Here, I thought, I would bring her home at last. I would tell her everything, my pinched circumstances when I met her father, how his words led me to Paris with an introduction to her husband."

"My father?" Julie felt the color drain from her face. "You knew he was alive?"

"Yes. Yes. I would tell her every detail and I would make her understand, make her forgive."

"Stop," she begged. "Please stop." But he was too set in his purpose to hear her.

"And here we were happier than I could have imagined in my wildest dreams. I waited, dreading the moment when I would see her lovely face change to hurt, disgust, disappointment. I let those golden days drift by, cherishing each moment—until the night she told me she was carrying our son. Then I knew the day of reckoning had come, and a strange thing happened. All my apprehension vanished, and I began to speak at last."

His eyes were seeing her now, compelling and dark with regret. "You know what happened then." He let his hands rest on the table, palms up and vulnerable. His words quickened, his tone becoming direct and urgent.

"I would have told you everything that night but for Jared's coming. Would you have forgiven me?"

She was too shaken to answer. He had known—known through all the years of their affair—that her father was alive. It was as if she had succeeded in detaching him from the men who had used her without love, and he had insisted on linking himself once more in that evil chain. When he spoke again she was almost afraid of what she would hear.

"Domenico died before you returned to France. When I read your letter... when I knew it was too late, that Guillaume would expose me, it was like another death. I wrote, poured out my heart—everything—begged your forgiveness. And I thought I had received it when you rushed into my arms weeping…but you had never read the letter. I tried to tell you everything that was in it, but I was inept, ill-prepared."

She had forgiven it all before this moment, she reminded herself. She had devoted the summer to hopes of a reconciliation. Her voice was cool and pale. "You knew my father was living in London?"

"Yes, yes, I knew. I met him once . . . he precipitated this whole accursed—" He forked his fingers through his hair in an anguished gesture then let his hands drop heavily to the table again, pressed his palms down and stood up.

"No! Not your father. I alone am responsible for what I did. No one else." In agitation, he began to pace the room.

"You want to know why I brought you here? Because at Bryony I botched my last chance with you. I thought at Bryony I might redeem myself. I cannot stop wanting you. After twelve years, my God, Julie—I thought I could—" He broke off and grimaced. "A life sentence? I have mismanaged everything."

Julie felt her body stiffen against the urge to yield. "Not everything, Sebastian. You have a fine son and you are extremely wealthy. Both thanks to me."

He was beside her in a moment. He looked down into her tense face, then squatted by her chair. "So you were never able to believe me. Julie, listen to me. Guillaume was never my protector. It was Napoleon. We are…related, Julie. Kin. I never lied about that. I learned the truth at Domenico's deathbed."

She crossed her arms tightly across her chest for a moment to counter the sensation that her heart was sinking. Then she let her hands rest on the table, moving her cup and saucer away with an angry little push. She stared straight ahead at his empty chair. "Related to Napoleon? How related?"

"God help me, Julie, I am not at liberty to tell you. Look at me, Julie. Can you believe me?"

If only she could. If only it had been a simpler confession. She'd been so anxious to put the past behind her, but now... Could she actually make herself believe such a far-fetched tale? Could that possibly be an act of will?

Love is based on trust, she thought desperately, and in spite of her efforts, she felt that trust stretched to the point of unraveling. She couldn't lose him now, and yet...

He reached for her hands and she let them rest limply in his. "I sensed a relenting in you today. I saw it in your eyes. You love me still. I know it. And yet you have hardened against me since you came into this room. Don't tell me now that what stands between us is merely the accident of my birth. Come back, Julie. Come back!"

"I want to believe you..." she said, and her voice faltered. She could feel through the clasp of his hands the great surge of sincerity, pulsing toward her. Whatever sins he had committed, hers was the greater. She had lacked the grace to forgive, to acknowledge that whatever his faults, he had never failed to love her. Perhaps this was the truth. What could he gain now from lying? Blessed are they who believe without a sign, she thought.

He straightened to his full height still clasping her hands. She rose from her chair to join him, answering the pressure of his fingers.

"I will believe you," she said slowly, wanting to convince herself.

"And you'll be my wife?"

"Oh, Sebastian, yes," she said, surrendering to his arms and at last meeting the pressure of his lips.

No moment, she thought, had ever been so painfully earned, and for all their past embraces, no kiss ever as sweet.

Lifting her off her feet, he whispered, "How I want to make love to you now! But we'll start right this time." He began to carry her, not toward his bedroom but to the front door. Years began to vanish and his face took on that dashing, impulsive look she had first seen in Paris. Words tumbled from his mouth, fast as buckshot.

"First, a marriage ceremony. Two weeks for the reading of the banns. And meanwhile we must tell Lewis— What do you want to do with Pocket Hathaway? But first— You have no mantle! Before the night draws in I must take you home and we'll—"

She stopped him with her palm across his mouth. Her body and soul, every fiber of her being, yearned to make up for all the years they had lost. "I am home, Sebastian. *I am home.*"

Chapter Twenty-five

Plymouth—August 1815

Sebastian and Julie had not spent a night apart since the previous October, and there was only one reason she was not with him now in Plymouth—Emily Juliette Ramlin. He had what for so many years he had never dared to hope for, a second child, a daughter just four weeks old. Julie protested that she was strong enough to accompany him, but the doctor forbade travel for another week.

"I'll be back in a few days," he promised. "Next time we leave Bryony it will be together. But to the west country— the roads are rough and arduous. It's too much for you yet."

Because she was not with him to see for herself, it had been wisdom not to mention the real purpose of his trip—his brother. Sebastian had no wish to probe the thin layer of her trust in him.

The British warship *Bellerophon* was the most celebrated vessel on earth at that moment, because Napoleon was on board. Two armed frigates flanked the ship like prison guards, but Captain Maitland had known Sebastian for twenty years and allowed him, at the emperor's request, to come aboard.

The brothers stood for a few moments, leaning over the gunwales. "I grew up in Somerset, not far from here," Sebastian said.

Nabu nodded. "The crew have been most kind. They have treated me with courtesy."

It was easier to look out to sea than to meet each other's eyes. It was easier to talk of trifles than the events of the past few months.

Nabu had escaped Elba in February. He had sailed for France with his little band of faithful. He had astonished the world by marching from the south to take Paris again, to take all France without firing a shot. Louis XVIII had fled Paris, obligingly leaving the Tuileries to its former occupant.

Everyone knew it couldn't last; it was impossible. But Napoleon always flew in the face of the impossible, and for a hundred days, the world wondered. Perhaps this was not a man at all but the devil incarnate. Old stories reemerged in the newspapers. The cardinal who had negotiated the concordat had worn dark green spectacles to soften the dazzle of Napoleon's eyes. The Duke of Wellington counted Napoleon's presence on the battlefield as the equivalent of forty thousand extra men.

Sebastian did not believe in devils. He knew from Letizia about Nabu's stomach ulcers and kidney stones. "He never admits it, but he's been in frequent pain since before Moscow."

In Sebastian's happiness was a profound sadness—for the man who stood beside him and for all he could not share with Julie about his heritage.

For a hundred days Sebastian had avoided the one name on everyone's lips. It was the one danger spot that might ruin what he had—for it could bring on a recurrence of Julie's distrust. Shutting off the outside world he had tended his new life with her like a fragile seedling garden that would not survive a strong wind.

When Napoleon was defeated at Waterloo, Sebastian felt a relief tinged with sadness. Nabu had many faults, but he was no devil, just a man who had run out of strength, out of hope, out of men.

But he had not yet run out of courage.

Nabu turned to face him on the stern deck, his brown hair lifting in the warm July breeze. "Well, I tried, did I not? I mourn all those sons of France who died to preserve a better way of life, but it wasn't all in vain.

"Some of the things I did will surely outlast me. I hope I will be remembered for giving them equality, just laws, prosperity—" He broke off and grinned. "Or at least the Rue de la Paix."

His gallantry was so painful to watch that Sebastian glanced away. The waters below the bows were infested with sightseers; every yawl and ketch and rowboat in England seemed to be bobbing below their starboard. The ship had only dropped anchor a few days ago, but word was out that Boney was on board, that Boney liked to walk the deck for exercise.

The small, crowded vessels below them jostled for a glimpse of the famous man, upturned gaping mouths, binoculars and spyglasses pressed to their faces like eyes on stalks. To Sebastian it was like the grotesquely animated flotsam of some sailor's nightmare.

"Come, you shall not remember me as a circus freak," Nabu said, and led Sebastian forward to his cabin.

He speaks as if this is the last time we'll ever meet, Sebastian thought.

He had spacious quarters in the fo'c'sle, the cabin of the first officer, but it was uncomfortably hot. They removed their coats and sat in their shirtsleeves on either side of a small table, nothing but a carafe of drinking water between them.

"Would you like some tea? I have only to ask that boy outside."

Sebastian shook his head.

Nabu patted his stomach and glanced around the cabin. "I surrendered to the British because although they were always my worst enemy, they were the most chivalrous. I hope they grant me a small plot where I can write my memoirs before I die."

The gray eyes smiled in a rare look of self-disparagement. "Did you know I wanted to be a writer? My father sent me to the French military academy because it was free. I was ten. I'd never left Corsica before. The first five words of French I learned were 'I want to go home.'"

The eyes flared with a sudden incandescence. "Still, I didn't do too badly as a soldier, did I?"

He's not done yet, Sebastian thought. He could see the glint of sabers in those steel-gray eyes. If he gets his hands on a ship, a half dozen men, by God he'll raise another army. He still hasn't accepted defeat.

"If I had a fraction of your persistence," Sebastian said, "I would..." His voice faded as the nostalgia returned. It was only a dull hurt now, the thought of those wasted years—like an old wound that still aches in rainy weather.

"You would what?" Nabu prompted. "You would have married the widow Farroux?"

"We are married, Nabu—since last October."

"Finally! My dear Sebastiano, my felicitations!" Nabu grasped his hands warmly then looked into Sebastian's eyes. "What's this? Is it so much less than you hoped for?"

Sebastian shrugged and shook his head. "No. But perhaps less than she hoped for...I don't think she'll ever recover full trust in me. She would deny it, but she still believes Farroux was my protector during the blockade."

"Farroux? That minor bureaucrat?" Nabu blew through his lips, a peculiarly disparaging sound. "He never had the power he let you believe. The old rogue was hoodwinking you. Didn't you tell her we are brothers?"

"I swore to you I would never do that."

Nabu sighed. "I'd forgotten. Mother is sixty-six years old." He looked around the cabin, his prison. "Do you think anything can hurt her after this?"

"I did tell her we are related," Sebastian admitted. "But brothers! Why should she believe it? No, it's best I never mention it again. At least we are together and that's more than enough after all the wasted years."

Nabu leaned forward, curious. "Why did you wait so long?"

"I wasn't waiting. I'd given up. If it were not for your words... But I'm not like you at all, Nabu. I generally *know* when I'm beaten."

Nabu frowned. "It's a concept I never quite grasped. How can one ever *know* that?" He reached for the water carafe and poured himself a glass with slow, deliberate movements. "I'd like to give you something to remember me by. Your wife's complete trust." He was still holding the carafe high, watching the thin stream of water trickle into his glass, smiling to himself.

"Bring her here. She shall hear the truth from me."

Sebastian straightened abruptly in his chair. "She's more than a hundred miles from here and she's recovering from... we have a new daughter."

Nabu responded to the radiance in Sebastian's face with a slow smile. "I am glad for you. Glad you're making up for lost time." He thought for a moment. "The Prince Regent hasn't decided what to do with me yet. We'll be sailing to Portsmouth tomorrow night." He blinked slowly. "I shall be there until he makes up his mind. How long will it take you to get to her?"

"Three days—less if I leave immediately."

Nabu gave a curt military nod. "Could she make the journey to Portsmouth?"

From Bryony it was not an arduous trip. "Portsmouth," Sebastian agreed. "God keep you till then." And before the words were out, his mind raced ahead of his body, already on the road for home.

Approaching the house where his daughter lay cooing in the nursery, seeing Julie on the front lawn pruning a rose-bush—it was so close to his old fantasies that his breath stopped for a moment. Had it really happened or would he awake soon to find the last ten months had been a dream?

Julie dropped the pruning shears at the sound of the carriage and ran toward it. Her warm embrace reassured him.

"Up and gardening already?" he asked fondly, and smoothed the tendrils of hair that strayed over her forehead. "Are you ready for that?"

"I have never felt better or stronger in my whole life than I do at this moment. You are back. Emily has learned to smile. Lewis will be home next week. He is bringing a friend from school."

They walked into the manor, their arms about each other, Julie filling him in on the household events of the past six days. In the nursery, Emily slept like a plump cherub. They tiptoed out of the room and did not speak until they were alone in the bedroom they shared.

She closed the door and embraced him again. Her body pressed against him as they kissed, as if her desire equaled his, but it was too soon after the baby, he remembered, and gently held her at arm's length.

"Another week," she breathed.

"I missed you terribly." He kissed her brow. "But it was almost worth it to have this homecoming."

"Almost, my love, but not quite. I trust you won't make a habit of it."

He grinned. "On the contrary, I shall cling like a barnacle. They're little creatures that attach themselves—"

She stopped his words with another impulsive kiss. "I may not be much of a sailor, but I do know what barnacles are, Admiral."

He laughed. "Are you sailor enough to board an anchored vessel?" He clasped her hands, and his face became suddenly very solemn and his voice cautious.

"Julie, the *Bellerophon* has sailed up to Portsmouth. Napoleon wants to see you."

Her voice didn't change but there was a slight dulling in her eyes. "Ah! So that's where you went! Of course I'll come, but why all the mystery?"

"I didn't want to...stretch your credulity again. Now I don't have to. Not ever. We can leave early tomorrow and be with him before noon. Napoleon has offered to reassure you that...that I am, after all, not an inveterate liar."

She stroked his cheek, trying to smooth away the troubled look. "Don't, sweetheart. Please don't speak of that again. I love you as you are. Have I not entrusted the rest of my life to you? Nothing else matters."

But it did matter. Much as she protested, he could see it in her eyes. A kind of resignation. An invisible veil of sadness between them. Tomorrow, God willing, it would be ripped away forever.

He avoided speaking of it until the following day when his grateful eyes spotted the *Bellerophon* duly anchored in the harbor. Clutching Julie's hand, he hurried down to the berth, preparing her for the revelation. "It's not a distant connection, Julie, it's close. You cannot imagine how much I've wanted to share it with you! But I was under oath to divulge nothing."

Under oath, she thought. Why could it not be the simple truth? Why would he insist on bringing her here? She could believe him—*did* believe him. She was almost convinced. "Before we see him, I want you to know that I do trust you," she said. "Truly I do." Somewhere inside her she could feel the last residue of suspicion melting, as if some hard, noxious substance that had attached itself to her soul for many years was at last crumbling, washing away in the cleansing currents of faith accepted.

Sebastian didn't answer. He was too intent on the ship, and her words drifted away on the salt winds. Still gripping her hand, he stopped in front of a naval midshipman who guarded access to the frigate, and handed the sailor a docket.

"Would you inform Captain Maitland that I request permission to come aboard with one guest for a private visit with the emperor."

The midshipman returned the paper back after a brief glance and gave a smart salute. "The captain's on leave, sir. And the emperor's no longer on board. He's been transferred to the *Northumberland*." As he spoke, the sailor's head dipped toward a much larger frigate. It was making canvas as it moved majestically beyond the sheltered water.

His voice dropped to a confidential whisper. "Saint Helena," he said.

Julie felt a convulsive spasm of Sebastian's hand as he turned his head to look. The frigate's foresails and main were already unfurled, and the mizzen sails were coming alive.

His voice was suddenly harsh. "But it can't be! Do you mean it's sailing *now*? For the south Atlantic?"

The midshipman nodded. "Exiled for life," he said importantly.

Drawing Julie by the hand, Sebastian walked along the narrow way between the dock and the deep-water berths until he found a gap in the forest of tall masts, a full window onto the departing ship.

It was far beyond hailing distance, beyond any hope of recall. A sharp gust of wind and the *Northumberland* surged forward on the wide water, its great canvases snapping in a last salute to the land. Sebastian's words were flat with shock. "We never said goodbye."

Julie turned from the majestic sight to Sebastian's face. His gaze was fixed on the ship as if *he* were the exile watching the coast retreat, as if for a moment he were leaving behind everything he held dear. Nothing could ever tell her more about kinship than the look she saw in Sebastian's eyes.

"You must have loved him," she said softly.

"He was my brother. We have the same mother." His words were so fraught with despair that they trembled as they came out.

There was no place left in her to doubt. If she had suffered duality through all those years of war, how much worse it must have been for him. She felt the grief he must have suffered, divided from a brother he had loved so much, burdened with a secret of such magnitude. With an intuitive knowledge, she was suddenly in possession of his pain. "Oh, my poor love," she cried out, "how terrible for you."

He could not tear his eyes away from the ship. "Saint Helena, a thousand miles from anywhere," he said, and his voice broke.

Blindly his arms went round her and he held her tight against the wind, watching the ship sail toward the horizon. Perhaps he could visit someday... No. Somewhere in his heart he knew they would never meet again.

Nabu had taught him what family meant, and something else he would never forget. Something about defeat.

"I'll take you to Letizia," he said, clinging to her fiercely, as though she, too, might slip through his fingers forever. "I'll show you all his letters to me. I'll not give up. I'll make you trust me again."

"You don't have to," she whispered in his ear. "You'll never, never have to prove anything again."

But he seemed too shocked to hear. "Saint Helena," he repeated bitterly. "They are chaining him to a rock in the middle of the ocean."

Julie reached up and brushed his solitary tear away with her finger, then cupped his face and drew his gaze away from the sight that brought him such grief. How she wanted to comfort him! "Why must they be so cruel?"

Then she looked into his face. His eyes were bright with tears and behind them she saw something she had never seen before. He was transfigured, his smile lit from within by the light of a thousand candles.

You'll never have to prove anything again. The sound of her conviction echoed in his ears like a peal of victory bells. The lost years faded into nothingness and the future was a sudden radiance in his voice.

"They *have* to chain him down," he said, at last turning away from the harbor. He drew his arm about Julie and began to walk with her, back to where their carriage waited. They could go home now and they would find the oneness they had lost for thirteen years.

"They have to chain him down, sweetheart," he said, his smile still dazzling. "If they don't he'll try again. He'll never give up. Nabu is not a man to settle for less than his dreams.''

Julie seemed a little puzzled by the fervor in his voice as he helped her into the coach. He nodded to the driver and the carriage leaped forward. He would explain later and she would understand; there was nothing they could not share now. But at the moment his heart was too full for more words.

They were going home.

* * * * *

A Postscript to the Reader

The frigate *Northumberland* sailed from Portsmouth on August 8, 1815, and reached the island of Saint Helena in October. Napoleon died there almost six years after my story ends. Traditionally he died of stomach ailments, but modern forensic medicine indicates that he was methodically poisoned with increasing doses of arsenic. Perhaps his captors couldn't quite believe that he had finally accepted defeat.

Joseph, the eldest brother, sailed for the United States and founded the Baltimore branch of the Bonapartes. Letizia lived on in Rome until 1836, outliving four of her children.

Sebastian and Julie, of course, live only in the author's imagination.

Harlequin Historicals

COMING NEXT MONTH

#47 STORMWALKER—Bronwyn Williams

Laura Gray was a casualty of the strife between the early colonials and the Indians of North Carolina. Raped and left for dead, Laura summoned her will to survive—only to be shunned by her own townsfolk. Could she bring herself to accept the only kindness offered her, that of the noble Stormwalker?

#48 DRAGONFIRE—Patricia Potter

Peking, China, was the last place Englishwoman Hope Townsend should have been at the turn of the century. The Boxer Rebellion was growing violent, and stodgy Marine Major Travis Farrell had enough problems without falling in love with Hope.

AVAILABLE NOW:

#45 THE HELL RAISER   #46 TERMS OF SURRENDER
Dorothy Glenn   Mollie Ashton

Have You Been Introduced To
THE GENTLEMAN
Yet?

If you enjoyed Dorothy Glenn's THE HELL RAISER (HH #45), you won't want to miss its companion book, THE GENTLEMAN, by Kristin James.

As a boy, Stephen Ferguson was taken away from his brother and his western home, then raised with all the comforts that money and city society could provide. As a man, he longed to be reunited with the family he'd nearly forgotten. In THE GENTLEMAN (HH #43) Stephen finds not only his father and brother but something even more precious—the love of a woman who is every inch his opposite—and absolutely his perfect match!

HARLEQUIN
American Romance®

THE LOVES OF A CENTURY...

Join American Romance in a nostalgic look back at the Twentieth Century—at the lives and loves of American men and women from the turn-of-the-century to the dawn of the year 2000.

Journey through the decades from the dance halls of the 1900s to the discos of the seventies ... from Glenn Miller to the Beatles ... from Valentino to Newman ... from corset to miniskirt ... from beau to Significant Other.

Relive the moments ... recapture the memories.

Look for the CENTURY OF AMERICAN ROMANCE series starting next month in Harlequin American Romance. In one of the four American Romance titles appearing each month, for the next twelve months, we'll take you back to a decade of the Twentieth Century, where you'll relive the years and rekindle the romance of days gone by.

Don't miss a day of the CENTURY OF AMERICAN ROMANCE.

A CENTURY OF
AMERICAN ROMANCE
1900's

The women...the men...the passions...
the memories....

CARM-1

Indulge a Little
Give a Lot

A LITTLE SELF-INDULGENCE CAN DO A WORLD OF GOOD!

Last fall readers indulged themselves with fine romance and free gifts during the Harlequin®/ Silhouette® "Indulge A Little—Give A Lot" promotion. For every specially marked book purchased, 5¢ was donated by Harlequin/ Silhouette to Big Brothers/Big Sisters Programs and Services in the United States and Canada. We are pleased to announce that your participation in this unique promotion resulted in a total contribution of *$100,000.*

*

Watch for details on Harlequin® and Silhouette®'s next exciting promotion in September.

INS

NEW YORK TIMES BESTSELLER!

POWER PLAY
Penny Jordan

If you have been unable to find this gripping novel of passion and revenge by bestselling author Penny Jordan in stores, why not order it by mail?

To receive your copy, send your name, address, zip or postal code, along with a check or money order for $4.95 ($5.95 in Canada), plus 75¢ postage and handling, payable to Harlequin Reader Service to:

In the U.S.
901 Fuhrmann Blvd.
Box 1396
Buffalo, NY 14269-1396

In Canada
P.O. Box 609
Fort Erie, Ontario
L2A 5X3

Please specify book title with your order.

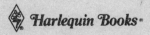 *Harlequin Books*®

PPM-1R